New Hunting Ground

The Vampire turned to look up at the large stucco villa that had been her home for the better part of the last two centuries. Behind it rose the hills surrounding Mount Etna and the dusty gray-green leaves of its fruitful olive trees. Beyond that were the valleys and vineyards, where the drunken god Bacchus himself still reveled with women young and old alike.

She would miss Italy, that much she already knew. But it was time to leave. After nearly twenty centuries, history had left this part of the world by the roadside. The blood of Europe had grown thin and tired, its people jaded. She thought of the letter from America, from the wife of a prominent senator she had met last summer on vacation on the Riviera. The Vampire smiled, remembering the eagerness in the woman's eyes, the quickening of her pulse when she spoke of her dreams of domination. The Vampire hadn't felt such enthusiasm, such ambition, since the early days of the Third Reich.

Yes, it was time to go west. America was a country just past ripening: She could sniff the first intoxicating traces of decay from all the way across the Atlantic. A field of grapes ready for harvesting.

She tapped on the glass partition that separated her from the hulking driver behind the wheel.

"Drive," she said, and the limousine pulled slowly away.

NOW THERE'S NO NEED TO WAIT UNTIL DARK!
DAY OR NIGHT, ZEBRA'S VAMPIRE NOVELS
HAVE QUITE A BITE!

THE VAMPIRE JOURNALS   (4133, $4.50)
by Traci Briery
Maria Theresa Allogiamento is a vampire ahead of her time. As she travels
from 18th-century Italy to present-day Los Angeles, Theresa sets the record
straight. From how she chose immortality to her transformation into a seduc-
tive temptress, Theresa shares all of her dark secrets and quenches her insatiable thirst for all the world has to offer!

NIGHT BLOOD   (4063, $4.50)
by Eric Flanders
Each day when the sun goes down, Val Romero feeds upon the living. This
NIGHT BLOOD is the ultimate aphrodisiac. Driving from state to state in his
'69 Cadillac, he leaves a trail of bloodless corpses behind. Some call him a serial killer, but those in the know call him Vampire. Now, three tormented
souls driven by revenge and dark desires are tracking Val down—and only
Val's death will satisfy their own raging thirst for blood!

THE UNDEAD   (4068, $5.50)
by Roxanne Longstreet
Most people avoid the cold and sterile halls of the morgue. But for Adam
Radburn working as a morgue attendant is a perfect job. He is a vampire.
Though Adam has killed for blood, there is another who kills for pleasure
and he wants to destroy Adam. And in the world of the undead, the winner is
not the one who lives the longest, it's the one who lives forever!

PRECIOUS BLOOD   (4293, $4.50)
by Pat Graversen
Adragon Hart, leader of the Society of Vampires, loves his daughter dearly.
So does Quinn, a vampire renegade who has lured Beth to the savage streets
of New York and into his obscene world of unquenchable desire. Every minute Quinn's hunger is growing. Every hour Adragon's rage is mounting. And
both will do anything to satisfy their horrific appetites!

THE SUMMONING   (4221, $4.50)
by Bentley Little
The first body was found completely purged of all blood. The authorities
thought it was the work of a serial killer. But Sue Wing's grandmother knew
the truth. She'd seen the deadly creature decades ago in China. Now it had
come to the dusty Arizona town of Rio Verde . . . and it would not leave until
it had drunk its fill.

DOMINATION

Michael Cecilione

ZEBRA BOOKS
KENSINGTON PUBLISHING CORP.

ZEBRA BOOKS are published by

Kensington Publishing Corp.
475 Park Avenue South
New York, NY 10016

Zebra and the Z logo Reg. U.S. Pat & TM Off.

First Printing: December, 1993

Printed in the United States of America

PART ONE

PRISONER
OF
LOVE

"I saw pale kings, and princes too,
Pale warriors, death-pale were they all;
Who cry'd—'La belle Dame sans merci
Hath thee in thrall!' "
—John Keats

"You are here to serve your masters."
—*Story of O*

ONE

The Vampire heard the gentle rap on the bedroom door and turned from the window that looked out over the blood-red hills of Sicily.

"*Sì,*" she called.

"*Scusi,*" the voice on the other side of the door said softly. "Your car, *Senora*. It is ready."

"*Va bene,*" the Vampire said wearily. "Come in then."

The door opened and the young man entered. He stood to one side against the wall and kept his eyes on the priceless carpet beneath his dusty work shoes. Those eyes, she remembered with satisfaction, had once been so bold and impudent. It had given her great pleasure to extinguish the spark of life that had once mocked her there. His not-so-white shirt, open down the front, showed off his smooth, muscular pectorals. Immediately, she could smell the not unpleasant aroma that the sun and the sweat of hard labor had left on his browned flesh.

"Did I teach you no better than that?"

She saw him flinch inwardly. The movement would have been imperceptible to the untrained eye, but to an experienced mistress it was as unmistakable as a brand burned into captive flesh. The small sitting room was suddenly redolent with a far more intriguing perfume than the boy's sweat: the universal scent of fear.

"Pardon, Senora, I don't know——"

If she had more time, she would have relished his confusion. As it was, she had less than two hours to make the drive to Comiso for her connecting flight to Roma's International Airport. To top it off, she still had unfinished business in the next room that demanded her immediate attention.

"Your hands, Carlino," she said.

"M-mio mani?" the boy stuttered, completely bewildered.

"Are in your pockets," the Vampire concluded.

The boy looked shocked. He pulled his hands from his pockets and stared at them disbelievingly, as if he had no idea how they could possibly have crept in there in the first place. He laid them on his thighs, open palms forward, on the front of his stained khaki trousers as he'd been trained.

"Did I teach you no better than that?" the Vampire said again in mock disgust. "Is this how you repay my efforts on your behalf?"

"Scusi mi, Senora," he began, desperately trying to make amends. "I make a small mistake. I no do it again. I——"

The Vampire held up her hand.

"Basta. Perhaps I shall tell Marcello about your 'small' mistake."

Beneath the thick fringe of his dark lashes the Vampire could see the cold terror in the boy's eyes, like a condemned man glimpsing his first sight of the guillotine that will claim his head. He fell to his knees, kissing the floor. If she were standing closer, his lips would have certainly rained their kisses on her feet.

"Mercy, *Senora,* have mercy on me!"

"Get up," the Vampire said coldly. "You are lucky I am in a good mood today. And that I am in a hurry."

"Grazie, Senora," he said, tears of gratitude shining in his eyes. *"Grazie."*

"Get up, I said."

The boy clambered to his feet.

"Fetch my bags to the car, you worthless son of a whore."

"Si, si, Senora," the boy said happily, lifting the heavy suitcases that stood next to the window. The Vampire watched appreciatively as the biceps bulged beneath the short sleeves of his shirt, watched with faint hunger the flex of his muscular buttocks beneath the thin, thread-bare trousers tied with a rope around his narrow hips. He was all smiles, bobbing his head agreeably, as he closed the door behind him.

The Vampire glanced at her gold Rolex and sighed. There never seemed to be enough time.

She turned and headed for the bedroom.

Beneath a slowly turning ceiling fan, on the large circular bed in the center of the room, was the body of a young girl.

She was naked, lying on her back on the white satin sheets, her long, shapely legs slightly parted. She might have been mistaken for dead, except for the slight rise and fall of her apple-sized breasts, though it was the faint but telltale vibration at the pulse points in her wrists and throat that the Vampire saw.

The girl's head had lolled to one side and her pale lips were slightly parted. Up close, the Vampire could see that her once brown skin had faded to nearly white. She touched the girl's flesh, damp and feverish in spite of the fan overhead.

The Vampire traced a line with her fingernail from

9

the girl's shoulder, down the gentle slope of her breast, to the tip of her left nipple. The girl moaned, as if her mistress's touch had scored her in both worlds, dreaming and waking—which it had.

In Southern Italy, the peasants still believed in the power of the *streghe* to affect their crops, their livestock, their health. So it was with the girl's father. She had given him a choice which child he would give as a gift to her and, needing all three of his sons to work the fields, he had given her the youngest—and therefore the most expendable—of his seven daughters.

He had given her up with the understanding that the Vampire would show her a different, more sophisticated world than that of the olive orchards of Nicosia, even if his daughter would exist in that world as little more than a slave. Such had been the lot of peasants since time immemorial. Such would always be their lot, in spite of what the communists, the Red Brigade, the social democrats, or the anarchists might say.

Nature itself had decreed that there would always be two classes of people—the predators and the prey—and the former lived off the blood and sweat of the latter and that was that. It was this instinctive, if fatalistic, understanding of the natural aristocracy of life that the Vampire loved most of all about the Italian peasantry.

"Angelina," she whispered, and the girl's eyes fluttered open. They were lovely eyes, the color of sunrise on the Mediterranean, but darkened now by the impending night of death.

"Ma Donna," she whispered, and smiled.

The Vampire saw the fresh blood staining the satin pillowcase beneath the girl's head. Her blood had lost the ability to clot and the wound at her neck had not closed. Neither had the strips and welts across the soft flesh of her belly.

"It is time," the Vampire said. "I must go."

The girl's smooth forehead furrowed. *"Perche?"*

The girl, uneducated at home, spoke little English, though she could understand it passingly well.

"Because my business here is finished," the Vampire said. She could have invaded the girl's mind, let the words bloom there like fatal black flowers, choking her with the perfume of despair, but she decided to speak to her instead, leaving her these last few moments of lucid consciousness as a special gift. She put a finger to the girl's cold lips. "No more protests, *va bene?"*

The girl nodded.

The Vampire smiled, and brushed back the girl's thick, damp, russet-colored hair with one hand. With the other, she caressed the girl's smooth flank. She cupped the handful of breast in her hand and kissed the girl's rosy aureole, cutting her teeth across the nipple. When the Vampire took her face away blood ran down the side of the girl's breast.

Angelina moaned and stretched her body like a sleepy cat. The Vampire reached down and stroked the reddish-brown triangle of fur between the girl's thighs. Then she leaned over the bleeding girl and gently lapped at her wounded breast.

"Mia seni . . . bella?" she murmured.

"Si," the Vampire said. "Your breasts are beautiful."

Angelina sighed, opened her thighs still farther, the skilled hand drawing her out of her herself like a man reels a fish out of the ocean. Her legs tensed and relaxed, tensed and relaxed.

"Mia piede," she rambled, breathless, her heart flip-flopping in her chest.

"Yes," the Vampire said, feeling a twinge of pity for the mortal vanity of the dying creature. "Your feet are lovely."

She held the girl's tiny left foot in her hand, kissing it, opening the delicate tracery of veins in her ankle.

11

"You are beautiful, my little angel," she reassured the girl, stretching out beside her on the bed.

She lowered her face again to the girl's left breast, which was now a ruined mass of blood. A ghost of a smile appeared on Angelina's lips, which had peeled back as her heart went into a fatal tachycardia, revealing her small, pearly white teeth.

With one practiced movement, the Vampire turned the girl's head to one side, baring her carotid. Her own long incisors slid forward from inside her gums, and she placed her mouth over the girl's pulsing artery. The blood, powered by the girl's irregular heartbeat, leapt eagerly into her mouth.

"Tu amo," Angelina wept hysterically, the constriction of the muscles in her throat, common in heart failure, making it all but impossible for her to breathe.

"Tu amo," she choked and gasped.

Lying on top of her now, the Vampire was able to control the powerful involuntary convulsions of the girl's dying body with her own superior strength. When her heart stopped with a terrible jolt of finality the Vampire felt it inside her teeth.

Of course you love me, you little fool, the Vampire thought, and planted the thought inside the girl's brain, the last thought the girl would ever have, giving it the force of revelation. *Don't you know who I am?*

The Vampire rose from the bed and looked down at the dead girl. If anything, death had not robbed her of her beauty; it had merely refined it. Gone was the ruddy peasant "vitality," replaced by a delicate and aloof quality that was almost classical in its perfection. Like one of the erotic sculptures by Balzini locked away in the secret vaults of the Vatican. On the girl's frozen features was a look of unabashed ecstasy.

At the corner of one of the girl's staring eyes, a fly had landed to deposit its load of eggs in her tear duct.

The Vampire brushed the fly away.

She leaned forward and kissed the girl's now marble forehead. Her lips left a bloody print on the cold white flesh.

In the courtyard, the white Mercedes limousine stood idling.

The Vampire crossed the red tiles of the driveway, beautifully landscaped on both sides with evergreens and lined with genetically engineered rosebushes bearing flowers of every color and variety. Marcello stood beside the car, holding open the door.

He was wearing a white linen suit that did little to civilize his powerful leonine build, a crisp white shirt gathered at the collar with a gold pin, and an extravagantly colored handkerchief. His black hair was oiled back and his eyes were hidden behind a pair of dark Wayfarer sunglasses. He looked less like the Italian noble that he was than he did a hit man for the Cosa Nostra.

"Take care of her," the Vampire said, indicating her bedroom window, reflecting a blinding white in the noonday sun. "She will make a delicious slave."

Marcello nodded, understanding that the girl was a gift she had given him.

"Thank you, M'lady."

The Vampire held out her hand and he folded it inside both of his own, covered with black hair like two immense paws. They were hands without conscience, the kind of hands that had strangled men, women, and children. He brought her hand up to his cruel and sensuous lips and kissed it passionately.

"Have a pleasant trip," he said, as she slid into the dark, air-conditioned interior of the car.

She nodded. "I intend to."

Marcello pushed the car door closed with a hermetic whoosh.

The Vampire pressed the button on the door and the tinted window slid down.

Marcello leaned forward. "Yes, M'lady?"

"One thing more," she said. "That slave, Carlino. I believe he took advantage of my haste this afternoon, thinking he could escape punishment. It was a small matter of disrespect, but as you know these things simply cannot go unattended."

"Your honor is mine."

"Good," she said, her face perfectly expressionless. "And Marcello, don't be lenient."

The swarthy man smiled, his capped teeth looking impossibly beautiful in his violent, pockmarked face.

"I understand, M'lady."

"Goodbye, Marcello," the Vampire said. She pressed the button and the dark glass of the power window slid slowly up its track, concealing her from sight.

The Vampire turned to look up at the large stucco villa that had been her home for the better part of the last two centuries. Behind it rose the hills surrounding Mount Etna and the dusty gray-green leaves of its fruitful olive trees. Beyond that were the valleys and vineyards, where the drunken god Bacchus himself still reveled on Lammas night with women young and old alike.

She would miss Italy, that much she already knew. But it was time to leave. After nearly twenty centuries, history had left this part of the world by the roadside. The blood of Europe had grown thin and tired, its people jaded. She thought of the letter from America, from the wife of a prominent senator she had met last summer on vacation on the Riviera, and remembered the eagerness in her eyes, the quickening of her pulse when she spoke of her dreams of domination. The Vampire hadn't felt such enthusiasm, such ambition, since the early days of the Third Reich.

Yes, it was time to go west. America was a country just past ripening: She could sniff the first intoxicating traces of decay from all the way across the Atlantic. A field of grapes ready for harvesting.

She tapped on the glass partition that separated her from the hulking driver behind the wheel.

"Drive," she said, and the limousine pulled slowly away.

PART TWO

LOVE
HURTS

"Despite its paranoiac optimism, considerably tempered by current events, contemporary American civilization can be termed a 'depressive' culture, one in which the true aggressive drive natural to men is institutionally *depressed*. With everyone equal, and institutions organized to soften out all differences of strength and intelligence, aggression is disposed of, it is hoped, like so much unpleasant garbage."—*S-M: The Last Taboo*

"Courage, my angel, courage: bear in mind that it is always by way of pain one arrives at pleasure."—The Marquis de Sade

TWO

Hillary Stanton was daydreaming again.

She was sitting in front of her make-up mirror when she remembered it, examining the ravages the night before had left on her delicate skin. Genetics had blessed her with a strong resistance to the weathering effects of time that all mortal flesh was heir to, but she was fast approaching the age when not even she could stay up all night partying without paying the price. At forty-five, she had begun to see the first indelible traces that would eventually transform her from what many had once considered a striking, if unconventional, beauty, into what was euphemistically called a "handsome" woman.

She stared critically at her reflection in the mirror, stretching between her fingers the fine skin at the corners of her eyes, where each clear green orb was caught in a tiny net of wrinkles.

She scooped a special cosmetic she had custom-made from crushed pearls, powdered rhinoceros horn, and other substances impossible to procure except where life was cheap and money more powerful than either law or conscience. She smoothed the cool concoction over the damaged skin. Almost instantly, the wrinkles disappeared.

Long ago, she'd had all the bulbs in the makeup mirror changed to a lower wattage to spare her such distressing sights, yet lately she'd been unable to avoid the stark evidence appearing nightly before her eyes. Perhaps that was why she seldom rose before sunset anymore, preferring the masking shadows of the city's nightlife to the harsh, unyielding light of its daily hustle-bustle.

Of course, Edmund didn't approve of her interest in the city's avant-garde scene or the contacts she made there, which he thought singularly unbecoming to the wife of a United States Senator, but it was only art, after all.

Who took art seriously anymore?

Hillary picked up her imported camel-bristle brush and started stroking her shoulder-length blond hair.

She remembered the blind rage she'd flown into when her personal image consultant had tactfully suggested that she was getting a little too old to wear her hair as long as she had in college and advised her to have it cut to its present length. After a blistering tirade during which she had reduced the poor woman to hysterical tears, Hillary had fired her on the spot. Two days later, she had hired a new hairdresser and instructed him to cut her hair exactly as his predecessor had advised.

Sure enough, the new style had taken five years off her appearance.

It was as she was brushing her hair, carefully counting each stroke, that she remembered the night before.

She was in the playroom getting ready when Degas came in with the girl. She was lying unconscious in his arms, her head thrown back, her long blond hair nearly touching the floor. She was wearing a black evening gown split up one side to reveal a dazzling flash of white thigh, a diamond necklace, and a pair of silver high-heeled sandals.

"Put her on the rack," Hillary said.

Degas carried her to an inclined wooden table she'd had specially constructed by an S-M enthusiast based on models of the infamous racks once used by the Inquisition to punish witches, heretics, and other enemies of the Church. It always amused her to contemplate how many of the best instruments of torture had been invented by the Church. She thought of mentioning it every time she met with the Cardinal, though she hardly expected he'd appreciate the joke.

Degas lifted the girl's arms above her head and secured them to a leather strap attached to a large spoked wheel at the head of the table. He grabbed her ankles, spread her legs apart, and tied each ankle with a leather strap bolted to the foot of the table. He removed the girl's shoes, leaving her barefoot, and walked around the side of the table to remove her dress.

"No, not yet," Hillary said.

She stepped forward from out of the shadows, wearing a one-piece PVC jumpsuit slashed with zippers. A pair of black latex gloves were stretched skintight all the way up to her elbows. On her feet she wore leather boots tied with no fewer than a hundred tiny laces. Her face was concealed behind a PVC mask so that her victim would be unable to identify her. She let a finger play delicately in the cleavage of the girl's dress, letting it linger between her breasts. She looked back at Degas, who stood by the spoked wheel at the head of the table, having already stripped down to the leather G-string she required he wear beneath his custom-made Armani suits. He, too, was wearing a black mask.

"Where did you find her?"

"Outside Lincoln Center," he said. "During intermission at the Pavarotti concert."

"Did anyone see you?" she said, cupping the girl's chin and lifting her head, brushing the silky hair from her face.

"No. She climbed into the wrong limousine. She was having a fight with her boyfriend, unfortunately, who had passed out in the men's room," Degas said with a sly smile. "I chloroformed her in the back seat and we were on our way in a matter of seconds."

"Poor dear," Hillary said, leaning forward to place a lingering kiss on the girl's soft mouth. "Wake up, my sleeping beauty. Wake up."

She popped an ampule of amyl nitrate under the girl's nose. The girl moaned, stirring against her bonds, and her eyes fluttered open.

"What's going on I—"

Hillary saw the fear in the girl's eyes when she saw her masked tormentor. She saw it intensify when the girl's eyes accustomed themselves to the gloom and the flickering candlelight and she caught a glimpse of the torture machinery standing grim and ominous in the shadows along the wall. She saw it turn to panic when the girl became aware of the straps on her wrists and ankles and understood something of what was happening. The girl threw herself forward, twisting and turning against her bondage, but all her efforts were in vain. Hillary waited until the girl fell backward against the wood, exhausted.

"Are you finished, darling?" she asked. "I hope so. Because you're going to need all your strength for the fun ahead."

"Please," the girl said. "Let me go. I haven't done anything to you."

"Shut up," Hillary said.

She produced a razor between her gloved fingers, which she held close to the girl's cheek. Terrified, the girl watched the razor with huge blue eyes as Hillary flicked it deftly through her fingers like a magician.

"I just can't decide where I want to cut you first. Perhaps I'll slit your nostrils," she said, holding the razor to the girl's nose. "Or perhaps I'll broaden that smile of yours a bit, give you a real ear-to-ear, so we can see all your pearly whites." She swept the hair back from the girl's left ear. "Or maybe I'll slice off one of your ears, send it to your boyfriend. Do a Van Gogh kind of thing. Would you like that? Well, maybe later. First, let me see if there's something more interesting to play with down here."

She hooked a finger in the cleavage of the girl's dress, pulled it away from her body, and swept the blade downward, the material ripping away all the way down to her ankles, leaving the girl in nothing but a pair of tiny black micro-panties and a lacy French-cut bra.

"No!" the girl gasped as Hillary threw the ruined clothes to the side. "That was a three-hundred-dollar dress. I wasn't even done paying for it. You crazy bitch. You're going to pay me back for that."

"If I were you, sweetheart, I'd be more worried about what I might do to this tight white skin of yours. Mmm, pretty sexy underwear. Were you planning on letting your boyfriend get lucky tonight? A girl doesn't put on underwear like this unless she's planning to let someone else take it off. Too bad you had that tiff. I bet you're both sorry now. You naughty little girl."

Hillary cut away the girl's bra and panties, leaving her totally naked, except for the necklace.

"Is it real?" she asked, holding it away from the girl's throat, staring through the stones.

"Please," the girl said. "It was my mom's. She passed away when I was little. It's the only thing I have left of hers. Please, I'll give you anything else—"

Hillary let the necklace fall from her hand.

"It's okay. We'll leave it on for now. It becomes you."

"Who are you," the girl asked, perhaps mistakenly seeing in the gesture a touch of humanity. "What do you want from me? Do you want money, is that it? Let me out of here and I'll call my daddy. He's a plastic surgeon on Madison Avenue. He's done all the famous movie stars. He can get you the money. Just let me go."

Hillary shook her head. From one of the pockets of her jumpsuit she pulled a pair of ugly-looking silver clamps attached by a short chain. "I'm insulted, darling. Do I look like I need money? I'm glad to hear that your daddy is a plastic surgeon, though. After we're through with you here tonight you're going to need one."

She ran her hands over the girl's smooth flanks, up her sides, under her breasts, rubbing the girl's nipples under her thumbs until they hardened.

"Please—don't do that."

"Don't do what?" Hillary asked, looking the girl in the eye as she took hold of her left nipple and with her other hand attached one end of the nipple clamps.

"Ouch," the girl shouted as Hillary flicked her fingernail over the captive nub of flesh. "Dammit, that hurts! I said, don't—"

"It's unfortunate you have such a low threshold for pain, seeing that in the next several hours you're going to experience so much of it." The girl screamed as Hillary grabbed the girl's right breast, squeezed the nipple, and attached the second clamp. She jiggled the girl's breasts, the chain between the clamps jingling. "Don't you look pretty. Maybe later on we'll attach some weights to your breasts and see how strong they are."

"You bitch," the girl spat when the pain subsided. "You better let me the fuck out of here right now. Or else."

"Or else what, darling?"

"Or else what?" the girl repeated. Every breath she took made the chain between the nipple clamps sway, causing a new wave of pain. "Or else what?"

"Yes," Hillary said patiently. "What is it you're going to do?"

"I'll—I'll call the cops on you. That's what I'll do. You're in big trouble, you fucking pervert. My boyfriend, he knows people. You know what I mean? When I tell him about this—"

Hillary smiled. "You really aren't too bright, are you?"

"Fuck you," the girl muttered, breathless.

"I don't think you fully comprehend your current situation. Let me explain it to you. See if you can follow me here. You are bound, naked and helpless, in the soundproof basement of a secluded house. There is not a soul within miles of the place. To top it off, even were I to let you go, you have no idea where you are or who I am. Have I left anything out? I don't think so. In short, you are completely at my mercy, so I would think you'd be interested in cooperating with me."

The girl seemed to see the logic in Hillary's argument, and the fear was back in her eyes. "What do you want me to do?" she asked, and this time there was no whine, no entreaty, no guile in her voice at all.

Only submission.

"That's better." Hillary nodded. "You're learning. My friend and I just want to have a little fun."

"Friend?"

The girl jerked her head around, trying to look behind her. She saw Degas at the head of the table, his massive chest oiled and crisscrossed by studded leather straps, his genitals bulging inside the skintight leather pouch of his G-string. He, too, was wearing a black zipper mask.

The girl saw the whip coiled in his hand. "Don't you dare," she said. "Don't you dare hit me with that."

"Oh, not yet," Hillary laughed. "But soon. We have to work up to it first. By the way, you aren't by any chance a devotee of yoga, are you?"

"What are talking about?" the girl said, shaken and confused. The woman had scared her badly enough, but in the back of her mind she really hadn't thought a woman would hurt her too badly. The appearance of the man, however, had raised the stakes. Now she was afraid for her life.

"Yoga, darling. The ancient Indian art of meditation and flexibility training."

"I don't understand—"

"Well then, are you naturally double-jointed?"

"No—"

"More's the pity, I'm afraid," Hillary said with mock disappointment. "I'm afraid the following is going to be a bit uncomfortable for you then."

She motioned to Degas, and the muscleman slowly turned the spoked wheel to which the girl was attached. She gave a sharp intake of breath as she was stretched, her spine straightening, her toes pointing. Her flesh was pulled tautly across her rib cage, her face a mask of pain. He turned the wheel until the girl's body was held tightly enough to restrict any movement but that essential to breathing. "Please," the girl gasped. "I'll do anything you want. Please."

"Of course you'll do anything," Hillary said brightly. "What choice do you have? You're a slave, after all."

"I'm not—a slave," the girl managed.

A cold, steel-smelling sweat had broken out over her body.

Hillary had smelled it often.

It was the infamous smell of fear.

"Oh, but you are," she said. "Think about it. If you

weren't a slave, would you be in the predicament you're in right now? What purpose do you suppose you serve if not for the entertainment of your social superiors?"

"You are—the slaves," the girl said, the tension in her body making it all but impossible for her to catch her breath. Every word cost her precious air. "For doing this—to me. For trying—to make—me a slave."

Hillary laughed. "Slave logic. Turn her up another two notches, please. Let's see what kind of music she plays."

The girl's mouth opened and a low animal-like moan escaped.

"Say it," Hillary said, brushing the girl's sweat-soaked hair from her face. "Say it."

There was hardly any breath left in her, but the girl choked out the words in the hope that by doing so the pain would end.

"I—am—a—slave."

Hillary nodded.

At the head of the table Degas turned the wheel again the girl's joints made small popping sounds. Her buttocks and shoulders lifted off the table, her entire body suspended by the tension of the straps fastened around her wrists and ankles. The girl opened her mouth again, but no sound came out; it was as if all the breath in her body had been squeezed out of her.

"How are you feeling now, darling?" Hillary cooed. She thumped the girl's taut belly with her forefinger. "Tight as a drum. Not the least bit of fat, not that there was any to begin with. You really keep yourself in good shape. I bet I could bounce a quarter off that belly of yours."

She casually walked over to one of the sconces set in the wall and removed a burning candle, carrying it back to the rack and holding it over the girl's stretched, supine body. She smiled down at her and tilted the candle a little to one side, letting the burning wax that had accumulated around the wick drip down the center of the girl's chest.

The girl moaned soundlessly.

Hillary tipped the candle again, concentrating on splashing the hot wax over the girl's breasts, paying particular attention to the sensitive flesh around her clamped nipples. Then she dripped a burning line of wax down her belly, filling her navel, all the way down to the top of her pubes.

"I wonder if you can guess where we put the flame?"

Hillary saw the girl's limbs trembling with tension and terror. She tried to pull away, but, stretched as tightly as she was, any movement was impossible. Hillary held the candle closer, her face rapt above the flame, like that of a saint. The flame sputtered and spat, the room suddenly redolent with the acrid stench of singed hair. Hillary smiled as she pushed the candle forward, and from somewhere the girl found the last reserves of breath to enable her to scream. The scream died down like a siren disappearing into the distance and the girl's eyes glazed over into a kind of shocked detachment. From between her spread legs the candle stub emerged, a small plume of black smoke curling upward from her sex to the ceiling.

"Degas?"

The muscleman stepped forward with the whip, brushing the triple-thonged leather across the girl's taut, sweat-glistened belly. He brought his arm back, shaking the whip free, and slowly and deliberately did what he did best. Hillary watched closely, her own eyes glazed over, heart pounding in her ears, flinching with each blow, growing more and more excited. Several times Degas slowed up, anticipating that his mistress had had enough, but she only impatiently motioned him to continue. The girl's body was striped with blood and sweat, her face a mask of agony. Degas had never gone this far before and he was beginning to feel sick to his stomach. The girl had already lost control of her bladder and she was shuddering with convulsions. He didn't think she could take much more.

"Enough," Hillary said at last.

She had stripped off the jump-suit and gloves and was now wearing only the boots and mask. She crawled onto the rack above the semiconscious girl, carefully lowering herself over her bound body. She squirmed against the girl's supine body, grunting and whining like an animal in heat. She worked her way down, kissing every inch of the girl, licking her clean from head to toe, growing more and more excited. Degas turned away, unable to watch anymore, his mistress writhing on the stone floor at the girl's feet, her body lathered in her victim's blood.

Afterwards Degas chloroformed the girl again, wrapped her in an old blanket, and put her in the trunk of the limousine for the drive back to the city. He would leave her on a bench in Tompkins Square Park.

Before he carried her to the car, Hillary took one last look at her, caressing her face gently with her hand and kissing her good night on the forehead. The girl was still wearing the diamond necklace.

"If you're lucky, darling," she said without the least trace of irony, "the cops will find you before the homeless do."

Hillary sloppily poured herself a half tumbler of Scotch from the cut-glass decanter on the table and drank it down with one long practiced swallow, hoping the alcohol would steady her nerves, knowing full well that it wasn't alcohol that she needed. Edmund had spoken to her about her drinking, and she had told him truthfully that it wasn't a problem, and though she

29

could tell by the patronizing look he'd given her that he didn't believe her, how in the world could she tell him what was really the matter?

The knock on the door nearly made her drop the glass.

"What is it?" she snapped.

She heard Degas's softly accented voice on the other side of the door politely ask her if she were almost ready. She was sure that wasn't how the message had been relayed to him. He told her that Edmund was already downstairs in the car and that they were due at the Waldorf in less than an hour.

"Tell him I'll be right down," Hillary said, spitefully retrieving her hairbrush and starting her count all over again. "When I'm good and ready."

"Yes, ma'am."

She and Edmund hardly ever spoke directly anymore. By mutual, if unspoken, agreement they had taken up residence on opposite sides of the sprawling Long Island mansion. On the rare occasions when they did speak it was to discuss politics; Edmund still rarely made a move without her consultation. But their talks were never personal and were always conducted with an audience of Edmund's closest political aides. Even when she'd been in the hospital he'd never visited her alone.

As for sex, he hadn't touched her in years, and that was just fine with her. In fact, the only time he acted like her husband was in public. For that reason, among others, Hillary hated the endless round of fund raisers, rallies, benefit dinners, and gala openings they were required to attend. She hated the grinning insincerity of the people who came to them, the vacuous well-wishers, conniving sycophants, and toadying nobodies, all of them putting down their bets and hoping their thousand-dollar-a-plate dinner would be their ticket to the political winner's circle.

But, as Edmund explained it a hundred times, they were a necessary evil to what was the only thing important to either of them anymore. The latest *New York Times* poll had Edmund up by nineteen points over his nearest rival in the list of likely candidates for next spring's presidential primaries, and with the President's popularity plummeting every day, it looked like whoever captured the Democratic nomination would be the next president. If he could avoid any major scandals, Edmund looked to be a shoe-in for the nomination. Yet Hillary was well aware that in politics six months could be a lifetime. She'd have to be careful; she hadn't waited this long to blow it all now.

She put down the hairbrush and added a little more blush to her cheeks, accentuating her rather undramatic bone structure. She consoled herself with the fact that Edmund had only flown in for the dinner tonight. She'd only have to endure his presence for a few more hours; he'd be flying back to Washington in the morning. She had already begun to feel the familiar tingle between her thighs, and that was what had her so worried. It was an addiction even stronger than alcohol or drugs, more powerful than sex. She was worried about last night. Not because of what she'd done; she had done such things a hundred times before. Not because she was afraid she'd be found out. As she had told the girl, there was no chance of discovery.

She was worried because last night had been the worst of all and still it hadn't satisfied her.

She was worried *because she hadn't gone far enough.*

THREE

On Eric's plate a large gray fly was sipping soy sauce.

Kelly had watched it moving from table to table, sampling dishes as if it were at a smorgasbord, finally landing on Eric's mu shu pork. Now it stepped gingerly around the lake of dark sauce, leaving tiny brown fly footprints on the edge of the plate, and climbed inside the ruined tunnel of Eric's egg roll.

Dammit, when did their relationship come to this? That it was easier to watch a fly picking through the remains of dinner than to look him in the eyes.

Once she had thought she had never seen anything more beautiful than his dark brown eyes. Now she saw nothing in them but anger, resentment, and judgment. Once she had dreamed of losing herself in their dark, inviting depths. Now they seemed as shallow and cold as frozen puddles.

Where had they gone wrong?

They were sitting in a red leather booth at a small Chinese restaurant on Twenty-ninth street called the Dynasty Ox. The Ox was the kind of place you'd never think of entering unless you were a public health inspector—or you'd eaten there before and happened to know that it had the best Chinese food in the city. How you got in the door that first time always made for a great story. Everyone who was a regular patron fondly remembered the happy accident that brought them to the Ox.

For Kelly it had been a sudden downpour that caught her without an umbrella and sent her running for cover in the nearest available doorway, which just happened to belong to the Ox. As she waited for the rain to let up, she was seduced inside by the delicious aroma emanating from the restaurant every time someone opened the door.

She had taken her place in line at the take-out counter and found herself standing behind a handsome man with dark curly hair and shoulders that stretched the fabric of his corduroy coat. On a whim, she tapped him on the shoulder and asked if he could recommend something from the take-out menu. He'd suggested that she get the pork lo mein, and the rest was history.

He was a cop, he had told her later that evening. He said it with an air of defensiveness: the way someone might say "I'm Kosher" at a Tennessee pig-pulling. It was his way of telling her who he was and what he believed in. He couldn't have been more specific. Eric Rossi was a cop with a capital *C*.

"There's nothing fancy about me, honey," he had told her another time. "I am what you see. Just an old-fashioned guy with old-fashioned values."

At first, Kelly had liked that about him. Eric was older; he was experienced; he'd been around the block. Her friends had another way of putting it. They warned her that he was carrying a lot of extra baggage: an ex-wife and two kids in Jersey, for one thing. Kelly saw it as giving him a kind of integrity. The man knew something about life. Real life. And that made him vastly different from the vapid arty types she ordinarily came in contact with in a life that revolved almost exclusively around her job at *NiteLife* Magazine.

But Kelly hadn't seen the flip side of the coin until much later. Eric just couldn't understand her job at *NiteLife* or her undeniable interest in those he ungenerously called the city's low-lifes. At first it was something of a joke between them, but eventually the joke began to wear thin, and beneath the increasingly shrill laughter, Kelly had detected Eric's seething resentment. Soon he no longer bothered to conceal his contempt for her work and lately had begun to badger her to quit the magazine.

"Why can't you get a regular journalism job? Like at *Time* or *Newsweek*. Even the *Village Voice*, for crissakes?"

How could she explain to him the irresistible attraction she felt for the dark side of city life, the indescribable high of being in the know, of being hip, of traveling in a world that most people didn't even know existed? It was the high that all reporters felt to one degree or another, of living at a depth that most people could not sustain. She was sure that for Eric being a cop held much the same appeal, though he didn't seem to see the similarity.

Their latest skirmish was about an article Kelly had contracted to do on the growing number of S-M clubs in the city. As part of her research, she planned to work undercover at one such club as a female dominatrice and to interview the men and women who frequented the scene. She had tried to explain to Eric that one of the most fascinating aspects of the clubs was that they had very little to do with sex—at least, in any explicit way. In fact, all the reputable clubs had a strict rule against any genital contact whatsoever; many of them even forbade the exposure of erogenous parts altogether. It was all a matter of theater, a carefully orchestrated psychodrama in which powerful and often forbidden issues of dominance and submission were ritualized, dramatized, and resolved in a safe environment between consenting adults.

But Eric wasn't buying it. To him, women who dressed up in leather and whipped paying clients were prostitutes, plain and simple, even if the laws of the City of New York didn't quite see it that way. When he had found out about the story idea he'd nearly hit the roof. Gone was all pretense of tolerance. He came down on her with patriarchal wrath, all but forbidding her to take the assignment. Her friends were all fools, her interviews and articles nothing but chronicles of human perversion, the magazine she worked for nothing but a porno-graphic rag pandering to the basest human instincts and representing everything that was wrong with the city. The storm had been a long time building and when it finally spent itself they both were devastated by the emotional destruction it had left in its wake.

Only one thing remained the same: her determina-tion to go ahead with the story.

Tonight she was paying the price for that determina-tion. The tension had been there all through dinner. For the most part they had eaten in silence. It was as if the table between them were booby-trapped with a complex of invisible wires that one stray word or look might trip, blowing what was left of the relationship to bits.

He pointed to her plate. She had barely touched her pork lo mein.

"Is that all you're going to eat?" he asked. It wasn't so much a question as it was a challenge: the opening salvo in what she could sense was going to be the final battle.

"I guess I'm just not that hungry tonight," she an-swered truthfully, still hoping to evade the inevitable.

"It's supposed to be your favorite." There was a note of sarcasm in his voice, as if he were accusing her of having lied to him. Or maybe she was just being too sensitive.

35

He pulled out a pack of Camels, shook out a cigarette, and lit it with the monogrammed silver Zippo she had given him for his last birthday. Kelly saw the couple at the next table turn and look disapprovingly at the drifting cloud of gray smoke. She silently prayed they wouldn't make an issue of it. In his mood, Eric wasn't above starting a brawl.

He blew the acrid smoke across the table. "Do you want to talk about this or what?" he snapped.

"No," Kelly said quietly.

Eric shook his head disgustedly, the color creeping up from the open collar of his shirt.

He stabbed the half-smoked cigarette into his plate instead of using the ashtray. It was as if he were unconsciously trying to do everything he could to disgust her, making it that much easier for her to walk away.

"Dammit, Kelly," he growled. "Why are you doing this to me? You know it drives me crazy."

"What am I doing to you, Eric?" she asked, hating the bitchy tone that had crept into her voice.

"Giving me this silent treatment shit."

"I'm not giving you any silent treatment."

"Then why won't you at least talk about this?"

"Because I know what you're going to say and—"

"And you're not going to change your mind."

"No."

Kelly looked up, eyes blazing to match the rage she knew she would see in his eyes. Only it wasn't rage she saw there, but hurt and confusion. Still she couldn't allow herself to back down. "No," she repeated, more to steel herself than to answer his question. "I'm not going to change my mind."

This time she saw the emotion drain right out of his eyes. It was as if a great chasm had suddenly opened, cutting her off from the dark mystery of his identity and leaving nothing but the cold, cynical eyes of a stranger.

36

"So this is it, then?" he said, his voice cool and hard. His police training was asserting itself, sparing him the pain of feeling. She felt as she imagined his suspects must during an interrogation: as if she were nothing but an insect in his eyes.

"Well, then, the hell with you," he said, so savagely she flinched. He slid out of the booth and reached into his pocket for his wallet. He pulled out a twenty-dollar bill to cover dinner and let it float to the table, where it landed in a small dish of hot mustard. "Go interview your precious perverts, you dyke whore. Maybe you'll get lucky."

From the corner of her eye, Kelly saw Cho Li by the register, watching them with concern.

So there it was: the final betrayal. In a rare moment of openness, she had trusted him enough to tell him about a brief lesbian experimentation she'd once done with a close friend of hers. Now he was using that trust as a weapon against her, hoping to wound her one last time, to leave her a scar to remember him by, before he walked out of her life for good. In spite of herself she felt herself blush with shame, and instead of hurting her as he'd intended, she hated him for it.

"I'm not a dyke," Kelly said, speaking calmly, hoping he couldn't see how much he'd shaken her. "And I am not a whore. And the people I write about aren't perverted by hatred and bigotry like you are. Now please go, Eric."

"Oh, they're not perverts, are they?" he said grinning unpleasantly, not bothering to wait for an answer. "Then tell me just what the fuck you call them."

Kelly had been trying to answer the same question ever since she'd decided to take on the story for *NiteLife*.

She had heard about clubs like Paddles and Masters, as well as the New York Eulenspiegel Society, which served as a kind of dating service for the whips-and-

37

chains crowd. But recently, S-M had gained a mainstream acceptance that was bringing it out of the dark closet of sexual taboos and putting it right out there on display for everyone to see. Everywhere you looked there were the images: from rock music videos to perfume advertisements, from punk chic to high fashion, from best-selling books like Madonna's *Sex* to the Donahue show to films like *Basic Instinct* and *9½ Weeks*.

It was this trend that Kelly's publisher at *NiteLife* had wanted her to follow, sending her out to dig below the surface of pop culture's faddish interest in images of pain and discipline to get at the scene's roots in the domination clubs and bars springing up with such frequency throughout the darker environs of the city.

And what Joan wanted, she almost always got.

Not that she'd had to twist Kelly's arm to take the assignment. Part of what made Joan such a good publisher was that she had an instinctive sense of what writer would be good for what story. It was an instinct Kelly had learned to trust over time.

Her first contact with the S-M underground had come the night before last at a party for the controversial surrealist "filmmaker" Ivan Koski at a SoHo art studio. Joan was well connected with the SoHo art scene, and she had managed to call in some favors to get hold of a ticket, which was as rare as a virgin in a seminary. The party was so exclusive, it was rumored that Senator Edmund Stanton's wife, a well-known avant-garde patron, was one of the invited guests.

Kelly studiously tried to avoid Koski's work. His most recent film was an ultra-sleazoid sicko called *100 Dead Girls*. True to its title, the movie depicted no less than 100 murdered women. No plot, incidental dialogue, no redeeming social message, just scene after scene depicting scantily clad women killed in a variety of increasingly bizarre and violent ways. Car wrecks. Stabbings.

Drownings. Crucifixions. Electrocutions. Sometimes singly, sometimes in groups. The climactic scene featured no less than fifteen women in a steam room gunned down in slow-motion detail by automatic weapon fire, à la Sam Peckinpah. The total effect was both mind-numbing and nauseating.

And, thanks to the caprice of a select group of effete East Villagers, it was also Art.

Kelly was greeted at the door by a pouty boy dressed in a French maid's uniform. Inside, she saw a wild scene suggestive of the nightmare paintings of Hieronymous Bosch. The studio was packed with people. Businessmen and society ladies in sequined ball gowns mingled with tattooed bikers and bottle-blond streetwalkers in skin-tight leather skirts, though it was hard to tell if they weren't all actors in disguise. There was a goat snacking out of a bowl of pretzels, an assemblage of human "mannequins," and a nude modeling a bikini made entirely of link sausages carrying a cryptic sign that read "Make me meat, too, daddy."

Kelly found Koski in the middle of the room. He was dressed in his trademark white: white suit, slacks, socks, and shoes. His white shirt was buttoned all the way up to his chin. His bleached hair hung in feckless bangs over his high forehead. He seemed completely unperturbed by the chaos raging around him. He had often called himself the Unblinking Eye: the ultimate voyeur. His horror of anything suggestive of active participation in reality had become legendary.

He was perched on a revolving platform. His "throne" was a large, uncomfortable-looking chair presumably made of human bone and skin. Elsewhere, Koski had claimed that the chair had once belonged to the infamous Wisconsin cannibal Ed Gein, upon whose real life and crimes the movies *Psycho*, *Deranged*, and *Texas Chainsaw Massacre*, among others, were based. An admiring private collector, he said, had given him the chair in exchange for one of Koski's most outrageous collages: *Foot Fetish, No. 1*.

Kelly was led to the platform by one of Koski's asexual catamites and offered the seat across from him: a small chair with a wooden armpiece like they used to use in grade school. Kelly started to put her notebook down when she saw the large plastic obdurator glistening with lubricant fixed to the seat of the chair. She saw Koski smile, appreciative of the embarrassment the crude practical joke had caused her.

"Art is sadism," he announced.

His coterie of crackpot followers clapped with delight.

Overhead, a huge spotlight flooded the platform with a harsh, unforgiving light. A man in a gold spandex jockstrap, a huge camera hoisted on one shoulder, followed the platform around and around, filming Koski as he sat pontificating. It was baking under the light, but Koski didn't seem to notice. In fact, he hadn't even broken a sweat.

In the middle of the platform, tied by the wrists to the post around which the platform slowly revolved, was a naked woman. Looped around her neck was a piece of rough butcher's twine from which hung a red china marker. It dangled between her breasts like a piece of jewelry. Her damp body was already covered with various slogans, many of which were obscene. Koski leaned forward and scrawled his latest aphorism across the girl's upper right thigh.

"Do you like my latest manifesto?" he asked Kelly, indicating the graffitti-clad nude. "I call it—"

He suddenly leaned forward again, apparently seized with inspiration, and grabbed the marker in one hand and the girl's sweating buttocks in the other. When he was done he turned the girl back to her former position.

40

Across her buttocks, emblazoned in large red capital letters, Kelly saw what he had written.

"Domination!" he cried.

His disciples oohed and aahed.

Later that same evening, a woman dressed in a five-hundred-dollar Olga Mano black evening gown pulled Kelly aside in the corner of the room and told her she had been to this outré new club in the Village. She was coked up, barely able to balance herself on a pair of thin silver spikes, and she kept trying to touch Kelly's breasts.

Kelly figured it was just some kind of bizarre come-on or, more likely, part of the evening's theatrics. But as Kelly tried to push past her, excusing herself to go to the bathroom, the woman pulled down her gown and showed Kelly a small red tattoo depicting two puncture marks on her left breast. She waved her hand wearily to take in the room behind her.

"They're all bloodsuckers you know," she sighed with stylish boredom and drifted off into the crowd.

"She's right," Kelly heard a voice at her shoulder. Turning, she saw a pretty, petite woman in a miniskirt and cowboy boots.

"Name's Valerie," the woman said, juggling her drink and offering Kelly her right hand. "Valerie Lawson."

"Kelly Mitchell."

"You interested in the S-M scene?"

"Yes," Kelly said, feeling as if she were in some kind of third-rate spy movie: the scene where the hero is approached by a member of the underground and has to guess the secret password. "I'm kind of new at this, though. It's a little overwhelming."

"Well don't let this shit fool you," Valerie said. "This has nothing to do with real S-M. Koski is just an old imposter. But it sure as hell is funny."

"Are you involved, then?"

"You might say that," the woman said. "To the out-

41

side world I'm Valerie Lawson, mild-mannered graduate student in anthropology at NYU. To my stable of loyal slaves, however, I am the beloved and dreaded Mistress Kane. I work in a dungeon on the Upper East Side."

Valerie laughed and tossed her long red hair. It was hard to imagine the cherubic little redhead as a leather-clad, whip-toting Amazon. She slipped a card out of the pocket of her motorcycle jacket and handed it to Kelly. "We're always looking for new talent. Stop by if you're interested. The pay's great, and it's a lot of fun having men groveling at your feet."

"What's the matter, food no good tonight?" It was Cho Li's wife, wiping her hands on a dirty towel.

"The food is delicious, as usual," Kelly said, and forced herself to smile. "It's my stomach that's not feeling so well."

"Ah. Stomach not good. I see," she said tactfully. Kelly was sure her husband had told her about the fight with Eric and sent her over to make sure everything was all right. She pointed to the lo mein on Kelly's plate. "You want me wrap. Yes?"

Though she doubted she would be hungry later, Kelly didn't want to risk hurting the old woman's feelings. "Yes. Thank you."

When she had gone with her plate Kelly sipped her tea, trying to appear as natural as possible. She was aware of the sudden quietness of the couple at the next table, could feel their eyes on her, searching her for clues. She was sure Eric had kept their conversation too low for them to overhear the particulars, though it must have been pretty obvious that they'd been arguing. If nothing else, Kelly was determined not to give them the

42

satisfaction of thinking they'd witnessed anything significant.

Instead, she looked casually around the restaurant for what she knew might well be the last time.

It was unlikely that after tonight she would ever be able to come back here again. She took in the grease-stained walls incongruously decorated with peeling travel posters of France and Italy and interspersed with amateurish oil paintings of seascapes and sunsets executed by Cho Li's brother.

She watched as Cho Li himself bustled in and out of the kitchen with his ever-present meat cleaver. She would miss the place, that was for sure. But she wouldn't want to risk running into Eric here again. Even if she could ensure that she wouldn't run into him, the memories of all the meals they'd shared in the restaurant would be too painful.

"Here you go," the Chinese woman said, depositing a small cardboard box on the table, along with a small white plate. "You come back soon, yes?"

"Sure," Kelly said, forcing another smile. She hated lying to the woman, but what else could she say?

There was a single fortune cookie on the plate in front of her. Kelly reached over, cracked it open, and pulled out the small piece of paper inside.

It was blank.

FOUR

Monica Caron stood in front of the huge floor-to-ceiling window with all of New York City lying bejeweled and abandoned at her feet. Her suite overlooked Fifth Avenue, and across the street stood the Metropolitan Museum of Art, in whose celebrated exhibits it had amused her to see what she considered inconsequential personal mementos preserved as priceless historical artifacts. Beyond that, she saw the vast green swath that was Central Park, sleeping like a dragon in a prison of concrete.

"Is the room satisfactory, Ms. Hunt?"

Monica turned from the view to the bellhop.

"It will do," she said.

She had registered under the name of Portia Hunt. The girl at the front desk had typed it carefully into her computer. When she asked for her credit card Monica had stunned her into speechlessness by pulling out eighteen crisp one-thousand-dollar bills. The girl stared at the money in her hand as if Monica had handed her a lighted stick of dynamite. From out of nowhere the night manager had materialized, all smiles, to welcome her to the hotel and to place himself at her disposal. He subtly took the money from the girl and slipped it into his jacket pocket, no doubt to have it checked by the resident currency expert to ensure that it wasn't counterfeit.

"Where would you like me to put these bags?" the bellhop asked.

"Take the large one into the bedroom. The small one goes in the bath. The others you can leave where they stand. I'll take care of them myself later."

She could sense the man's hostility beneath his carefully cultivated solicitude. His contempt was masked, but it was expressed in an infinite number of subconscious communications: the way he held his head, the cast of his shoulders, the inflection of his voice. Most of the rich people he served, having lost the ability or the will, no doubt would never have noticed it. He might not even have been aware of it himself. But to a natural master it was obvious in his very posture. Circumstance, not nature, had made this man a slave.

Monica watched him with interest, as a scientist watches the behavior of a rat in a maze.

Like all the hired help, he was dressed in a special uniform meant to identify him as a hotel employee. In his case the uniform consisted of gray pants with maroon piping, a French-cut shirt with a cranberry cravat, and a maroon waistcoat with epaulets that would have embarrassed a South American dictator. On his head he was required to wear an Australian fedora sporting a long maroon plume.

Like all uniforms, it negated his individuality. But worse, it singled him out as one whose duty it was to serve. How many people would he come in contact with today? Fifty? A hundred? And how many would see his face? How many others would see nothing more than that preposterous uniform, nothing more than a faceless, nameless drone whose sole duty in life it was to carry their bags, open their doors, hail their cabs?

How he must hate getting up every morning and put-

45

ting on that uniform! What, Monica wondered, kept a man at such a job?

As he grabbed the handle of one of the suitcases, she noticed the gold wedding band encircling the ring finger of his left hand. Ah, she thought, love doth make slaves of us all. He might as well have had that golden ring welded through his nostrils.

She eased into his mind, eavesdropped on his thoughts, not surprised at what she found there.

He was grabbing her roughly around the arms, stifling her cries with his palm as he pushed her down onto the antique sofa. He ripped away the fabric of her clothes, his need angry and urgent, his breath hot in her face with profanity and threat. His hands were everywhere at once, her breasts, her buttocks, between her legs. He entered her brutally, vengefully, as if she were life and fate themselves and he was fucking them back. All the while he breathed curses in her ear, telling her how much she wanted it, how much she deserved it, how much she loved it.

Underneath the angry rap Monica read the subtext of his violent stream-of-consciousness. The thoughts of rape were harmless, only compensatory. They were the result of his own feelings of inadequacy and the frustration he felt recognizing that he would never be her social equal no matter what he achieved in life. The simple fact of the matter was that he did not want to hurt or humiliate her at all; he instinctively realized it wasn't in his power. The truth was far more shocking than that. What he really wanted to do was to make love to her.

Monica watched, amused, as the images of violence changed until the movie playing in his mind was one of soft and romantic sensuality. In his fantasy she was lying on the king-size bed, gloriously naked, while he crouched between her legs, gently worshipping at the altar of her sexuality, his tongue singing the goddess's prayer. Paradoxically enough, he was still wearing the uniform.

The bellhop jerked his head up, like a fish with a hook in its lip.

He had felt the invasion as she purposely stepped out of hiding and make her presence felt inside his mind.

She heard him thinking that he was being ridiculous, that she couldn't read his mind, telling himself that it was only his imagination. She intensified her consciousness inside his mind, flooding the inside of his skull with her awareness, revealing everything that was hidden there. She enjoyed the look of confusion contorting his features, the deep blush coloring his flesh, the way he immediately dropped his eyes to the floor, his voice thick and choked as he forced himself to ask her if that was all.

Monica let him stand there and contemplated his embarrassment. He seemed to physically wither under her unrelenting gaze. Even from across the room she could smell the perspiration breaking out under his armpits. Inside his jockey shorts, his penis had retracted, his testicles shriveling up protectively, hard and small as two acorns.

No more rape fantasies there.

"You may go," she said finally.

His body sagged, crucified by tension.

"Yes, ma'am," he whispered.

He hurried from the room.

Monica laughed. He hadn't even waited for his tip.

Monica sat behind the antique French hunt desk that stood by the window. She opened the drawer and removed two sheets of expensive vellum embossed with her family's gold and scarlet hereditary crest. She

47

paused for a moment to run her fingers over the texture of the paper.

Real lamb's skin.

On such paper, writing was more than just a means of communication: It was an act of sensuality.

Such quality was lost today from the lives of most people. Alas, the days when the old magicians wrote their grimoires in human blood on human flesh were gone forever. And so, too, she feared, had the quality of literature. The last time she had been to a B. Dalton Bookseller she had been shocked to see the classics crowded onto four shelves crouched forlornly at the back of the store, surrounded on all sides by all manner of mindless schlock. In the old days the elite knew that only if the means of writing were expensive and limited would anyone think twice about whether what they were writing were important enough to be recorded for posterity.

She uncapped her Mont Blanc fountain pen and began to write.

She lifted the pen from the paper and stared out the window. The lights of the city twinkled from a million windows. Down below, she could hear the sounds of traffic, like the trumpeted echo of prehistoric beasts. In the middle of that great sea of lights, the park was an oily slick of blackness.

Monica knew that somewhere down in the darkness there was a man getting mugged by three youths armed with sawed-off baseball bats. A woman had just been raped at knifepoint and left for dead, her face needlessly slashed from eye to lip. A teenage runaway was kneeling on sharp stones behind some bushes giving a blow job to a horse patrolman, whose partner stood lookout on the path. And at that very moment a large gray rat had waddled out from the sewer near the lake and attacked a skinny cat licking the secret sauce off an old Big Mac wrapper.

She read over what she had written, blew on the brownish-red ink to make sure it was dry, and then carefully folded the paper in threes. She slipped it into an envelope and printed the address of Hillary Stanton's Long Island mansion on the front. She tore a stamp off the roll provided by the hotel, licked it, and placed it in the corner. She would have to remember to drop the letter down the mail chute at the end of the hall in the morning.

She leaned back in the wooden chair and rubbed her eyes lightly with her fingertips.

There was a soft knock on the door.

Right on time.

"Enter," Monica said.

The door opened and the bellhop came in wheeling a silver ice bucket in which rested a single bottle.

He stopped just inside the doorway. He looked around the darkened suite and saw Monica sitting by the window, his heart skipping a beat. She was dressed in a sheer black negligee she had once worn when sharing the bed of Tsar Nicholas and Alexandra.

"Champagne, ma'am," he stuttered, looking immediately uncomfortable, as if he didn't know where to put his eyes. He appeared to have recovered nicely from his earlier embarrassment, though he probably thought he'd recovered a lot better than he did now that he was actually in the room with her once again. All in all, he seemed like a man torn in opposite directions, the desire to bolt for the door equally as strong as the desire to be in her presence, leaving him paralyzed by indecision, like a man tied between two powerful horses. "Compliments of the house. Hope I didn't disturb you."

"Not at all," Monica said.

"Can I pour you a glass?" he said.

"Yes do."

He crossed the room to the small wet bar in the corner. He was still wearing the demeaning uniform, but he had somehow managed to dispense with the hat. She watched his movements carefully, appraising the slope of his shoulders, the shift of his buttocks, the strong clean line of his jaw. Throughout the centuries she had stood beside countless auction blocks, in China, Egypt, Greece, Rome, and the United States, wherever there was commerce in naked mortal bodies, and her experience had made her nothing short of a connoisseur. In another time and place he would have made an excellent pleasure slave. Still, she was sure she could find a use for him during her stay in New York.

He took down an elegant long-stemmed champagne flute from the overhead rack. He set the glass on the tiled bar top a little too hard. Monica noticed that his hands were trembling.

She moved to an armchair for a more comfortable view and watched as the man carried the glass over to where she sat, looking as if he were walking on a highwire suspended miles above the ground.

Even in the dim lamplight Monica could see that he was handsome. His thick but neatly trimmed black hair contrasting nicely with a striking pair of blue eyes that reminded her of sunset on the Aegean. She imagined that beneath the uniform his body was brown and sculpted, powerful pectorals shaded by dark curling hair tapering over his washboard belly. She licked the edges of her teeth in anticipation.

"What is your name?" Monica asked.

"My-uh-name?" he asked, as if stumped. In spite of himself, he'd been unable to take his eyes off her body, which was all but exposed beneath the diaphanous material of the negligee, her white flesh glowing like the moon behind a cloud.

"Yes," Monica repeated patiently. "Your name."

"Daniel," he said, almost apologetically, as if it were preposterous that he have a name at all.

"Daniel," Monica said, delighted. "Do you want to fuck me, Daniel?"

The man looked at her, stupefied. "I—um. I think I should be going."

"I'm sorry. I didn't mean to frighten you. But I'm used to speaking my mind. I didn't scare you, did I?"

"No, ma'am."

"Good. Have a seat, Daniel," Monica said, motioning to the armchair across from her. "You will sit with me for a while, yes?"

The man nodded his head dully. He sat down in the chair, still holding the forgotten flute of champagne.

"Good. I do so hate to drink alone. Go ahead," Monica said, nodding to the glass.

The man drank half the ginger-colored liquid; he came up for air, and then drained the glass dry. Monica could sense the color rising to the man's cheeks, smell the warmth of his blood in the air, and beneath it, the first stirring of sexual excitement.

"Take off your tie," Monica said. "I want you to be comfortable."

He pulled the the cravat out of his shirt, loosened it from around his throat.

"Good," she said. "Very good. I want to make you a little business proposition, Daniel. First, though, I want you to unbutton your shirt."

The man did as he was told, numb fingers clumsily pulling at the buttons of his shirt, until it lay open to his waist. The lamplight played over his burnished flesh, leaving an intricate and pleasing play of shadows over his muscular torso. "Oh, yes," she said. "That's very nice."

51

She let her hand drift over the thin material covering her breasts.

"I would like you to come work for me," Monica said. "I need a—bodyguard. Does that sound interesting to you, Daniel?"

The man nodded. His eyes were staring, unfocused, his mind clouding with desire.

"Very well, then," Monica said. "The first thing I want you to do is take that uniform off."

The man did as he was told, quickly stripping off his clothes, standing naked and erect before her.

"From now on that is the only uniform you need wear in my presence."

Monica spotted the gold band on his hand. "The ring, Daniel."

The man stared down at his hand.

"Take it off."

With difficulty, the man pulled off the ring, letting it fall to the carpet.

"Where you're going, you must leave everything behind. Everything. Do you understand?"

"Yes, ma'am," he whispered.

"Come, Daniel," Monica said, her voice barely audible in the still room.

The man fell to his knees before her chair.

"I thirst, Daniel," the woman said, "Do you understand?"

The man nodded, eyes downcast.

This time Monica thought the words instead of saying them.

Then serve me.

FIVE

"He said that?"

Kelly stared into the golden depths of her second Scotch and soda. "Uh-hum," she said, taking another sip. The alcohol had loosened her tongue and she found herself in the mood to talk. "He all but accused me of leaving him for another woman."

She wasn't accustomed to drinking the hard stuff, but she had needed something stronger than her usual light beer to take the edge off the pain of the night before. She had watched "The Tonight Show" and "Late Night" and then some lame horror movie on HBO about a glowing stone that turned its possessor into a man-eating wolf before finally drifting off to sleep on the couch at about three in the morning.

Even though she had seen the breakup with Eric coming for quite some time, she didn't find it any easier to accept. Twice already today she'd had to fight off the urge to pick up the phone and call him. In the back of her mind there was still the nagging hope that she could make everything between them all right again.

But it wasn't all right. She knew that. And what's more, it could never be all right again. Eric had let his mask slip down last night, the mask everyone wore during the first golden days of a relationship. The mask that said "I'm all right, you're all right; I eat what you eat; I believe what you believe; I want what you want." But what Kelly had seen in the face behind his mask last night had shocked her.

It was the face of something alien, something hostile, something carniverous. And what it wanted to do was to devour her life.

Still, there was that damned urge to call. It orbited inside her body, like a physical need, each time coming back a little stronger than the time before. The last time it had come back she had called Gwen and asked her to meet her for a drink. Somehow it seemed appropriate. Out of all her friends, Eric had disliked Gwen the most. Predictably enough, the feeling on Gwen's part was mutual.

Gwen's effect on men had always mystified Kelly. She was undeniably attractive—blonde, green-eyed, and freckled—with a pixielike, aerobicized body and a dynamite smile. Definitely more small-town cute than big-city chic, but knock-down sexy all the same, even in the blazer-and-skirt uniform of an NBC page. Still, all but the most obtuse men seemed to know to keep their distance. It was as if she gave off some kind of sexual pheromone that let them know they'd just be wasting their time.

"He wanted me to quit writing."

"Fuck him," Gwen said a little too loudly. A pair of businessmen along the bar turned and looked curiously in their direction. Gwen didn't seem to notice.

T.G.I. Friday's was one of those goofy theme restaurants with looseleaf-thick menus and all kinds of junk hanging from the walls. But the bar was large and comfortable, and it was the kind of place where two unescorted women could sit at lunch and share a drink without feeling like bleeding meat in a shark tank. At this time of the afternoon the restaurant was filled with office workers from Time Warner and the NBC building across the street, as well as the omnipresent tourist crowd who'd drifted over from Rockefeller Center, looking for a cheap place to eat.

"You know I never liked that sonofabitch," Gwen said, sucking the last of her banana daiquiri through a straw. "I warned you about cops."

"Cops are okay."

Gwen snorted. "They're all fucking Nazis. You're an artist, Kell. A free spirit."

Kelly rolled her eyes.

"No kidding. I read that piece you did on the new bohemians. Great stuff. Real genius. You want to know where you would have been in two years if you stuck with him? I'll tell you. Cooped up in some overheated apartment in Bensonhurst, standing in the kitchen with his mother, for crissakes, stirring a pot of tomato sauce and watching his kids while he was out playing softball with the boys."

"His kids are nice," Kelly said, a little sentimentally, remembering how Eric's younger girl had taken to her right off.

"You're missing the point."

"Which is?"

"He was poison for you, Kell. If he could, he would have sucked the life right out of you."

"You're just jealous," Kelly teased.

"Damn right I am."

"Aw come on, Gwen." Kelly laughed.

"Well, if you ever get the inclination to walk on the dark side again . . ."

"Thanks, Gwen. It's comforting to know your available for stud service. At least I won't have to fear becoming an old maid. I have to warn you, though, my sex drive is insatiable."

"So's my appetite."

"I remember."

"Seriously, Kell," Gwen said, "if you ever need someone—no strings attached—I . . ."

"Oh, knock it off." Kelly waved her off, as if it were a joke. But she knew it wasn't. There was something sad and desperate in Gwen's face.

Something vulnerable. And terribly naked.

"I just wanted you to know . . ."

"I know," Kelly said quietly. She wondered how the hell Eric had figured it out. "Gwen?"

"Yeah?"

"Thanks."

"No prob."

The mask had slipped back on and once again it was the same old Gwen. Cool. Hip. Cynical.

Kelly was thankful. She didn't need any more psychic grief.

Gwen checked her watch. "Well, I guess I should be heading back to the studio. I got a busload of fucking Mormons to lead through "The Tonight Show" set. Do you believe that? Mormons, for crissakes. It's amazing how far people will come to see a pressboard desk and a couple of cheesy chairs that Chevy Chase and Jaclyn Smith farted in."

Once again Kelly noticed the businessmen looking in their direction. She wondered if they worked at NBC.

Gwen pulled out a twenty to cover the drinks.

"Oh, no," Kelly said, grabbing for her pocketbook. "I asked you."

Gwen waved her off. "Don't worry about it. You're treating me to lunch next time."

"I am?" Kelly said, amused. She dropped her purse back into her open pocketbook.

"Your damn right you am."

They pushed their way through the crowded bar to

56

the revolving door, which disgorged them into the noon-time hustle-bustle of Fiftieth Street.

"Bye, love," Gwen said and kissed Kelly softly on the cheek.

She stood there gazing at Kelly, her mask once again slipping, the woman beneath looking perfectly helpless, like a doe stopped for a moment at the crest of a hill, the dogs hot on her trail.

Kelly was about to say something, but before she could Gwen turned and dashed across the street. In her wake, a yellow taxi screeched to a stop and some guy who looked like an assassin leaned out the window, gestured with his fist, and started screaming curses in Farsi.

SIX

Rossi drove west down Fulton Street toward the World Trade Center and the docks along the Hudson River. He split his attention between the chaotic traffic pattern and the temperature gauge of his old Grand Prix as the needle nudged past the halfway point and moved perilously close to the red area.

It was an unseasonably warm November afternoon, even for New York City, and the compressor in his air conditioner had been busted since August. He buzzed down the power windows and the air that blew in was hot and fetid, full of carbon monoxide, rotting garbage, and the sour stink of human frustration. He buzzed the window back up.

It wasn't even rush hour yet, but already the streets were filling up. In another hour the city would be tied up in knots.

A yellow cab swung out in front of him, and Rossi slammed on his mushy brakes, nearly taking out a bicycle messenger riding the slipstream on his flank. The cyclist whipped past him, raising his middle finger. The cab was now wedged catty-corner between Rossi and the city bus in front of him.

Rossi elbowed his horn.

He felt the sweat jiggling down the side of his face. It felt cold as mercury against his warm skin.

He glanced at the rearview mirror and caught sight of his face. He looked like death warmed over. And no wonder. After leaving Kelly in the restaurant, he'd gone straight to a bar in Brooklyn to get shitfaced. He gave himself a headstart and then staggered home to finish the job. His plan was to drink himself into oblivion, and in New York City you just didn't do that in public unless you were looking to wake up in a metal drawer wearing nothing but a toe-tag.

He finally accomplished his aim at about five in the morning, passing out on the couch. The first thing that greeted him at three-thirty the following afternoon was the sight of an empty bottle of Dewars lying on its side on the coffee table. The second was the call from Graham. He grabbed the phone merely to shut it up, each ring like a nail being driven into the space between his eyes. On the other end, Graham sounded as if he were speaking through a megaphone. Rossi held the receiver about three inches from his ear. As it was, it took him several minutes to process exactly what his partner was saying.

The gist of it was that they had found a body down by Pier 25 that they thought he should see. Rossi told Graham to give him half an hour and spent nearly all that time trying to get up off the floor and cursing himself for having picked up the phone in the first place. He stumbled into the bathroom to pee, shoved a half-dozen aspirin in his mouth, stuck his gun in his pants, and grabbed his sportscoat from behind the couch, where he had thrown it the night before. He was on the Brooklyn Bridge into Manhattan within an hour.

Now, as he sat stuck in traffic, his mind went back to the night before. He had regretted his behavior at the restaurant from the moment he had left. What the hell had gotten into him, anyway? He could feel himself losing it, knew he was going to be sorry, and yet he had not been able to stop himself from saying what he knew would hurt her. How could he have lost control like that? He had known from the day they met how important her career was to her. He had accepted it then, in the first blush of their relationship, perhaps hoping in the back of his mind that he could change her. He should have known better. His ex-wife had tried to change him. It just doesn't work. He wanted to call Kelly, to apologize, but what could he possibly say that would exonerate him from being such an ass?

If there was anything he'd learned from the breakup of his marriage, it was that there were some truths no relationship could survive, emotions that, once released, could never be put back in the box again. Last night he had ripped up some old rotted boards and showed her where the slimy, crawling things were: It was a sight she would never forget, a sight she would remember whenever she looked into his eyes.

God, he felt awful. He hadn't felt this bad since his divorce. He and Margie had had nothing left by the time they'd finally called it quits, yet leaving his home and his kids had been the hardest thing he'd ever had to do. In a way, this was even worse—worse because he still loved Kelly. He felt just plain empty, hollow, as if someone had stuck a vacuum cleaner hose up his asshole and Hoovered out his insides.

The traffic started moving again, and Rossi swung onto Greenwich Street and from there to the West Side Highway, along the river. He glanced to his left. Through the window the Hudson River lay flat and brown and lifeless. So polluted, nothing could live in it anymore. So full of chemicals and waste and garbage, it had turned into a river of poison. It was like the River

Styx, separating the living from an island of the walking dead.

Along the sidewalks Rossi saw men dressed in blood-stained white smocks, looking like trauma surgeons after five or six hours in the ER. Some were pushing large wheeled frames, like they did in the garment district, only instead of wholesale coats and suits, from these frames hung the butchered carcasses of cattle and pigs. This was the city's meat-packing district. Most of the city's meat supply was brought in here, processed, and distributed to supermarkets throughout the five boroughs. The area had a well-deserved reputation as one of the rougher places of town. Maybe it was the raw, coppery smell of blood that seemed to hang in the air. It was no secret to the cops that worked homicide that not all of the blood routinely spilled in this part of town was animal.

It was also no secret that the area was a favorite mob burial ground. There were some pretty persistent rumors that the mystery of Jimmy Hoffa's disappearance could be solved right here. Though there were those who vociferously insisted that the late teamster boss was planted under the end zone of Giants Stadium in the Meadowlands, there were others as passionately convinced that Hoffa's postmortem care had been conducted right here under the supervision of a local mob butcher. The theory went that when Labor Day rolled around that year, Americans all over the East Coast had a little bit of Jimmy in their hot dog bun beneath the mustard and sauerkraut. Rossi had to admit that the hot dog theory had a certain convincing ring to it. To be sure, it had all the imprimatur of the mob's poetic sense of justice. Not to mention their macabre sense of humor.

He found the warehouse he was looking for without any problem. Even without the address he would have recognized it by the flashing lights of the squad cars and

EMT vehicles parked along the curb. A small detail of uniformed officers had set up a perimeter, marking off the area with yellow tape, keeping back the small group of curiosity-seekers who had gathered in the hope of catching a glimpse of the latest New York City carnage. It was always the same. Whenever the crime was committed no one was ever around to see a thing. But five seconds after the corpse was discovered, people started appearing from out of nowhere, like flies on a fresh-dropped dog turd, buzzing with excitement, each of them anxious to be outraged by the brutality of their fellow citizens. It was as if they drew some kind of sustenance from death. You could see it in their faces: a smooth, radiant, excited look that made everyone appear at least ten years younger. Just once he'd like to see one of them have to go to the door of some poor bastard at three in the morning and inform them that their mother, father, son, daughter, husband, or wife had just been found murdered. He was sure that would squelch the light right out of their silly faces. Death was the kind of news that *aged* a person ten years, whether giving it or receiving it.

Rossi pulled up to the curb, climbed out of the car, and started toward the warehouse.

He raised his detective's shield and the crowd parted reluctantly to let him through. A uniform stepped forward from behind the tape to check his identification. The young cop looked suspiciously at the badge and then at Rossi, as if he expected some kind of ruse, and then held up the tape and waved him through.

Rossi met Graham at the loading bay where the big cop had gone to get some air and smoke a cigarette. Rossi noticed that the seasoned homicide investigator was fumbling with his matches and cigarette.

Not a good sign.

"What the hell happened to you?" Graham asked, finally getting the match lit. He dropped it to the ground without lighting the cigarette. "You look like shit."

"I feel like shit, too," Rossi said. "So step carefully."

Graham grunted and led him to the freight elevator at the side of the warehouse.

"You don't look so hot yourself," Rossi said as they headed up to the third floor of the building. "What's going on in here that's so fucking important you had to wake me up from a drunken stupor to see?"

Graham told him that three meatpackers on their lunch break had snuck into the abandoned warehouse with a prostitute and some beer, looking to have a good time. What they found instead was a dead Jane Doe hanging from her tootsies like a side of beef. From what they could tell so far it looked like she had been killed right there in the warehouse sometime late the night before.

They exited the elevator, and Rossi found himself in a huge, loftlike room that ran nearly the entire length of the third floor of the building. There were more uniforms patrolling the area, radios squawking from their utility belts, making sure that no one from the *Times* or, God forbid, the *Post*, had found their way past the outer perimeter.

"Back this way," Graham said.

Rossi followed him to the rear of the huge room. There, in a kind of recessed alcove, more yellow tape was stretched across the doorway.

"In there," Graham said, pointing. "If you don't mind, I'll wait here."

Rossi stepped inside.

The orange-suited technicians from the crime lab were just finishing up. If he'd come earlier, he would have had to don one of their orange uniforms, complete with hair net and booties. As it was, the scene had probably already been compromised when the meatpackers first stumbled in hours ago. Now the last of the ident techs was carefully laying up his plastic Ziploc bags of fibers and hair samples and closing up his bag of tricks.

"All yours, captain," he said, as he passed by Rossi.

Suddenly Rossi was alone in the close room. There was a broken pane of glass on the boarded-over window. A large wooden table, scarred with knife marks. A barrel of old rags stood in the far corner. On the ceiling there was a metal track from which hung, one after another, a series of large, cruel-looking iron meathooks.

On one of these hooks hung the naked body of Jane Doe.

Her ankles had been lashed together with a pair of leather cuffs. She had been turned upside down, hoisted, and hung from her bound feet.

Though he hadn't wanted to look, he couldn't help it. His eyes traveled down the length of her body to her face. It wasn't morbid curiosity that caused him to look, but a need to personalize this horrendous crime, to help remind him that the victim was a human being with hopes and dreams, not simply a lifeless corpse to be tagged, bagged, and forgotten, just another number in the city's mounting homicide rate. He felt the need to see the face of the person who'd met with such an end, to form some kind of silent communion with her, to promise her he'd do his best to find whoever was responsible. At least that was what he told himself.

It was the faces that always haunted him. The faces that would come back in his nightmares.

Sometimes the faces he saw looking back from the other side were shocked, or outraged, or just plain sad. Most disturbing of all was that most of the time they looked as if they were at peace.

Rossi looked down to where her face should be and saw . . . *nothing*.

And then, as if by a whisper, his eyes were drawn to the left.

There, on an overturned metal bucket, her head had been propped.

Rossi felt his stomach roll at the sight. He closed his eyes, as if trying to adjust them to a sudden darkness, and then opened them again, hoping to see things in a clearer light.

That's when he realized the second odd thing about the murder scene.

Of all the rooms in this particular part of the city, this was probably the only one in which there wasn't a single drop of blood.

SEVEN

Father Paul wiped his forehead with a handkerchief. He picked up the bottle of warm Snapple and quietly sipped the iced tea through a straw. In the closeness of the confessional he could smell the cheesy heft of his own sweating body. He shifted his weight on the hard wooden bench, the bones in his buttocks feeling sore and bruised. He stared at his watch in the gloom, barely able to pick out the time.

Thank God.

Only another ten minutes to go.

On the other side of the screen he listened wearily as Sima Harrison confessed to spending her welfare check on crack while her baby went hungry. She had told him the same story the month before and the month before that. When she was done he told her to say five Our Fathers and seven Hail Marys. Then he waved his hand in a lazy semblance of the Holy Cross and bid her take care of the precious gift God had entrusted to her.

"Go in peace," he muttered.

"Thank you, Father," she said, sounding genuinely relieved.

He slid the panel closed and sighed.

His parish was one of the poorest in the city. As a younger man, fresh out of the seminary, he had seen the glamour in that. Now he saw nothing but the squalor and the hopelessness. Then he'd been inspired with a sense of mission and the conviction that he could make a difference in people's lives. In the beginning he firmly believed that faith could conquer the despair that surrounded him on every side, the poverty, the crime and, worst of all, the apathy of society itself. Now he himself stood among the vanquished.

In his years inside this booth he'd heard every degradation of which the human animal was capable. A man who stabbed his best friend for twenty dollars to pay for drugs. A teenage girl who left her newborn infant in a trash bin. A father unable to resist the temptation of sleeping with his nine-year-old stepdaughter. There were others, too, not so dramatic, but every bit as ugly; uglier in a way, for they illustrated the everyday evil of the human mind: the jealousy, the lust, the anger, and the pettiness of the people who stood beside you on the subways, at the traffic lights, in the grocery lines. Inside the confessional he could eavesdrop into the mind of Man, and what he'd heard there over the past twenty-seven years had sickened him unto death. He had heard it all; he had forgiven it all.

If only he still believed in what he was doing with his life. If only he could muster a belief in *God*. But the fact was, he didn't believe in Him at all. Sometimes he wondered if he ever really had.

How easy it would have been to blame his lack of faith on failed ideals instead of a basic flaw in his own character. Perhaps the bishop would better understand his slide into sin and degradation if he were to blame it on his constant exposure to the unrelenting misery of the human condition. There were other priests who'd had his kind of trouble. Priests who were quietly removed from their parishes, given counseling, and sent to work elsewhere. Yet, in the confessional of his own conscience, he could not lie. The seeds of his monstrous sins had lain dormant in him all along. Perhaps, unconsciously, that was the reason he had chosen this parish in the first place. Where else could he have found such fecund soil for his own evil?

The Devil works in mysterious ways His souls to steal.

Behind him another sinner knelt, ready to receive his benediction.

Not his benediction, of course.

Christ's.

He was just an instrument of the Lord's mercy, a vessel that transferred the cleansing water of God's forgiveness to those on earth. Not even his own sins, his own failings, or so he'd been taught at seminary, could spoil the purity of that mercy. But what if the vessel were shattered?

If he no longer believed in God at all?

He shifted his weight to the other side of the confessional. He imagined himself inside a coffin buried deep underground, haunted by the voices of the dead, each confessing to him their sins throughout all eternity. Suddenly, he felt painfully claustrophobic, dizzy, as if he were going to faint. His breath came in short gasps and his heart beat rapidly, like a small, sharp-beaked bird pecking at his sternum. He felt like he was suffocating.

He wanted to bolt from the confessional, to run away from it all.

What in the world was stopping him?

He brought the bottle of tea to his clammy forehead, trying to leech the last bit of coolness from the glass. He felt his heart slow, his breathing grow normal. He'd had these attacks before. Often while he stood delivering his Sunday sermon, he would look out at his congregation and see in their blank, staring faces such an impenetrable wall of human stupidity that he felt the uncontrollable urge to run screaming from the pulpit. Somehow he'd always managed to stem the rising tide of panic. They were anxiety attacks. He had read all about them. By sheer force of will he waited until this one passed, breaking over him like a fever, leaving damp patches under his arms, along his spine, in the crotch of his pants. He took a deep breath.

On the other side of the booth another crippled soul was crouched, waiting for absolution. Whoever it was, he or she was unusually quiet. He could usually hear them clearing their throats, shifting around uncomfortably in the cramped space, nervously awaiting their appointment with the Almighty.

Only Father Paul knew he no longer spoke for the Almighty. When he forgave them their sins, he was speaking strictly for himself.

As one sinner to the next.

He slid the panel open and the voice on the other side spoke the timeworn formula with a quiet intensity that made the priest's hair stand on end.

"Forgive me, Father, for I have sinned."

There was a pause on the other side of the waffled screen, as if the man was trying to collect his thoughts, as if he was trying to figure out where to begin. In the silence of the small confessional, Father Paul could hear nothing but the sound of his own breathing. If he listened closely enough, he was sure he would be able to hear the sound of his beating heart.

"Go ahead, my son," the priest prompted.

"Father, I am going to murder a woman."

The priest's first thought was that he hadn't heard the man correctly. He was tired, after all, and looking to return to the rectory for a nap. His next thought was that the man was just blowing off steam. Perhaps he'd gotten mad at his wife or girlfriend and had had the foresight to come to the church first in order to cool down. People who were reasonable enough to see him before doing something rash were not the kind of people to do something rash to begin with. Still, you couldn't be too careful.

"Do you know what you are saying?"

"Yes, I do."

The priest tried to identify the man's voice. Quiet, intense, strong: It was a voice that commanded attention, a voice used to being obeyed. He couldn't place it.

He stared instead with morbid fascination at the dim shadow moving behind the yellow-orange screen. The shadowy figure was ominous, like some kind of monstrous black angel that it was his great misfortune to interview, the image of death and evil itself, ready to devour his soul. Was this man telling the truth, or was he just some kind of nut off the street? Father Paul wanted to believe the latter, but something told him the man was not a lunatic. It was the voice.

It was the voice of someone telling the Truth.

Father Paul was afraid to move, afraid to say a word. He felt as if he was hypnotized, as if what he was experiencing were taking place in a dream.

"Father," the terrible voice continued, "I am afraid this is the last confession you will ever hear."

"What—"

"I have been sent by the bishop."

Father Paul felt his blood turn into columns of scampering red ants.

"He knows about the boy—or should I say *boys?* I am here as your replacement."

For years now he had lived in dread of this moment, yet now that it had come he felt nothing but an overwhelming sense of relief. How had the bishop known? Had there been a complaint? All he knew was that he was glad it was over. He had rehearsed his confession a hundred times, a thousand times, planning exactly what he would say. As it turned out, he didn't have to say

70

anything. The bishop already knew, the matter was already resolved, he needn't say a word. They would do with him as they saw fit and he would accept whatever punishment they meted out. For the first time in years he felt that perhaps there was a Divine Providence.

"Thank you." He bowed his head and whispered through the screen to the man on the other side. "My God, thank you."

In the first rush of relief he had forgotten all the man had said. Now it came back to him, nibbling at the edge of his brain.

"But you mentioned a woman," Father Paul said. "You said you were going to kill a woman. I don't understand."

"I have been sent here on a mission from the Church. Your role is incidental but vital to my success."

Father Paul had heard of many things the worldly Church supported that contradicted its established tenets, support and aid to political tyrants, especially those opposed to communism, no matter how repressive, came immediately to mind, but he'd never heard the Church openly sanctioning murder. If the man hadn't spoken with such conviction, he might have doubted he was who he said he was and instead mistaken him for a homeless lunatic, or worse, considering the knowledge he'd had about his personal life, an irate father who'd discovered what he'd been up to with his son.

"I don't believe you," Father Paul said.

"Ah, but you do," the shadow on the other side of the screen said. "I can hear it in your voice."

It was true. His voice held little conviction even to his own ears. The fact was that he did believe the man. He had seen enough evil in the world—and in himself—to believe it existed almost anywhere.

"Who is this woman? Why does the Church want her dead?"

71

"I was little more than a boy when I met her for the first time," the shadow began. "Eighteen, maybe nineteen. The world was new then; it was still nearly forty years before the birth of Christ. In Britain we knew little of the outside world. Our bards were our rulers, poetry our law. Druids, they called us, because in their ignorance and crudity they thought we worshipped trees. Murderers, they called us, because we practiced human sacrifice. Meanwhile they butchered thousands in their filthy ampitheaters for nothing more than entertainment.

"I remember the afternoon the soldiers came, men with breastplates like the sun and helmets crested with terror. They came and burned the sacred oaks, groves that had stood for thousands of years, burned them in the name of Caesar. For years we'd held them at bay with magic and superstition, but in the end Roman greed and pragmatism wore us down. Now there was no stopping them. They swept through the forests like wildfire, and everywhere they passed they left a trail of death.

"They slaughtered our priests, our warriors, our leaders. The rest of us they herded up and put in chains and marched off to Rome. Oh, how I've wished a thousand times that I had fallen beneath a Roman sword then and there, that my blood had watered the ashes of the place where I was born. Instead I lived. I survived. Survived—it's a theme that haunts my long and tortured life. My curse.

"Many died on the long march to Italy; many of the best of us were left by the roadside. I've often wondered at the paradox of that: how the strongest had the will to die. Needless to say, I did not. In Rome we were a novelty: the wild men of the north. They put us in cages for public display and in their gladitorial shows, trained us to fight, to kill each other like animals. The only thing that saved me was the crowd's insatiable appetite for something new. Like your television today, their sadism had no artistry. It was consumption for consumption's sake. The mob grew bored with us. So I was placed in chains again and sent by Caesar as a gift to the land of the pharaohs.

"In Egypt at that time there was a queen whose beauty, they said, was such as no mortal had ever seen before or would ever see again. I laugh now, for I can see her now from the perspective of history. Cleopatra was quite common: dusky, short, and fat. But she possessed a glamour that made men and women flock to her bed like lambs to a valley red with slaughter, knowing as they did the price for their evening's dalliance: that to sleep with the Queen of the Nile meant death.

"I saw firsthand the power of this glamour, for it was in her house that I was engaged as a slave. To her bedchamber I conducted hundreds of pretty boys and girls from the best houses in Egypt, their bodies nude and trembling like reeds in a field waiting for the cruel scythe. In the morning I took them out again, cold and stiff, their passion drained with every drop of blood, while the heartless Queen lay against her purpled cushions, fat and surfeited, like a leech. To look at her then, the hair on your neck would rise and the blood in your veins turn to ice. There was no thought of pleasure then—only pain, death, and the unspeakable corruption after death.

"It was there that I met her for the first time. She was tall and pale and beautiful as a snowstorm, her eyes blue as veins below the flesh. Her hair was like the sunshine and her lips red as the poisonous berries of the mistletoe. At the time she called herself Nepthys, after the Egyptian goddess of the underworld. On the surface she was little more than a handmaid to the Queen. But it was clear that she had cast a spell over the woman, had her firmly in control. In my land they had a name for beings of her kind: Thekyll—life suckers. They roamed the midnight forest, luring men and women into their arms, leaving them to face the morning soulless husks.

"Cleopatra went nowhere without her at her side. They were lovers, but more than lovers, for the power she exerted over the Queen was far deeper than merely erotic. The Queen relied on her in everything, so that soon Nepthys was the real power behind the throne: It was her we feared to displease, for at her word Cleopatra would condemn anyone to death. To my horror, I found that I attracted Nepthys's attention. I resisted her advances, knowing that to consummate the urge she coaxed in me would surely mean my death.

"My reward was to be thrown into the dungeon, where Nepthys visited me every night with some devilish new torment to break my soul. The might, the wealth, the wisdom of an ancient nation had refined the instruments and protocol of pain to the heights of a religion. Whip and chain and burning brand were its instruments of worship. But of all the tortures she visited upon me, none were worse than the blessed promise of relief. In the swell of her breasts, or the softness of her hands, or the cradle of her thighs she tempted me with the cessation of suffering and the ecstasy of sweet oblivion. And yet I would not give in. I'm sure that's all that saved me: my fear of death. Saved me as well as damned me.

"What follows next still pains me to recall, in spite of all the lives I've take since, for it is the first that was the turning point that led me down damnation's road to hell.

"She was a slave, just like myself. From Asia, I think she was. I can see her now, a tiny thing, no bigger than a boy of eight, and yet a full-grown woman of her race, her body in its unmistakable first flower. She stood before me, naked, bound in chains, her eyes cast down be-

74

tween her feet, the tears falling on her peach-sized breasts as our mistress explained to us the cruelest facts of life: that life could only be where life had ceased to be, that some were meant to rule and some to serve, and that all of life was naught but domination.

"She handed me the whip and bid me rule. And rule I did, knowing it was either her or I, until that poor girl's pleasure screams had died in agony and the blood began to flow and my mistress bid me taste the sweetest wine of all, the wine you taste but once and crave forever—

"Not long after, word came from Rome of Caesar's assassination. Whether she truly underestimated the strength of those who backed Augustus, or merely had grown tired of playing mistress to the Egyptian Queen, she seduced Mark Antony to Cleopatra's bed. To say the least, it was an affair badly begun and ended worse. Mark Antony fell upon his sword at Actium and Cleopatra—

"The fatal puncture wounds upon her breasts, they said, were those of poisonous asps. But I know better what breed of serpent she had suckled there.

"I escaped the wholesale slaughter that followed, the piteous wailing of slaves and masters alike, butchered on the marble floors and disappeared into thin air. For years I stalked the Roman nights, seeking my victims from every class. Noble men and ladies, merchants, senators, and slaves fell in my path, drawn by some calling in their blood to seek me out in the dark corners where I reigned supreme. I did not disappoint them. Often I recognized others of my kind, skulking through those bloody alleys, but never the woman who had changed me. We passed each other like ex-lovers of the same woman, with eyes averted, brimming with hatred, embarrassment, and a thousand unasked questions.

"In those days I think Rome must have been the

vampire capital of the world. Every morning the Tiber was choked with our naked, bloodless victims. It was a squalid, greedy, superstitious age, but one that understood dominance and submission better than any other than perhaps your own.

"I spent a lifetime of idle afternoons lolling on the bleachers of the Coliseum, sleepily taking in the gruesome entertainment of the day. Here was tried every perversity of which the human mind could conceive in the name of domination. Here a handsome Persian youth, no more than a boy, was armed with a light stick and pitted against a lion raised on human meat. Here a Greek slave, playing Pasiphaë, was sewn inside a reeking cow skin and introduced to a randy bull, who was lewdly encouraged by experienced prostitutes to consummate a union most unnatural. Here again a beautiful virgin from Demeter's temple was tied to a stake for some petty offense and painted with honey, the flies and ants ensuring that she suffered a slow and painful death. And just in case anyone should object to the impropriety of putting a virgin to death, we were duly reassured that, under the authority of Caesar, the girl had been repeatedly raped beforehand by her Roman guard.

"It was here one sunny August morning I first saw those they called the Christians. Sated on blood and pain, nonetheless I was amazed at how those noble souls went to their grisly ends while looking to the sky in rapture, the strange name of their prophet, Jesus, upon their abused and bloodied lips. I quit the city, determined to find this man who could make the dead walk, the blind to see, and people choose contentedly to die.

"Travel then was not as travel now, and by the time I got to Jerusalem he'd already been arrested and framed by the Pharisees and delivered onto the Romans to be sentenced to die. I met him on the rod to Golgotha, beaten, mocked, half-naked, crowned with thorns,

76

and on his back the wood on which he'd presently be nailed. He begged me for a drink of water, and so disgusted was I at this poor excuse for God, I spit upon him and hit him with the quirt I used to spur my mules. His cheek lay open and his blood spurted on my robe, but it was I who flinched, for in his eyes I saw that he had cursed me, not with anger, nor with threat of retribution, but with mercy. And I heard a voice inside my head as gentle as a lover's. *You shall walk the earth forever and never shall you rest until you've found your death, for what you fear is what you love the best of all.*

"I wanted to ask him what he'd meant, but the soldiers prodded him with their lances and spurred him on. They hung him on Golgotha between two thieves that afternoon. I didn't stay to watch. I was already on a ship to Rhodes.

"I've wandered through the centuries ever since, searching for the woman who damned me. I saw her traces scattered all through history, wherever reigned man's inhumanity to man. I saw her bloody hand in the Inquisition. She was there in England, goading the Witchfinder General. I caught a glimpse of her again during the Black Plague and during the trial of Gilles de Rais, better known as Bluebeard, who it's said sodomized and killed some two hundred boys at her instigation.

"She's gone by a hundred names throughout history: Kali, Lillith, Baalat, Sekhmet, Lamia, Succubae, Vampire, and others it is forbidden to speak. But one thing remains the same: her insatiable thirst for blood and pain. I've been in this city scarcely a week and already I see her disciples everywhere I look. I've seen them carrying briefcases on Wall Street and Park Avenue and pushing shopping carts filled with their mortal remains through Central Park. I've seen them cruising the bars of Greenwich Village and riding the subway below the earth. The streets are populated by the living dead and you see them not. They walk among you, glare at you hungrily from every corner, their blood thundering with the siren song of domination. She has heard them and she has come, and so has one whose soul is dear to me, whose innocence I have sworn to keep no matter what the cost. She has come of age and I must find her and bring her knowledge of who and what she is before it is too late."

"You're insane," Father Paul whispered, awed at the magnitude of the man's delusion. "Why are you telling me all this?"

"To prepare you for your part."

"My part?" the priest asked incredulously. In his guilt and terror he'd already felt a premonition of the answer. "What is it that you want from me?"

"Nothing that you haven't given up already," the shadow said. "Nothing but your soul."

EIGHT

Tonight was the night Hillary had dreamed about all her life.

In the lives of all great personages there was always a moment of destiny after which nothing would ever be the same again, a turning point that led an individual chosen by fate for greatness away from the masses and onto the lonely road of immortality.

Tonight was such a night.

Hillary breathed deeply, trying to fix the scene in her mind's eye, for she knew she would want to remember it for the rest of her life.

They were sitting in the den, the walls lined with Edmund's leather-bound law books, a huge oak fire crackling in the flagstone fireplace that covered the entire east wall, and across from her on the burgundy leather couch that had been occupied by innumerable governors, senators, congressmen, and two presidents sat the woman of her dreams.

Until she had met Monica at a reception the year before, Hillary had been unable to put a face to the god-like woman of her recurring dreams. On a veranda overlooking the twinkling lights along the French Riviera, the sweet scent of oleander and hibiscus in the summer air, Hillary had fallen under the spell of a beautiful woman in a black sequined ballgown whose sensuous red lips seemed to be speaking a second, more intimate language beneath the polite small talk usual at such affairs.

She described herself as an intimate of a rich and reclusive Italian countess who Hillary knew only by name and who was rumored to be a descendant of the Borgias. About six months later, back in New York, Hillary had read a small note buried on the obit page of the Sunday *Times* mentioning the death of the countess under mysterious circumstances. Through Edmund's European connections Hillary was able to learn some of the details kept out of the newspapers. The countess had been found floating nude in the swimming pool of her estate outside Trieste. She had apparently been strangled to death with a length of red rope, the ends of which were found clutched in her own fists, as if she had strangled herself. Some thought that perhaps it was the macabre work of the Red Brigade; what they had really done to the industrialist Aldo Moro the government had forbidden the papers to print. Others hinted that the countess had a drug problem. A chambermaid was eventually charged with engaging the countess in certain dangerous sexual pastimes, including the practice of self-asphyxiation. The case was ruled an accidental homicide and closed. The chambermaid later died in a single-car traffic accident outside Rome.

Hillary had received a letter from Monica about three months earlier, announcing her impending trip to the States on some affair for the Italian government. Hillary wasted no time wiring Monica back at her estate in Sicily, inviting her to visit at the Long Island mansion. Now, at last, their reunion was taking place.

Hillary glanced at the woman sitting across from her with a mixture of fascination and embarrassment. She sipped her wine, trying to hide both with an air of sophistication, but only succeeded in making herself feel more self-conscious. She'd had Degas select one of Edmund's precious bottles of California vintage that he only reserved for presidents, premiers, and dictators.

"Do you like the wine?" she asked hopefully. "My husband says it's the best in America."

Monica sipped slowly, her eyes leveled at Hillary, who suddenly felt hot.

"It is good," the woman said. "But it lacks the depth and complexity of the wines of Europe." She held up the glass and stared thoughtfully at the red wine. "Still, there is a delightful *exuberance* about it. There is a simple, barbaric strength to it that I find quite exhilarating. Distinctly American."

Across from Hillary, the woman's cool and flawless beauty was a constant reminder of her own girlish nervousness. Every movement Hillary made seemed awkward by comparison; even the way she was sitting caused her the most intense torture. It was stupid to say anything about the wine. Of course, being an Italian, she had tasted the best wines in the world. She felt a touch of anger. She had sat in this very same room with some of the most powerful men in the world and she had never felt so stupid and clumsy. What was it about this woman that made her feel this way? Was it possible that she was in love?

"It's been such a long time," Hillary said, trying a different tack. "It's good to see you again."

"Have you thought about me then?" Monica said, her gray eyes as ambiguous as clouds.

"Oh, yes," Hillary said, before recognizing the slight note of sarcasm in the woman's voice. By then, it was too late to retrieve her own enthusiasm. She felt herself blushing.

"I have thought about you, too," Monica said, relieving Hillary of some but by no means all of her embarrassment. "Often. I have even visited you in dreams. Perhaps you remember some of them?"

Hillary remembered the dreams of the forgotten temple, of the long colonnade, the statues of the famous men and women of history. She remembered the obscene fountain, the red-veined pillars, the ominous chain terminating in a hook orange with rust. But most of all she remembered the marble woman seated on the throne, her cold and perfect features, her lips freshly painted red.

Was it possible those dreams were something more than dreams? Her study of the occult, of the principles of astral travel, of psychic vampirism, told her that they could be.

"I remember them," Hillary said, finding herself naturally drawn into this strange conversation about shared dreams as easily as if they were discussing a shared experience.

"Interesting dreams," Monica said. "Were they not?"

"Yes," Hillary said. "So—realistic."

Monica smiled, but it was the way marble smiled. "What men can dream they can achieve," she said, and then added cryptically, "if they are willing to pay the price. Are you willing to pay the price?"

Hillary nodded. "Yes."

The Vampire looked at the woman sitting across from her. She was wearing a white sheath dress cut low in the front, her breasts half-exposed, her feet naked inside a pair of silver mules. Even from across the room the Vampire could smell her perfume, not the expensive designer scent she wore, but beneath it, the unique musky aroma that nature gave her to attract her prey. The Vampire was amused at the mortal's clumsy attempt at seduction, as if such an attempt were calcuable or even necessary, as if it were something so effervescent as beauty or even sensuality that made her hunger. To be sure, the Vampire had far more beautiful and delicious lovers in her time but few who seemed as eager to damn themselves as this poor mortal.

"Come here," the Vampire said.

Hillary stood up, forgetting her glass, which spilled down the front of her dress, staining the white fabric. She crossed the room and knelt on the floor between the Vampire's knees, lifting her bright, expectant face, as if waiting for a benediction, her eyes fixing on those of the Vampire, which had taken on the color of the fire.

Monica reached out and touched the mortal's face, tracing her fingernail along her warm carotid, contemplating with philosophical detachment that with one flick of the wrist she could cut the tenuous thread that connected the woman to life. Monica stared into the woman's eyes, seeing her victims pupils dilate, her heart beating light and fast, her breath coming in short, hard gasps. The woman's lips parted, and Monica leaned forward, taking Hillary's head in her hands, tilting it back like a goblet, and gently kissing her. Hillary sighed when she felt the teeth bite into the soft flesh of her lip, her consciousness melting away like a wafer, flowing into the wound and pouring with her blood over the Vampire's educated tongue.

In her blood Monica could taste Hillary's entire life. She tasted a father, successful, articulate, dazzlingly handsome, a mother troubled, frustrated, inexplicably sad, and a bright, precocious, pretty child who knew instinctively how to play one off the other to her own advantage. She tasted a child whose father's job in government intelligence forced her to move from place to place too frequently to ever have a friend, who understood humanity to be a fleeting thing, to be drained and discarded without conscience. She tasted a young woman who passed through school on the strength of her charm and beauty, seducing her male teachers and intimidating the females, leaving classmates of both sexes panting in her wake. She tasted a young woman resentful of her father's ignominious death in a Washington, DC, brothel after a massive coronary and disdainful of her mother's slow descent into madness that left her a permanent resident of a Connecticut sanitarium to this day.

She tasted a young woman whose obsession with sex and power led her inevitably to a study of the occult, in whose principles she found the basis for a new faith that held no commandment more sacrosanct than the one that exhorted its faithful to do as they will. She tasted a woman who to this day kept a note from a distraught lover mailed the day she hung herself in her dorm room, deriving a perverse thrill from its profession of endless love, which she read not as a desperate plea for help from a lonely and misguided girl, but as a prayer of sacrifice to her as a superior being. She tasted a woman determined at all costs to regain the status she felt she had lost with the death of her father, even to the point of marrying a man she despised, of weaving about him a web of sexual intrigue and black magic, and threatening him with destruction when he'd come to his senses. She tasted a woman who'd come close to death when the lump was discovered in her left breast and whose will to live, always powerful, had raged into a pyre of monomania that kept the opportunistic cancer cells still in her body at bay. But most of all she tasted a woman who loved no one and no thing so much as she loved herself, a woman whose first and last loyalty was to her own survival, a woman who with her dying breath would throw the switch obliterating the world for no better reason than that she had done with it and no one else should have it.

In short, she tasted a vampire.

Monica broke the kiss. She had tasted enough of the

woman's life to guess the rest. Roughly, she pushed her away, and Hillary fell back on her heels, staring up at her, breathless, her lips red with blood, her eyes glazed with adoration. Her dress had come open in the front and her silicon-enhanced breasts had popped out, orange in the firelight, heaving with passion. Each of the hardened brown nipples, Monica noted, had been pierced with a slender golden ring.

"That was only a taste of the ecstasy that awaits you," the Vampire said huskily, brushing the sweat-dampened hair from the woman's face. "Soon I will take you all the way. Together we will rule the world if you dare. A life for a life, just as I promised."

"When?" the mortal panted, eager, so eager, for her own damnation. "When?"

"Soon," the Vampire said coldly, patting the foolish woman on the head absently. "Soon. First we must have a victim."

NINE

Kelly stared at her computer screen in utter exasperation.

The sentence she had just written staggered forlornly across the dark monitor like the remnant of a beaten army. She backspaced along the line, highlighting the words with her cursor, and sent them hurtling into never-never land. That was the best thing about writing in the computer age: There were no wastebaskets overflowing with crumpled paper, no pencils nibbled away in frustration, no desktop archipelagoes of pink eraser crumbs. You could eliminate with a single keystroke every trace of your humiliating and futile pleas to the muse for inspiration.

She had been trying to describe the scene at Koski's earlier that week, but in spite of the notes she had taken she wasn't having much success. She thought that putting a couple of days between herself and the event might help clarify things in her mind; instead it had only made them more chaotic. She'd been at it for nearly five hours now and she was no closer to getting a handle on the story than when she started. Earlier in the evening she had forced herself to stop for a half hour to grab a hamburger at Gus's, the Greek diner down the street from her building, thinking that a break might do her good. But when she had returned to the apartment the word elves hadn't come to write the story for her and she had sat down in front of the same cold blank screen. She sat there still, the cursor blinking in the corner like a vein in her temple.

Outside, the November wind rattled the window over the fire escape as if an invisible cat burglar were trying to break in. It was chilly in the apartment, and Kelly pulled her bathrobe closed and sipped a cup of herbal tea. Somewhere outside that window Eric was passing the night. She thought of all the rotten things he had said about her job at *NiteLife*. She looked down at her notes and had to admit that some of the assignments she'd covered, including the current one, hadn't exactly been Pulitzer Prize material. Still, she felt her job had a meaning, her work had purpose. Hell, she didn't need to justify it to herself. She did what she did because she enjoyed it. Nothing else mattered.

She remembered coming to the city from Illinois six years ago with the dream of becoming a writer. Of course, she had thought that she would become the next Bob Woodward or Carl Bernstein. She had never pictured herself prowling the Manhattan night in search of stories of surrealist perverts and female dominatrices. Yet she had discovered in herself a strange fascination for the after-hours clubs and bars inhabited by people living habitually on the edge. She felt like a cross between a sociologist and an archaeologist. Each story was like charting a lost continent and cataloging a fabulous and endangered species.

In fact, if the truth were told, her job at *NiteLife* was the most important thing in her life. She had no home, no family she could rightfully call her own. Her mother, she'd been told by a tactless social worker when she was barely six years old, had died in childbirth. Her father had simply abandoned her. Nonetheless, Kelly was thankful for the truth, no matter how cruel, knowing that as time went on the truth would probably have been lost. Even at the age of six she hadn't remembered feeling any special pain about hearing the facts surrounding her genesis. Like most six-year-old kids, she had a penchant for the melodramatic and a natural affinity for the underdog that made her pleased to be able to consider herself with more justification than most in the role of the orphaned princess who was the star of every fairy tale. Whereas most children could point to their parents and clearly see they sprang from no magical origins, Kelly could legitimately conjecture that her parents might be anyone she desired. It was a sentiment her adopted parents, Bob and Glenda Mitchell, a loving, gentle couple who gave her those first six wonderful years, did nothing to discourage. They were both killed on a rainy Saturday evening when their wood-paneled Ford station wagon skidded off an embankment and into the Skerry River.

Kelly was brought to a local Catholic orphanage, where she stayed for nearly two years while her adoptive parent's estate was settled in court during a bitter challenge involving various surviving family members. It was during that time, while in the care of the priests at the orphange, that Kelly began to have nightmares of a hooded figure with eyes glowing like coals who visited her in the dead of night. She would wake up screaming, bringing the matron running and waking all the other kids in the hall. In spite of threats the nightmares did not abate, and eventually they had to put her in a private room to keep her from scaring the other kids. The strange visitor continued to visit her, sitting quietly by her bedside with his red, glowing eyes, fingering the beads of his rosary, while Kelly lay stiff and still as a little corpse, her fists doubled up, her nails leaving half moons of blood in her palms until the mysterious visitor vanished near dawn and she was finally able to sleep.

By the time she left the orphanage for a series of foster homes, Kelly had all but forgotten about the nightmare visitor, though he returned for a brief time while she was a teenager. By then her adopted parent's estate had long been resolved and the court had appointed a financial guardian over the money they had left in their will for her education. The money had been managed poorly, if not downright criminally, but by the time she was ready to leave her last foster home at the age of eighteen, there was still enough left for her to enroll in the journalism school at the University of Chicago. Six years later she gathered up her degree, her suitcase, and what little money was left from her bequest and headed for New York. She wanted a fresh start in a new city and a future that would be all her own.

Now, at the age of twenty-eight, she was old enough to realize that she was a long way from fulfilling her dream and yet young enough to hope she might still get there. She thought about her meeting tomorrow with the dominatrice she'd met at Koski's party. She had reached Valerie Lawson at Captive Hearts and arranged to sit in on a session or two with a couple of her regular clients. Weird how it was all falling into place so conveniently. In the beginning she had always found it kind of strange—downright creepy—the way the events of her life slowly organized themselves around a story she was writing, like metal filings around a magnet, forming a definite pattern. But over time she began to grow used to the phenomenon.

Synchronicity, Joan had called it, and said that all the best reporters had it.

Some old-timers called it instinct, or a nose for news, or just plain luck; in fact, it was something even rarer and more nebulous than any of those things. It was the gift that only a few reporters had for coming up with the revealing interview, the incriminating document, the right informant that breaks the big story. It was something in the air that allowed certain reporters to get that edge on everyone else that made all the difference between a scoop and yesterday's news. By tomorrow morning, Kelly half expected everyone in the city to be buzzing with talk about domination.

She remembered the leather freaks she had seen coming home on the train after Koski's party. They sat together on the bench, listless, androgynous, vaguely menacing in their motorcycle boots, studded jackets, and metal chains. Their hair was bleached and teased to resemble the aggressive manes of wild animals. They stared at Kelly, their kohl-lined eyes huge and empty in pale, washed-out faces, like the eyes of predators already sated. No doubt they were returning from some after-hours haunt. Kelly had seen their kind before, of course, but for the first time she saw more than the threat; she saw the seduction implied in their post-punk, nihilistic posturing.

Still, they scared her.

She thought again of tomorrow afternoon's appointment at Captive Hearts. She had half a mind to call up and cancel it. Yet at the same time she felt compelled to see it through. Often, she discovered, it was the very stories she'd found the hardest to do that had yielded the greatest rewards. There was a rightness to doing this story that she couldn't explain.

Kelly pushed her chair back and crossed the room to stand in front of her fish tank.

On the wall above the tank hung one of the Matisse prints she had bought after she and Gwen had gone to the exhibit at the Metropolitan Museum of Art last fall. Inside the illuminated rectangle of water and glass, the brightly colored fish passed gracefully back and forth.

Usually watching the tank relaxed her, but tonight nothing could quell the restlessness that seemed to be blowing through her.

She stared back at the computer screen, black and ominous as the mask of Darth Vader.

She knew she should get back to her writing, but suddenly there were a thousand and one things she could think of that she'd been meaning to do: clean the bathtub, repaper the kitchen shelves, defrost the refrigerator, alphabetize her bookshelves, *give Eric a call.*

Experience had taught her that when she started feeling like that, there was nothing to do but force herself back to the computer and bull her way forward with the writing, no matter what the results. She sat down in front of the screen, determined to make something happen. She used one of the old tricks for overcoming writer's block that she had learned from a creative-writing teacher at a course she had once taken at the New School. She put her fingers on the keyboard and just started typing the first thing she remembered about the night at Koski's.

When she finished typing two hours later she was surprised to find that she had knocked off nearly seven pages. After reading what she'd written, she deleted half the pages and saved the rest for tomorrow. Then she turned off the computer and headed for bed. She set her alarm for noon and climbed under the cold sheets, drifting off to sleep just before sunrise.

TEN

The bone-white limousine moved quietly through the darkened streets. Inside, the senator's wife sipped ice-cold Absolut and lit a menthol cigarette. She looked out the tinted window at the night's offering, the women standing along the curb, each groomed and plumed as outrageously as a tropical bird.

Hillary usually had her "victims" delivered to her at the mansion. Degas selected them, knowing her peculiar tastes, and had them brought through the delivery entrance to her private playroom to avoid attention. The senator didn't object, so long as she was discreet. How could he? She had known about his stable of Washington, DC, mistresses for years. They had worked out a mutually fulfilling agreement. They would each pursue their own pleasures and keep each other's secrets. He asked her only that she restrict her activities to times when he was away in the capital and that she choose her paramours carefully lest they find themselves at the center of a public scandal.

Being the wife of a senator could be such a bitch. Sometimes it was like living in a fishbowl. Not that the press hadn't had the chance to call her out on more than one occasion. The fact was, her husband was one of the most popular liberal senators in the country. He was an advocate for all the right causes and all the right people: The fags, the hags, the niggers, the kikes, and the spicks had made him their darling. No one in the liberal media was anxious to tear him down, even if his personal life was something less than sterling, so long as he didn't abuse their editorial license.

So she usually restricted her playmates to the rolls of the local agencies. They were professional escorts, would-be actresses, and struggling models, for the most part. They knew the moves, the talk, the cues. Lately it had begun to seem a little too perfect, as if the whole thing were choreographed, which in a way it was, and that ruined it for her. It made her feel cheap and pitiful, like one of those married businessmen who sneak off for a twenty-dollar blowjob on Eighth Avenue during their lunch hour.

She needed the edge that only the live action could give her. The uncertainty, the danger, the genuine fear in the eyes of her victims.

And that meant occasionally sending Degas out to "kidnap" someone or cruising the streets herself for the rough trade.

Outside her darkened window, the world was a chaos of leather, rhinestones, feather boas, fishnet, and flesh, flesh, flesh. Where did they all come from, these hard-faced, hard-bodied girls? What desperate need of their own brought them here to the streets, strutting along the gutter, selling themselves to satisfy the hungers of people like herself?

It was not a question of morality. There was no right or wrong to it. Rather, it was the natural order of things. These girls were prey, pure and simple, and she was a predator. They needed each other. Neither of them could have changed the rules of the game even if they wished. Hillary pressed the button on the console beside her with one long lacquered nail. "Stop up ahead, Degas. The cherry-blonde."

The girl was standing in front of a mailbox covered with graffiti. She was wearing a red leather skirt so tight you could see the crack of her ass. In spite of the November chill she had on a tiny middy blouse, and she wasn't wearing any stockings. She was perched on top of a pair of red alligator heels so high Hillary wondered how she could walk in them, unless they were nailed to her feet. (An interesting thought, that.) Around the girl's neck was a long black cord from which hung a large stainless-steel Egyptian *ankh*.

Hillary watched as Degas walked up to the girl, pointed back to the car, and explained the game. She took another sip of the chilled vodka and drew deep on the mentholated cigarette. The girl looked to the car, back at the dark, handsome, ponytailed man, and then back at the limousine again. Hillary could tell that the girl was interested. Degas could be particularly persuasive. His expensive, tailor-made suit fit his powerful, *v*-shaped body like hard-on granite. He had a face like one of Michelangelo's angels.

He was gay, but he was man enough to reach down a wiseguy's throat and pull his asshole out through his lips. The only difference was that he would probably get a hard-on while he did it.

Whatever it was he said turned the trick. The girl was coming to the car, mincing along on the high heels like a trained pony. Hillary took a last toke on the cigarette and stubbed it out in the ashtray. She touched her finger to the console, and the bullet-proof armored door unlocked from inside. Degas pulled open the door and the girl leaned forward to check out that everything was as she had been told, and then she climbed inside.

Degas shut the door; it locked automatically.

"Wow," the girl said, snapping her gum. "I been in

94

limos before, but this one takes the cake. It's bigger than my fucking living room."

She was younger than she looked standing on the corner, and somehow older at the same time. It was the kind of look all whores got, even after a short time on the street, a kind of natural camouflage that made them look as hard as the concrete jungle that was their habitat. Something about the eyes: flat and passionless, like the soporific look of a mouse in the cage of a boa constrictor.

"Hey, don't I know you from somewhere?" the girl said, looking carefully at Hillary. The car pulled away from the corner and began to move up the street, picking up speed as they turned the corner and headed for the expressway that led out of Manhattan. The girl didn't seem to notice that they were leaving the city.

"I doubt it," Hillary said dryly. "Would you care for something to drink?"

"No thanks."

Hillary poured herself some more Absolut. She lit another cigarette.

"I know," the girl said, this time snapping her fingers and gum in unison. "I've seen you in the papers."

"Doubt it," Hillary said. "I'm not a cartoon character."

If the girl was offended she didn't show it. Perhaps she was used to being insulted; perhaps she expected it as part of her job.

"It's okay," she said. "I meet lots of famous people. You'd be surprised. Just the other night I met that actor, the one who was in all those cop movies, you know the one I mean. Big guy, lots of muscles, talks with an accent. He wanted me to pee on him. Can you believe that? This macho movie star and he pays me to come back to his penthouse and piss on him while he lies in the bathtub. You don't have to worry, though. I'm very discreet."

Hillary watched the girl as she talked, fascinated by the play of the expressway sulfur lights on her face, the effect like a pair of gloved hands, one white, one black, gently slapping her over and over again.

"Do you mind if I take my shoes off?" the girl asked, interrupting herself to rub her left ankle. "My feet are killing me."

"Yes, I do," Hillary said. "Leave them on."

The girl shrugged. "It's your nickel," she said.

Hillary listened to her stream-of-consciousness ramble until she finished her cigarette. She crushed out the cigarette and reached down to the Gucci travel bag on the floor of the limousine. She came up holding a ball gag.

"Shut up and put this on," she said.

The girl took the gag, holding it by its leather straps.

"Your driver told me what you're into. That's cool. I've played that scene before. The way he told it, he doesn't lay a hand on me. It's just you and me getting it on, right?"

"Right."

"Good. I wouldn't mind him playing along, but I don't want him whipping me. He looks like he'd cut me to ribbons."

He would, Hillary thought.

"And I want a safe word."

Hillary nodded. "Of course. How about 'mercy'?"

"Mercy," the girl said, as if trying the word on for size. "I like that. You gotta stop if I say 'mercy.' "

"I promise."

"Okay." The girl took the gum out of her mouth and looked around, and Hillary handed her a tissue. She wrapped the gum and put it into the ashtray. Then she opened her mouth and eased her lips around the orange rubber ball. She ducked her head forward, lifting her hair, and fastened the leather thongs behind her head, holding the gag firmly in place.

"Put these on your ankles." Hillary handed the girl a pair of leather restraints.

The girl bent forward, snapping the cuffs around her ankles.

"Good. Very good," Hillary murmured. She could feel the blood thudding at her pulse points, the warmth washing over her like a red tide. "Now the bracelets," she said huskily.

The girl took the steel handcuffs, snapped one closed around her left wrist. She was about to snap the second closed, her hands in her lap.

"No. Behind your back," Hillary corrected.

The girl shuffled forward on the car seat as best she could with her ankles bound, her skirt riding up over her bare thighs, her split crotch panties showing. She snapped the cuff closed around her right wrist and leaned back against the car seat. Hillary forced her breathing to slow, took a long swallow of the Absolut, and gazed at the bound girl, thinking of what was to come, of the playroom, of Monica waiting for them to return with their victim. Tonight she would go farther than she ever had before. Tonight she would go all the way. Hillary could feel her heart skipping beneath her reconstructed left breast like a record.

The girl turned her head and stared out the smoked window, watching the scenery flicking past, the limousine slowing down slightly as it turned onto the ramp of the Long Island Expressway. She looked slightly bored, as if she found herself in this particular predicament at least two or three times a week.

The stupid bitch hadn't figured it out yet.

Hillary lit a third cigarette, her hands shaking with anticipation.

If she were wearing a gag, how was she ever going to say the safe word?

ELEVEN

Captive Hearts was located smack in the middle of midtown Manhattan. From the outside the building looked like any other nondescript commercial/residential brownstone. Inside it had all the clean efficiency of a well-run modern office.

Kelly found herself standing in a brightly lit reception area with gray carpeting, chrome chairs, and potted plants. In one of the chairs sat a middle-aged man in a gray business suit. Across the room a pretty black woman sat behind a desk, reading a Hemingway novel and eating a green apple.

If she hadn't known better, Kelly might have thought she had stumbled into the office of a successful midtown dentist. The secretary looked up from her reading when Kelly entered and gave her the once-over as she approached the desk.

"I'm here to see Valerie Lawson," Kelly said.

The woman frowned. "You mean Mistress Kane."

"Yes," Kelly said, remembering the woman's inquisitional pseudonym. "I'm Kelly Mitchell."

"You'd be the new girl, then?" she said with a slight expression of disapproval that Kelly interpreted as jealousy. How long had the girl behind the desk waited to become a mistress?

"That's right."

"She'll be right with you. She's with a client right now. If you care to take a seat—"

"Thanks."

Kelly crossed the room and sat down at the end of the line of chairs stretched against the wall. She tried not to look at the man at the opposite end, but she could hardly keep herself from stealing a sidelong glance for curiosity's sake. He was a typical middle-management type, a banker or assistant marketing director, not the kind of man you'd expect to be visiting a house of dominance and submission. Kelly surreptitiously checked the hands folded in his lap. Sure enough, the man was wearing a wedding ring. She couldn't resist taking a quick glance at his face. He was staring straight ahead, his eyes fixed on nowhere, looking vaguely ashamed of himself, as if he were afraid he might be recognized.

Kelly forced herself to look away.

On the table beside her she saw a pile of magazines that provided the only indication that this wasn't any ordinary midtown office. The magazines had titles like *Female Superior, Dominatrix,* and *Goddess Worship,* and featured luridly staged photographs of aggressive, leather-costumed women standing threateningly over naked, kneeling men. They were the kind of magazines you could find on any newsstand in the city, yet the images were unlike most of those Kelly was accustomed to seeing on similar skin magazines. Instead of the woman being a passive participant, a mere object of male masturbatory fantasy, here were images of strong, active, even frightening females, women with power and authority, as witnessed by the submissive and obviously excited male subjects cowering docilely at their feet. It was true they were only staged photo shoots; it was also true that the fantasies depicted were catering primarily to men. Yet the message conveyed was totally opposite from that in most such magazines. In both, the woman was an object of pleasure. But there she was usually an object to be manipulated. Here she was an object to be worshipped. To be sure, something about the images stirred Kelly. She picked up one of the magazines for a closer look and had started flipping through the pages when Valerie came into the room.

Kelly remembered the petite redhead she'd met at Koski's party and how she'd had trouble imagining her as a whip-toting Amazon. Now, seeing the woman dressed as she was, she saw what she had apparently missed before, or what the clothes themselves served to bring out in the seemingly unprepossessing girl.

It was the unmistakable air of domination.

Valerie saw the look of surprise on Kelly's face and laughed. "It's me all right," she said. "Some costume, huh?"

"It's quite—ah, impressive."

Valerie was wearing a pair of black leather pants that laced up the sides, a studded leather belt, a leather harness bra festooned with chains, and a pair of fingerless PVC gloves that stretched all the way over her elbows. The entire ensemble was designed to provide a maddening blend of exposure and inaccessibility. She couldn't have looked sexier if she were completely naked. Kelly admired the confidence Valerie exhibited as she navigated on a pair of four-inch spike heels. Kelly was uncomfortable at half that height. Looped in her left hand, Valerie was holding a short whip of braided black leather.

"I'm glad you decided to come," she said, and shook Kelly's hand. She turned to the woman behind the desk. "Brenda, I've got Mr. Cooper in suspension in Dungeon Two. Give me about twenty minutes. We'll be in the lounge."

"Okay, mistress," the girl said, and returned to her book.

100

Valerie led Kelly to a small room behind the reception area that was equipped with a microwave, a refrigerator, a television, and several comfortable, well-worn couches. On one wall she saw a framed poster of Michelle Pfeiffer dressed in the leather fetish costume she wore as the Catwoman in the *Batman* movie. On the side of a cluttered metal desk pushed against the opposite wall someone had stuck a bumper sticker that read: *The more I learn about men the more I like my vibrator.*

Valerie poured herself a cup of black coffee from the coffee maker on the card table and introduced Kelly to some of the other dominatrices who were using the lounge, reading or relaxing between sessions. There was Satana, Payne, Lady Severa, and The Countess. They were playwrights, artists, or students in their outside lives, but they had all discovered in domination a passionate and profitable sideline.

For Valerie, it had been her graduate school study of prehistoric matriarchal societies that had opened her eyes to the reality of female power. Immersed in books like Robert Graves's *The White Goddess* and Merlin Stone's *When God Was a Woman*, she began to lament the fallen station of her once proud and indomitable sisters. She started to feel more and more as if she had been born at the wrong time, in the wrong country, far from her spiritual home. Others sensed the change in her personality, especially men, who seemed to be suddenly uncomfortable, even afraid in her presence, which suited her just fine, as she'd always found men more of a nuisance than anything else.

Strangely enough, it was a man who had introduced her to Captive Hearts. He was a fellow Ph.D. student in her class, a shy, nervous, intense type, who she had immediately noted for his good looks and intelligence, and had as quickly discounted for the wedding band on his finger. One evening, during a break in the cafeteria, she

101

asked him to elaborate on the work he was doing on vestigial manifestations of goddess worship in contemporary culture. He told her about clubs he had visited like Captive Hearts, where men paid to be dominated by women and to be chastised for their sex's grievous insult to the Goddess. She doubted that many men shared as politically correct a motivation for frequenting such clubs as her sensitive classmate, at least not consciously, anyway. Nevertheless, she was intrigued enough to check it out for herself. The rest was history.

Or, in this case, "herstory."

"It's great to be in control," Valerie said. "Exhilarating, really. Think of how much crap we have to take as women. Boyfriends, husbands, bosses, jerks on the street. In here I am a queen, a goddess, a nightmare harpy from hell. A Woman. And the funny thing is, when I leave here I carry a little of that aura with me. People treat me differently, because I feel differently. I carry myself with authority. Or so I've been told."

Kelly thought of the man she'd seen in the waiting room. "What kind of people come here? I mean, what drives them to be—"

"Dominated? You name it. We have businessmen. Lawyers. Accountants. They're often successful, creative, powerful people. There's an element of guilt involved, I guess. They have to be so dominant in their ordinary daily lives, it's a great release for them to come here and be dominated in return. In spite of their outwardly aggressive natures, something inside them needs to submit to a higher authority. Helps them relieve the pressure of command, I guess. We get quite a few famous people, too. Politicians, soap opera stars, athletes. You'd be surprised. In lots of cases, though, they're people just like you and me. Store clerks, banktellers, housewives—"

"You mean you get women?"

"Sure. We get a lot of couples, too, where both partners are submissive and need someone to take control. We're an equal-opportunity torturer. Sometimes I feel like a psychiatrist."

"And what does it cost someone to be analyzed?"

"Anywhere from one hundred fifty to three hundred dollars an hour. Excluding tips, of course. It depends on what they want."

"It costs a lot to be a slave," Kelly said.

"That's probably why we tend to get such an upwardly mobile clientele. Generally speaking, the riffraff can't afford our prices. I guess they have to content themselves with self-flagellation."

"And there's no sex?"

"Absolutely not. If any woman here accepted money for even so much as a handjob, she'd be fired on the spot. Not that such a thing would ever happen. All the women working here have become far too dominant to allow themselves to be exploited in that way. Occasionally, if we know the customer really well and we like him and want to give him a special reward, we may allow him to masturbate himself in our presence, or we may even press a vibrator against him, but there's absolutely no physical contact involved. The rules are very strict and very strictly enforced. Ilana—she owns the club—sees to that. They say she is a descendant of the Hungarian Countess Elisabet Bathory. You know, the one who killed all those virgins to bathe in their blood so she could stay forever young?" Valerie laughed. "As you might guess, no one is anxious to get on her bad side."

Just then, the man Kelly had seen in the reception area came into the lounge, his sleeves rolled up, an apron tied around his waist. He gathered up the coffeepot and cups and carried them over to the sink and began washing them.

"Is he a slave?" Kelly asked.

103

"Robert? Oh, yes," Valerie said offhandedly. "He's our houseboy. He comes in whenever he can get away from the office and does odd jobs around the place, vacuuming, moving furniture, washing dishes. He's very helpful. He's what we in the business call a servitude slave. That means they get off on serving women. You haven't lived until you've had a man naked on his hands and knees scrubbing your bathroom floor or cleaning your refrigerator while you're out shopping or having lunch with the girls. It's one of the perks of being a dominatrice. Hell, it's almost enough to make you believe there really is a goddess, after all."

"And he doesn't expect anything in return?" Kelly asked incredulously.

"Oh, they usually expect some kind of attention. They are men, after all. But the important thing is that you control the game. Most of the time they're satisfied to kiss your feet or to be verbally humiliated, something like that. You've got to remember, it's not sex these folks are primarily looking for. Not sex as you understand it. For them, the act of submission provides a sensual charge that goes beyond mere genital explosion; instead, it's a prolonged psychic orgasm that reverberates throughout their whole being for days at a time."

Kelly felt as if they were talking about a whole different species of being from the men and women she knew. She couldn't imagine what drove such people to the unique passions they pursued or to go to the expense and inconvenience that such a pursuit so obviously cost them. Yet she had no doubt it must be a powerful stimulus. On the other hand, she felt more than a little empathy with Valerie and the other dominatrices of Captive Hearts, who defied the conventions of patriarchal society and dared to explore the untapped reserve of their own feminine power.

"I think I understand what you're saying," Kelly said.

"But there's one thing I don't quite get. If you're acting out their fantasies, accepting their money, giving them pleasure, are they really slaves? Aren't they really still in charge?"

Across the room, Satana and Lady Severa interrupted a conversation they were having about an upcoming psychology final to share a laugh with Valerie.

"Right on, sister," Lady Severa said. "You're a woman after my own heart."

Satana turned to Valerie. "She's a natural, all right."

"We have this argument all the time," Valerie said by way of explanation. "Who really holds the whip. Fact is, it's a two-way street. We're getting pleasure out of the session or we wouldn't be doing it. We're also the ones in control. The slave decides the limits of the fantasy, but a good dominatrix knows how to push those limits, how to get them to go just a little farther than they intended. That's where the real sense of power comes into play. And the slaves, they're generally very appreciative when you show them how much farther they can go. It's almost a matter of pride to them. They offer their submission to you as a gift and you take it, much the same way the Goddess takes a sacrifice or a prayer. After all, even a Goddess needs to be worshipped in order to survive."

The receptionist stuck her head in the lounge to remind Valerie about Mr. Cooper, still suspended in Dungeon Two.

"Thanks, Brenda," she said, and turned to Kelly. "Come on, I'll show you what I mean. We can talk about domination all day long and you'd never understand. You have to experience a session firsthand, and then you can tell me who you think is really in charge. One thing, though: Once we're inside the dungeon I'm no longer Valerie Lawson. I'm Mistress Kane."

TWELVE

Kelly followed Mistress Kane past the bathroom and the office and down a short corridor to three heavily paneled doors.

Inside the second room, Mr. Cooper was standing, his naked body suspended by a block-and-tackle arrangement hanging from the ceiling. He was suspended so that his toes barely touched the floor, all of his weight supported by the trembling muscles of his calves, his ankles locked in a spreader bar that forced his legs apart and left him with only the more painful option of hanging from his wrists. He was naked, of course, except for a rubber ball gag and a couple of well-placed plastic spring clothespins.

In spite of his obvious discomfort, he was fully erect, his penis sheathed in a condom.

"In case we have an accident," Mistress Kane explained. "But we're not going to have any accidents, are we, David?"

The man muttered through the ball gag, sounding a little like Elmer Fudd, assuring his mistress that there would be no accidents.

"That's good," she said. "I've brought a visitor to see you, David. She is here to see for herself what a beautiful thing your submission can be. Do you have any objections?"

The slave murmured again, shaking his head no. Kelly wondered if it made any difference what he said.

"I thought not," Miss Kane said. She turned to Kelly. "David enjoys being shown off to other women. He likes to show how agreeable and obedient he is. Don't you, David?"

The man stared at the floor between his spread feet. His face colored with shame.

"Yes, Mistress," he mumbled.

"Let's begin, shall we?"

There was something shockingly impersonal and yet strangely touching about seeing the man on display like this, the knowledge that he'd been waiting alone in this room, silently suffering the whole time they'd been speaking, the way his body trembled with anticipation at the mere sound of the dominatrice's voice. Kelly felt as if she were intruding on some deep and private mystery between this man and woman. Dare she call it love?

She glanced around the room, and everywhere her eyes fell she was confronted with some instrument designed to administer pain. There was a large wooden wheel with leather straps, a wooden bondage cross, and a chair covered with rounded spikes. Along the walls, Kelly saw the tools of this bizarre discipline: whips, canes, paddles, cuffs, ropes, as well as various fetish accoutrements such as harnesses, gags, clamps, lingerie, high heels, hospital gowns, adult diapers, and wigs. There were also supplies of a more practical nature, including paper towels, body oil, electrical tape, surgical gloves, and a bucket and mop. The room looked like a cross between a medieval torture chamber and an autobody shop.

Kelly turned back to the man hanging from the padded leather cuffs.

Mistress Kane had added a leather eyeblind to the man's costume and he was taking mincing steps, the blindfold making it difficult for him to keep his balance as she stalked around him menacingly, poking him with the handle of the braided leather whip.

He looked to be no older than thirty, his body well proportioned, smooth, and muscular, like a Wall Street whiz kid who played squash three times a week and jogged in Central Park. From what she could see of his face behind the blindfold, he was quite handsome. Certainly he must have a girlfriend or, like the man in the lobby, a wife. Did whoever it was know the secret passion that drove the man she loved? If she didn't, what would she think if she found out?

"The purpose of the blindfold," Mistress Kane explained, "is to heighten a slave's level of anxiety. Through the imaginative use of restraints and gags, a good dominatrice seeks to render a slave as helpless as possible. The key is to keep the slave guessing what's coming before he finally gives up guessing altogether and just accepts whatever comes. Good—or bad."

During her little speech, she had put down the whip and picked up a long leather paddle covered with silver studs. Without warning, she swung her arm forward, the paddle smacking sharply across his buttocks, leaving a faint stain of crimson across his white flesh. She swung the paddle again and then again, the man flinching each time in obvious pain. The dominatrice stroked the reddened flesh, her voice filled with what sounded like genuine sympathy for the man's suffering. "There, there," she said sweetly, as if comforting a child. "I know it hurts. But just a little more. You can do it. I know you can."

She turned to Kelly. "The trick is to show equal parts severity and mercy. That heightens the mood and tends to help a slave achieve greater levels of submission. Any

108

sadist worth his or her salt knows that a little tenderness goes a long way."

She stepped back and let the man have it with the paddle again, this time even harder than before, until the force of the blows caused his body to rattle against his chains. The man was moaning behind the gag, but whether they were moans of pain or pleasure it was impossible for Kelly to tell. If she understood the dominatrice correctly, it didn't matter. The whole point was to bring the two extremes together.

Mistress Kane dropped the paddle to its place on the wall and returned to the hanging man. She grabbed him around the waist, pulling him up against her, and began flicking the spring clothespins attached to his nipples with her forefinger.

."The funny thing about clothespins," she said, "is that after awhile they actually stop hurting. Until you take them off."

She pulled the clothespin off the man's left nipple and once again he moaned. The dominatrice held him closer, as if trying to drink the pain running through his body. She pulled off the clothespin attached to his other nipple. She rubbed the sore buds of pink flesh, laughing as the man tried halfheartedly to squirm out of her grasp. Before she stepped away she reattached the clothespins.

"Better?" she cooed into the man's ear.

The man nodded.

"The key," Mistress Kane said, going to the wall and selecting one of the larger bullwhips hanging there, "is to know exactly how to gauge a slave's limitations. It's really not that difficult once you get the hang of it. There is a current that runs through them during a session. All you have to do is tap into it, and it's almost as if you become one person. It's quite amazing what can be accomplished when this occurs. You can take a slave almost to the very end. Of course, if the two of you aren't working together, you can really end up hurting somebody. And I hate to mess anybody up." The dominatrice smiled. "I like to use people again and again."

She emphasized her point by snapping the long bullwhip against the floor. It sounded like a gunshot going off in the small room. Kelly appreciated the importance of what the woman had said about establishing a rapport with her clients. She had no doubt that the dominatrice could cut the man to ribbons with the whip if she wasn't careful.

"Naturally, it's a little easier with men." Mistress Kane pointed at the man's erection with the whip handle. "As you can see, they have a built-in indicator. It's one of the ways that Nature made us superior to them. Not only are they more vulnerable physically, but they are more vulnerable psychologically because they can't hide their arousal from us."

The dominatrice stepped back and lazily let the whip unfurl to the floor. She extended her arm backward, swinging it forward in a graceful, sweeping motion that reminded Kelly of a movie she had once seen about fly-fishing. There was a booming explosion of leather and flesh, and Kelly saw the first pink welt rise across the man's back. Before the mark could even redden a second was added, parallel to the first, and then two more in the opposite direction, forming a neat crosshatching.

"I like to make designs," Miss Kane said, pausing for a moment to admire her own handiwork. "It's much more interesting that way. You must remember that what we do here is not just punishment, it's a form of art."

For the most part, the man stood quietly during the whipping, groaning a little and struggling to stand still as the whip marked him. Kelly saw that between his legs

110

his penis bobbed, heavy and erect, showing no sign of wilting. He was breathing heavily and his body was slick with sweat in spite of the room's air conditioning. The dominatrix had stopped talking, her attention riveted on the task at hand, her eyes shining with a strange light that suggested she had reached that state she had spoken of only minutes before, where she and her victim had become as one.

When she was done whipping him Mistress Kane removed the ball gag from his mouth and pulled a tube of red lipstick from the zippered pocket of her leather pants. She uncapped the lipstick, grabbed his cheeks, and told him to pucker up. She smeared the lipstick thickly across his lips, and then she removed the leather eyeblind, reaching up almost maternally to brush the sweat-soaked hair off his forehead. The man kept his eyes lowered to the floor.

The dominatrix walked to the wall and turned the winch that lowered the block and tackle so that the man was now able to stand flat-footed on the floor. She continued to turn the winch until he was able to sink to his knees, but whether he did so out of humility or simple exhaustion Kelly couldn't tell. Meanwhile, the dominatrix lifted each of her legs, reached back, and slowly and deliberately pulled off her spiked heels. She crossed the room in her bare feet and stood menacingly over the naked man, grabbed him roughly by his sweat-soaked hair, and shoved his face into her leather-covered crotch. She looked up at Kelly.

"He's trembling," she said with obvious satisfaction. "You see before you a man who has learned his place among women. A man who has learned to submit." She looked back down at the kneeling man as if he were a dog whose obedience had pleased her. "You may now kiss my feet," she said.

The man fell prone before her and enthusiastically

kissed each of the dominatrice's feet, each kiss leaving behind a vivid red lipstick print.

"Thank you, Mistress," the man murmured. "Thank you."

She released the man from the leather cuffs and unlocked the spreader bar around his ankles. She also removed the clothespins, which hadn't fallen from his body during the whipping.

"Now I want you to crawl across the floor on your knees and thank our visitor for watching your submission."

Kelly stood, too shocked to say anything, as the naked man worked his way across the floor on his hands and knees, lowering his head to her feet, right, then left, gently kissing her insteps.

"Thank you, mistress," he murmured and backed away.

Looking down, Kelly saw two faint red lipstick prints where he had kissed her.

She stared dumbly after the man, blood thundering in her ears, warmth spreading over her face and neck, sweat breaking out over her body. The rush was so overwhelming, she was sure for a moment that she would faint right then and there. When she looked up she saw Valerie staring out at her from her dominatrice costume, and the expression in her eyes was too intimate to be anything other than one of recognition.

"Congratulations, sister," she said solemnly. "You've just learned the first and most important lesson in domination."

THIRTEEN

Hillary Stanton sat at the head table reserved for dignitaries and celebrities and cut listlessly at her bloody prime rib.

She stared out at the crowd packed into the Grand Ballroom of the Waldorf-Astoria for the New York City AIDS Foundation Banquet and felt nothing so much as a profound and general disgust for the entire human race. She hated these gatherings of do-gooders and self-serving activists, the majority of whom were interested in nothing more elevated than lining their own pockets and protecting their own interests. The room was full of people who stood to lose a great deal if a cure for AIDS were discovered tomorrow. She wondered how many of these earnest and dedicated crusaders would trade their six-figure salaries, their limousines, their status as "experts" in exchange for such a cure.

Of course, the reason she was here was just as self-serving. Edmund needed the liberal gay vote to carry New York City in the statewide election, and that meant Hillary needed to become a lay expert on the disease that was decimating so much of the homosexual population. Consequently, she had talked to doctors, held AIDS babies in hospitals, and visited hostels where dying gay men clutched at her ungloved hand with a desperation bordering on the obscene. The result was that she was able to look at a person and recognize the otherwise invisible shadow of death that marked those destined shortly for the grim reaper. She saw several such men in the crowd tonight, dressed in their tuxedos, the guests of honor at a ball honoring Death itself. In spite of their immaculately tailored dress, they looked like nightmare figures from a painting by Chirico, their bodies frail as skeletons, their flesh blemished with disease, their eyes huge and limpid in their wasted faces.

The eyes were the worst: They burned with a hunger for love, for acceptance, for redemption that consumed them from the inside, as if they were men possessed. Hillary found looking at them both irresistible and impossible at the same time, like staring into the sun.

On her right, the fat, bespectacled wife of the mayor of New York City was whispering in her ear, congratulating Hillary on a beautiful, heartfelt speech. She was here on behalf of her husband, as well, who was upstate somewhere watching a pro-am celebrity tennis match. He was up for reelection, too, and he needed the gay vote as badly as Edmund did, having alienated most of the heterosexual white population with his ethnic pandering. The mayor himself didn't feel it necessary to be at the fund-raiser himself, perhaps because he was attending a tennis match in honor of the late Arthur Ashe, the black former Wimbledon champion who had only the year before died of AIDS.

Hillary politely thanked the woman for her praise, but the truth was, she hardly remembered what she had said at the podium. The speech had been written weeks before by someone on Edmund's staff, and she had memorized it using a mnemonic trick that was totally independent of the meaning of the words. She'd given enough such speeches to know where to put the accents, where to pause for effect, where to appear momentarily overcome by emotion. She was a natural actress; in fact, she'd even briefly considered the profession shortly before she'd met Edmund. It was an ability she still depended on to carry her through interminable nights like these.

Hillary was nodding away to whatever it was the mayor's wife was saying, eating her undercooked roast beef and smiling whenever she sensed the lens of a camera passing like cross hairs over her face. Her mind, however, was on the night before, on the girl she had picked up and brought back to the mansion. There were huge gaps in her memory, but the images that kept flashing back to her had her worried.

She remembered the girl's face, white and terrified, her mouth formed around a silent scream the shape and color of an orange rubber ball gag. She remembered a whip lying on the floor, red and long, like a snake turned inside out. She remembered Monica standing in the light, her body clothed in gore like a scarlet bodysuit, her hands on her hips, laughing. She remembered drinking a glass of wine unlike any she had ever tasted before that had given her such towering visions she had passed out.

On the drive to the Waldorf she had worked up the nerve to ask Degas if they had taken care of the girl. She was relieved when he told her that he had driven the girl back to the city early that morning. Monica had hustled her out of the house before dawn and instructed him to drop her off where they had found her. When she'd asked if the girl seemed okay he'd looked at her strangely, but answered that although she was a little worse for wear, she wasn't complaining. Monica had stuffed several crisp one-hundred-dollar bills into the pocket of her skirt.

The mayor's wife had finally stopped wetting her ear and turned to talk to a controversial black councilman.

115

Hillary sighed with relief. Not only was the woman an insufferable cow, but she had a terrible perspiration problem. She smelled like Chinese cabbage.

A gay man with eggplant-colored splotches on his face stepped up to the table to thank Hillary for her concern and to urge her to convince Edmund to do all he could should he be elected president to find a cure for AIDS. She felt like telling him to go fuck himself; she had battled cancer, which killed more people in a year than AIDS had in the last decade. If she were to lobby for the cure of any disease, it would be one she were personally threatened by.

Instead, Hillary smiled politely, nodding her head appropriately, her eyes resting on the bejeweled mountain of celebrity flesh that was Elizabeth Taylor, who had been cornered by some reporters. She'd just been released from the hospital after yet another bout of pneumonia. Hillary wondered if the rumors she'd heard about Taylor were true, and that her almost evangelical interest in the government funding of AIDS research was due in large part to the fact that she herself had the disease.

Self-interest.

It made the world go 'round.

Idly, Hillary touched the place on her throat where she'd found the puncture wounds. She didn't remember how she'd gotten them, but she could easily guess. She had placed a bandage over the wound and hid it beneath a high-collared blouse. Now, as her fingers brushed lightly over the marks, she felt a tingling warmth spread through her body, registering most intensely in her erogenous zones. She closed her eyes and felt the pleasure wash over her, making her shudder all the way down to her toes.

Shaken, she picked up her water glass.

"Are you okay?" the mayor's wife asked, a note of concern in her voice.

"I'm fine," Hillary said, smiling nervously. "It's just a touch of flu."

FOURTEEN

Rossi watched Graham dunking his raisin bagel in his coffee and felt his stomach turn. Graham had called him up and told him to meet him at Ron's to discuss the coroner's report on the Jane Doe they'd found in the old warehouse.

They were sitting at the small breakfast counter on Tenth Avenue about a half hour after dawn. Ron's was the kind of place where the local drug dealers grabbed a bite to eat before going to bed after a long night on the streets, the kind of joint where, if you found a roach doing the backstroke in your egg yolk, you had two choices, and neither of them was to complain to the management.

Ron's was a misnomer, anyway.

The original owner had sold out and moved to a Florida rest home five years earlier, after he was shot in the head during an armed robbery that left him with a brain as soft as one of his infamous two-minute eggs. The place was currently owned by a Jamaican couple who kept the place open twenty-four hours a day and never had any trouble because their three sons ran the local drug posse. They used the place to cut deals, and cops like Rossi and Graham used it to find out what was really going down on the streets. In addition to the free donuts and coffee, the two detectives got the occasional piece of information that could help them break a big case.

The old saying was true: When you lay down with dogs you got up with fleas. But the fact of the matter was, every good cop Rossi knew was crawling with fleas.

"Hinton's pretty sure she wasn't done at the warehouse," Graham said, biting off a big chunk of soggy bagel.

Rossi winced. He stared suspiciously at his spoon before using it to stir his tea. "No fooling. There wasn't a drop of blood in the place."

Graham shrugged, using the bagel to shove scrambled eggs onto his fork. He shoveled the eggs into his mouth, took a sip of coffee, and chewed meditatively before he spoke, the contents in his mouth reduced to a brown paste. Rossi deliberately looked away, and his eyes fell on an ancient no-pest strip hung above the grill, studded with what looked like round, hairy raisins.

"Well, I guess he figured the guy might have used a bucket or something to catch the blood."

"Guy?" Rossi said, looking back. "He's sure it's a guy?"

"Either that or a fucking Amazon. You saw yourself how she was trussed up there. You'd have to be a guy, and a pretty damn strong one at that, to hang her up like we found her. It'd be a tall order. Even for me."

That was saying something. Graham was big. Not particularly tall, but wide as the front of a truck, and just about as solid. On more than one occasion, Rossi had seen him flatten a locked door simply by running full tilt into it.

"Maybe it's more than one. Maybe a cult?"

Graham nodded. "Could be. They cut the head off. Why do that? Could be ritualistic. Maybe some kind of wacko blood thing."

"Or someone who thinks he's a vampire. Remember

119

that guy we busted last year for robbing the city blood banks?"

"Whatever happened to him, anyway?"

"I don't know," Rossi said. "Got warehoused in some mental institution the last I heard. I lost track."

Graham stabbed toward the window with his fork as a homeless man shuffled past. "Some do-gooder doctor could've had him released. Seems like they're letting them all out nowadays."

"True," Rossi conceded. "I'll check it out."

Graham looked up from his plate, his smooth jowels wobbling, and grunted.

"Do we know who she is yet?" Rossi asked.

Graham extended his pinkie and flipped open the folder on the counter next to him containing a copy of the coroner's report. "Name's Walsh. Heidi Walsh. Forty-two years old. Married. Two kids. Vice-President of Marketing for Stillwell Enterprises, a California pharmaceutical company. Here on business."

"So what's a nice woman like that doing found naked in a warehouse?"

Graham closed the folder. "Don't know. Hinton says there's no sign of a struggle. And—get this. There's evidence she engaged in sexual intercourse immediately prior to her death."

"They found sperm in her vagina?"

"Nope."

"In her ass, in her mouth?" Rossi said as Graham shook his head each time. "Where then, for chrissake? In her fucking ear? Give me a hand here; I'm running out of orifices."

"No sperm at all."

"Dildo? Then it could have been a woman."

"Nah, it had to be a man."

Rossi slurped his tea. "So what does Hinton think? The woman know this guy or what?"

"He thinks maybe she met him at a club and let herself get picked up and taken somewhere for fun and games. He thinks maybe it was some kind of S and M thing."

Rossi felt Graham's piggy blue eyes on his face like flies. He wanted to brush them away.

"What makes him think that?"

"The leather cuffs on her ankles. Standard issue S-and-M gear. You can find them in any sex-novelty shop in Manhattan. They also found a copy of the *Story of O* in her hotel room."

"That doesn't make her a freak."

"It don't make her fucking Donna Reed either," Graham concluded.

Rossi knew what he was thinking. You didn't spend as much time with a man as Rossi had spent with Graham without developing a kind of telepathic sympathy with him. They had shared things with each other that they hadn't shared with anyone else, not even with the women in their lives. The fact was, the longest relationship either of them had had with any human being was the one they had with each other, a relationship that had begun in their days as rookies at the Academy and continued as they followed each other up the chain of command to the rank of homicide detectives. Along the way they'd had their backs to the wall on more than a few occasions, and they had learned to trust each other with their lives.

"Eric," Graham said, "if you want to talk about it—"

Rossi shook his head. "Nothing to talk about."

Graham stopped eating. "Yeah, well, you were there for me when Darlene walked out with the kids. If it weren't for you, I would have gone off the deep end for sure. I just want you to know that I remember. And that I'm here to return the favor."

Rossi was both amused and touched. He'd never

heard Graham talk like this before. As he remembered, about the only support he'd been able to offer Graham was getting drunk with him. It was about as close to sensitive as the big cop could get.

Rossi waved him off. "Darlene was your wife, for crissake. Kelly, she was just a good fuck. You were right about her and me: two different worlds."

Rossi knew he didn't sound very convincing, but Graham had the good sense to let it go. He doused his bagel in his coffee again, leaving one of the raisins floating in the cup. At least, Rossi *thought* it was a raisin.

"Christ," Rossi said, disgust twisting his features. "Don't you know it's not polite to dunk? Don't you ever read Ann Landers?"

Graham pushed the soggy bread into his mouth.

"Fuck Ann Landers," he said, his voice muffled by wet bread. "If I don't give my stomach a head start digesting these godamn things, they'll sit there all day long like a fucking horeshoe."

"Why the hell do you eat them, then?"

"Are you kidding? They're delicious."

Rossi shook his head and stared out the window. It was still early, but already the streets were crowding up with people on their way to work. He watched them lock-stepping up the street, briefcases in hand, eyes straight ahead, looking through the filth, the disease, the despair that clung to the city like an old woman huddling against the cold in a tattered coat. He watched them on their way to their offices in the pristine glass buildings uptown.

He thought of Kelly.

She was one of them.

For a few months he had been a part of her world.

That was over now.

Now she was just part of the scenery.

FIFTEEN

Connor Scott stood motionless, the music from the stereo blasting Iron Butterfly's "In-A-Gadda-Da-Vida," his attention fixed on the black bag hanging from a beam in the ceiling of the loft, imagining it were an enemy approaching with intent to kill him.

Suddenly his body exploded in a series of well-practiced movements. His fists striking the bag twenty-four times in rapid succession, right-left, right-left, so quickly that if anyone was observing, all they would see was a pink blur. The bag itself, though weighing only twenty-five pounds, hardly moved on its chain. Scott knew it didn't take much force to kill a man. If you knew where to strike, you could snap a man's spine like a dry stick, punch a hole through his skull with your thumb as if it were no more than an eggshell, crush his windpipe like a paper cup.

Connor knew where to strike. It was his job and he was good at it.

So damn good at it he sometimes scared himself.

He had seen what happened to others in the Craft, good, solid magicians who had slipped over the edge. It wasn't hard to do. It took a special type of human being to kill without conscience or passion, and yet still preserve within oneself a code of honor. Not everyone was morally capable of it. Connor could kill a man with a ballpoint pen or with a deadly poison made from dandelions and common household vinegar. He was also a master of transformation, possessing the powers of mimicry and disguise that made it seem possible for him to change his shape at will. He could be your mailman, your boss, your husband, or your wife. As a result he was, among other things, the ultimate secret agent. In his long career with the Craft he had been called upon to assassinate a South American strongman, strangle an organized crime lord, and poison a wealthy and corrupt industrialist so that it looked as if he died of a massive coronary.

He took pride in his Craft and his abilities. He enjoyed what he did, and he had long since stopped trying to deny it. He felt a great sense of pride knowing that he was one of a select few chosen to be a weapon of the spirit, a soldier of the aethyr. The odds were clearly stacked against them. A browse through the pages of any daily newspaper was enough to cure an intelligent man of optimism. The world had clearly lost its soul.

Connor finished with a series of sidekicks, timing them to the music, and then let loose with a high roundhouse that exploded into the sawdust-stuffed canvas and sent the bag swinging wildly just as the tape clicked off.

He grabbed a towel draped over a nearby chair and wiped the sweat that shined his face and chest, tossing the used towel into the small utility room that housed the washer and dryer. The loft was long enough to run a fifty-yard dash and still have a few yards left over to slow down. There were separate areas set aside for his bed, his desk, and his bookcases, and a cozily arranged setup of couches and armchairs surrounding a large-screen Sony Trinitron home theater that served as a living room. Except for the bathroom and a dark room built into one of the closets, there were no doors anywhere in the loft.

No doors. No room. No walls.

No places to hide.

They had arranged for him to move into the loft months ago, stocking it to suit his personal preferences, right down to the portable 5419 Braun electric razor in the top drawer of the bathroom cabinet and the twenty-five crisp white L.L. Bean button-down shirts hanging on the clothes bar in his sleeping area. The cabinets and refrigerator had been stocked with his favorite food and beverages. The organization he worked for believed in taking good care of its own.

Connor walked to the barred window that faced east and stood in the spill of yellow sunlight that warmed the floor under his bare feet. He stood erect, breathing deeply, until he could imagine five distinct spheres of energy opening in his body like flowers opening to the light. From the lower-most, located just below his feet, he drew a narrow current of blue-white light, pulling it up through the sole of his right foot and letting it flow upward through his right leg, along the right side of his spine, under his jawline, all the way through the top of his head, where it opened the uppermost sphere like a great spotlight. He pulled the energy back down through the left side of his body, opening each of the negative circuits in turn, letting the energy run down his left leg and out through his left foot, completing the circuit.

He repeated this exercise several times, circulating the light until he felt his entire body sheathed in light, filled with a tingling, protective electric energy. He allowed himself the luxury of existing inside the cocoon of light for several minutes before taking a deep breath and absorbing the energy into his body. It was a trick he had learned years ago from an Illuminated Master in East

Germany, and he'd used it religiously every morning to keep himself alert and energized. The fact that he hadn't caught a cold or flu in a dozen years was probably the least beneficial effect of the exercise.

His morning rituals complete, Connor hit the shower, taking it ice cold as usual. He wrapped a fresh towel around his waist, draped another around his shoulders, and padded toward the small kitchenette on the south side of the loft. On the way he grabbed the remote from the leather armchair and flicked on the morning news. Katie Couric and Bryant Gumbel were sharing a laugh over some inanity. He was about to flick it off to C-Span or CNN, but something about their combined idiocy appealed to him, so he left them on. He opened the refrigerator and scanned the shelves until he found the bottle of orange juice he had squeezed the day before.

It was nearly empty.

He pulled open the chiller bin and found a lone orange among the various fresh fruits and vegetables stored there.

Damn.

He'd have to run down to the market and get some more. He toweled dry his sandy hair, threw on a dark jogging suit and running shoes, and took the freight elevator down to the street.

In the loft it was almost possible to forget where you were. There, Connor could lose himself in a book of poetry by Keats or Blake, or a piece of music by Mozart or Verdi. But once he hit the street the city sat on his chest like a five-hundred-pound woman with bad breath.

Connor hated New York.

He hadn't been to the city in two years, but in that short time it had deteriorated to a degree he would hardly have thought possible. He was trained to register danger, and everywhere he went in New York he felt his

126

system overload with warning signals. There was an atmosphere of tension on the streets that was palpable, a sullen look in people's eyes that threatened instant violence, or the meek submission to violence. It was the law of the jungle, which was fine by Connor; he operated best in situations where might made right. But for those poor souls who clung to the vain hope that they still lived in a civilization, the laws didn't protect them; they merely got in the way of their ability to protect themselves. It bred a citenzry of placid victims, like cattle, who would sooner or later be plucked from the herd, fleeced, and slaughtered at the whim of those whose only law was that dictated by their own unchecked appetites.

Only last year there had been riots in Crown Heights during which a black teenager had stabbed a Hasidic Jew to death in the street. The police had arrested a suspect who had confessed to the killing. In his pocket they had found a knife and money, both soaked in the victim's blood. Bleeding to death on the hood of a car, the dying student identified the youth as his killer. Still, the predominantly black and Hispanic jury declared that there wasn't enough evidence to convict him. He was set free. The mayor, who'd been accused of holding the police back when the rioting started to let the mob "vent," stood by the verdict, hailing the process of American jurisprudence and suggesting that the city hold a parade to promote interracial harmony.

That, for the history books, was what passed for justice in the city of New York during the last days of the twentieth century.

On the corner outside the Korean grocery where he did his shopping, Connor saw three black kids who should have been in school hassling an elderly Korean woman trying to push a handcart of groceries to her apartment. They blocked her path, taunting her, snatching at items from her cart and tossing them back and forth. When she pleaded to them in broken English to let her pass they responded by demanding that she pay a "toll" in order to proceed up the street. One of them grabbed a bottle of milk and let it fall to the sidewalk.

The woman turned and looked towards Connor for help.

Connor felt his mind empty, his body get that loose, elastic feeling it always got when it was readying itself for action. His mind was already imaging where the first blow would land, how it would catch the tallest boy under the chin, instantly snapping his neck, how he would spin underneath the knife the second boy would pull from the pocket of his Georgetown jacket, throw an elbow into his ribs, driving shards of bone into his lungs, how he would then come up out of his crouch to deliver a sword strike to the carotid of the last boy, destroying his windpipe and causing him to die less than three minutes later of asphyxiation.

"What you looking at, whitey?" the tallest boy said. He was wearing a black baseball cap with a large silver *X* sideways on his shaved head. He grinned unpleasantly to show a gold-capped tooth.

Connor held the boy's eyes for a moment and then dropped them submissively to the dirty pavement.

He shrugged apologetically, grinned, and hustled past the woman into the grocery, bent under the weight of the disappointment he felt in her eyes.

Connor wished he could explain. He had no choice. He couldn't draw attention to himself. His cover required him to act like everybody else, and so he did just that. He became just another of the many people on the streets of the city who minded their own business, kept their eyes straight ahead, their ears deaf to the cries for help assaulting them from every side. He became one of the soulless multitude who had become so used to the victimizing of their fellow citizens that they hardly noticed it at all anymore. It was part of his disguise.

He had become, in the parlance of the times, an innocent bystander.

SIXTEEN

It was the middle of November, and the subtle perfume of decay was everywhere in the air. It was the scent of the leaves turning on the trees, of unpicked fruit souring on the vines, of small, unseen things dying.

The Vampire breathed deeply.

To her, it was the smell of ambrosia.

She stopped to observe a yellow jacket, weaving drunkenly over the pavement, its time run out, and plucked it up between her thumb and forefinger. The insect's abdomen pulsed, driving its stinger into her flesh like an impotent lover until it was exhausted. She stared into its honeycombed eyes, trying to drink in its insectoid awareness. She placed the insect in her mouth and chewed it, the taste something like Aspergum, only better, because it had once been alive.

She walked along the path that wound through Central Park, the heels of her black boots clicking on the macadam, and everywhere the Vampire looked she saw corruption.

Between a pile of broken stones she saw the sleek head of a black snake staring into eternity. Under a small stone bridge she saw a large gray rat waddle into a drainage ditch with something wriggling in its mouth, its nude tail lashing the air behind it. Through a sewer grating she saw a dead cat, flattened by decay and laid open by maggots, lying on its back in an oily puddle, its face withered with pain. In every corner, in every windbreak, she saw the rotting garbage left by passersby, spilling over the trash cans, blowing along the ground, sustenance for the flies who sought the rot for food, warmth, and procreation.

And everywhere she saw the homeless, shambling soullessly on the fringes of the park, lying in boneless piles on park benches or staggering from the shadows, their hands always out, hoping to leech a few drops of life's blood from anyone who passed, a few drops of life's blood that took the form of a handful of pocket change.

Brother can you spare some blood?

One such man approached her.

He was black, cankerous, his matted hair alive with lice. No more than thirty, he looked as if he were twice that age. From his ragged clothes came the stench of alcohol, sweat, and disease. He lurched toward her from a small stand of shrubs, calling out some sexual crudity, mistaking her for some rich society bitch on a Wednesday afternoon stroll before her lunch with the girls at the Top of the Sixes.

He realized his mistake from ten feet away.

He stopped dead in his tracks, his yellowed eyes widening, his dark flesh blanching, his lips peeling back in a toothless grin.

"M'lady," he mumbled, shuffling backward as if struck a blow to the forehead, recognizing her.

He stumbled to his knees in a grotesque parody of courtly respect, a puddle of bloody urine forming beneath his knees.

Her slaves were everywhere, too numerous to count.

She left him there, his head to the pavement, muttering to himself. Anyone who saw him would think he was just another homeless lunatic. The city was full of them.

She stopped and found herself standing before a life-sized bronze statue of William Shakespeare. The immortal bard of Avon stood at the head of poet's row, pensive, as if hatching one of his timeless verses while a fat gray pigeon sat on his head. He, too, was one of her slaves, but a slave of a different sort. She had met him when he was little more than an itinerant stagehand for a traveling theater company. She had taken him one night on the very boards he loved too well. He had declined her offer of immortality for a mere taste of vampire blood and a knowledge of the eons, for he was smart enough to know that great art was born only of great suffering, and that to lose his mortality was to lose that part of himself from which all great art sprang.

Fool, the Vampire thought, as she saw the statue now, all that was left of the man—besides the poetry, of course—just a bronze likeness covered in pigeon shit.

And not a very good likeness, at that.

The man himself was gone. Dust. Molecules. Memory.

What would he give to come back, to be a living, breathing, eating, drinking, lusting man of flesh and blood and bone again? Would he give up his treasured poetry, his fame, his paper immortality?

Oh, to have a body again, eh, Willie?

The Vampire looked at the bodies of the young office workers, secretaries, and businessmen walking through the park, as well as those jogging, bicycling, or pushing baby prams. She savored the sight of those stretched out on the huge gray rocks that rose from the grassy hills like pagan altars, baring their flesh as they attempted to drink in the last days of sunlight before the cold days of winter.

She caught their perfume in the air as she passed, the warm and inviting aroma of flesh and blood. They were like ripened fruit, waiting to be plucked, their fresh and ruddy youth dying to be tasted. All around her acres of humanity ready for the harvest, and yet only a relative few would be selected. She saw those who had already not made the grade. They sat alone on park benches feeding the pigeons, old and infirm, their time long past, withered and soured; no one wanted them anymore. They were like compost from which next year's harvest would be grown.

Nature was wasteful.

And yet only through such profligacy could nature ensure such a bounteous variety as she provided. Only by letting some fruit fall could the seed for the following year's harvest be set.

Ah, youth.

She felt the eyes of both men and women upon her, eyes wet and hot as kisses. If she cleared her mind, she could pick up their invisible fantasies, which filled the air like television signals. Fantasies of warm, willing flesh, of mouths and orifices moist with eagerness, of limbs compliant to her each and every command.

Her passage through the park was like that of a powerful underwater current, dragging after her the wills of all whom she swept past.

On Central Park South there was a long line of hansom cabs offering tours of the park to the tourists. The Vampire walked up to a splendid sky-blue carriage with a canvas roof trimmed with silver fringe. The horse was a handsome black gelding with the lines of a thoroughbred who'd no doubt seen his best days on the track and had been sold to the carriage trade by a sentimental owner, instead of to a dog food factory. There was a nobility in its aspect, in the way it held its head, that its current degraded state had been unable to erase. There was a natural aristocracy even among animals.

The Vampire stroked the neck of the horse and felt it

lean toward her touch, whinnying softly and nuzzling her wrist.

"He likes you," said a voice behind her.

The Vampire turned and saw a young man in a billowy white blouse, black vest, and muddy riding boots approach.

"He usually tries to bite," he continued, somewhat less sure of himself now that he could see her face.

The old-fashioned blouse was open down to his breastbone, and the Vampire stared at the pulsating blue vein that ran down the side of his thin white throat.

"Would you like a ride?" the man asked.

"Yes," the Vampire said. "I would very much."

He looked curiously at the small tanned pouch she pulled from inside her coat, hardly noticing it when she handed him a crisply folded hundred-dollar bill.

He helped her up and she settled into the beautiful carriage as the man climbed up on the box, grabbed hold of the reins, and shook them. The horse immediately took up a sprightly gallop, its hooves clip-clopping on the street like the rhythm of a beating heart.

The Vampire sat shielded from the sunlight beneath the gaily fringed awning, staring out at passersby, remembering riding in similar carriages in England more than a hundred years ago. She snapped the small pouch closed, stroked the soft wrinkled flesh with her fingers, and fondly remembered the lover whose organ it had once graced.

She laughed.

And no birds sang.

SEVENTEEN

The past week had been sheer torture for Hillary.

She had been unable to sleep, unable to eat, unable to think straight. She'd had no word from Monica since the night in the playroom, and she could hardly stand the separation. She'd never expected to feel so strongly for the woman. She had never felt this way for anyone in her entire life. Certainly not for Edmund. Nor for any of the other men and women she'd had affairs with during her twenty-five-year marriage. It was as if she'd been infected with some kind of strange fever. She was acting like a high-school girl, except she hadn't even acted this way when she was in high school.

If she didn't know better, she would say she was in love.

She had picked up a girl the night before on Tenth Avenue and brought her back to play with, but not even that took her mind off Monica. It was terrible, this need she'd felt for the woman, this hunger to be in her presence, to hear her voice. She'd had Degas drive her to the old hotel on Central Park where Monica was staying and had Degas go inside to ask after her at the desk. He'd returned with the news that Monica had left for the day. Desperate, a thousand and one nagging thoughts popped into her head. Did Monica have another lover somewhere in New York? Where else could she be?

Hillary called the hotel desk from the phone in the limousine and heard for herself the operator tell her that Ms. Caron was not answering her phone, could she please take a message? Hillary hung up, furious, desperate. She considered charging up to Monica's room and banging on the door to satisfy herself that she really wasn't in. Perhaps she was just avoiding Hillary's call? If she had to, she could have Degas pick the lock on Monica's hotel-room door. She would search the woman's belongings, find out for herself if she had any reason to doubt Monica's loyalty. If Monica had a lover, she would have him or her killed, or she would have Monica killed, or she would kill herself.

In the end, she contented herself with driving around the block for hours, hoping to catch Monica either on her way in or on her way out. She realized that she was being hysterical, yet the realization did nothing to relieve the gnawing hurt in the pit of her stomach. Every half hour she called Monica's room, and every time she received the same answer. Finally, she had Degas drive aimlessly around the city. Though she told herself she'd given up, she continued to scan the faces of the crowds moving through the streets, hoping to catch a glimpse of Monica.

During the past week she'd gone to an opening at Lincoln Center, the dedication of a statue to Edmund's father in Connecticut, and a Democratic fund-raiser upstate, but she hardly remembered any of it. She had only been going through the motions, smiling, shaking hands, making polite chatter. She was on automatic pilot; all her attention was focused on Monica. She set up appointments in order to have something to do and then found herself rushing through them in order to call Monica's room or pass by the hotel. She called her hotel room repeatedly throughout the week, finally being told by the manager that Monica had left town for a couple of days. Shamelessly, Hillary pretended to be a relative who needed to contact her because of an emergency. The manager apologized and informed her that Ms. Caron had left no forwarding number at which she could be reached. Hillary exploded, called the man a liar, and hung up. An hour later she was on the phone to the hotel again, trying to disguise her voice, using the same ploy.

She was humiliating herself and yet she couldn't help it.

She had called again a few minutes ago and received what had become the stock answer: Monica was not in the hotel.

Hillary stood on the balcony outside her bedroom and stared out at the ocean that lay beyond the jumble of rocks forming the eastern border of the estate. The cold Atlantic heaved black and monstrous against the sky, the moon laying down a silver pathway into the night. She was dressed in nothing but a sheer peignor that the damp November air penetrated at will. She wanted to feel the cold, feel it take her without mercy, paw her with its brutal selfishness. She didn't care if she caught pneumonia; it would be better than the sickness she felt in he heart.

Below she saw the floodlit grounds of the estate, the pool and gardens covered with black tarpulin, the fountain white and dry, and beyond that the electric fence that kept out would-be intruders, curiosity seekers, and possible assassins. She had always thought Edmund was being a bit overly cautious about the latter, but his family had angered a lot of people through the years and the memory of his older brother's assassination at the hands of an Arab extremist still haunted him. Hillary knew that downstairs in one of the control booths Degas was watching the monitors that covered every inch of the grounds. An intercom had been installed in every room, allowing her to alert him at a moment's notice in case she needed him. She played with the idea of calling him to the room, of greeting him naked, of seducing him into her bed. She knew he was gay. He had seen her naked dozens of times with no discernible reaction. But he was a man, and she was sure that his unfailing sense of duty would take care of the rest. It would be humiliating to throw herself on him like that, but perhaps that was just the kind of thing she needed to pull herself back together again. She was humiliating herself anyway. Why not drink the bitter poison to the dregs?

She was so damn lonely. She had always been lonely, but somehow she had never noticed it before. For the first time in her life she needed someone to fill the void. Monica had shown her the empty place in her heart. Now that she was gone, Hillary suddenly felt what she had never known was missing in herself. The only place she found relief was in her dreams. Each night for the past week she had dreamed of Monica. Each night they lay in each other's arms, and yet in the morning the dream only left Hillary less satisfied and more desperate to see her.

Damn her, she cursed the woman who had brought her to this. *Damn her to hell.*

Hillary touched the place on her throat where Monica had kissed her. For she had determined that, indeed, it was a kiss that had caused the wound. She had taken off the bandage even though it hadn't entirely healed. Sometimes it burned, other times it merely ached, and yet other times it sent such a sweet longing through her body, Hillary thought she would die. She touched it now and felt such a longing, one that made her heart swell to bursting and triggered a spasm of pleasure between her legs. Just then the breeze picked up from the sea, smelling of salt and deserts, and the moon tore away from the clouds, and she heard a whisper behind her and she knew who it was even before she turned.

Hillary.

She was standing just inside the French doors to the bedroom, her own black peignor transparent as the web of a spider, her hair loose around her shoulders, her lips red as the blood of a wounded animal traveling over the snow. Hillary stood as still as a statue, afraid that her slightest movement would disturb the air, disrupt the gossamer-thin weave of fantasy and desire on which her image had been woven. But something in Monica's eyes willed her forward, and she found herself walking toward her, her feet moving of their own accord, yet carrying Hillary where she wanted more than anywhere else in the world to go.

Monica reached out, and Hillary touched her hand and felt a thousand avenues of pleasure open in her body. In an instant, her week of suffering and loneliness was forgotten, all the anger and outrage, all the melodramatic plans of murder and suicide. Suddenly, everything was all right again. Monica's mere presence in her bedroom had changed the world, and Hillary would do nothing to jeopardize her happiness. She had Monica's hand in her hand, felt flesh on her flesh, breath on her breath.

"You're not a dream, then?" she barely whispered the word.

"No, I am not a dream," Monica said. "The rest of it. The pain, the loneliness, the despair. That was a dream."

In her left hand, just below her breast, Monica held a silver goblet. Hillary noticed it for the first time. Now the woman held it out to her, warming the bowl in both hands.

"Drink," she said.

Hillary took the goblet and stared into its clear red depths, depths like expensive red leather, the flare of the sunset in New Mexico, the fires of hell. Suddenly, she remembered the wine from the night in the playroom. She had taken the same beverage then and it had made it difficult to remember what happened. She looked up doubtfully.

"What is it?" she asked.

"It's the rarest of wines," Monica explained. She brushed away the gauze and bared her breast, white and perfect, marred only by a small cut just above the small dark nipple. "Drink," she said. "It'll make what must happen next hurt less."

Hillary lifted the goblet to her lips and drank, the wine flowing slowly and intimately over her tongue, warm as a living thing. When she was done Monica took the goblet from her hands and led her to the bed. She cupped Hillary's face in her hands, and Hillary didn't object when Monica turned her head sharply to one side and tore open her throat. It was like no kiss Hillary had ever felt. It was cold and savage and the pain poured through her like liquid lightning, flooding her sickened body like a heavy dose of radiation. Hillary could feel herself growing weaker, and yet she did not fight back, did not want to fight back. Instead, she felt herself spooling away into the darkness until her ego was nothing more than a faint star about to disappear in the black maw of empty space.

This is what it is to die.

Whether the thought was hers or the other woman's, Hillary didn't know, but she was sure it would be her last. She was suddenly in the ruined temple again, propelled forward down the colonnade by two black-robed figures, her bare feet not even touching the marble. They threw her onto the floor before the marble Lady who stared down at her from her throne with a stone-cold look of haughty contempt. Hillary peered up from the floor and saw that the woman's marble lips were wet and red as berries. She let her eyes fall discreetly over the woman's alabaster breasts, the erotic curve of her belly, the lithely carved muscles of her thighs and calves. In her stone lap someone had laid flowers that had long since dried, their petals crumbling to red dust. Hillary's eyes came to rest on the woman's slender marble feet, which were covered with the rust-colored lip prints of all those who had worshipped her throughout the centuries.

Hillary suddenly doubled over with erotic spasm. She rose slowly to her feet, as if her body were being pulled by invisible strings, her hands rising to her hair, by dream logic long and full again, and rotated her hips, grinding them sensually and shamelessly like a Forty-second-Street stripper, thrusting her breasts out to the bald marble eyes of the statue. As she danced, the temple around her seemed to change, the red-veined marble pillars turning to flesh, the pink curtains pulsing with membranous life, while throughout the entire temple came the rhythmic percussion of a beating heart that grew ever more rapid. Hillary felt as if her body were on fire, as if she were slowly burning away to ashes from the inside, consumed by her own passion. Her nightgown lifted off her like smoke, her body clad only in the perspiration of her excitement. She moved like a woman possessed, determined to coax some response from the immobile stone, and all the while the beat of the heart grew louder, as if the temple were the heart itself and she were dancing inside it. She fell at the statue's cold feet, writhing on the warm red tiles like a severed snake, rising slowly to her knees once more, bending backward until the top of her head touched the beating floor beneath her, her arms flung outward to either side, her muscles trembling with the pain of her unnatural and vulnerable position. And still the Lady sat without expression. Hillary flung herself forward, exhausted and breathless, defeated yet again by Her implacable nature. The heartbeat slowed, the flesh turned back to marble, and once again she found herself in the ruins of an ancient temple dedicated to a forgotten goddess.

She was grabbed roughly around the arms by the black-robed figures who pulled her away from the statue and dragged her weeping toward the large concrete fountain. Hillary struggled in their iron grasp, but it was useless. One of them grabbed her kicking feet, crossed her ankles, and lashed them together with a leather band. As they hoisted her upside down into the air, she saw the outside circumference of the fountain, intricately carved with figures of satyrs and nymphs engaged in every variation of sexual congress. From the ceiling, she caught only a glimpse of the terrible orange hook before they thrust it between her bound ankles, leaving her dangling over the cracked bowl of the fountain and disappeared into the shadows. She hung there for several moments, her eyes moving from the dry concrete beneath her head to the beautiful stone Lady on the throne, to her bare feet crossed so small and far away above her pounding head.

From out of the shadows the robed figures came once more, and Hillary tried to twist away on the chain as one of them grasped her around the waist and the other pulled from his robe a gleaming silver crucifix. The crucifix flashed before her eyes and the robed figures suddenly stepped away, bowing their heads as they retreated once more into the shadows. Hillary didn't understand until she saw the bright red blood splashing over the concrete below her head. They hadn't tied her hands and she grabbed at her throat, trying to stop the blood arcing from the severed artery, squeezing out between her fingers in powerful jets with every beat of her heart. She looked down into the basin and saw that it was already half filled with blood, *her* blood, and knew that it was hopeless.

She dropped her scarlet hands from her throat, her eyes glazing over, her life running out of her as a terrible chill crept over her from her toes to her scalp.

She felt the tears roll down her cheeks, the embarrassing warmth scald her thighs, and from far away she heard the woman laugh. It was a harsh, impersonal sound, like the rumble of distant thunder or the destructive power of great machines. She felt the woman pull her head roughly to her breast and force the warm nipple between her numb lips. And Hillary recognized the sweet perfume that emanated from the breast as the smell of her own body.

And without even knowing what to do, responding to some primal instinct for survival beyond human knowledge, Hillary bit the breast offered her and drank, the warm blood filling her mouth, giving her back to herself in a rush of gratitude and love.

Hillary woke up eighteen hours later.

Her heart slammed against her sternum, pausing for what seemed an eternity, and then began beating madly. She sat up in bed, the sheets damp and cold with perspiration, as she had passed the time in a crisis of fever. The pungent odor that assaulted her nostrils told her that the release she'd felt in the dream had been physical as well as emotional.

Monica was gone.

But then, what did she expect?

It *had* been a dream. Hadn't it?

Hillary pulled the soiled sheets from the bed and rolled them into a ball that she shoved in the back of her closet. She didn't want the maid to find them. She would dispose of them herself later on.

143

EIGHTEEN

Life was just beginning to get interesting again.

Connor Scott was sitting in the back of a yellow cab, heading south on the New Jersey Turnpike. Rush hour was over, but most of the traffic was still heading in the opposite direction. Outside the window, Connor saw the distinctive moonscape of northern Jersey, with its petro-chemical drums and storage facility complexes built over the surrounding swampland. In spite of the barren terrain, he felt the old familiar excitement thrilling through his body, as if his nervous system had just been connected on-line.

It always started the same way.

Last night it had been a call to a phone booth halfway across town. The drop-off point was given in a code incorporating the tones of a standard touch-tone phone. That was the way the best codes worked: a combination of the unusual and the mundane.

This morning he stood on the corner of Sixty-seventh and Fifth Avenue at nine-thirty sharp and waited for the game to begin. He'd been given no indication of what cab to take. They relied on his intuition to fill in the blanks. If this intuition wasn't sharp enough to figure it out, he wouldn't be in this business very long one way or another anyway. He saw the pentagram sticker on the dented right front fender right off and knew instinctively that was the cab to hail. Sure enough, as Connor jogged up the street, the cab veered sharply to the curb and let out a pretty woman in a business suit and Reeboks. He would have bet anything that the briefcase she carried was filled with important-looking but totally bogus documents. He climbed into the car and, without saying so much as a word, the driver made a beeline for the Lincoln Tunnel.

Connor glanced up at the driver's face in the rearview.

It matched perfectly the picture on the photo ID identifying him as a New York City cab driver. Not that fake IDs would be any problem for the Craft to produce. Of course, it was entirely possible that the man really was a cabbie. Or he might be an agent operating under Level 6 anonymity: a man who lived and died believing he was a cab driver, or an investment banker, or a store clerk, never suspecting that he had actually served a far greater purpose. It was the ultimate deep cover. Connor looked carefully at the man's face in the mirror. Who was this cab driver, really? He knew better than to ask.

They were approaching Newark International Airport, and Connor watched a huge 747 lifting itself off the runway and passing overhead, making the sky tremble. He wondered what kind of mission they had for him this time. He hoped it wasn't anything like that business in New Orleans. After six months in a maximum security prison he'd begun to believe that they'd forgotten him, or worse, that he was being abandoned as a form of punishment for unintentionally violating one of the Craft's many inviolable rules. He'd needed all of his mental reserves to combat the paranoia and rage that had threatened to overcome him during that trying time. Prison was like that. It truly fucked with your mind. Of all the things he'd experienced, confinement was the most terrible.

The driver had turned off the main road and was bouncing along an unpaved trail so narrow that the yellow fronds of the surrounding swamp brushed the windshield and made it almost impossible to see. Nonetheless, the cabbie hadn't slowed down any. Connor buckled himself in and held on to the seat, bracing himself with his feet to keep from hitting his head on the car roof. They made it through the overgrown road and came out on a small island of mud surrounded by huge expanses of weeds and dead water. Here and there, half sunk in the mud, Connor could see old tires, box springs, and other refuse dumped by less than scrupulous disposal companies. On what looked like the skeletal arm of a submerged crane, he spotted the slim, graceful, startling white figure of a heron.

The driver had stopped the cab, and Connor climbed out of the car, methodically stretching his legs as he looked across the little mud island and sized up the situation.

Up ahead, idling, was a black stretch limousine with tinted windows. He turned back to say something to the cabbie, but the man had already thrown the car into reverse, the front grille disappearing into the tall fronds, leaving Connor alone with the limousine, the heron, and miles of barren swampland.

There was a raw stinking breeze blowing from the west, carrying with it a combination of the stench of chemical waste and decaying vegetation, and Connor pulled his coat closer. The fact was, he had been to these swamps before. This was a popular mob burial ground, and Connor had dumped one or two bodies here himself. There was a lot of secrets sleeping under the scum film of that stagnant water. For a moment Connor played with the idea that this might be what they had in store for him. He'd known magicians who, for one reason or another never explained to them, had been unexpectedly terminated in this way. Instead of a pink slip, the Craft issued you a .22-caliber bullet behind each ear.

Connor shrugged.

It that was the deal going down here, there wasn't a whole hell of lot he could do about it. He reached into his coat to take his Wayfarer sunglasses out of his pocket and flicked the safety off the .38 special in the shoulder holster under his arm. If they did it right, he wouldn't have time to so much as sweat under the armpits. If they did it wrong, maybe he'd have a chance to take one of them into the Void.

He started for the limousine. Halfway there he saw the front door spring open and a man in a gray suit step out of the car. He was tall and thin, with receding blonde hair and silver wire-rimmed glasses. He looked like any other shallow-chested, nearsighted, asthmatic CPA, but Connor knew that appearances were deceiving. This man could fuck your wife, eat your kids, kill your dog, and go home that night and still get all misty-eyed over those sentimental AT&T television commercials.

Connor knew the type. He was the type.

He felt his feet sticking to the mud as if the earth itself was reluctant to let him go to the car. The man in the gray suit reached down and pulled open the back door of the limousine. Up close, Connor could see the earphone in his left ear, the wire running down into the collar of his Brooks Brothers shirt. The man nodded toward the dark interior of the car. Connor caught the man's eyes as he slid into the car, but they were as expressionless as the heads of two nails. As he lifted his legs inside, the man swung the door shut. It made a sound as if it were being hermetically sealed.

"Good morning, Mr. Scott."

Connor slid his sunglasses off, but he heard the voice before his eyes adjusted.

Sitting in the far corner of the limousine was a man in an open-collared shirt years out of style and a tan safari jacket of the variety made popular by Manuel Noriega and other self-proclaimed South American revolutionaries. He was bald as a light bulb, no eyebrows, his eyes hidden behind a pair of mirrored wraparound glasses His head was held up by a metal brace that constituted what Connor at first mistook for the man's shoulders, his chin resting in a small cushioned cup. His hands were covered with white gloves, with which he held a plastic mask up to his face in order to breathe. From the bottom of the mask a ribbed white hose led to a large green tank bolted to the floor. But the oddest thing about his comportment Connor discovered when he used his second-sight to discern the psychic aura that surrounded every living creature. He had none.

Connor had no idea who the man was, but his bizarre appearance touched off alarms in his subconscious. His sixth sense told him that this was one bad dude.

"What have you got for me?" Connor said.

He felt the man probing his mind, trying to penetrate through the facade of complacency he'd put on to hide his involuntary shock at seeing the condition of his caseworker. He didn't know how well he was succeeding until the man gave a small, sly smile, like a snake winding sideways through tall grass.

He handed Connor a sheet of paper with a sketch depicting a beautiful woman. She had long hair, the perfect bone structure of a model, and eyes that the unknown artist labored hard to get right before he finally gave up, contenting himself with two smoky clouds of graphite.

"Who is she?"

"Her name is Monica Caron. She is a terrorist suspected of sabotaging that American Airlines flight last year in Australia. You remember the one?"

Connor did. The plane had exploded in midair over Sydney, killing all 273 people aboard. He was sure they hadn't found a definitive cause for the explosion, although a bomb had been suspected from the start. Perhaps they hadn't seen fit to release the information to the public. More likely, the Craft had their own sources they weren't willing to share with the authorities.

"What is she doing here?"

"We don't know yet," the man said. "We think she is here to commit an act of political terror, possibly to assassinate a major political figure. She is thought to have arrived in New York two or three weeks ago, but it is impossible to tell where she is now. We have people in every major city trying to track her down. You're our man in Manhattan."

Connor held up the sketch.

"We don't have a photo?"

"There are no photos on record of Ms. Caron. You might say she is rather camera shy."

There was the smile again.

Connor felt his insides crawl.

"Do we have any leads? Any idea where she might go. Who she might contact?"

"We think she may have infiltrated the S-M underground. She comes from a rich European background. Her family goes back centuries, very influential, even more powerful than the Agnellis, and with some confusing ties to the Vatican. She was abused by her father from the time she was six until the time she was sixteen, when she strangled him. I guess you might say she's been rebelling against authority ever since. She is a sophisticate and a decadent, with a taste for both men and women. She's ruined the reputations of more than a few lovers back in Europe, not to mention costing a couple of them their lives."

The man paused for a moment to bring the mask to his face, gasping into it until he caught his breath, his lungs sounding like a damaged bellows.

"Don't underestimate her," he said, still sounding a little out of breath. "She is extremely dangerous—and totally ruthless. She is said to have an almost hypnotic power over those she targets. I don't suggest getting any closer than you have to in order to find out what she is up to."

"And then?"

"Do nothing. Someone will contact you."

Either the man was being overdramatic or there was more to this little-rich-girl-gone-bad story than he was telling him.

Connor strongly suspected the latter.

"Good day, Mr. Scott."

Connor understood that he was being dismissed. No more questions were allowed. As if on cue, the door was opened from the outside.

"Oh, Mr. Scott," the man said. "By the way . . ."

"Yeah?"

"Those three black boys you put in the hospital . . ."

Connor cringed. He had followed them out to Brooklyn one evening, catching up to them in the alley of an abandoned tenement where they'd gone to buy some cocaine, and beat all three of them badly, though not mortally. Of course he'd been in disguise. Interviewed by a police detective in the hospital the one whose jaw wasn't wired shut told her that they'd been attacked by a gang of nine Hispanics armed with baseball bats. He'd been too embarrassed to admit the truth: that they had been whipped by a skinny black teenager in an L.A. Raiders parka. Connor had taken the money they'd brought to buy drugs to make it look like a simple robbery. The next morning an elderly Korean woman found an envelope containing a check for two-hundred-fifty dollars in her mailbox with an official-looking letter from the Internal Revenue Service, explaining that she was entitled to the money due to an organizational error.

The man shook his head disapprovingly.

"That kind of thing," he paused, making a face of horrified indignation, as if someone had sneezed and left a booger on his shirt. "It calls attention to oneself. You know the rules."

"I'm sorry."

"Please don't let it happen again."

"Yes, sir."

Connor stepped out of the car, back into the sticky, smelly, black-green mud. The man in the gray suit shoved the car door closed behind him and climbed in behind the wheel of the limousine, putting it into gear and slowly turning the big car around. Connor stood out of the way, his hands in his pockets, and watched the limousine disappear between the fronds. Then he followed it down the access road back to the turnpike, walked three miles to the nearest tollbooth, told them his car had broken down, and called a cab to take him back to the city.

NINETEEN

Power *was* the ultimate aphrodisiac.

Kelly felt the transformation begin the moment she began to change into her domination outfit. It was like suddenly being connected to some incredible source of power that slept deep inside her. The first time she had experienced the change it had scared her, but gradually she had gotten used to the low-level hum of erotic energy running through her, and after a few sessions she had even started to look forward to it.

To grow hooked on it.

For today's session she had chosen a wet-look PVC nightie, garters, and a pair of fishnet stockings. To top it off, she had selected studded leather wrist cuffs and a pair of knee-high leather boots with four-inch heels.

Before working at Captive Hearts, Kelly had never fully appreciated the erotic potential of clothing: the cool impersonality of leather, the implied invulnerability of a studded choker, the slippery untouchability of PVC. Like most women she'd worn leather on various occasions and felt a faint erotic arousal by its smell and touch, but not until now did she truly recognize the full extent of its power. She thought of the Roman legions, of Cossack horsemen, of Nazi storm troopers. To each, leather had been a symbol of power, authority, and will.

Of domination.

Unlike many women she knew, Kelly had always felt uncomfortable dressing to accentuate her natural feminine attributes. Raised in the era of Gloria Steinem and NOW, she always thought that "dressing like a woman" was somehow demeaning to her as a person and a legacy of the days when a woman's sole reason for existence was to make herself pleasing in the eyes of men. Though she hadn't followed the route of some of her more radical feminist friends and gone out of her way to make herself look as sexually neutered as possible, she studiously avoided the more flagrant examples of sexist fashion: mini skirts, high heels, perms, and makeup. She kept her nails trimmed and unpainted and seldom wore anything more provocative than skirts and sensible pumps for business functions, and, on her own time, jeans and T-shirts.

But Valerie had shown her that far from being a method of pleasing men, a woman could use her wardrobe to empower herself and gain control over them. It was a point lost on most feminists, who in her experience saw no deeper than the surface of most things, that a woman should set her sights not on equality, but superiority, and her best chances of that were not in being treated as one of the guys. As any objective look at the history of nations or corporations plainly showed, men treated other men with terrifying disdain and disregard, constantly struggling to defeat each other in endless games of power. Rather, a woman's superiority rested in how different she was than a man and the paralyzed fascination that most men had for that difference. How many times had a man of awesome power—an emperor, dictator, president—men rendered invulnerable by their ruthless domination of other men of power, fallen victim to a woman whose only discernible weapon

153

was her natural sexual allure and a mind shrewd enough to know how to employ it?

To a limited degree, Kelly had seen the principle at work hundreds of times in her own everyday life. She remembered the evening of Eric's birthday when she had dressed up in that frilly black nightie she'd bought from the Pink Pussycat. She'd felt rather silly and embarrassed until she saw the look of hunger in his eyes, hunger mixed with awe, passion with submission. She hadn't thought much of it at the time, but now she recognized the moment for what it was, as well as the intense erotic arousal she had experienced at realizing she had the power to elicit such strong feelings from another human being. It was all a matter of witchcraft, really, of illusion and allure. It was no coincidence that the word "glamour" was originally used to describe a form of magical enchantment.

All women, Valerie contended, were natural witches.

"We have to come up with a name," Valerie said before her first session.

"What's wrong with my name?"

"Nothing. Kelly is a perfectly fine name for an office worker or a housewife. What you need is something more exotic. Something that separates you from your ordinary everyday role and expresses your dominant identity. Something that commands immediate respect. And fear." She thought for a moment and snapped her fingers. "I know. You'll be Lady Domina."

"Lady Domina?" Kelly said, trying the name on for size. It seemed kind of silly to her.

"Don't you like it?"

"I don't know—I."

"Don't worry," Valerie said, confidentally. "You'll get used to it. It's perfect for you."

Kelly painfully remembered her first client, a middle-aged Jewish toy manufacturer from Hoboken who fantasized about being interrogated by a beautiful concentration camp warden. Knowing what she knew about concentration camps, Kelly found the man's fantasy repellent, until Valerie reminded her that fantasies had no obligation to be politically correct. In fact, the taboo nature of most fantasies was usually what made them so powerful as fantasies in the first place. If she wanted to learn domination, and, in the process, a good deal about human nature, she first had to put aside her judgmental attitudes. Within the walls of the dungeon there was no right or wrong; only what was true.

Valerie had assisted her during that first session. She helped Kelly tie the man to a straight-backed wooden chair and had fixed a white-hot spotlight on him, while Kelly stalked around him with a leather riding crop, barking out questions and berating him before he could answer. Finally they put him in a homemade wooden stocks, his head and hands secured by padlock, his legs spread and ankle-tied to a runner bar at the base. Whip in hand, Kelly stood behind him, sweating, her heart pounding as the moment of truth arrived. Of course she knew this moment would come eventually, but now that it was here the reality of it overwhelmed her. She felt her arm go weak and was sure that she couldn't go through with what she knew she had to do next.

The man's middle-aged back, pink and defenseless, seemed so incredibly vulnerable. Throwing that first blow was the hardest thing she had ever done. It was like standing at the edge of a high place and forcing yourself to jump. Somehow she knew that once she brought the whip forward it would be like getting the urge to take that first step off the precipice: There would be no going back. She was frozen there for what seemed an eternity. Across the room, Valerie waited and watched, but Kelly was aware only of the whip in her hand and the man's waiting back. She might be standing there still if not for what happened next. The man suddenly whimpered—with anticipation or impatience or simply discomfort, Kelly didn't know—but somehow that pitiful human whimper triggered something deep inside her that enabled her to overcome her inhibition and to lash him.

She hit him again and then again, each blow feeling better, more right than the blow before. She began thinking of Eric, and suddenly all the frustration and anger of the past several weeks poured down her arm and into the whip like a hot current and onto the soft flesh of the faceless man before her. If Valerie hadn't been present, Kelly might have hurt him badly. Before she could do any real harm, however, Valerie had jumped in and grabbed the whip from her. Kelly stared in astonishment at the blood streaking the man's back. Later, Valerie explained the importance of always remaining in control, that one never struck someone in anger, as that could lead to serious injury. Kelly was too shaken to continue, so Valerie had finished the session, whipping the man who stood patiently in the stocks, never once complaining.

Kelly did better with her second client, a mild-mannered CPA who'd wanted to be spanked while wearing nylon stockings. He huddled on the floor afterwards, spontaneously ejaculating and begging her not to be mad at him. Kelly had felt an extraordinary mixture of invincibility, benevolence, and pity for the man, though she knew she could show nothing but stern annoyance in order to keep the fantasy intact. She had never so completely felt her power as a woman than at the moment that anonymous man lay at her feet and orgasmed merely from being in her presence. It was exhilarating in a strange way, just as Valerie had said, and a little frightening, if the truth be told, to realize she possessed so much power. She suddenly understood the almost sensual enjoyment so many gun owners professed to feel for their weapons. The power she possessed was even more intimate, but no less explosive, than the one that came from the barrel of a gun.

Over the next several weeks she had dominated others, both men and women. Outside the dungeon she had consciously begun to dress more provocatively: wearing shorter, tighter skirts, more revealing blouses, and even makeup. She practiced walking on high heels and went to a local beauty parlor for a complete makeover, getting her hair permed into a cascade of red-brown curls and allowing herself the decadent luxury of a manicure and pedicure.

She noted the difference in the way people reacted to her almost immediately. The men stared after her with the dazed and lovelorn look of caged bulls. The women followed her with eyes filled with a stupefying mixture of envy, lust, and adoration. For her part, Kelly had begun to look at the people she met in a different way: imagining, for example, how a well-dressed businessman on the subway might look naked and kneeling reverently at her feet, or how some pretty but snotty salesgirl she'd encountered while shopping might look with chains around her delicate wrists and ankles.

Kelly told Valerie about her experiences the next time they met at Captive Hearts and the woman smiled, explaining that it happened all the time. It was just a matter of her discovering her true dominant personality.

"You are going through a phase we all go through," she said. "You're seeing the world through the eyes of a mistress. Ilana calls it finding your place on the scale of dominance. You'll get used to it. In the meantime, sit back and enjoy it."

Kelly stood up in the small dressing room off the women's bath and checked her appearance in the full-length mirror. The PVC material stretched seductively over her body like a second skin, pushing up her breasts and molding itself to her buttocks. Her hair fell loose around her white shoulders and her face, above the studded leather collar, looked haughty and disdainful in spite of the sensuous pout of her rouged lips. She took a couple of steps in the high-heeled boots, turned around, and caught a glimpse of herself from behind. The boots took some getting used to but they were extremely effective, the heels bringing out the natural s-shape of her spine, forcing her to thrust out her breasts and buttocks to achieve a new and more sensual balance.

Kelly looked in the mirror with a mixture of fascination and awe.

The woman looking back at her was no longer Kelly Mitchell.

It *was* Lady Domina.

She felt a shiver of anticipation. There was a man waiting for her in Dungeon Three. She reviewed one last time the information sheet that each new client was required to fill out. Valerie explained that in addition to the survey, each prospective client was screened twice by phone and once in person to weed out the wackos, the wiseguys, and the merely curious. Her client that afternoon was a professional photographer. It was his first visit to Captive Hearts, and in the box provided indicated that he was interested in mild to moderate pain. His name she noticed only in passing.

Connor Scott.

TWENTY

The black Grand Prix trolled slowly down Forty-second Street.

Rossi felt the neon lights scroll up his face. He watched with flat eyes the endless procession of peep shows, sex-video shops, and X-rated theaters. His damp flesh bore their lewd, garish messages as if his own most secret thoughts were being broadcast across his forehead for everyone to see. He grabbed the Camels on the dashboard, shook one free, and lipped it from the soft pack.

He threw the pack onto the dashboard, reached inside his leather jacket, and stared at the expensive lighter in the palm of his hand.

Shit.

ER. The monogram was delicate, scripted, worked expertly into the elegant design of the silver. She had bought it for his forty-second birthday. They had gone to a new Indian place she had read about in the weekend section of the Sunday *Times*. She had given him the lighter during dessert. She told him that if he insisted on smoking, he should at least have a safer lighter. It might take him another twenty years to die of lung cancer, but it would be a shame if he accidentally immolated himself due to the vagaries of his Bic lighter. He had laughed and said he would think of her every time he lit up and hammered another cancer stick into his coffin.

Now, unexpectedly, the jest had become a curse.

His hand trembled as he poked the tip of the cigarette into the flame.

Later, she had invited him back to her place for a surprise.

"Another gift?" He feigned boredom as he waited, amused and aroused, on the sofa. In the next room she had slipped into something a little more comfortable.

She came out of the bedroom wearing only garters, a push-up corselet, and black seamed stockings. She must have gotten the outfit at one of those sexy boutiques in the Village. She never wore such things to bed, preferring instead an oversized T-shirt or one of Eric's old flannel shirts, and somehow that had made it seem all the more exciting. But that wasn't all. She had several other surprises in store for him that night, including a most unusual way of serving birthday cake that proved the lie to the old saying that you can't have your cake and eat it, too.

But the biggest and best surprise of the evening came when he let it slip out that he loved her—and she put her head on his chest and told him she loved him, too.

He snapped the lid of the lighter shut and stuffed it deep inside the inside pocket of his coat, where he hoped never to find it again. He pulled the unfiltered smoke deep into his lungs like the kiss of some dark and poisonous lover he had tried in vain to escape only to return once again to her ghostly, cancerous arms.

He gazed out the open side window of the car into the cold, light-splashed night.

Even at this hour the streets were crowded.

But gone were the businessmen and office workers, in their suits and skirts. Or if they still inhabited these streets, they were wearing different plumage. Now the streets were filled with pushers, punks, parasites, and perverts. Everyone out there had something to sell—either their innocence or their experience, and every gradation in between.

Rossi watched the great temples of sin roll past. He knew only too well what went on behind their glittering facades. He had seen the truth behind the empty promises of their opulent marquees. In dimly lit rooms that smelled of sweat and sex, he had experienced what it meant to lose every ounce of self-respect.

Surely by now he should know that whatever it was he was looking for he would not find it here. This was a fool's game, a con.

The first time he'd played was when his marriage had broken up. He had needed it then. He'd been filled with so much frustrated rage that he had needed to strike back, even in an oblique way, at the impersonal forces that were destroying his life. He had volunteered for the undercover assignment knowing full well what he would be required to do, the role he would have to play. He had descended into the secret underworld of leather bars and bondage clubs as if he were going home, speaking the language of the dominants without a lesson, recognized by those who lived there as if he were a native.

Indeed, he had gone native.

When it had come time to resurface he hadn't wanted to come back. It was Graham who finally rescued him, dragging him forcibly with him from that basement club in SoHo where Rossi was appearing on the stage of a makeshift dungeon four nights a week under the name of Master Rod. The police psychologist had explained it in terms of the Stockholm Effect, arguing that although Rossi had entered the situation voluntarily, he had nonetheless been subject to a variation of the subtle form of brainwashing that often caused hostages, political prisoners, and kidnap victims to sympathize, identify, and, in some cases, even join the cause of their oppressors.

Rossi gladly accepted the diagnosis, yet deep inside he knew it was nothing but a pile of happy horseshit. Still, he was not yet ready to admit to anyone, least of all himself, the truth about what he had experienced, or the fact that he was regularly returning to the clubs to feed a need for power he could no longer control.

It was Kelly who had saved him.

A few weeks after meeting her at the Dynasty Ox, the urge that had nearly driven him mad had completely disappeared. His sickness—and he did regard it as a form of sickness—had gone into remission. Master Rod had been put back into his cage and the hungers that had driven him into the night seeking satisfaction had abated, satisfied instead by a diet of old-fashioned love and romance. It was goofy, but it was also true.

He had convinced himself that his violent urges were nothing more than a form of frustrated love. He didn't need them anymore. It was one more thing for which he could thank Kelly.

Now that it looked like his relationship with her was over—

Looked like it was over?

Come on. Time to smell the coffee. It was over.

Now that Kelly and he were through, the need had resurfaced with a vengeance. It hadn't been a month yet, and he had already taken to cruising the streets, his darker half no longer willing to remain obligingly in the background. He demanded his night on the town, so to speak, and Rossi had no choice but to follow him around like his obedient shadow, content to make sure he didn't get them both in trouble.

A hundred times a day the images came. Quick, fleeting, but enough to tweak him into awareness. The dispatcher down at the station. The CUNY student who lived in the apartment down the hall from him. The checkout girl at the Korean grocery where he bought his Camels every morning. An anonymous secretary working her way down Fifth Avenue at lunch hour in a tight mini skirt and red high heels . . .

The thoughts were not his. They came from some dark place in his mind. The same place those dreams came from of leaving the house in the morning without your pants.

It was Master Rod again. No doubt about it. He stood just to one side of him, whispering in his ear.

Rossi clung to that fantasy. He clung to it because it was the only way he could look at himself in the mirror each morning to shave without drawing the razor across the big, throbbing blue vein in his throat. As it was, he often thought he'd like to see his blood blossom slow and red through the white shaving cream like a hot-house carnation.

Rossi had never been an alcoholic. Never been addicted to anything, except tobacco. In his line of work, he met addicts of one sort or another every day. He had little sympathy and no respect for people whose compulsions drove them to cross the line. And yet he could hardly consider the need that drove him to cruise these streets anything less than an addiction. Now, ironically, Kelly was descending that same dark, damp stairway. How could he tell her the reason he didn't want her to do the story? How could he warn her without telling her the truth about himself?

He watched the night people walking along the avenue. He had been around long enough to recognize at a glance which were the predators, which the prey. And to understand something of the hidden need that drew them both into the game, the eater and eaten; it was the law of nature, and both played the role allotted to them.

It was the need of the antelope for the lion, of the rabbit for the fox, each seeking consummation in an orgasmic rush that transcended the danger of pain, disease, violence—even death itself.

For the most part, they made their illicit transactions in plain sight. They knew that after midnight, after the office workers had commuted to the safety of the suburbs, after whatever foolishly curious tourists from those distant planets of Ohio and Idaho, drifting down here from the theater district, had scurried back to the hotels where they belonged, the street—and anyone still foolish enough to be on it—belonged to them. Now they peddled cocaine and flesh and other more exotic pleasures out in the open, hawking their wares like Arab merchants. Prospective buyers strolled among them, comparing prices and quality. And bathing it all, giving the scene of a look of hellish unreality, was the bald glare of a thousand lights, as if the entire street and everyone on it were being x-rayed. Here there was no privacy. Here the maggots of society were forced to wriggle out in the open. It was the kind of hard, cold, intrusive light that made it possible to wear dark glasses even at midnight.

It was a good thing.

Down here, the last thing you wanted to do was look anyone straight in the eye.

Rossi wore dark glasses.

He rolled to a stop at the corner of Eighth Avenue and Forty-second Street. Across the way, on his left, was the Port Authority bus terminal, its massive, rusty steel girders a singular monument to ugliness. Everyday it served as one of the city's main terminals for the influx of fresh victims: runaway teens, bored housewives, young naifs of all descriptions full of trust and ambition come to this mecca of decadence to sacrifice their innocence on its neon-lit altars.

It was relatively quiet now: the hustlers, pickpockets,

confidence men, and psychos had slunk back to their lairs for a few hours of precious sleep. In a few short hours, it would be feeding time again.

Rossi pulled forward as the light changed.

On his right, along a fence guarding an empty lot, was a cardboard city housing the bums, alcoholics, and deinstitutionalized insane who only those who hadn't yet been assaulted by them physically or verbally euphemistically called the "homeless."

Up ahead, Rossi saw a small group of street hustlers dressed in tight leather skirts and heels. He sped through the cross street, barely beating the changing light, and screeched to a stop at the curb before the one he was looking for could disappear in the alley behind her.

Rossi leaned out the window. "Going somewhere, Joey?"

The others, looking relieved, scattered like frightened birds. In their wake they left behind a trail of cheap perfume, clicking heels, and lisping voices full of telltale outrage.

The young prostitue turned and smiled.

He was wearing a sleeveless Day-Glo T-shirt tight enough to show the perfect outlines of his grapefruit-sized breasts, a pair of red nylon short shorts, fishnet stockings, and high heels. His red-brown hair was tied back off his heavily painted face, through which you could still see a trace of the acne scarring his cheeks.

He sauntered up the car window, suddenly all cocky confidence, and leaned in on his skinny, white, depilated forearms. "I told you," he pouted theatrically, "when I'm out here the name is Bethany."

Rossi stared straight ahead out the windshield. "Get in the car, faggot."

The prostitute flinched as if struck, and then obediently minced around the front of the car to the passenger side. He slid into the seat next to Rossi and hardly

165

had time to pull the door closed before the car sped away from the curb.

"What's this all about?" he asked, pulling open his sequined evening bag and removing a package of scented cigarettes. He fumbled a light. The short chewed nails on his stubby fingers were painted black.

"Nervous?" Rossi asked tonelessly.

He hated playing this game. Almost.

"Look, I'm clean," the prostitute said, holding out both arms. "No drugs. No diseases. I just had the test."

"I don't give a shit about that."

Rossi sped quickly down Eleventh Avenue all the way to the lower twenties. He made a left down one of the side streets and slowed down as they passed a row of abandoned buildings that some city renovation plan had long since forgotten. Last year, in the hall of one of the buildings, they had found the half-consumed remains of two teenage prostitutes, their throats slashed with a broken bottle. Everyone had hoped that the dental pattern on the gnawed bones would prove to be rodent or canine.

They hadn't.

Rossi pulled the car to the curb and stopped the engine, but left the headlights funneling off into the urban sprawl.

Joey looked around uneasily at the darkened doorways lining the street like a trembling mouse sensing the presence of a snake. He knew that regular visitors to this particular section of Manhattan real estate did not generally have a long life expectancy.

"Why'd you bring me here?" he said, the falsetto in his voice real this time.

"There's a fifty in the visor," Rossi said.

Joey's painted eyes lit up when he saw the money. They flicked back to the street outside and then uncertainly at Rossi.

"You sure like to live dangerously," he said. "What do I have to do?"

"Just talk."

"That's all?" Joey asked, sounding leery, suspicious of the hook.

Rossi nodded.

Joey looked relieved. "About who?"

"Herbert Martin."

The prostitute looked nervous all over again.

Rossi had followed the trail of the "Blood Bank Robber" through three different state psychiatric facilities, five different psychiatrists, and what seemed like half the social workers in the state. Sure enough, as he and Graham had feared, Martin had been released after only thirteen months of observation. The trail had come to a dead end.

"I want to know where he is," Rossi said.

"I don't know," the prostitute said. He saw the look on Rossi's face and pleaded innocence. "That's the truth. He came around here for a while, it's true, but he took off after that and I haven't seen him since. He was still hooked up on this blood thing. I'm telling you, he was just as whacked out as when he got put away. More so, if that's possible. He was looking for someone to suck his blood. Can you believe that? You know I don't go in for any weird scenes like that."

"Who does?"

"Who does what?"

"Who does what Mr. Martin wants done?"

Joey looked out the window into the surrounding darkness, then back at Rossi. It was a look Rossi knew well. The punk was weighing which of the two he could best afford to have mad at him, which of the two it would be easier to bullshit. Finally he ground his cigarette out in the ashtray, the filter stained pink with lipstick. He blew the smoke toward the ceiling of the car, as if resigning himself to the inevitable.

"I don't know his name. I've only seen him around a few times. Tall, dark, handsome. He always dresses in black. All the boys are nuts for him. They say he hangs around a lot in the subway and picks up some of the rougher trade downtown. There are all kinds of rumors flying around about him. That he's some rich Wall Street broker, a member of British royalty, or even a secret agent of some kind. He's sexy in a scary kind of way, like he might cut your throat while you're doing him. Like I said, I don't go in for the weird stuff, but there's a lot of kids who do. That's all I know, honest."

Joey reached up for the bill clipped to the visor and Rossi nodded. The punk stuffed the money into the top of his skimpy T-shirt, between his budding breasts.

"Cute," Rossi grunted. "Real cute."

Joey smiled.

"Get out," Rossi said.

Joey looked incredulous, the smile fading from his face.

"You heard me," Rossi said. "Get out."

"You've got to be kidding."

"Do I look like I'm kidding?" Rossi asked, his face dead as stone.

"You can't let me out here," Joey whined. His eyes rolled around the deserted street, taking in the broken sidewalks, the husks of abandoned buildings, the cruel galaxies of broken glass. "The niggers'll be picking me out from between their gold teeth before I make it to Tenth Avenue."

"Then I'd turn on that feminine charm of yours, sweetheart, and hope for the best. Now beat it."

"Damn it—" Joey muttered. He jerked open the car door and stepped out onto the street. He looked both ways, each end of the street stretching away like a tunnel with no light at either end.

"And Joey—" Rossi said.

"Yeah?" the whore simpered hopefully, bending down to the passenger window.

"I'd double up on those hormones if I were you. You've got a bad case of five o'clock shadow."

"You bastard," Joey said, kicking at the car door and nearly losing his balance.

Rossi hit the gas, peeling away.

In the rearview he saw the prostitute yank off his heels and sprint like a track star for the relative safety of Eighth Avenue.

TWENTY-ONE

Father Sylvestri dipped his fingers in the bowl of holy water and traced the sign of the cross over his forehead, chest, and shoulders. He carefully lowered his large body onto the padded kneeling bench in front of the small altar dedicated to the Virgin Mary.

In the alcove, the statue stood bathed in the light of dozens of white votive candles, lit by men and women seeking comfort from the Blessed Virgin. Father Sylvestri looked up at the peaceful face, the irregularity of the candlelight giving an almost lifelike quality to her ceramic features. Like many of his new parishioners, Father Sylvestri felt more comfortable addressing his petitions to the Virgin than he did to her Son. There was something about the blue-robed woman that was reassuring in a way that Christ, with his bleeding hands and feet, his grimace of stoic spirituality, was not.

The priest had just begun to whisper the first words of his impromptu prayer when he felt the cold black air rush past him. The candles guttered, throwing spidery shadows around the alcove, the Blessed Virgin suddenly looking horrified. Some of the candles went out entirely, as did the hopes and prayers they represented, turned to smoke and hot wax instantaneously in the presence of evil.

Father Sylvestri started to his feet.

On more than one occasion in the last several weeks, he'd had to fight off the neighborhood junkies who wandered in from the streets, looking to rob the church of some fixture or other in order to pay for their next fix. Or those who hadn't yet heard of Father Paul's dismissal, who'd come to hustle the corrupt priest out of a few bucks in exchange for a couple of sweaty minutes in the darkness of the confessional. But Sylvestri knew it wasn't they who had interrupted him this time.

"Stay where you are," the voice behind him said, lashing the air like a whip.

"You've no power here," the priest said. He hadn't yet turned around but, still facing the Virgin, he recognized the irony of his words.

"Oh, don't be so gothic, Sylvestri," the Vampire said calmly. "You forget how old I am. I remember when Christianity was a cult among a hundred cults and the cross nothing more than an instrument for the capital punishment of common thieves and murderers. Don't forget, it was I who sat beside Tiberius and Nero at the Coliseum and whispered in their ears the ideas for all those wonderful tortures your Church historians are so devilishly fond of chronicling. All this," she waved her hand dismissively around the chruch, "baroque paraphrenelia has no effect on me."

He turned slowly to face her. She was standing a dozen feet away, her face masked in shadows, a black cloak covering her leather-clad body.

"The Blood of the Lamb has power over all unclean spirits. The Blood of the Lamb casteth out evil."

"Oh, put a sock in it, will you, Sylvestri?" the Vampire said, the heels of her boots echoing throughout the empty church.

She stopped at the end of the aisle between the pews. In spite of her bravado, the priest noted that the Vam-

171

pire ventured no closer to the altar. Still, he knew better than to feel safe.

Instead, the priest felt the sweat beading on his forehead like mercury.

"The Cross of the Savior will destroy you," he said with more confidence than he felt.

"Perhaps you'd like to test your hypothesis," the Vampire said drily. She waited, tasting the priest's fear in the cavernous air between them. "I thought not. That's always been your problem, *Father*. You lack the courage of your convictions. Where was your faith in the Blood of the Lamb on the road to Golgotha, when he asked you for a drop to sustain him on his way to execution and you denied him?"

She saw the pain of the memory register on his face.

"What do you want from me?" the priest growled, like a whipped animal who didn't know its own strength.

The Vampire laughed. "Why, I want you, Father. I want that hunger you try to pretend no longer exists under your cassock. I want you kneeling before me, offering your essence, just as you were kneeling a minute ago at the feet of that sanctimonious plaster whore you call the Mother of God."

Sylvestri started forward, his hands rigid with murder, and stopped cold when her face shed its mask of shadows.

She had lost none of her beauty or power since he had seen her last; if anything, her glamour had increased. He'd seen her hand in the genocidal slaughter of the Khmer Rouge, the Nazi concentration camps, and the Great Purge of Stalinist Russia, as well as the Manson murders, the Jonestown massacre, and the ethnic purging in Bosnia. Wherever man had made a religion of pain and death he found her bloody fingerprints. And yet, somehow, the suffering she had witnessed hadn't added a single line to her face, nor had it dimmed the luster of her brilliant eyes. If anything, it had served as an elixir of eternal life and youth and beauty, just as she had promised it would, nearly two thousand years before.

He felt her invading his mind, the power of her attention like a naked blue laser, illuminating the dark half of his brain, showing him the sins of his past. He saw the unwelcome images shuttling behind his eyes, images of bondage and humiliation, of men and women humbled to his lust, of nude bodies lying spent in shallow graves wearing the red initials of his unspeakable rage. Were they fantasies or memories?

Or both?

He had tried to atone for those acts, to seek forgiveness, and yet nothing could erase them from his conscience.

"Go to hell," he whispered, so quietly he might have only thought the words.

The Vampire shook her head with mock disappointment. "I see you haven't changed a bit. You say one thing, but your heart says something else entirely. You have domination in your blood the same as I do. You have my blood, or have you forgotten? When will you stop trying to fool yourself?"

"It's you who are the fool," the priest said. "I want nothing to do with you or domination."

The Vampire shrugged. "It's not you I want, Sylvestri."

Her confidence was even more unnerving than her threats.

"What do you mean?"

"I've found someone," the Vampire said.

The priest felt his heart sinking. "Who?" he asked.

"A young woman of exceptional promise. Naturally, she doesn't yet understand what attracts her to our world, but she shows a remarkable unconscious receptivity to our ways. That is something you cannot teach. Or unlearn. Something that is only passed on through the blood."

Father Sylvestri had thought the vampire had come for him, that she had followed him to New York. He had never suspected that the truth was far worse, that he was only a bonus on the way to a greater prize. That she was after *her*.

"You bitch," he gasped. "You can't have her. I won't let you have her. She's mine. Do you understand? Mine!"

He started forward again, and this time he felt her mind probe deeper into his, unleashing a new torrent of images, doubling him over with forbidden ecstasy.

He staggered forward, hands clasped. "Oh, Father in Heaven," he prayed. "Deliver me from evil . . ."

"You silly fool," the Vampire sneered. "Don't you know you can't resist me? Your god is nothing. He has forsaken you long ago. Your soul is mine, Sylvestri. And so is your body."

The priest fell to his knees, as if someone had cut his hamstring. His body jerked and danced on the cold marble like an epileptic's, his hips bucking wildly, his eyes rolling back in his head until only the whites showed. He struggled to speak, his voice choked with passion.

"By God," he swore, "I'll kill you for this. I'll—"

"Save your breath Father," she mocked. "Enjoy the pleasure I give you now. The next time I come I'll come with the power to send you back to your bleeding god, you dog of Christ."

His body spasmed, as if electrodes surgically implanted deep inside his brain had suddenly been activated, his penis leaping up and down, the humiliating warmth spreading over his thighs, ending nearly thirty years of abstinence. He lay there in a heap as the Vampire retreated up the aisle between the pews to the big double doors leading onto the street. Throughout the empty church her laughter rang in his ears like the sound of angels, like the sound of madness.

TWENTY-TWO

On Saturday afternoon Kelly and Gwen had lunch and went window shopping together in the Village. Thanksgiving was still more than a week away, but already the local merchants were getting ready for Christmas, and frantic tourists bustled in and out of stores, laden down with bags and packages.

"So who is this Mr. Wonderful anyway?" Gwen said, trying her best not to sound too sarcastic.

"His name is Connor Scott. He's a photographer. He's got an exhibit of his stuff in a small gallery uptown. He's really very talented."

"Where did you meet him?"

"At the club."

"You've got to be kidding! You mean he was one of your clients?"

Kelly felt herself immediately on the defensive. "It's really not that unusual," she said. In fact, it wasn't. Many of the mistresses went out with clients at one time or another. Valerie had told her that she herself had once dated an investment banker—client of hers for three months. "It happens all the time."

"I don't know, Kell," Gwen said. "Call me old-fashioned, but it all sounds kind of fishy to me."

Kelly supposed it did. If you had told her a month

ago that she'd be working as a dominatrice and dating one of her clients, she would have thought the idea as crazy as Gwen did now. Even now, she found it a little hard to believe. But the fact was that Connor was not like the regular clients that came to Captive Hearts. He was an artist, a photographer, and, like her, he was working on a project exploring the subject of domination. He wanted to experience firsthand what it was that fascinated so many people both inside and outside the scene and to use its powerful and bizarre images as part of a new exhibit he was planning.

As he put it, he wanted to capture the "soul" of domination on film. It was no different, he'd argued, than the research he did for any of his other assignments, whether the subject was skydiving or a celebrity portrait. He needed to know his material. "You couldn't take a picture of the Grand Canyon," he argued, "without going to the Grand Canyon." Kelly understood perfectly. He was seeking authenticity. It was the same thing she was trying to achieve in her article.

She remembered how uncomfortable he had appeared during their session. He'd been waiting for her in Dungeon Three, crouched, fully clothed, inside a large wire dog cage, and looking profoundly embarrassed. He was a strikingly handsome man with clear blue eyes the color of glaciers and sandy hair that curled slightly at the back of his white oxford shirt collar. At her command, he undressed hurriedly in the cramped cage, cursing under his breath as he struggled to pull off his clothes in the tight quarters. Kelly could hardly help but notice his well-cut physique, the fluid muscles of his arms and chest, the lean and explosive power of his thighs. He looked like a caged tiger, sullen and dangerous, and Kelly felt a thrill of genuine fear at the thought of dominating such a man. It was the same thrill, she imagined, that a real-life lion tamer felt, stepping into the cage with the big cats, knowing they had the physical power to easily rip him to shreds and that all that kept them from doing so was the snap of his whip, the superiority of his mind, and his audacity to take command.

She let him out of the cage, and he trundled across the floor on his hands and knees, his face flushed, his eyes lowered. It was clear that he wasn't used to this kind of treatment and judging from the evidence between his legs he didn't seem to be getting a great deal of enjoyment out of it, either.

"Look," she offered. "We don't have to go through with this if you're having second thoughts."

"No," he said. "I want to. I need to know what it's really like. If I'm going to photograph this scene I need to be a part of it, not just a bystander."

"Well, it'll be a lot easier if you just relax and let me take control," Kelly said.

"How?"

"Think of it as a play. And we're the actors. You're acting the role of the prisoner and I'm your wicked warden. Or your kidnapper. Or whatever you like. Leave yourself behind and just get inside whatever fantasy comes to mind."

"Okay," he said playfully. "Your wish is my command."

"That's better. Kiss my boots, slave."

He looked up at her incredulously.

"You heard me," she sneered in her best bitch-goddess tone, feeling herself assuming the role. "Kiss my boots."

Slowly, almost condescendingly, he lowered his face to her feet, kissing the black leather.

She struck him across the back for his impertinence, and he looked up sharply. In that instant she saw something pass behind his clear blue eyes, something dark

178

and vicious, like a fish emerging from the bottom of a lake to snatch something from the surface.

Kelly felt an instant of real fear and remembered Valerie's warning about how some men reacted to the reality of being hit for the first time. Even though they paid for it, wanted it, or thought they did, they sometimes responded violently. Kelly was thankful for the video cameras mounted in the corners of the room and the intercom that Kurt, one of Captive Heart's beefy bodyguards, monitored from a small room downstairs. But just as suddenly as the shadow appeared it vanished, leaving nothing but the cool blue gaze she'd seen before and then the expression she had come to expect because she had seen it so often. In his eyes she read the universal language of submission.

Tied to the whipping post, he stood quietly as Kelly stalked around him with her bamboo switch, taunting him as she'd been taught, building the suspense, feeling her own excitement growing.

She gazed at the evidence of her success between his legs and felt a dizzying jolt of power.

She had broken through the man's embarrassment, his male-oriented conditioning, even his artistic objectivity, to enable him to surrender to his desire to be dominated. Yet her instincts told her there was still something he was holding back, some part of himself that he was not giving up, holding it in reserve against her. She began the caning, seeing him relax under the blows, which, though they were not hard, were hard enough to be mildly painful. Remembering the earlier look she'd seen in his eyes, she was thankful for the leather restraints around the man's wrists and ankles. In the end, it was not the most successful session she'd ever had, but it had proved to her that she had the resolve and the power to bend even this proud and arrogant man to her will. Maybe she'd been too physically attracted to him, maybe even a little too scared of him, to be quite stern enough. Or perhaps he'd just been too strong-willed to submit totally. In any event, he seemed satisfied with the session.

As he dressed hurriedly, he thanked her for her patience, told her he thought the session would really help his project, and surprised her by asking her out to dinner. Caught off-guard and undeniably attracted to the man, she said yes before she had time to reflect on how the balance of power had suddenly changed. She saw him smile confidently as she accepted, then turn and stride from the dungeon, leaving her standing there feeling sort of silly in her domination costume and whip, a man used to getting what he wanted.

"I'll say one thing," Gwen commented. "You two are sure gonna have one helluva story whenever someone asks you how you met."

"Yeah, I suppose so." Kelly nodded. "I'll tell you, though: He's really a great guy. I've never met anyone quite like him. He's funny, intelligent, passionate, and open-minded. He doesn't make me feel suffocated. After Eric, it's such a relief to be around a man who lets you breathe."

"Have you done it?"

"Done what?"

"You know. *It.*"

"Sex?"

"No, Parcheesi." Gwen snorted. "Of course sex, you moron. Don't look so aghast. You've whipped the man, for crissake, and you're embarrassed at the suggestion that you might have sex with him? You're a weird chick, Kelly baby."

Kelly had to laugh. She supposed it did seem that way to Gwen. But the last few weeks had proved to Kelly what she had found hard to believe herself at first: that domination had little to do with sex, at least the

180

way people usually thought of sex. In a strange way, it had replaced sex after her breakup with Eric. Kelly thought of what Valerie had said one afternoon, sitting in the lounge between clients and painting her nails. "I've been celibate for three years. No sweat. I'm just not interested in vanilla sex anymore. it bores me. I don't understand what I ever saw in it. I mean, there's no imagination to it."

Kelly hadn't come to the same conclusion exactly, but she had begun to understand what led a woman like Valerie to say such a thing. With Connor, however, Kelly had definitely felt the first sexual stirrings since Eric, but she had no desire to jump into anything just yet, least of all bed. She remembered going up to his loft after their first date and seeing some of his photographs. She was sure he'd try to put the move on her then, wasn't quite sure she'd even refuse him if he did, but he'd done nothing of the sort. Instead, he'd been the perfect gentleman, and she had found herself only wanting him more.

"No, we haven't gone to bed yet," she said to Gwen. "But soon, I think."

Gwen shrugged, shook her head. "A man who kneels at your feet and begs to be whipped. Well, I guess you could do worse. Really, though, Kell. I'm worried about you. I think you're getting in too deep with this domination thing. I wish you'd quit."

Kelly waved her off. "It's just the story, Gwen. Honest. I'm just in it for the story. As soon as I've got enough research I'm out of there."

"Don't you have enough information already?"

"Almost. I've got an interview tomorrow afternoon. Her name is Ilana Florescu. She claims to be a descendant of a real Hungarian princess. Valerie set it up. It seems I'm one of their most promising new employees."

Gwen made a face.

"Anyway, they say this Ilana runs an underground club, and I'm talking deep underground, that caters to some really big clients. Movie stars. Politicians. Intellectuals. No one gets to talk to her. I mean, she's practically *invisible*. I'm getting to the center of something here, something real important. I can feel it in my gut. Just a little longer."

"Promise?"

"I promise."

It had begun to rain, a light rain that the air had chilled almost to the point of freezing and that stung the flesh wherever it was exposed with tiny, fiery darts. As coincidence would have it, they found themselves standing in front of a leather boutique. In the window stood a sexless mannequin dressed in full leather domme regalia. On the mannequin's head, in deference to the season, someone had added a red Santa Claus cap.

"Come on," Kelly said. "Let's go inside a minute. There are a few things I need to pick up."

Later, at home, as she unpacked her purchases—a leather zipper mask, a pair of PVC spiked heels, and a small egg-shaped vibrator—Kelly felt a shiver of fear. She wondered if what she had told Gwen was true: Was it really all just for the research? Or was there something more insidious going on here? She looked at the items on her kitchen table.

Perhaps Gwen was right.

Maybe she was getting in too deep.

TWENTY-THREE

In the back of the cab on the way to the interview, Kelly shuffled nervously through her list of questions. She had crossed out and added items to the list so many times, it had begun to look like a diagram for the Star Wars Defense system. She stared at what she had written with a mounting sense of futility. She knew that once she was alone with Ilana there would be no more opportunity for her to consult her notes; she'd be pretty much on her own.

Ever since Valerie had relayed the invitation to meet with Ilana, Kelly had felt a combination of eagerness and trepidation. On the one hand, it was no doubt a sterling opportunity to get the behind-the-scenes story of one of the most ultraexclusive clubs in the country. On the other hand, Kelly wondered what to expect of a woman who made a business out of putting on S-M shows for some of the most powerful and influential men and women in America.

From the first time she'd heard of Ilana, Kelly had wanted to get an interview with the elusive diva of pain. As the weeks went by, she kept her ears open for any rumor about her or her underground theater club. In the circles Kelly traveled, people were always looking for something new and outrageous. Domination, whatever it was, would have seemed the logical choice to capture their jaded imaginations. Yet none of her acquaintances seemed to have heard either of Ilana or the club. Even Joan, her editor at *NiteLife*, reluctantly admitted ignorance on the matter.

So Kelly, had been patient, dropping only occasional references to their invisible boss to Valerie, trying not to seem too eager. Suddenly her patience paid off when Valerie unexpectedly informed her that Ilana had been pleased with her work and wanted to meet her. Kelly had detected a trace of envy in Valerie's tone, but she was too excited to let it bother her. The only catch was that Kelly had been summoned to the inner sanctum the same week. It didn't give her much time to prepare.

Kelly made the most of it.

She hustled around, following up what few leads she had, trying to find out everything she could about Ilana, but there wasn't much to find. She had emigrated to America from Hungary some time after the Second World War. She was supposedly the scion of old money, though no one seemed to know who her family was or how they made their fortune. The rumor that Valerie had recounted, that Ilana was a descendant of Elisabet Bathory, the notorious sixteenth-century countess who had slaughtered over six hundred innocent virgins to bathe in their blood and thereby ensure her eternal beauty, seemed to be more than just good copy, given her current profession, though Kelly had not been, so far, able to validate it.

Stuck in traffic on Fifty-fourth Street, Kelly kept looking at her watch. She cursed herself for not allowing more time to get to Ilana's uptown penthouse. She had lived in New York long enough to know that you always gave yourself an extra twenty minutes to get anywhere. She had also interviewed enough of the rich and famous to know they were exceedingly funny about time. They acted as if the old adage that time was money were literally true.

To them, maybe it was.

Kelly finally arrived at the grand old building on Central Park West about fifteen minutes late. The polite but officious security man at the desk made it worse by refusing to give her an elevator pass until he cleared her arrival upstairs. Nearly twenty minutes later, and now over half hour late for her appointment, Kelly found herself standing outside the solid oak door of Ilana's penthouse apartment.

She took a deep breath, prayed the woman hadn't already written her off, and pressed the buzzer beside the polished brass wall plate.

The woman who answered the door was beautiful; not merely pretty or even drop-dead gorgeous, but breathtakingly beautiful. The kind of beautiful you don't see in the real world, only in the air-brushed, cheesecloth-covered pseudoworld of magazines and movies. Tall, high cheekbones, cat-green eyes, she had the poise and regal looks of a *Vogue* model. Was she Ilana's lover? A business partner? Or perhaps one of the actresses who worked at Domination? Kelly had never seen her before at Captive Hearts. With her beauty and poise, she would surely have been a most sought-after mistress. Kelly felt a pang of jealousy.

"Kelly Mitchell," she said. "I have a one o'clock appointment with Ilana." She shrugged by way of explanation. "I'm a bit late."

The woman nodded and said nothing. She turned form the door, motioning behind her with her hand in a bored, almost langorous manner, indicating that Kelly should follow her.

The jealousy Kelly had felt initially was replaced by sudden and irrational hatred. Just who the hell did this arrogant bitch think she was, anyway? As she trudged along behind her into the sitting room, Kelly felt like giving her a kick right in her perfect fashion-model fanny. Instead, she contented herself by sticking out her tongue.

The woman turned suddenly, motioning to an elegant-looking chair, and Kelly felt her face flush with embarrassment. But if the woman had seen her, she had the good breeding and manners to give no indication. Not an emotion dented those calm inscrutable, maddeningly flawless features.

Kelly sat down and took in the breathless elegance of the room. She was certainly no antiquarian, but if the room wasn't furnished in genuine period antiques, then they were damned good fakes. There were ornate, gold-inlaid mirrors, China vases delicate as eggshell, furniture made of wood whose surfaces shone like dark glass and were carved with such feathery deftness, the effect could only have been achieved by a true artist. Everything seemed to glow with that intrinsic and intangible inner light that shone through objects of real quality. Against one paneled wall, Kelly saw several paintings that looked familiar. She was sure that more than one of them was a priceless original. Kelly had been in the homes of some of the world's most famous rock stars, socialites, and celebrities, but she had never seen quite the display of opulence that she did here. It made Madonna's Madison Avenue penthouse look as if it were furnished at a Sears blowout sale.

She was looking down at the plush Victorian carpet beneath her feet, figuring that it must have cost more than she'd probably make in a lifetime, when a pair of elegantly brocaded slippers stepped into her field of vision. Kelly jerked her head up and found herself staring into the largest pair of eyes she had ever seen.

"I didn't mean to frighten you," the woman said, amused.

186

"No, it's my fault," Kelly said. "I was just—" What the hell *was* she doing, anyway? "Admiring your carpet," she blurted, unable to think of anything more clever than the truth. "I'm I sorry I'm late. The traffic—"

The woman waved her off. "Don't worry about it. Time," she said dismissively, "is such an American obsession. You Americans eat by the clock, sleep by the clock, fuck by the clock. In Europe, in the old country, we follow our appetites, not our watches."

She held out a slender white hand tipped with five perfectly manicured and lacquered nails.

"I am Ilana," she said.

The woman gave the impression of being tall, but when Kelly stood up to shake her hand, she was surprised to find they were roughly the same height.

"Kelly Mitchell."

"I've heard some very exciting things about you, Kelly Mitchell. It is not often one comes across a young woman with so much natural talent for our business." Ilana smiled and motioned to the armchair. "Please sit down."

Kelly tried to take a mental photograph of the woman. She knew from experience that her readers liked to know what her subjects looked like, what they were wearing, whether they were relaxed or uptight, whether they seemed tired or suspicious or constipated or just plain folks. The woman who sat before her now resisted such easy characterization. If the girl at the door's beauty was flawless, then Ilana had the kind of flawed beauty that was even more captivating for being so unusual. Her long dark hair was piled on top of her head, her face small and delicate, her nose perhaps a shade too long, her mouth just a little two wide, with the slightest hint of overbite. It was her eyes, however, that made the difference. They were the most expressive eyes

187

Kelly had ever seen. The eyes of a natural actress. They appeared cold as black stone one moment and molten with emotion the next.

Ilana might have been as young as twenty-five or as old as sixty. Her face was smooth and unlined, and yet there was something unnameable about the woman that made her seem a lot older than that. Kelly reminded herself that according to her research Ilana had already been a young woman when she came to America in the late forties. That would put her at least in her early sixties by now. What was her secret? In her work with celebrities, Kelly had seen the length and depth to which the rich and famous would go to maintain an illusion of perpetual youth, but no matter how much money they had, there was a limit to how long even they could cheat time. Pretty soon they all managed to end up looking like wooden mannequins held up by invisible strings. What was Ilana's secret? Lamb hormones? Genetic alteration? Yoga? The blood of virgins?

Once again she found herself staring into those mutable eyes.

If eyes were the windows to the soul, then Ilana's eyes were a pair of peepholes into . . . what?

A dark grotto where pale lovers lounged naked by a stone fountain.

A rainswept night forked by lightning, trees bent double, wind howling.

A newly dug grave.

"Excuse me?" Kelly said, embarrassed. First she was a half hour late for the interview, then she was caught staring at the woman's feet, and now she was daydreaming while Ilana was talking to her. What could the woman possibly be thinking of her?

"I said, would you like something to drink?"

"Um, yes," Kelly said. "Some Perrier, if you have it. Thank you."

"Of course." She turned to the *Vogue* model, who had quietly reappeared behind Ilana's chair. "Paulette, bring us two Perriers."

Paulette nodded and left the room.

"Paulette cannot speak," Ilana said. "She has no vocal chords. A birth defect, as I understand. But quite a fortunate, if rare, trait in a domestic servant. Don't you think?"

So she was not Ilana's lover, after all, but her servant. Kelly felt a moment's guilt for her earlier uncharitable thoughts over what she had mistaken as the woman's rudeness. At the same time, she was taken aback at Ilana's offhand comment about the poor girl's handicap.

"Oh, yes," Ilana said laughing, "I always forget. You know it amuses me. You Americans believe in nothing. You call your presidents liars and burn your country's flag. You blaspheme the Pope and rip up his picture on national television. You defy the commandments in your Holy Bible and deny the existence of God Himself. But when it comes to the idea of equality, you are more sensitive than the most fanatic Islamic fundamentalist. The only profanity you know are words like kike, wop, spick, and nigger. Especially nigger."

Kelly flinched at hearing the words Ilana used so fluently. The priests in the orphanage had taught her never to use such words. To this day, she always referred to the latter as the N-word. "We don't use those words in polite society. They hurt people's feelings," she said.

"But that is precisely my point," Ilana countered. "Such words represent the only form of blasphemy you know. Democracy is your religion, Lady Liberty your God. Your prophets aren't Moses, or Isaiah, or even Jesus Christ, but Jefferson, Adams, and Franklin. The idea that all men and women are created equal is the only commandment you hold to be true."

"Don't you believe that?"

189

"Why, of course not," Ilana said. She took a glass of sparkling water from the tray that Paulette had carried into the room. "Just look around you, dear. No one is equal. One person is stronger and dominates with his strength. Another is prettier and dominates with her beauty. Still another is smarter and dominates with his intelligence. Or richer. Or more power. Or better-connected. Or just plain lucky. Look at Paulette and I," Ilana said, as the woman returned to her post behind her mistress's chair. "She is quite lovely to look at, yes?"

Kelly found herself looking at the girl's photogenic face. She felt another brief flash of jealousy. She couldn't help it. The servant was simply the most beautiful woman Kelly had ever seen. "Why, uh-yes. I guess so," she answered.

She felt uncomfortable discussing the girl's looks while she was standing in the room, as if she were a rare antique vase or a priceless painting. The girl, on the other hand, did not seem to mind. Rather she seemed to be quite used to it.

Ilana gazed at her like a connoisseur. "I have no doubt that with her beauty she could beguile any number of lovers, drive rich men to poverty, strong men to self-destruction, proud men to servitude. Yet she finds total satisfaction in her utter submission to me. Why?"

Ilana didn't wait for Kelly to answer.

"I am her superior and she worships me because of it."

Kelly searched the girl's face. If she was insulted, or even surprised by this outrageous declaration, she didn't show it. Kelly wondered whether her placidity was due to the fact that she was used to this kind of talk from her impetuous mistress.

Or was it because what Ilana said was true?

"Don't look so surprised," Ilana said. "Every relationship is based on the same principle: two people try to ex-

190

ert their will over each other. In the end the stronger one wins. The weaker party accepts the terms of the stronger in order to earn his or her right to stay in the relationship. He or she gets the love, the money, the beauty, etc., that they value more than anything else. In the meantime, the stronger party gets a devoted slave submissive to their desires. If you look closely enough at any relationship you'll see the same dynamic at work."

"What if two people refuse to force their will on each other? If they have respect for each other's desires as they have for their own?"

"Ah," Ilana said. "You speak of love. An interesting aberration. I've never had the disease myself."

So much the pity, Kelly thought.

She wondered if that had been the problem between her and Eric. They were both so stubborn, so full of pride. Neither of them would ever give in. What would happen, however, if someone were to love someone so much that they surrendered not out of weakness, but out of strength, so great was their love for another. Kelly dared not argue the point with Ilana. She was sure the cynical woman would just laugh outright at her. It didn't matter anyway. She and Eric were through. Finished. Kaput.

"I suppose it must have been a great deal different in your country than it is here," Kelly conceded.

"In Hungary, before socialism each person knew his or her place. The peasant was born to work the soil, tend the animals, and serve his or her master. The aristocrat was born to rule, to cultivate the arts, to advance the race. For centuries it was like that, each person knowing his place in the grand scheme of things, each fulfilling the particular duty to which he or she was born. In such a society true stability exists. There is no need for psychiatrists or employment counselors or self-help books to help people find themselves. In such a society no one feels left out, or useless, or confused because each and every one of them has a purpose."

"To be a slave?"

"Slavery is a highly underrated institution. Every truly great civilization since the birth of time has employed it to one degree or another. The Egyptians. The Mayans. The Romans. Even the Greeks, the founders of modern democracy, had a slave class. As a plant is comprised of both roots and flower, so a truly beautiful society blossoms only when it consists of those who serve and those who rule. Only when there are slaves whose duty it is to take care of mankind's lowest needs can those at the top be free to pursue the finer arts of true culture."

"But how do you determine who is the master and who is the slave?"

"There exists a natural aristocracy among men and women, just as there is among animals. In America you have your slaves and peasants just as any society does. The only thing different about America is that your slaves have been brainwashed into believing the myth of the Constitution. Of all the falsehoods ever foisted upon humanity in the name of ethics and religion, the most pernicious is the myth that says everyone is equal to everyone else. Nothing could be further from the truth.

"In America every mother tells her child he or she can be anything they want: a doctor, a lawyer, even the President of the United States. Is it any wonder that there is so much chaos in your society, so much violence, corruption, misery, and unhappiness? Is it not obvious that when one is told he or she can be anything they want and they realize that, in fact, they cannot, because they are not smart enough, pretty enough, talented enough, or whatever, they feel a terrible resentment toward those who do succeed? If they were merely slaves or peasants, they would not seek the heights they cannot attain, nor would they burn with jealousy at seeing others, who they understand to be inherently better than they, enjoying the fruits of life."

Considering her ideology, Kelly wondered if Ilana had been a member of the Nazi party during the war. Until now, Kelly hadn't considered the political ramifications behind the philosophy at Captive Hearts. She had thought of S-M simply as a psychosexual phenomenon. Could there be more to it than that?

"Still, you have to admit," she offered, "democracy is the best system in the world."

"I admit nothing of the sort," Ilana said. "Do you know what Plato said about democracy? He said that in a democracy even the mule refuses to get out of the middle of the road in the belief that he has just as much right to be there as a citizen. No, my dear, democracy is far from the best of all possible worlds. Your founding fathers were drunk on liberty when they wrote the Declaration of Independence, and two hundred years later you Americans are suffering from the hangover."

"Why did you come here to open Captive Hearts?" Kelly asked. "It seems you would have been better off somewhere else in the world."

"Ah, but that's where you're wrong," Ilana said, smiling, the slight overbite becoming more apparent. "You see, nowhere do people hunger so much for authority than in a place gone soft with license and decadence. Europe learned that lesson at great cost not so long ago. You Americans, with all your talk of equality and sexual liberation, are among the most repressed and easily dominated people in the world. Like a child let run wild, you secretly crave discipline. Rightly, you perceive the hidden truth: Discipline is order, beauty, love. There is no one more desperately unhappy than a slave without a master. He or she literally begs for discipline. America is full of such unhappy slaves, men and women desperately seeking someone to tell them what to do, what to think, what to feel. You see signs of their desperation everywhere. Your politicians are fond of saying that education will cure the crime problem, the drug problem, every problem. It is not rehabilitation but humiliation that is the answer. Humiliation administered by a strong and caring master. I have become a fabulously wealthy woman in this country by providing people with the authority they so hungrily seek. In the last several weeks, I suspect you've seen ample evidence of that."

Kelly had to concede a point of Ilana's there. But she was hardly ready to accept Ilana's success as a professional dominatrice, no matter how impressive, as a reason to embrace a return to institutionalized slavery. As a political philosopher, the woman's logic left a lot to be desired.

"Kelly," Ilana said, "you are obviously a bright young woman. I see in you a great deal of promise. But there is still a great deal you have to learn about the world and about yourself. I want to help you."

"Why me?" Kelly asked.

"I think of myself as a teacher. And it is one of the few genuine pleasures in the life of a teacher to find a pupil who shows an aptitude to carry on the work that she has started. Are you willing?"

"I don't know," Kelly said uncertainly. What was she getting into? She had a sudden urge to bolt from the room. "I mean, I think so."

Ilana nodded. "An honest answer. You confirm my impression of you. I have a club called Domination; perhaps you've heard of it?"

"I've heard rumors. I—"

"Rumors. Lies. Propaganda. They are what separate us from the truth when the truth is painful. It would please me greatly if you would come to a private party I have scheduled at Domination this Saturday night. I think it will answer some of the questions you still have, as well as educate you on the practical points of our philosophy. I trust you will see that we are not the bloodless, aristocratic parasites you take us for, but the very flower of humanity."

As Kelly accepted the invitation, her heart pounding in her ears, she could hardly help but think again of what she'd read about Elisabet Bathory, the Bloody Countess of Hungary. In the end, the fiendish woman had outraged even her own royal kin and was sentenced to spend the last four years of her life bricked up in a small, windowless room in her castle, completely cut off from all human contact. Now, nearly four hundred years later, Kelly had the feeling that Ilana's infamous ancestor would take a great deal of pleasure in recognizing in the hypnotic beauty who sat across from Kelly a good deal of herself.

TWENTY-FOUR

Connor Scott was invisible.

He was sitting at the entrance to an alley between two buildings about half a block down the street from Kelly's brownstone. Across the street was a Greek diner. On the corner there was a small collection of shops, including a laundry, a newsstand, and a barber. Connor had been standing there since early that morning, but no one had paid him any notice.

For most apprentices to the Craft, waiting was the hardest part.

They got into trouble because they lacked the patience to sit quietly and let events unfold according to their natural evolution. They jumped in and forced the issue, and as a result distorted events and brought bad karma down upon themselves. The extensive training he had received had taught him the immense practical value of what every mother tells her child: that all good things come to those who wait.

To prepare himself, Connor had meditated for several hours before dawn on the grid for invisibility found in the *Book of the Sacred Magic of Abramelin the Mage*.

Of course, he wasn't really invisible.

The idea was that our thoughts gave us substance in the world. If you emptied your mind through concentration on the magic squares, you would become as invisible as any other unconscious object people saw every day and passed by without noticing. Connor could easily have been a lamppost, a parked car, or a homeless man. He had dressed himself in a tattered, oversized coat, a pair of baggy, shamelessly stained trousers, and broken-down cardboard shoes stuffed with that morning's *Wall Street Journal*. He had blackened his face and glued a ratty gray beard, stained yellow with tobacco juice, along his jaw.

Kelly had been down twice today; once at 10 A.M. to buy a newspaper at the newsstand and again shortly after 12 when she stopped at the diner, took a seat in a booth by the window, and had a lunch that consisted of a hot turkey sandwich and three cups of black coffee.

Connor had been watching Kelly's apartment for the past two weeks, ever since he had met her at Captive Hearts. He had been out with her twice in that time, and he had come to the conclusion that she was just an innocent woman playing around with a life-style that could be more dangerous than she suspected. Connor knew from experience what could happen when you submerged yourself in an identity not your own. Oftentimes you discovered parts of yourself that you didn't even know existed, parts of yourself that had never been given a chance to emerge, would never have emerged if you hadn't been thrust in an unfamiliar environment. Sometimes the new personality staged a revolt, and when it was time for it to return to the closet of the subconscious it refused to go back, instead destroying the person you had once been and taking over for good.

Being a guerrilla of consciousness was a dangerous business.

Connor had no reason to believe that Kelly was anything other than what she had told him. Her story about being a reporter for a local avant-garde newsmagazine checked out. But his highly developed sixth sense told him there was something more to her than met the eye. He couldn't put his finger on it exactly, but if was there nonetheless, an aura that singled her out as a person of importance in the overall scheme of things. He had felt it during the session at Captive Hearts when she had played the dominatrice. There was a raw, undisciplined power in her that coudn't have been acted, and though she seemed perfectly normal afterwards, the impression he'd gotten during the session hadn't left him. His gut told him to keep an eye on Ms. Mitchell, and his gut was seldom mistaken. If she wasn't at the center of this case, then she was certainly a satellite orbiting the central mystery.

He recalled the information in the report he'd accessed from the Craft's central computer files.

Her mother had died in childbirth. Her father had never been identified. The girl had had a tough childhood, bounced from foster home to foster home, the only parents she'd ever really known killed in a traffic accident. Was it really an accident? Connor didn't think so. He didn't believe in accidents. Things always happened for a reason, and if you followed the seeming random trail of coincidence closely enough, you always found evidence of conscious manipulation. According to the rules of his universe, Connor was certain that someone wanted to make sure that Kelly Mitchell did not have a family, that she was essentially alone in the world, that she would grow into exactly the kind of woman who would suit his plans.

But what were those plans, and who was behind them?

That, Connor still had to find out.

He had already submitted his first field report to the Craft, and they had confirmed his decision to keep an eye on the girl. It was hard to figure out their motives.

Connor had long since given up trying. You could throw your brain into permanent neutral trying to decipher their directives. More talented magicians than he had tried. The insane asylums were filled with them. He knew that the mission he was on could all be a big sham, an exercise in misdirection, for all he knew, a feint to the left while the real action was happening in the opposite direction. It was likely that no matter what the outcome, or his role in it, he would remain in the dark as to the real purpose behind his efforts, if his efforts had any purpose whatsoever.

Better to just go with the flow.

He thought about his date with Kelly the night before last. They had gone to an Indian restaurant in the East Village and he had watched her with great interest throughout the meal, knowing full well from the report he'd read just that morning, that she had gone to the opening of this very same restaurant some months before to celebrate the birthday of her ex-boyfriend. He found it interesting that she hadn't made up some excuse not to come to this particular restaurant—Indian food didn't agree with enough people for it to be a common enough excuse—but she had readily accepted his suggestion with a look of stunned graciousness. He knew what she was thinking: What a coincidence it was that he had to pick *that* restaurant of all the restaurants in the city. Throughout dinner, it was clear to Connor from subtle cues in her emotional affect that Kelly still felt a great deal for Eric Rossi. No doubt she had decided to come to this restaurant to prove to herself that she was ready to give up her relationship with the homicide detective once and for all. It was a courageous if unnecessary act. In Connor's experience, people were often far too hard on themselves.

After dinner they took a taxi uptown to visit the gallery that was showing his photographs. The gallery was legitimate, as were the photographs, all taken by Connor himself, submitted to the gallery in the usual way and accepted purely on the basis of their merit. The Craft had pulled no strings to get him the exhibit. That was the way they liked to work, keeping things as close to real-life as possible. It was a philosophy that made the Craft the most omnipotent and invisible secret organization in the world. They left very few loose ends for everyone to detect in their intricate web of deception.

Kelly had seemed genuinely impressed with his work, especially with the photographs he'd taken of the S-M scene, including some of those he'd snapped without her knowledge of her in her role as Lady Domina. She looked at the latter pictures with a strange fascination, mesmerized by the leather-clad woman in the mask and spiked heels. Only later did Connor fully understand the strange nature of her interest. Kelly did not recognize the woman in the photographs as herself.

He rode with her back to her apartment in Queens, and she invited him up for coffee. Her apartment was much as he pictured it would be. The furniture was too worn to be trendy, but comfortable all the same. Brightly colored framed prints from the Metropolitan Museum of Modern Art hung on the walls. There were magazines and books spread out on the coffee table and desk and piled beside the couches. Last evening's dishes were still in the sink and a basket of clean laundry waiting to be folded stood outside the door to the linen closet. In short, it was exactly the kind of living arrangement you might expect of a bright young single woman living alone in New York City, right down to the sparkling clean fifteen-gallon fish tank in the corner of the living room.

She apologized for the mess, told him to make himself comfortable, and retreated into the kitchen to fix the coffee. During that time he quickly reviewed and memorized the numbers on her caller ID hooked up to the phone next to the couch. She took a seat on the armchair across from him and they sipped their coffee and talked, and Connor knew that in her mind she had already decided to sleep with him if he made a move. She wanted to erase as permanently as she could the physical memory of her ex-boyfriend from her sexual circuit. Though she didn't think of it in exactly those terms, that was basically what she intended, whether she was conscious of the fact or not.

Connor knew that eventually it would become necessary to have sexual relations with her, if only because she would expect it as the next stage in a normally developing relationship, and that to do anything else would be productive of nothing but discord. He had done similar work in the name of the Craft before, and though he found her immensely attractive, both physically and psychically, he was still reluctant to begin this phase of the relationship. Not because he shied away from the deception that was necessarily involved; deception was his business. But quite simply because the act of love required a discharge of precious magical energy. He had learned from experience that in his line of work any dissipation of magical energy could be extremely hazardous to his health.

A staring passerby alerted Connor to the fact that he was no longer "invisible." He had lost his concentration on the grid, and his thoughts had begun to stray. At the corner he saw a cop swinging a black riot baton and bearing down on him, ready to send him on his way.

He glanced up at Kelly's window.

It was already dark, and the light had come on behind the shade, one more yellow square against the already deepening autumn darkness.

In less than two hours he would be back to pick her up for their date.

Connor stood up slowly.

Sitting slumped against the wall, his mind a thousand miles away from his body, he hadn't realized how cold it had gotten. He gathered his tattered overcoat around him, and hobbled toward the subway station.

He felt the eyes on him—not the cop's eyes, but other eyes.

They were like spiders crawling over his skin, which had been sensitized by years of paranoia training. Connor had felt the eyes before: in the theater with Kelly, in the restaurant, in the park. He was sure it wasn't the Craft; they would know better than to think they could go undetected. He was equally sure that he wasn't the primary target. No, he was positive that whoever it was, they were watching Kelly. He looked back along the street and saw no one out of the ordinary.

At the subway entrance, he glanced over his shoulder at her lighted window.

She was important, this Kelly Mitchell.

He was sure of it.

But why?

TWENTY-FIVE

Rossi was the last to arrive in the conference room, where an impromptu meeting had been called that morning for the detectives working the case of the headless woman found in the warehouse by the pier.

They'd been able to keep the most sensational details of the murder out of the papers, and so the case so far lacked one of those colorful nicknames that made such great newspaper-selling headlines. Of course, there was no shortage of sobriquets for the case circulating around the squad room, and most of these ranged from the mildly distasteful to the downright obscene. It sounded heartless and they were forbidden by regulation to refer to cases in that manner, but they did it anyway, even at the risk of incurring disciplinary action. The simple fact of the matter was that more often than not, humor was the last and only defense they had against the horrors they were forced to witness day in and day out.

Rossi saw Evans and Mantucci in the front row. Hoffman and Washington were sitting behind them, the latter regaling them all with the story of his sexual exploits of the previous night. If only half of Washington's stories were true, he qualified as a modern-day Casanova. Whether true or not, however, the man was undeniably entertaining. He was wasting his imagination as a cop.

He should be writing stories for *Penthouse*. This morning he was telling a triple X-rated whopper about twin gymnasts, a trampoline, and a turkey baster.

It sure as hell beat the way Rossi had spent the night.

He had cruised the sex shops along Forty-second Street and Eighth Avenue, hunting for clues, but aside from the usual collection of perverts and marginal characters, he'd found out nothing. Later, he'd driven through the tenderloin district, with its converted warehouses turned leather bars, but no one had been picked up by anyone with a taste for blood. Tired and frustrated, Rossi had ended the night in a third-floor walkup with a seventeen-year-old prostitute he'd helped out of a few tough spots over the past six months. She'd offered him a freebie on several occasions in return for his kindness, and last night he had decided to call in his marker. As she knelt in front of him, his pants around his ankles, his hands in her hair, he kept his eyes open for fear that if he closed them he might see Kelly.

Rossi was no choirboy: he'd been to prostitutes before. He wasn't expecting her to fall in love with him, but the girl was cold and disembodied even for a whore. She took care of him with a mechanical efficiency, her eyes flat as coins, her body lifeless as rubber. When it was done he felt emptied of more than just his pent-up lust.

Still, as unsatisfying as the encounter had been, in its own small way it had helped to ease the ache of losing Kelly.

Rossi had been shot once—a stray bullet through the hand during a drug shootout. Nothing serious. But for the first two days, the pain had been great, it was as if his entire existence had been reduced to a shot hand. He'd had to undergo weeks of physical therapy to strengthen and retrain the damaged muscles, and several times he was close to giving up. Even after he was reinstated to duty the hand bothered him, unexpectedly sending jolts of pain up his arm, keeping him awake at night, leaving him weak and nauseated. But as the time passed the pain slowly faded until eventually the excruciating agony he'd experienced became nothing but a distant memory, a mere shadow pain that still ached on occasion when the weather was bad or when he was exceptionally tired or stressed, leaving him to wonder if imagination alone hadn't exaggerated the original hurt; if anything, in fact, could really have hurt that badly. Little by little, helped by encounters like the one with the prostitute the night before, Rossi was emptying himself of the need and the pain left after the breakup with Kelly.

There were coffee and donuts on a card table in the corner of the conference room. Rossi filled a Styrofoam cup at the large silver urn, tore open three packets of sugar, and stirred the black coffee with a red plastic stick. He tossed the stick into the trash can, passed on the donuts, and took a seat in the back row next to Graham, who was working on the first of three powdered jelly donuts on a small paper plate perched on his right knee.

"What's up?" Rossi said, blowing on his coffee.

"Don't know," Graham grunted, exhaling white sugar powder. "Cap called the meeting. Maybe we finally got a break in this damn case. Or he's gonna chew our asses. My money's on the second."

They didn't have long to wait.

Captain Sweeney stalked into the room at nine o'clock sharp, his hands stuffed into the pockets of his corduroy coat. Following hard on his heels was a man in an impeccably pressed gray suit and a flattop so level you could have landed a helicopter on it. Sweeney introduced the flattop as Agent Greene of the Illinois office of the Federal Bureau of Investigation. Sweeney could have saved his breath. The guy had Federal Agent written all over him. He looked like he probably could shit in triplicate.

"Good afternoon, gentlemen," Agent Greene said.

Graham looked around theatrically, as if to see if someone might have sneaked into the room when no one was looking.

Rossi grinned.

At the front of the room, Sweeney shot them both a warning look. If Agent Greene noticed any of the exchange, his poker face didn't show it. Instead, he went straight into his pitch.

"Over the past eight years," he began, "Chicago has been victimized by a series of brutal murders quite unlike any the city has ever known. The bodies of thirteen people—nine women, four men—have been found in deserted or semideserted locations, each stripped naked, each hung upside down from their ankles, each decapitated. In each case the head was found nearby, gagged, facing east. The cause of death was always a traumatic blow struck through the shoulder blades by a broad-bladed weapon of some kind, perhaps an old-fashioned battle sword. The oddest thing, however, is that in every case, though post-mortem evidence clearly indicates that the victims were murdered at the location at which they were found, little or no trace of blood was found at the site.

"The last victim was found in the locker-room shower at Wrigley Field nearly six months ago. Naturally, we hoped that we'd heard the last of the killer; there's always the chance that people of this kind, because of the element in which they commerce, meet with a bad end on their own, but we knew that most likely he'd just moved to a new location. Sure enough, it looks like he might have turned up in New York. There is good reason to believe that your warehouse victim is one of his."

"Thirteen murders," Evans said from the first row. "You must have some kind of physical evidence."

"Almost nothing," the agent said. "Aside, of course, from the aforementioned and other random deductions we've drawn from the victims. He doesn't sexually assault them and, curiously enough, there is never any sign of struggle. Consequently, we don't have any blood, semen, or skin samples. We've got a few clothing threads, but that is about all. Whoever this guy is, he's the type of character who can murder thirteen people without losing so much as a single hair. I think that in itself tells us more than any DNA sample the kind of monster we're up against."

Even among these hard-bitten homicide cops, there was a collective shudder. Rossi felt it, though he knew that later on no one would admit having been spooked, including himself. Later on, there would be the same old jokes, the same old macho posturing. It was all part of the code.

"Maybe he ain't human," Washington said to break the spell.

The agent didn't even blink.

"I'll guarantee you one thing," he said. "Whoever he is, he's not like anything you've ever run across before."

He nodded to Sweeney, who produced a large manila envelope. The captain opened the clasp, removing a sheaf of papers, which he began to distribute around the room.

Rossi took a sheet from Hoffman, passed one to Graham, and stared at the badly reproduced picture next to the printout of the suspect's vital statistics and characteristics. The agent waited for them to digest the information before continuing.

"The description and psychological profile are purely speculation, courtesy of our team at Quantico. They caution that considering the paucity of hard information, they don't have much on which to base their conclusions."

"Who is he?" Rossi asked. He was looking at the figure of a broad-shouldered man in dark clothes moving away from the camera. He seemed to be jogging up a wide stone staircase. His face, turned away from the camera, was blurred.

"His name is Pietro Sylvestri. Interpol has been tracking his movements for some time. Over the last thirty years they have attributed over twenty-five hundred murders to his credit, which would make him the most prolific serial killer in history, discounting, of course, political mass murderers like Stalin, Hitler, and Pol Pot. That photograph was taken at the Vatican sometime in the early sixties."

"Thirty years," Mantucci said. "He must be a middle-aged man by now."

"Older," the agent said. "Interpol estimates his age to be closer to eighty."

"Eighty!" Mantucci shouted. "We're looking for an eighty-year-old serial killer?"

There were exclamations of open disbelief throughout the room. Once againt the agent waited for the agitation to die down before continuing.

"No one said he's the killer. But we are very interested in locating the man, if he's still alive, which we believe he is. Gentleman, I know the facts as they appear in this case challenge conventional thinking, but what we have here is a highly unconventional killer. If we are going to catch him, we must begin to think in unconventional ways."

"The Vatican," Rossi mumbled, staring closely at the face, the features swimming in a gray soup. "Why the Vatican?"

"We think he may be a priest," the agent said. "Or that he used to be a priest."

"A priest?" Graham snorted.

"I've heard it all now," Hoffman said, shaking his head. "And you guys wonder why I don't convert."

"We know that the Church circulates priests who've gotten into trouble," the agent said. "Adulterers. Child molestors. Even murderers. Remember how quickly they hustled Father Ritter out of the country after that flap at Covenant House here in Manhattan? With the Church's vast international economic and political resources, it is extremely hard for us to keep track of those it is determined to protect from prosecution, let alone for us to bring them to justice."

"But why would they want to protect a serial killer?" Mantucci said.

"We think he may have once belonged to a radical Jesuit organization known as the Assassins of Christ. The AC operated behind enemy lines in communist countries during the cold war, defending the rights of the faithful against the atheists and Marxists who were trying to forcefully stamp out the practice of Catholicism. It is believed that they conducted assassinations of communist political leaders and sympathizers with the unofficial sanction of the Order of Cardinals in Rome. Sylvestri may have been a loyal soldier in that cause who went over the edge, and the Church feels the need to protect him. And, of course, their own interests. But that is all speculation. I'd rather not go into that here."

The agent continued to answer questions, but Rossi had stopped listening. Instead, he was thinking back to the night he'd picked up Joey and what the prostitute had said about the man in black with the obsession for blood. Could he and this rogue assassin-priest be one and the same man?

Rossi kept his mouth zippered.

He'd seen enough of these hotshot FBI punks riding to glory on the grunt work of ordinary cops like Rossi and the rest of the men in the room to let it happen again.

He waited until Sweeney dismissed the meeting before cornering Graham in the hall and telling him what he suspected.

PART THREE

THE ART
OF
PAIN

"The road of excess leads to the palace of wisdom."
—William Blake

"Our Lady of pangs and pleasures,
Teach us the indifference that kindles love anew,
Make known to us the truth about this world—that it
has none,
And grant us strength to live up to this verity of veri-
ties."
—*Caligula*, Albert Camus

TWENTY-SIX

The club Domination was located on the lower West Side, a few blocks south of what was commonly known as SoHo. It was housed in an old theater that had closed down after most of the neighborhood's movie-going population had migrated out of the area to more civilized environs north of Houston Street. As it was, no one would ever suspect it to be the location of the city's most exclusive night spot. The only clue that it was anything other than a symbol of the city's economic and cultural decline were the two limousines idling out front.

"Well, it's no Studio 54, that's for sure," Gwen said.

Ilana's invitation entitled Kelly to bring a guest, and she had asked Gwen along. She often counted on her friend's droll commentary and down-to-earth viewpoint as a sure tonic to the disorienting alternate reality of the punks, freaks, and ravers that populated the club scene.

Kelly looked at the crumbling movie house, its blind marquee and empty ticket booth a grim reminder of what used to be. She double-checked the address Ilana had given her.

"Is this the old Concordia?" she asked the cabbie.

He looked up in the rearview mirror, narrow eyes beneath an awning of greasy curls. "That's it, lady," he said in a harsh accent that could have been either Israeli or Iraqui.

Kelly shrugged, dug in her purse, and paid the driver. A moment later, they were standing on the sidewalk in front of the forbidding theater as the cab sped away down the street.

"I sure hope we're in the right place," Gwen said, looking around her at the abandoned cars and graffiti-splashed walls. "Or we're in a lot of trouble."

"Well, we've got high-class company, anyway," Kelly said, nodding towards the two limos.

"Could be a mob rubout."

"That's what I like about you, Gwen," Kelly said. "Always looking on the bright side."

They walked toward the stairs leading up to the theater's main entrance and found it impassable. The tile floor that once greeted moviegoers had been dug up by vandals, who had broken the glass out of the ticket windows and display cases, ripping the posters of long-past coming attractions. The entrance was shielded by a locked iron grate; nonetheless, the glass doors behind it had been smashed and boarded over, sprayed with obscenities. Beer bottles, crack vials, and old syringes were scattered on the ground, where addicts had taken refuge from the elements under the awning.

"What the hell do we do now?" Gwen asked, wrinkling her nose at the suffocating stench of urine.

Kelly was about to suggest they ask the inhabitants of one of the limousines when she spied the stairway around the side of the theater, leading down to what appeared to be a small basement entrance. Underneath a bare red bulb that cast the entire area in a dim blood-hued light, she saw two men checking the pass of a couple dressed in evening clothes.

"Look," Kelly pointed. "Down there."

They went around to the side of the theater and

down the stairs in the semidarkness, Gwen complaining literally every step of the way.

Even from outside they could hear the relentless, monotonous throb of electronic music.

At the bottom of the stairs they came upon the two doormen.

They were both big, their powerful *v*-shaped physiques unconcealed beneath their leather dusters, their hair slicked straight back off chiseled faces. They wore black wraparound shades and each wore a tiny earplug in his right ear. They looked like a cross between Secret Service agents and *GQ* outlaws.

"Hey, how about throwing a few extra watts on those stairs back there," Gwen said. "I nearly broke my neck."

Neither of the men answered. They merely examined the pass Kelly handed them and motioned them inside.

"Hey, guys," Gwen said, "I'm talking to you."

They stared stonily at Gwen from behind the dark glasses.

"Come on," Kelly said through gritted teeth. She smiled apologetically at the two bouncers. "She needs a little discipline is all. She's a bad girl. You know how it is."

She pulled Gwen with her toward the black steel door that led inside the theater, but not before Gwen was able to turn around to get off one final zinger.

"I think it's time to get the batteries checked in those Miracle Ears of yours," she said, touching her finger to her ear. She turned to Kelly. "Jeez. Can you believe those guys? You'd think the President of the United States was coming."

Kelly rolled her eyes. "I don't know why I take you anywhere," she muttered.

They passed through the door and ran straight into a wall of sound that cut off all further discussion.

Kelly had seen some pretty wild sights club-crawling

through the city's sexual underbelly as a reporter for *NiteLife*, but nothing that quite compared to the scene that confronted her inside Domination.

The room before her was splashed with colored lights from strobes that sprayed the floors and ceiling like a severed artery. Patterned explosions of light blossomed everywhere, opening and closing on the crowd like gunshot wounds. On the walls, hidden projectors simultaneously played various famous vampire moves. Kelly recognized Bela Lugosi staring from behind his black cape, as well as George Romero's *Martin* and Catherine Deneuve seducing Susan Sarandon in *The Hunger*. Meanwhile, in metal cages suspended from the ceiling, young men and women wearing nothing but gold and silver glitter dust performed highly stylized dances simulating various acts of tabooed coitus.

"I think we overdressed," Gwen yelled.

The music was so loud as to make it nearly impossible to hear oneself speak. At the same time, the searing light of a Tazer gun flashed in time to the hypnotic beat of the music, syncopating the movements of the crowd. They were dancing to music it should have been impossible to dance to, moving in a strange herky-jerky fashion, as if each blast of light sent an electric shock through the floor.

Kelly stepped out of the way of a drag queen dressed to look like Marilyn Monroe, conspicuous puncture marks inked on his neck, blood spilling over his plastic breasts. Against a far wall she saw a statuesque black woman in gold platform shoes leading a beautiful blond zombie in a leopard-skin bikini by a rhinestone-studded dog leash. And there were a parade of others, each more preposterous than the one before: a bald man wearing leather chaps and bandeleros that crisscrossed an oiled, muscular chest pierced and tattooed; a woman mummified in gauze and plaster that left only her breasts and genitals exposed; a man wearing a barbed wire jockstrap and a leather zipper mask; an androgynous albino creature in a sky-blue feathered unitard and sporting a mohawk pink as cotton candy.

"Look," Gwen shouted into her ear. "Isn't that Messalina?"

Kelly looked to where Gwen was pointing and spotted the famous eroto-rock musician. She was surrounded by her entourage of costumed party boys, arm in arm with her latest lover, an acerbic, horse-faced feminist comedienne and performance artist. Even in her trademark costume of frilly underwear and peek-a-boo black leather, the bad girl of rock-and-roll barely stood out in the crowd. She was talking to a tall, handsome Hispanic man who Kelly also recognized. He was a well-known baseball player who played with one of his New York teams. Eric had once taken her to one of the games at Yankee Stadium. They disappeared as suddenly as they appeared in the relentlessly blinking lights.

"Wow," Gwen said, sounding genuinely impressed. "Messalina. This place must be hot."

They worked their way through the hot, frenzied crowd, in search of the stairs that led up to the main floor of the theater. Along the way they passed a couple of domination tableaux. In one, a woman dressed in a latex bodysuit administered a whipping to a man in a silver G-string who was bound to a bare boxspring suspended from the ceiling. In another, a pretty redhead was being artfully immobilized in an elaborate and beautiful spiderweb bondage by a man who looked so much like her he could have been her brother. Kelly made her way to one of several bars located around the floor and asked one of the bikini-clad bartenders how to get to the main floor. She had been invited upstairs to watch a special performance in what Ilana had called the Theater of Pain. The theater was considered the club's inner sanctum, reserved for the club's most important members, and Kelly couldn't help noticing the look of jealousy and awe on the face of the bald and tattooed girl when Kelly shouted her request over the pounding music.

Probably trying to figure out what famous person I am, she thought, amused.

They found the door exactly where the bartender had directed. At the landing there were two more security guards dressed in expensive-looking Italian suits, as well as the ubiquitous dark glasses and earplugs. The taller of the two looked at the passes Kelly had handed him and, satisfied that they gave them clearance to enter the theater, opened the door behind him and motioned with his head up the stairway.

They squeezed past his bulky body and no sooner started up the stairs than the guard slammed the door shut behind them, cutting off the wild cacophony of music below, plunging them into a deafening silence.

Gwen, a few steps up, turned back.

Kelly shrugged.

They continued up the stairs.

At the top they found themselves inside a movie house that on first glance was no different than any other. Carpeted floors, vaulted ceiling, the hush of anticipation. Strangely enough, none of the noise and excitement downstairs filtered through the thickly curtained walls. Kelly handed her pass to a young woman in a white ruffled tuxedo shirt and bowtie. She read the seat number with a small penlight and led them down the worn scarlet carpet, pointing with the penlight to a pair of seats about six rows from the stage.

They excused themselves as they shimmied their way through the crowded aisle to their seats.

"Oh, wait," Gwen whispered, a little too loudly, a big grin on her face. "I forgot to get the popcorn."

"Ssh," Kelly said.

The stage was shielded by a great curtain of red velvet, edged with silver brocade. On its faded surface Kelly could just make out a heraldic crest: a strange dragonlike beast hanging from a cross.

"Great seats," Gwen said, softly patting the plush armrests.

Kelly nodded.

She was surreptitiously scanning the audience in the seats around her. There were none of the avant-garde, post-punk polyglot seated up here. For the most part, everyone was dressed in formal or semiformal evening clothes. A few rows up, Kelly recognized a well-known author of best-selling vampire novels sitting with her hands folded demurely in her lap. Behind her, Kelly saw the tanned, handsome face of one of Hollywood's most distinguished actors. And in the first row sat a flamboyant and famous real-estate tycoon and his equally famous supermodel mistress. Overhead, there were special boxes overlooking the stage. Kelly could just make out the dim faces of the people seated in the shadows, but she recognized only one. It was Senator Edmund Stanton's wife, Hillary, who Kelly remembered from Ivan Koski's party. She was just about to turn to Gwen when the lights overhead dimmed, throwing the stage into spotlight, where the lone figure of a woman stood before the scarlet curtain, as if she had materialized out of thin air.

She was wearing a leather mask, but Kelly knew that it was Ilana. The mask left the lower part of her face exposed, exaggerating the delicacy of her small white chin and the sensuality of her painted red lips. The dominatrice was wearing a one-piece suit of shiny blue-black leather that fit her like a second skin. She moved with the feral grace of a black cat on a pair of high-heeled black boots. There was no mistaking the dangerous beauty of the woman. From the eyes that burned with sultry intensity to the riding crop she held in her gloved right hand, Kelly saw in Ilana the epitome of the type. She was the woman Keats saw as he lay dying of tuberculosis, the woman who lured steadfast Odysseus to the rocks of doom. She was the black widow of the human variety. To mate with her once was death irresistible.

There was an audible sigh from the audience at Ilana's appearance, a spontaneous expression of collective desire. Kelly felt it herself. Beside her, Gwen gave a little involuntary gasp. Then there was a smattering of polite applause.

"Welcome, friends," Ilana said in her accented voice, "to the Theater of Pain. I know that many of you have come from far away to be here tonight. Some of you are old acquaintances. Others are here for the first time. But we are all wanderers of the same solitary path, come together on this night of the full moon to share the sweetest of sacraments—the sacrament of blood that binds us all in eternity. Here, be assured, you are truly among family."

There was more applause.

"I know that you will enjoy tonight's performance. I am pleased to present a pair of wonderful new actors. Their names are Kathy and Steven Bennett. He is a systems analyst for a midtown bank. She is a part-time teacher and homemaker. They have two young children, live in a pleasant Connecticut suburb, and are both active in their local PTA. They've been married for seven years and were sweethearts in high school, where he was a star quarterback and she was a cheerleader. In their school yearbook, they were voted cutest couple.

"Their sexlife was tender and loving, if somewhat predictable. Something was always missing. Sometimes

220

he would play the agressor in their little love games, sometimes she, but they were unable to fool themselves. They both needed the same thing, and by a strange ironic twist of fate it was the one thing they were unable to give to each other. They were two identical substances in need of a catalyst to make them ignite.

"For the past two years they had been talking about finding another couple who would complement their needs, who could give them what they needed. It had remained a fantasy at first, just pillow talk, but with repetition it had begun to grow more feasible, until Steve began renting videos, buying bondage magazines, and logging onto S-M computer bulletin boards. Three weeks ago that was where he found the ad placed by a dominant couple seeking a pair of submissive playmates. Kathy was reluctant at first, but Steve convinced her to give it a try. All they had to do was meet with the other couple. He promised her that if either of them felt the least bit uneasy they'd call the whole thing off. Eventually, she agreed. After all, it was something she had fantasized about for so long. I wonder if she's sorry now."

Ilana turned and swept her arm elegantly toward the stage behind her as the lights dimmed and the heavy velvet curtain was slowly raised.

For several suspenseful moments they sat in total darkness.

Then, all of a sudden, light flooded the stage.

And the play began.

TWENTY-SEVEN

When Steve and Kathy Bennett regained consciousness the first thing they realized was that they were no longer sipping wine in a living room and nervously sharing their sexual fantasies of domination, which was the last thing they remembered before becoming terribly disoriented and passing out on the couch. The second thing they noticed was that they were bound to two crude wooden crosses standing upright in front of a bank of blinding Kliegl lights.

They were naked, helpless, and understandably terrified.

"What's going on here?" Steve yelled into the wall of light. "Where the hell are you? Answer me, goddamm it!"

A few of yards away, Kathy twisted against her restraints, trying to catch sight of Steve. She was bound tightly at the wrists and ankles, her hands and feet already going numb. "Steve?" she cried. "I'm scared. I want to get out of here. You promised."

"Don't worry, honey," her husband said, carefully examining his bondage. The ropes were tied so tightly, the tips of his fingers had begun to turn blue. His hopes sank. "I'll get us out of this somehow."

The loud, mocking sound of two hands clapping

broke the silence, and Ilana stepped out from behind the light. In spite of his anger, Steve could already feel his cock thickening at the sight of the leather-clad woman.

"How sweet," Ilana mocked. "It's nice to see that chivalry hasn't died out completely in this age of equal rights. Not yet, anyway. But tell me, Steve. Between me and you, just how is it that you intend to escape, anyway?"

"Look, this has gone far enough," Steve said in his most commanding tone. It was the tone of voice he used to discipline subordinates at the office or to deal with recalcitrant business associates, but it sounded far less convincing given the present state of affairs. "I don't know what kind of game you're playing, but we don't want any part of it. Do you understand? Now let us down."

"I'm afraid that isn't possible, Steven," Ilana said.

"I'm not fooling," Steve said, thinking that perhaps the woman had misunderstood his objections as submissive playacting. Hadn't they said something about that earlier, while they were getting acquainted? "We really don't want to play. We want to go home."

"You're so cute when you get mad. But I'd save my breath if I were you. You have a lot of screaming to do."

"Listen to me, you psycho bitch. You're going to let us down now. Right now. Or there's going to be trouble. Kidnapping, for starters. Assault. Drugging us with whatever you had in that wine. We're going to the police. Do you hear me?"

Ilana laughed and turned to Kathy. "My, how forceful he sounds, how assertive. How *dominant*. You'd almost forget that he came here to have his ass whipped and to see his wife fucked by another man, wouldn't you? Unfortunately, his change of heart comes a little too late."

"I'm not telling you again," Steve screamed. "Let us down, now!"

"Amusing as your little tantrums are, Steven, I'm growing tired of hearing your voice. I think I'll have you gagged for now. But don't worry. Later on I'll let you scream all you like."

Ilana snapped her fingers, and from out of the light a beautiful coma girl appeared with a rubber ball gag. She was dressed in a black leather corselet, shiny black boots that stretched to midthigh, and studded leather wrist bands. Two tiny black triangles of leather left her nearly naked in front and in back. Her breasts, pushed up by the corselet, were bare.

Steve tossed his head from side to side, but the girl eventually forced the orange rubber into his mouth. She tied the leather straps securely behind his head. Steve continued to curse and shout behind the gag, but the words sounded like little more than baby talk.

"That's better," Ilana said. "A little easier on the ears."

She walked over to Kathy, who watched the woman with wide, terrified eyes. "Please . . ." she whimpered.

"Nice tits."

Ilana reached up and put her hands on Kathy's breasts, and the woman tried to pull away. Ilana smacked Kathy across the face, stunning her for a moment, tears standing in her pretty blue eyes. Ilana grinned wickedly, licked her lips, and roughly grabbed the woman's breasts. She traced her fingers around Kathy's pink nipples until they hardened.

"I'll bet your hands and feet have gone numb by now, haven't they?"

"Yes," Kathy whimpered.

Ilana gave her nipples a hard tweak.

Kathy cried out in pain.

"Yes, what?" Ilana said.

"Yes . . . mistress," Kathy said softly.

Ilana produced a small pliers from inside her leather jumpsuit. She grasped the tender flesh of the woman's left nipple beneath the serrated edge and twisted. Ilana waited until Kathy's scream had died away.

"Louder," she said calmly.

"Yes, mistress," Kathy shouted, breathless.

"Well, you'll thank me for that numbness later when the nails go in and you're in enough pain to last a hundred lifetimes. That's the first thing you have to learn. You see, that's the way God works. What at the time seems to be needless pain and suffering later turns out to be for your own good. In fact, since you probably won't be in any condition to thank me later, why don't you do so now."

"Thank you for letting my hands and feet go numb . . . *mistress!*" Kathy shouted.

"That's it," Ilana said brightly. "You're getting the hang of it now."

She placed the pliers around Kathy's sore nipple and squeezed until bruised flesh emitted several drops of bright red blood. Kathy screamed and thrashed against her bonds but to no avail. She couldn't shake the iron jaw of the pliers from her abused nipple. Finally, when it seemed as if she were about to pass out, Ilana removed the pliers.

"Why . . . why did you do that?" Kathy stammered as the pain faded. "I did what you said."

"That's the second thing you have to learn. No matter what you do, no matter how well you behave, you have no power over your fate. It's all out of your hands now, Kathy. You are completely at my mercy. I have the power to make you feel good. Or to make you hurt. And there is nothing you can do to change it one way or another."

Kathy started crying.

"What's the matter, Kathy? Is this a little more than you bargained for? Well, like the old saying goes, be careful what you wish for, you just might get it. Look at Steve over there. For all his aggressive histrionics, he still has quite an erection for a man who's not enjoying himself. Can't help yourself, can you, Steven, you naughty boy?" Ilana turned back to Kathy. "I'll bet he's hoping this is all part of the game. Well, take heart, my pets. It is a kind of game—a show, actually. I call it "The Pain Show." And I think it's high time we got the show on the road."

Ilana left Kelly to contemplate her fate and turned back to Steve, who watched the dominatrice approach with a mixture of fear and rage in his eyes. She motioned to the coma girl standing behind Steve's cross, who reached up and removed the ball gag.

"I think we should start with you, Steven," Ilana said, massaging his half-hard organ until it stood erect against his smooth belly. "You seem to be up for it."

"Get your hands off me, bitch," Steve growled, unable to control the swelling of his traitorous cock.

"You fool," Ilana sneered. "Before long you'll be begging me for this kind of attention."

She reached between his legs with the pliers and grasped his left testicle. She looked up into his face, enjoying the look of terror stamped there, and slowly squeezed the jaws of the pliers closed.

Steve tried frantically to think of some way out when a wall of white pain blinded him to any thought whatsoever. He prayed he would pass out, but he didn't. Instead, he felt every excruciating second of the pain. After what seemed like an eternity she released his testicle, and a wave of nausea rose inside him, drowning him in agony.

"Let me go," he yelped, breathing raggedly. He felt the iron close around his other testicle.

"But we've only just started." Ilana feigned disappointment. "Don't tell me you want to quit already?"

Whatever attraction S-M had once held for Steve, he realized now that it wasn't for him. The pain he had felt wasn't erotic or sensual; it was simply pain.

"I don't care. I've had enough."

"I don't think so," Ilana said.

Steve could feel the pliers tightening its grip on his testicle.

"Please," Steve said, deciding to try humility. Under the circumstances, he didn't have much choice. It was his last hope before he was forced to accept his worst nightmare. "I mean it. Please let us go."

"I can't do that, Steven."

Steve felt the sweat breaking out over his body. "Why not? In your ad you said you'd respect our limits."

"And I will. But you haven't reached your limit yet," Ilana said.

"What do you mean by that?" Steve asked, fearing her answer.

"You're still alive."

She squeezed, and Steve felt his remaining testicle squashed inside the pliers like a small, overripe plum. Once again he was hurled into the white wall of pain, only this time he felt as if he were being pushed straight through it and out the other side, into some new, heretofore uncharted territory of agony. He tried to protect himself from the pliers, but there was little he could do with his ankles tied to the base of the cross.

The pain went on and on.

"Shut up," Ilana snapped. "Or I'll cut off your worthless balls and gag you with them, you pitiful wimp. Not that it makes any difference. You can scream your fucking head off and no one will help you. Here, I'll prove it to you."

She turned to the coma girl, who had reentered from

227

stage left with a partner. The second girl was carrying a wooden mallet and several large iron nails.

"Begin," Ilana said.

The coma girl stood just below the left arm of Steve's cross. Her partner handed her one of the nails. She reached up as casually as if she were about to hammer a picture hook in the wall of her apartment and placed the point of the large nail in the hollow of his wrist. She then reached back and took the large wooden mallet from the other girl.

Steve began to form a conception of the enormity of what was about to occur and panicked.

"No," he wept, "Jesus, no. You can't do this. I *beg* you!"

"There's the proper tone," Ilana said. "Keep your eyes open, Kathy," she called back. "Maybe you can learn something."

The sound of Steve's screams rent the air, but worse than that was the steady, hollow sound of the hammer as it pounded the nails into his hands and feet. Kathy closed her eyes tight to the sound of her husband's agony.

"You're not watching, Kathy," Ilana called back. Her voice had an ominous singsong sound to it. "Don't make me have to cut your eyelids off."

Kathy forced herself to look. Steve's hands and feet were bloody. His face, chalk-white with pain, was thrown back, but he was no longer screaming. Instead, his chest was heaving as he tried to gulp down air. Every muscle seemed to be jumping with the strain, his contorted body a hierogylph for pain. In spite of herself, Kathy dropped her gaze to his crotch. His unflagging erection was enormous. The observation confused her, and she quickly looked away.

"Let him down," she pleaded. "Please, mistress, let him down."

Ilana ran her hands over the straining muscles of Steve's thighs and buttocks. She touched her finger to the wound in his wrist, licking away the blood and sweat, and put her finger to her lips. "Ssh," she said. "Don't let him hear you. You don't want to scare him, do you?"

Steve moaned.

"Kathy," he cried. "Help me!"

"Please, mistress," Kathy begged. "Please let him down. Don't you have any sympathy?"

"I'm sorry." Ilana shrugged. "But you simply have to expect a little pain in these cases. After all, it isn't easy for a man to become a god."

"Please don't talk like that. We'll give you anything you want. Money. Is it money you want? If you let us go, we'll give you everything. We won't tell anyone. I promise."

"Poor Kathy," Ilana mocked. "Poor dimwitted Kathy. You still don't get it, do you? There's only one thing you have that's worth anything to me."

"What?" Kathy asked, pitifully hopeful, as if there were suddenly some way out of this insane madness. Over Ilana's shoulder she could see Steve twisting on his cross. She knew she had to hurry. "Tell me. Whatever it is—"

"I want to hear you scream."

Kathy felt her heart sink. She knew then that the woman was crazy and that this terrible thing was going to happen. The coma girls were already kneeling at the foot of Kathy's cross, waiting for their mistress to give them the word to proceed.

"What do you think, Kathy." Ilana asked conversationally, like one woman asking another her opinion on the color of a nail polish. "Should we nail those pretty feet of yours side by side or one on top of the other?"

"Don't do this, please, don't do this . . ."

"I say side by side. It'll be twice the pain, but it'll be worth being able to see all ten of those pretty little toes of yours squirming."

Kathy felt the sharp point of the nail on her instep. She closed her eyes and tried to prepare herself for the pain to come. The coma girl raised the wooden mallet and, without preamble, slowly and methodically drove the first iron nail through Kathy's left foot.

Ilana turned and stepped toward the light.

"Crucifixion is perhaps the oldest and most revered method of putting someone to death. Contrary to popular belief, it was not invented by the Romans, though one might say they perfected the method through their special genius for variety and by using it to execute its most famous victim. In spite of that, Jesus Christ was only one of millions of men, women, and children to decorate the gruesome tree, nor was he its sweetest fruit, by far.

"I suppose the greatest misconception about crucifixion, however, is that it was invented primarily as a form of capital punishment. The fact is that as early as the sixth century B.C. there is evidence that crucifixion was the preferred method of offering up human sacrifice to the gods, often in return for a bountiful harvest. The tradition survives today in the practice of posting a scarecrow in a field of crops, though any farmer will tell you no crow was ever scared by a couple of sticks dressed in old clothes. Psychologically, the cross is a perfect symbol of the basic duality of the human condition, which is the source of all suffering. On the cross, a man finds himself torn between irreconcilable opposites—between good and evil, male and female, his mortal body and his immortal spirit—and it is this suffering that ennobles him. It is this struggle to transcend his own limitations that we never grow tired of aiding in our quest to free mankind from the bondage of flesh."

230

Ilana turned back to the crosses at center stage.

"The interesting thing about crucifixion," she said almost conversationally, "is that there are several ways to die. The Romans used numerous varieties of crosses, exhausting the possibilities of the human anatomy. They used y-shaped crosses, x-shaped crosses, even l-shaped crosses. Sometimes the victim was nailed upside down, as in the case of Saint Peter. Other times they merely tied the victim to the cross, letting him or her starve to death over a period of days, pestered by insects and birds. By far the easiest and quickest way is to drive the nail into the wrists in such a way that it severs an artery and the victim bleeds to death. As you can see for blond Steven and blond Kathy, we have chosen the variety of cross that, ever since Golgotha, has been associated with the passion of the savior of mankind, Jesus Christ.

"In this case the manner of hanging is similar as well. The nails have been driven through the wrists and feet, but not so as to sever any major arteries. This particular variation is an especially cruel and painful way to die. The position of the limbs and the attitude of the body make it extremely difficult to breathe. The victim has to struggle upwards against the wood at a great expense of energy and in excruciating pain. Eventually, the victim suffocates as fluids collect in the lungs and he becomes too weak and exhausted to lift himself up to breathe. Depending on the strength and will of the victim, death can take anywhere from one to three hours. It is almost always a dramatic and transfiguring event. They do not call it the 'passion of Christ' for nothing."

Kathy heard little of the dissertation.

Through a haze of pain, she looked down at her fine young body stretched and nailed to the cross. The pain was worse than anything she could ever have imagined. It felt as if all the bones in her hands and feet had been methodically smashed. They were already horribly swollen around the cruel iron nails, leaving Kathy to wonder if she would ever be able to walk again.

Ilana was standing beneath her now, looking up thoughtfully into Kathy's face, enjoying her agony.

"How's it going up there?" she called out pleasantly. "You don't look so good."

"It hurts," Kathy whimpered. "It hurts so bad."

Ilana laughed. "Pain's the name of the game, Kathy. That's what you came here for, isn't it?"

"Not this. Oh God . . . not this."

"You came here to submit, didn't you? Well, one cannot choose the manner in which one submits. You must give up that which you find the hardest to give. That is the only way to true liberation."

"But my body," she sobbed, thinking of her hands and feet, of being crippled and disfigured for life. "You've ruined me."

"Don't think of what you've suffered as injury," Ilana reasoned. "Think of it as decoration. Here, the more such wounds you suffer, the more beautiful you are."

"You're insane," Kathy said. "You can't get away with this."

"Oh no?" Ilana said, amused. "I'll bet you didn't let a lot of people know what you were up to when you and your husband decided to answer my ad. After all, it's just not the kind of thing you tell people, is it? Even if you had, the name I used was fictitious. The apartment? It's already been cleaned out. As far as anyone knows, you've fallen off the end of the earth."

Kathy knew what the woman said was true. They hadn't told anyone about answering the ad. They'd told their baby-sitter they were driving into the city that evening for dinner and a show. What else could they have said? She had known that this was a bad idea, that they shouldn't have done it, and now they were trapped here with this insane woman and her strange friends. It didn't seem fair that it should come to this. She had always been so careful all her life. It didn't seem fair that one mistake should have such terrible consequences.

"I don't want to die," Kathy cried out, for the first time formulating her worst fear.

"No one does," Ilana said matter-of-factly. "But let's not talk about that just yet. You still have awhile to go. After all, you're in pretty good shape. What's your secret, anyway? Thighmaster? Slim Fast? Power walking? I remember when a woman your age would have been considered an old hag. But you're still quite a tasty-looking little thing."

Kathy struggled upward on the cross, rising on her bare tiptoes as best she could, the nails tearing at the flesh of her hands and feet, and gulped the air. After a few painful breaths, she sagged back down against the wood and moaned.

"Now, remember what I told you about conserving your strength. Don't be too greedy with that air. I'd like you to at least last the hour. A lot of people have come a long way just to see you two."

"You mean there's people—watching?"

The idea was inexplicable. Horrific. But perhaps it was her only hope.

"Legions darling. You should be honored."

Kathy stared frantically into the blinding light. If she could just catch sight of a single face, make eye contact with one of those silent bystanders . . .

"Help us . . . someone," she cried out, her lungs burning with the effort. "Someone please—help us."

Her body was racked with a fit of coughing that threatened to strangle her. She suddenly felt incredibly exhausted. The pain in her hands and feet intensified, and she realized she was sagging against the cross. She was too tired to lift herself up.

233

"Save your breath. No one is going to help you. They came here to see you die, to sip from your pain."

"No," Kathy rasped. "I don't—believe that."

"Oh, but it's true!" Ilana said cheerfully.

"Who are you people?"

"We're sadists, Kathy. True sadists. You should know what a sadist is by now. *We enjoy seeing pain.* We get off on it. When the whip cracks across the back of some naked and compliant slave we get the same jolt of pleasure—only in the opposite direction. It's like a switch, Kathy, at the moment a connection is made and an energy released, and the sadist sucks it up. Are you paying attention, Kathy? I'm trying to teach you something important."

Kathy's head had fallen forward and a thin line of bloody drool connected her lower lip to the nipple of her right breast.

"Kathy, I'm talking to you!"

Hearing her name, Kathy stirred and lifted her head. It felt so heavy, heavy as a cannonball; already it was nodding toward unconsciousness.

She was shocked.

Was it happening already? Was she already dying?

She forced her mind to clear, knowing that if she allowed herself the luxury of fainting it would all be over. She had to stay awake, stay alert for some opportunity, any opportunity, to escape. She couldn't give up yet. It was the only way she and Steve had any chance. . . .

Steve . . .

She looked up and caught a glimpse of her suffering husband, head back, eyes closed, body rigid, tears streaming down his grimacing face. He looked for all the world the way he did when he was having a powerful orgasm.

It was ridiculous; she must be hallucinating to even

think such a thing. But there was the evidence: His penis was still standing erect against his belly.

What the hell was the matter with her, even thinking to look at a time like this? She must be slipping into hysteria.

Still, even under all the pain, Kathy was aware of the first glimmer of her own erotic arousal. Could this all be some kind of bad trip; had the wine they'd been given earlier in the evening been spiked with some kind of drug? She had never done drugs, not even as a teenager, but it seemed possible to her that what she was experiencing might be the result of a drug like LSD. If it weren't for the terrible pain—the pain was real enough. Too real. Kathy was having trouble breathing again. She shimmied upward on the cross, feeling splinters from the rough wood catch her skin. The effort made her head spin. . . .

Ilana reached out and grabbed Kathy by her short, sweat-soaked hair, pulling her face up.

"Kathy!" she called out sharply.

Kathy's eyes fluttered open.

"I'm afraid you dozed off again," Ilana said, sounding disappointed.

Kathy fixed her gaze on the dominatrice; her vision had started to roll a little, like the picture on a broken television.

"That's better," Ilana said when Kathy's eyes refocused. "You were gone for a little while there, but now I see you're ready to give me your undivided attention. As I was saying before you took your little nap, all sadists are vampires. I see you look confused. Did I fail to mention that we are vampires? I hate to cloud the issue with semantics. Sadists. Vampires. Angels. It's all the same. The point is that we draw nourishment from the pain of others. We mainline on the stuff. Blood, essential though it is, can hardly compare to the pure essense of

235

human suffering. It's like flounder compared to caviar, Hamburger Helper to filet mignon, muscatel to Dom Perignon. But do you know what's the best of all, Kathy?"

Kathy was suddenly aware of the terrible thirst that now raged through her body. She would have given her life for a mouthful of cool water.

"Water," she said. "Can I please have—some water?"

"I'm afraid not, dear," Ilana said. "I know dying like this is terribly thirsty work, but water will only make you sicker in the long run. Trust me. You'll thank me later. Now I asked you a question. Do you know what is the best of all?"

"No," Kathy whispered hoarsely.

"I'll give you a hint. It's the ultimate submission."

A terrible wave of nausea washed over her, as if her stomach had been pumped full of helium. Suddenly, Kathy wanted nothing so much as to end this terrible charade, to withdraw her full attention into her suffering body.

"Death," she said resignedly.

"Not quite. But I have to hand it to you, darling. Considering the circumstances, you're really trying. There's nothing quite so delicious as an educated slave. I'm afraid, however, you're wrong. The ultimate submission is not simply death, for that can be taken with or without your permission. No, the ultimate submission is when a slave gives his or her life willingly to the master. Oh, that is pure ambrosia, the food of the gods, the fruit of the original tree of life!"

Illana stepped closer to the cross, her hands stroking Kathy's sweating, trembling thighs, her breath cool and sweet on the dying woman's face. She whispered so low that Kathy had to strain to hear her.

"That is what we want from you, sweet Kathy. That is what we need. That is the only thing that will make

236

the terrible pain in your poor hands and feet go away. Give us your life, Kathy. Give up your life and the suffering is over."

Kathy felt herself floating, moving toward Ilana's voice, drawing her out of herself like a snail from its shell. But at the last moment something held her back.

"Never," she swore. "Go to—hell."

Ilana merely laughed. "Never is a long time, Kathy. A long time to suffer. I'll check with you in a couple of minutes. Right now, I'm going to look in on Steven. Something tells me his idea of "never" has suddenly gotten a lot shorter."

Wearily, Kathy watched as Ilana turned and sauntered over to Steve's cross. At some point she had stripped off the leather suit and was now wearing nothing but the boots, the mask, and a leather thong. Kathy watched how Ilana's hips rolled seductively on either side of the thong that split the flawless white hemispheres of her perfect ass.

Why am I even noticing such things . . .

And yet she couldn't help it. Couldn't help but feel a perverse attraction for the woman who was killing her and her husband.

As if she truly were my mistress. As if it were perfectly natural that I should submit to her.

Kathy looked up to where Steve hung helpless against the wood and saw that he had raised himself mightily against the back of the cross to breathe the cool clean air above the reek of his sweating, straining body. She could see the strain the effort was costing him, his arms and legs shuddering, his nailed feet standing on tiptoe on the blood-soaked wooden wedge. He looked the way he did when he was lifting weights, holding the bar above his head with two hundred pounds of iron, his face red and swollen. Except he never held it up for this long . . .

What was he trying to do?

She heard his voice, low and hoarse but clearly audible through the auditorium's excellent sound system.

"Our Father who are in heaven . . ."

Steve was praying. In seven years of marriage they had been to church only a handful of times, and here was Steve praying. Kathy felt her heart lurch in her chest. She knew it could only mean one thing.

Steve was dying.

For a moment Kathy felt nothing of her own pain, nothing of the nails piercing her hands and feet, nothing of the dehydration and nausea, the cold chills and muscular spasms that wracked her dying body. All she felt was a blinding white-hot rage and an all-consuming urgency to go to her husband's aid. She pulled at the nails with all her strength, as if by some superhuman effort she might pry them right out of the bloody wood, little realizing that in her rapidly weakening state her savage effort amounted to little more than a few pitiful and lascivious writhings for the entertainment of the crowd.

"Don't give up, Steven," she shouted, the exertion of raising her voice nearly causing her to black out. "Don't give up!"

"I love you, Kathy!" he cried out.

"I love you, too," she wept, and heard the polite titter of laughter from beyond the lights. "Listen to me—please. Don't give up."

His voice called back, weaker. "I'm sorry. Please forgive me!"

The lights came up all around her until she could see nothing but a blinding wall of white brilliance. From somewhere inside that incomprehensible heat and light she heard a sound she had heard hundreds of times before. The unmistakably intimate sound of her husband reaching orgasm.

"No!" Kathy screamed. "Steven. No!"

But the sound of her husband's dying passion followed her into unconsciousness.

Kathy was drenched in sweat, her body writhing on the cross in a grotesque parody of sexual passion.

One last time she struggled upwards against the rough wood, trying to draw breath into her burning lungs, but the effort made the pain in her body unbearable, and she sagged back down. She knew she would not try again.

Her head fell forward.

She had begun to bleed from the nostrils.

Hot tears splashed her breasts.

Ilana stepped forward, pushed the sweat-soaked blond hair out of her eyes, and bent down to look into her face.

"Kathy," she said quietly. "Can you still hear me?"

Kathy opened her eyes, glazed by pain and shock. They focused for an instant, and seeing it was only her tormentor come back to torture her some more, they slowly closed again.

"Kathy, I want to help you."

The note of genuine compassion in Ilana's voice brought Kathy back. Even now, she clung to hope.

"Can you hear me?"

Kathy's lips trembled but no sound came out.

"Good. Then listen to me carefully. Steve is gone."

"No." The sound was little more than a hoarse croak. "No."

"Yes. It's true," Ilana explained patiently, as if speaking to a child. "If your eyesight weren't all but gone, I'd show him to you. He died just a few minutes ago. Broken on the cross, as the cross is breaking you."

"I loved—"

"Yes. Yes, I know. You loved him. Let it go now,

Kathy. Give up. There's no hope left. You've suffered long enough. It's over."

"But—my kids . . ."

"Will be better off without you," Ilana finished.

"No," Kathy croaked. She shook her head frantically. "They still—need me."

Ilana was amazed at the young mother's stubbornness. Still, she knew just where to strike the coup de grace.

"You're not fit to raise them."

"I'm a good—mother."

"If you were a good mother," Ilana said, measuring the effect of her murderous words, "you'd be home with your kids right now instead of here with me, wouldn't you? This is your punishment, Kathy. You must accept that now. Your time has come."

It took all her remaining strength, but Kathy raised her head to her inquisitor one last time.

Ilana was transfixed. The pain in the dying woman's face was exquisite. It surpassed anything Ilana had ever seen in any art gallery anywhere in the world; it nearly took her breath away. In the woman's once pretty eyes Ilana could read the end of the story, the magical moment they all came to sooner or later. The moment of ultimate submission. The moment they gave up their lives to a higher purpose. It was what Ilana lived to experience. It was how her kind had survived for millennia.

Kathy was trembling, but not in pain or fear. It was relief that flooded her now—relief, and something else.

Gratitude.

What Ilana had said was true. Her eyesight was failing and she could hardly hear anymore, yet she kept what was left of her fading consciousness fixed on the dominatrice. It suddenly seemed to Kathy that the leather-clad woman who stood before her covered in

240

her husbands blood was the kindest and most beautiful woman Kathy had ever seen.

And then the truth of what Ilana had tried to tell her before hit her like a jolt of electricity, threatening to overwhelm her.

Ilana was an angel.

"How—"

"What?" Ilana said loudly. "I can't hear you. You'll have to speak up."

"How do I—"

"Die?" Ilana asked, amused. How quaint. The poor thing was asking her how to die. "That's easy," she said. "It's the most natural thing in the world. Just let it happen."

Kathy closed her eyes tight, her face straining with effort.

"Help me," she croaked.

Now that she had decided to die, the darkness that had seemed so close seemed to have suddenly retreated.

"No, no," Ilana said more gently. "You don't have to do anything. Just let it happen."

"I don't—Oh!"

Kathy's eyes snapped open, the pain and tension draining from her body. It was as if death, when it finally came, though she had been dreading and avoiding it, had nevertheless surprised her, as if it were the very last thing in the world she had expected.

They were always surprised.

"That's it," Ilana coached. "That's it. Just let it happen."

"Omygod, omygod, omygod," Kathy rambled, delirious. "I'm—I'm—I'm *coming!*"

"Yes." Ilana couldn't help but suppress a laugh. "You're coming."

Kathy moaned as her sphincter relaxed, amazed that

241

she could still feel shame as the warmth spread down the backs of her thighs.

Ilana stood on the wedge at the foot of the cross, balancing herself on either side of Kathy's pierced and bloodied feet, and pressed against the woman's convulsing body, her hands caressing the dying woman's breasts and face and hair.

"Don't be ashamed," she whispered. "You have never looked more beautiful in your life."

She kissed Kathy's blue lips with her tongue, nibbled the lobe of her left ear, and teased her way down the side of Kathy's throat to the place where the pulse beat strongest and loudest. Meanwhile, one hand worked its way down Kathy's belly to the furry golden triangle between her legs. Ilana bared her incisors in what could almost have been mistaken for a smile. Beneath her fingers she felt Kathy's body responding.

"I have to admit you gave it your best shot. I guess it was your love for your kids that kept you going. But it was also your guilt that did you in. Love is a double-edge sword, sweet Kathy."

With that, amid the aphrodisiacal stench of blood, sex, sweat, and feces, Ilana slid her teeth into Kathy's defenseless carotid.

For her part, Kathy was aware of nothing in her new world of darkness but the slightly unpleasant, slightly sexual feeling of someone sucking her throat. One by one the cells in her brain winked out. Her dying mind mercifully confused what was happening with past memories of nursing her babies, only she couldn't figure out why they were sucking her throat instead of her breasts.

In any event, the last thing she was conscious of was a tremendous feeling of love as another used her body to draw warmth and life and nourishment.

That and the sound of enthusiastic applause.

TWENTY-EIGHT

"So what did you think of this evening's performance?"

Ilana was sitting in front of the makeup mirror in her dressing room backstage while Paulette, dressed in a short leather dress that barely covered her ass, slowly brushed her mistress's long dark tresses. Ilana had sent one of the security men into the audience after the show to invite Kelly and Gwen backstage, and now they sat together on a sofa in the elegantly appointed room. From the angle of the chairs they could not see into the mirror, but Kelly had the distinct impression that Ilana was studying her face to decipher her true emotions.

She decided to be honest.

"I have to admit," she said, "I was somewhat shocked."

"Really," Ilana said. "May I ask what exactly disturbed you?"

Kelly hardly knew where to start.

She had seen more than her share of slasher movies, as well as the spurious "art" films of such schlockmasters as Dario Argento and Ivan Koski, and so had become jaded at the misogynist violence and indiscriminate bloodletting that dominated so many contemporary movies. As far as she was concerned, such films were nothing more than the wet dreams of would-be rapists, psychopaths, and serial killers, and their popularity among a growing number of the American population was a cause for genuine fear. Yet none of the gore-soaked masterpieces by either of those directors or a dozen less talented and stylish imitators could compare to the level of realism or the sheer, unadulterated violence, that she had seen in the Theater of Pain.

If she hadn't known better, she would have sworn that what she had seen on the stage had been real. She had watched in horror the torture of the man and woman on the crosses, and no matter how closely she observed she could find no seam in the performance to suggest that she had witnessed anything other than the actual suffering and death as it was portrayed by the two actors.

Of course, common sense told her that the man and woman did not really die onstage. To have believed that would have been preposterous. It would put her in the same category as the country bumpkin who rushes up onstage to protect the heroine from the villain, mistaking illusion for reality.

Still, the feel of her skin *crawling* on the back of her neck when she heard the woman screaming for help seemed visceral proof of what her mind insisted could not be happening.

"I don't know exactly," Kelly said, trying to answer her own confusion. "The violence—"

"Certainly you've seen its equal on film."

"Yes," Kelly agreed. "That just it. This was . . . live."

"And that disturbed you?"

"Not just that. The way it was depicted. There was no story. No moral. No socially redeeming message of any kind. Just violence for the sake of violence. It almost seemed to be . . ." Kelly stopped, groping for the word.

"Yes?" Ilana prompted.

"A . . . celebration."

Ilana turned in her chair and smiled. "A celebration. I like that. Yes, I like that very much. That's enough, Paulette," she said. "Please go fetch our young stars of the evening."

Ilana rose from the dressing table. She was wearing only a thin silk dressing robe, through which the outline of her elegant limbs were clearly visible. As she turned, the robe fell open, exposing her belly and the dark hair between her thighs. Kelly averted her eyes. She didn't want to think that the woman was being flagrantly sexual. Instead, she decided to give Ilana the benefit of the doubt. She reminded herself that in Europe they had different standards of modesty than they did in America.

Ilana sat down on the red velvet chaise across the room, letting the gown open farther, exposing the inside curves of her perfect white breasts.

"And why shouldn't violence be a celebration?" she asked. "What better way to transcend a necessary evil? As the Marquis de Sade once said, the only way to accept death is to eroticize it."

"But you are encouraging it," Kelly said. She had quickly reached into her handbag to switch on her microrecorder while Ilana was moving to the chaise, and now she dropped her eyes to make sure that it was working. She saw the tiny plastic wheels turning. "Aren't you afraid that by eroticizing violence you will encourage more people to commit violent acts?"

"Look around you," Ilana said. "Can you possibly argue that my little shows can be responsible for even a fraction of the violence that exists in the world? On the contrary, I propose to you that our existence itself is violent—and I'm not speaking of what you find on the crime-beat page of the daily paper. I mean the price of life is violence."

The robe fell open even farther, and Ilana's breasts

and belly were now fully exposed. It was impossible to believe that she was unaware of her nakedness, or that she wasn't deliberately using it to make them uncomfortable. Was this one of Ilana's lessons? Or a blatant attempt at seduction? Kelly tried to keep her eyes fixed on Ilana's face, but she felt her eyes flick almost involuntarily over the woman's voluptuous body. Each time she did so, Ilana seemed to catch the lapse in her attention. Kelly blushed, and thought she saw a smile playing on the other woman's sensuous lips.

"We cannot live a single day," Ilana continued, "without doing violence to some form of life, whether it's the food we consume, the microbes in the air we inhale, or the thousands of cells that perish each day within our own bodies so that new cells may be created and we may continue to live. No religion has adequately handled the basic immorality of life. The Jains went to perhaps the greatest lengths. They used to go about sweeping the ground before them with small brooms, lest they should inadvertently crush some hapless insect that crossed their path. What they didn't realize was that every time our immune system repels a flu virus, or destroys a cancerous cell, or eradicates a germ that has invaded our body unbeknownst to us, we are guilty of holocausts. We cannot escape the fact that there is no way to live except to deliver death to some other form of life that wants to take our place."

"You said no religion resolves this paradox. Is that what you're trying to do in the Theater of Pain?"

"No," Ilana said bluntly. "The Theater of Pain is a safety valve, a way to express our outrage at the fundamental violence at the heart of existence and to transmute it through the erotic into a form of art from which we can all take pleasure. Outside these walls, the violence of the world is an ugly, squalid, brutal affair. What we do is make the unavoidable beautiful. Is that not humanity's highest calling? To give meaning to suffering, to ennoble the struggle against disease, to bring hope to the finality of death? Is that not what all of the greatest artists throughout history have tried to accomplish? That, too, is what our much maligned practice is all about. S-M is not a sexual dysfunction. Or a fetish. It is a religious calling. It is an artistic response. It is the stamp of a superior mind."

"I was surprised," Kelly said, "at how many famous people there were in the audience."

"You shouldn't be. Think about it: For the most part, people who have accomplished something in their lives have usually done so at the expense of others. They understand better than most the principles that I have been discussing." Ilana turned to Gwen. "What about you, my dear? You have been extraordinarily quiet. What did you think?"

Gwen had been uncharacteristically tongue-tied throughout the entire interview. Now she blushed a bright cherry-red as Ilana questioned her.

"Come on." Ilana smiled. "Don't be shy. As you can see, your friend Kelly feels quite free to challenge me, as she should. It is only when all doubts are quieted that one hears the voice of truth. Speak your mind; I won't bite."

"It was . . ."

"Sexy?"

"Yes," Gwen muttered, blushing even more furiously.

"I am glad you enjoyed it," Ilana said, as if she and Gwen shared an intimate secret. "Ah, here are my pets now."

Kelly looked up and saw that Paulette had reentered the room leading the two young actors from the playlet. They were fresh from the shower, no longer in their stage makeup, each wearing nothing but a tiny white G-string that left little to the imagination.

"Bravo," Ilana clapped her hands. "You were magnificent. Come here, my pets, let me kiss you."

The man and woman padded obediently over to the chaise, kneeling on either side of the chair, as Ilana turned to one and then the other, kissing each of them deeply on the mouth.

If they noticed Gwen and Kelly in the room, the pair didn't show it. They seemed to share their mistress's lack of modesty, staring with wide, worshipful eyes at their patron. Kelly began to wonder if this, too, was all part of the performance.

"As you can see," Ilana said, "they've suffered no serious damage from the night's entertainments. Have you, my pets?"

"No, mistress," they replied.

It seemed to be true. As far as Kelly could tell, their bodies bore no trace of the grievous mortal wounds they seemed to have suffered on the stage.

Ilana touched the woman on the breasts. "I was lucky to find them. They really are husband and wife. There's a certain chemistry you just can't fake. Not only that, but they are true submissives. They need the pain. Don't you, my pets?"

"Yes, mistress," they chimed.

Ilana continued to fondle them absently.

Later, she ordered the husband and wife to remove their G-strings and make love on the floor while she continued, completely unaffected, her lecture on domination.

TWENTY-NINE

Ilana insisted on having a car take them home after the show in spite of Kelly's protests that they could just as easily catch a cab outside the club. "In this part of town the streets are dangerous at this hour," Ilana argued. "I'd feel responsible if anything were to happen to you."

Kelly relented once it became clear that Ilana wouldn't take no for an answer. Satisfied, Ilana summoned her driver and instructed him to take them home. The driver was no steroid-pumped pretty boy like the club's doormen, but a tall, muscular, middle-aged fellow with a receding blond hairline and the chiseled features of a Gestapo chief. "Take good care of my friends, Henrik," Ilana told him when he arrived at the door of the dressing room. "Make sure they get home safely."

"Yes, mistress," he said in a crisp German accent. He turned to Kelly and Gwen. "Follow me."

He led them out the back of the club to the limousine waiting in the alley. He held the door open until they climbed inside and then walked around to the front of the car.

There was a shield of smoky privacy glass separating the front and back seats of the spacious limousine.

Nonetheless, Kelly was careful not to say anything about what they had seen at the club, for fear the driver might overhear them through the intercom. Instead, they sat quietly, looking out at the early-morning city streets, the homeless picking through the rubble as if it were the day after the apocalypse.

On the other side of the glass, the driver didn't say a word until they crossed Forty-second Street, and then it was only to ask them where they lived. His harsh voice, made harsher by the heavy German accent, cracked through the intercom, startling them both. A short time later they were speeding down a deserted Queensboro Bridge out of Manhattan.

Kelly directed the driver to drop them off in front of Gus's, half a block away from her building.

"Sorry, *fraulein*," the driver said. "I am to see you to your door."

"It's okay," Kelly explained. "I live nearby."

"I have my orders," he said. He explained that he had been instructed to take them home; where they went after that was their business. He said it in the polite but unyielding tone they used in those old World War II movies, when they were trying to get information out of some poor captured Allied soldier.

Kelly felt herself growing angry, but she realized there was no use getting into an argument with the man. He was set on having his way.

Ilana's way.

He had made it abundantly clear that she was his mistress, and he obeyed no one but her.

Reluctantly, she directed him to her building, trying to convince herself that she was only being paranoid about not wanting the man to know where she lived. After all, Ilana could find out easily enough through her employment records at Captive Hearts. The driver came around and opened the door, and they climbed out of the car. He stood on the sidewalk and waited until they had unlocked the outside door, stepped inside the building, and waved from the vestibule. Only then did he get back into the limousine and pull away.

"Asshole," Kelly muttered.

They stood in the vestibule and waited until they saw the limousine slow down at the end of the block and round the corner before they stepped back onto the street and doubled the half block back to Gus's.

Kelly took her usual seat in one of the booths by the window, and Gwen slid in across from her. Kelly often came to the diner for coffee on her way home from a club she was reviewing in order to collect her thoughts and look over her notes. It was a quiet neighborhood place, and she had been coming here for such a long time that all the waitresses knew her, letting her sit as long as she liked, scribbling into her notebook, and they refilled her coffee cup without her even having to ask.

Doreen was on duty tonight.

Kelly liked Doreen. She was an aspiring actress who had come to New York from Wisconsin over fifteen years ago to make it big on Broadway. She was nearly forty now and well past her prime, but she hadn't given up her dream, still scanning the trade papers, going on auditions during the day, and waiting tables at Gus's at night to pay the rent. There must be tens of thousands like her all over the city, men and women who spent the best years of their lives barely scraping out a living in dead-end jobs, just for that one chance to grab the brass ring. If there was ever any trace of bitterness in Doreen, it certainly didn't show. Though delicately lined by age and smudged by years of burning the candle at both ends, her face still glowed with the unmistakable light of eternal hope that kept her looking a good ten years younger than she really was.

"Evening, Kelly," she said, practicing her Irish brogue, armed with a pot of Gus's blackest brew.

"Evening, Doreen," Kelly said, turning over a heavy chipped cup. "How goes it?"

"Same old same old," Doreen said. "Pretty slow tonight. Gus's prostate is acting up so he's cranky as hell, one of the girl's called out sick, and my feet are killing me. How about you?"

"Okay. Just got back from one of the lower rungs in the Inferno. Place called Domination. Ever been there?"

"Nope," she said. "Don't think so."

"Believe me, you'd remember if you had."

Doreen laughed. "Coffee, hon?" she said, swinging the pot Gwen's way.

"None for me, thanks," Gwen said.

Across the table, Gwen was obsessively tearing an empty sugar packet into pink confetti. She seemed wired, preoccupied. She hadn't said more than a half dozen words since they left Domination. It was as if she were lost in her own thoughts.

Kelly didn't blame her. She was preoccupied herself. What she had seen at the club was unsettling, and yet somehow provocative in a way she was not yet ready to admit even to herself.

"I feel like I just stepped out of the Twilight Zone," Kelly said. "What a scene."

"I think I'm in love," Gwen said. "What a goddess."

"Calm down." Kelly laughed. So that was her problem. Typical Gwen. "She looks like she had her hands full to me."

Gwen shook her head. "I thought she was going to suggest a group scene right there."

"Hoping, you mean."

"Bitch." Gwen grinned. "What was it with those two actors anyway? They looked like zombies."

"They were supposed to be love slaves."

"Yeah," Gwen said. "I should be so lucky. You could keep the guy, but the housewife wasn't bad. Do you suppose the whole thing was an act?"

Kelly shrugged. "It was a fantasy scenario. They probably got off on the idea."

"Who would fantasize about being crucified?"

Kelly thought of some of the fantasies she'd encountered at Captive Hearts. In the beginning she, too, had found many of the fantasies bizarre, if not downright repellent. But in time she had begun to have a more tolerant view of the men and women who came to her. More often than not, they had suffered for years with guilt and shame over their fantasies. Yet even in the most violent and perverse fantasies, Kelly could recognize touching instances of genuine humanity. She had begun to feel a certain amount of respect, even love, for those who had the courage to face their darkest desires. In time, Kelly had come to think of her job as a dominatrice as more therapist than anything else. Like a therapist, she helped people confront the truth about themselves.

"You'd be surprised. People fantasize about the damndest things."

"What do you fantasize about?"

Kelly shot her a look.

"Sorry," Gwen said. "Can't blame a girl for trying. Anyway, it was a pretty convincing act they put on."

Was that all it really was, an act? Something to outrage a jaded public?

Or was it something more sinister?

Certainly the two actors did not appear to bear any lasting ill effects from the treatment they had received. The nails, the pliers, the mallet must have all been stage props, though a more realistic demonstration Kelly had never witnessed. She had seen the nails piercing the flesh, seen the couple's bodies quake with pain, their faces drain of expression as death finally came to them.

Kelly remembered what Ilana had said at their first meeting in the penthouse, about equality being the great American sacred cow. How we held to religious belief that all men and women were created equal, when, in fact, the idea that there were two unequal classes of people, one meant to serve and sacrifice itself to the other, was far older, far more powerful. Was that what Domination was, a place to provoke that one and only American taboo?

Perhaps that was the angle she could take on her story. She pulled out her pad, jotted down a few notes.

"Yoo hoo," Gwen said. "Hey, didn't anyone ever tell you it was rude to start writing in the middle of a conversation?"

Kelly looked up from her pad. "Sorry," she said.

Gwen yawned, stretched. "That's okay. I'm going, anyway. Gotta get up for work . . ." she checked her watch ". . . in about three hours. Got a ten-o'clock tour to give."

"I'll call you."

"Thanks for the invite."

"Thanks for coming along and providing some instant sanity."

Kelly glanced out the window. False dawn. The street was brightening, but the sun wouldn't come up for another hour or so. "Will you be okay?"

"Are you kidding? I've got my Mace, my dog whistle, my penny-roll. I'm a walking arsenal of feminine self-defense. Besides, haven't you heard? Crime is down two whole percent in the subway this year."

Kelly shook her head.

She had long since given up worrying about Gwen. It could easily become a full-time job.

Kelly watched as her friend walked down the damp

254

street to the subway entrance at the corner, descending down the dark stairs. Just then, Doreen came to refill her coffee. Kelly was going to need it. She had a long morning of work ahead of her. Her story on domination was due to Joan by the end of the month, and she wanted to catch her impressions of the night past while they were still fresh in her mind.

Kelly reread the notes she had jotted down so far.

What had Ilana said about life needing death and how had it tied in with her theory of domination?

Kelly rummaged around in her bag until she found the microcassette recorder she had used to record their conversation. She pushed the reverse button until she was about halfway through the tape and punched the playback.

Nothing.

She reversed the tape a little farther and played the tape back. She heard her own voice through the speaker finishing one of the questions she had asked Ilana, but in the space afterwards there was no answer.

Kelly shook the recorder, rewound the tape, and played it all the way through.

At regular intervals she heard her own voice, but in every place Ilana spoke there was nothing but the blue fuzz of eternity.

THIRTY

Rossi parked his car across the street from the railyard and walked across the tracks toward a group of parked subway cars near the front of the platform. The M train terminated at Metropolitan Avenue by the old Lutheran Cemetery in Queens. Rossi spotted a uniformed cop standing guard outside one of the passenger cars and headed in his direction. He was no more than halfway there when he spotted Graham waving to him from the open door.

"Same as before?" Rossi said as he made it to the car's stairs.

Graham nodded. He made room as Rossi squeezed past him into the car.

"Jesus Christ. What's that smell?"

"Someone lost his breakfast," Graham said, pointing to a milky-white slick that looked like creamed chipped beef on the floor. "Watch your step."

The girl was hanging upside down from one of the straphandles, naked as meat, her pale feet crossed above the leather handle as if in prayer. His eyes followed the inexorable line of her body, down her long legs, over her pubis, her flat belly, her small, pointed breasts.

"Where's the head?" he said flatly.

Graham pointed to the seat behind Rossi.

There, on a sheet of yesterday's *New York Post*, sat the head of a young Oriental woman, her long dark hair combed away from her delicate face. Her dark eyes were fixed, bulging almost comically, as if surprised to see her body asserting its independence. Under the head, a small ring of blood had stained the paper around the blackened neck stump. Other than that, Rossi saw no other blood in the car.

"Who found her?"

"The conductor," Graham said. "He's in there."

They went to the next car, where Mantucci, inexplicably stripped to his shirtsleeves in the chill car, was taking the statement of a young black man doubled-over on one of the plastic seats. The conductor was clutching his knees to his chest, holding his head between his legs, as if he were seasick. Whenever he answered a question he lifted his face, and Rossi could see the misery etched into his features, not to mention the vomit stains on the front of his shirt.

The man explained that he had been walking back through the train after it pulled into the station, as he always did after a run, to make sure that there were no homeless people aboard, when he found the dead woman. When Rossi interrupted his statement to ask why he hadn't noticed anything out of the ordinary earlier, the man was too sick to deny that he had been asleep in the conductor's car for most of the evening.

Another black man in a transit uniform was standing by the open door, nervously smoking a cigarette. He was about twenty years older than the conductor, mid-forties, his hair receding up the front of his skull like brown foam. His red-rimmed eyes kept jumping around the car, looking everywhere but at Rossi. The man had a bad case of the sniffles, and, in late November—with hay fever season long over and flu season still weeks away—that could mean only one thing.

"You the driver?" Rossi asked.

"Yes, sir," the man said.

"You see anything?"

"No, sir."

"Think hard," Rossi said. He had half a mind to send the man downtown for a drug test. Not long ago, a transit driver on crack had caused an accident killing nearly a dozen riders. "No one get on that looked suspicious?"

"I remember a man getting on with a woman who looked drunk."

"When was that?"

The driver shrugged. "I dunno. Sometime early. Three in the morning, mebbe."

"Where'd they get on?"

"Fulton Street," the driver said. "I forget. Maybe Essex . . ."

Fulton, Rossi thought.

Not far from Chinatown. That sounded about right.

"The man. What did he look like?"

The driver shrugged again. "It was dark. I didn't see his face."

Rossi pulled out the sheet of paper in his pocket and showed it to the driver.

He studied the figure of the faceless man in black ascending the Vatican stairs. He looked up at Rossi, his red-rimmed eyes showing recognition.

"I dunno," he said. "Could be him. Like I said, I didn't see his face."

Rossi folded the paper and put it back in his pocket. The driver had recognized him, even if he hadn't realized it consciously. Subconsciously, he'd made the match.

The smell in the car was making Rossi sick. He stepped outside onto the platform into the open air. It was a gray, overcast day, the clouds black smudges inching across the sky. Every time the wind gusted Rossi felt a sprinkle of hard rain against his face.

He reached inside his jacket and pulled out his cigarettes. Lighting up, he stared out at the yard of parked subway cars, some only temporarily out of service, some derailed and waiting for repair, all of them looking especially forlorn in the late autumn air. He considered the lines of track that met from all over the city, like a river of steel and electricity, and marked its terminus here, carrying the body of the girl in the car to this desolate place, not far from the cemetery.

Rossi heard a click and a whirr and jerked his head to the side.

Alongside the train, a reporter was talking to the uniformed cop standing outside the train. A few yards behind him, a skinny photographer in a bulky military-style jacket was pointing a telephoto lens through one of the train windows.

Rossi saw red.

Throwing away his cigarette, he charged up the platform, shouting at the man with the camera, who started backing away, a look of alarm on his face.

Rossi passed the cop and the reporter, frozen in tableaux, and grabbed the photographer by the coat, throwing him up against the train. He grabbed for the camera, trying to wrestle it away, but it was secured to the man by a strap that passed across his chest and underneath his arm.

"Give me that film, you sick bastard," Rossi spat in the man's frightened face. "Give it to me now or I'll break your fucking neck!"

He slammed the man against the train again and was about to do it a third time when he felt a heavy hand clamp down on his shoulder and effortlessly spin him around.

Rossi suddenly found himself staring into Graham's

meaty face. The big cop was shouting at him, but for the first few seconds Rossi heard nothing but the roar of his own blood rushing through his ears.

"What the hell're you doing?" Graham growled under his breath. "We don't need a problem with the fucking newspaper, man."

"You're right," Rossi muttered, feeling ashamed of himself. He knew what he'd done was stupid. It could cost them both a suspension, at the very least a reassignment. "Sorry. I just lost it."

"You're lucky he didn't have that camera focused on you. We don't need no front-page exposure on the cover of *Newsday* of you beating up on a reporter while a serial killer roams free."

"You're right," Rossi said. "You think you could put me down now?"

Hardly realizing it, Graham had lifted Rossi nearly off his feet. He lowered him gently and jerked his partner's coat back into place.

"Let me go see if I can straighten things out with his buddy over there," Graham said.

The big cop walked over to the reporter, turning on the Irish charm.

"My partner there," he smiled, "he didn't mean anything by what he did. He was just a little upset by what he'd seen in there. It's pretty gruesome. Please apologize to your photographer for us."

"My photographer?" the reporter said. "I thought he was with you guys. I never saw him before in my life."

"What the fuck—" Graham turned to Rossi, who looked down the platform, over the tracks, and between the cars parked in the railyard.

The man with the camera was gone.

THIRTY-ONE

Hillary stared at the article with a feeling of dread.

She was sitting in the observatory in her nightgown, reading the papers. Outside the glass walls of the room the gray Atlantic swelled ominously, the black clouds swooping down on the water like vultures. She had already read the article three times, as if half expecting to find her name there. It was a short article buried on page three of the city section of *The New York Times* about a woman found murdered in a Queens subway terminus. The article identified the woman as Nancy Li, twenty-four, of Chinatown. It went on to say that she was the single mother of a three-year-old girl and had worked as an assistant manager in a midtown bookstore.

Hillary remembered the pretty Oriental woman they had picked up outside an East Village club the night before.

They had drugged her and stripped her in the back of the limousine while Degas drove them back to the mansion. Monica had instructed Hillary to kneel before the girl and serve her orally, while Monica took a small razor and opened a vein in the girl's breast and sucked the blood that ran down her nipple.

Hillary grudgingly did as she was told, though she didn't like the idea of going down on the girl one bit. To her, it seemed an act of humility. She thought that Monica was going to teach her the art of torture, and instead she had her playing the role of geisha. Still, she didn't dare disobey Monica. The idea that Monica might leave her again was too terrifying to contemplate. So she crouched on her knees on the floor of the limousine. In spite of her state, maybe because of it, the girl began responding to Hillary's oral ministrations, though Hillary spitefully made sure to mix the girl's pleasure with pain, nipping her clitoris and the inside of her labia with her teeth whenever she thought the girl might come.

By the time they arrived at the mansion their victim had fully revived. Frightened to the point of paralysis, she hadn't struggled at all as they laid her on the stone floor, tied her wrists behind her back, and shackled her ankles together with a thick leather cuff. They attached a hook to the iron eyelet bolted into the ankle cuff and hoisted her body into the air by winch over a tub of ice-cold water. They let her contemplate her predicament for a few moments, twisting helplessly in the air above the water, babbling incoherently for mercy, before Monica gave the signal for Degas to slowly lower her into the water until her head and shoulders were totally submerged.

The girl writhed and thrashed and tried to jackknife her body at the waist in a vain attempt to raise her head out of the water. Monica waited impassively until the struggling stopped, the girl's held breath exploding from her lungs, making the water boil, her body hanging motionless from the chain, before she gave Degas the signal to turn the winch. Once clear of the water, the girl had begun choking violently, expelling water from her lungs, gasping so hard it almost sounded as if she were drowning on air instead of water. They did this over and over again, one time even waiting until the girl's skin had turned a steely blue and Hillary thought for sure that she was dead, before pulling her up out of the water.

After the fight had gone out of her they had led the girl to a specially constructed torture stool that resembled one of those ergonomic chairs they sold for high-tech offices, except this one was designed to render its occupant as helpless and accessible as possible. Once strapped onto the stool, the girl's body was thrust forward, providing access to both her buttocks and her genitals, all her weight thrown against her bent knees, leaving even the soles of her feet exposed. Her wrists were secured above her head to a Y-shaped bar running from below, which left her breasts free, while a heavy rubber band cinched around her neck and knotted through the back uprights ensured that her head remained relatively immobile.

Monica took a candle from the wall and walked around the bound girl. She brought the flame close to her face, her breasts, her genitals. The girl tried to pull away, but she was bound too tightly. She walked behind the stool and brought the candle close to the girl's squirming feet. Monica held the candle to the defenseless flesh, methodically burning the soles of each foot until they could smell the flesh roasting. She returned to the front of the stool, lowering the candle to the girl's small breasts, letting the warmth lick the tender flesh, and then letting the flame kiss her nipple.

The girl screamed, but Monica did not move the flame until it burnt itself out.

Pain sobered her, and the girl found the words to plead. "What do you want with me?"

"We need you for a ritual of magic," Hillary said, as Monica returned to the wall to relight the wick of the candle.

"Ritual," the girl said breathlessly. Hillary saw a

shudder pass through her. "Are you some kind of Satanists?"

"Satanists?" Monica said, returning with the lighted candle. "I'm afraid not. There is no such thing as Satan."

Slowly the fire did its work, reducing the soft pink bud of the girl's nipple to a nub of charcoal. Monica repeated the process with the other nipple.

"By the time we are done with you," she said, "you'll be begging me to let you die. No one will want you."

Monica proceeded to burn the girl, roasting her lips, her fingers, her toes, her genitals. When she was done with the flame she produced a collection of long steel needles and, heating them until they were red-hot, she grabbed the girl's buttocks and pierced her with the needle until it had all but disappeared into her flesh. Hillary could hardly tell whether the girl screamed louder when the needle entered her flesh or when Monica pulled it out, but the sound was making her delirious with a kind of passion. She watched as Monica turned the girl's buttocks into a pincushion, then turned her attention to stabbing other tender parts of her body with the long needles. Monica thrust a needle through the girl's nostrils, skewered her breasts together, and finally sealed her lips together with two large needles that made it all but impossible for her to scream.

The girl slumped forward on the stool, held up only by her bondage and the rubber strap around her head and jaw. Where she had once been quite lovely to look at, she was now a hideous mass of burns, bruises, and blood. Monica produced a strange contraption of leather straps and metal thumbscrews that she called the fool's crown, explaining that it was used during the Inquisition to punish heretics. She grabbed the girl by the sweat-soaked hair and shook her awake by lightly slapping her on her swollen cheeks. She placed the leather contraption over her head, tightening the straps until it fit securely around her head, the metal screws coming into contact at various places around her skull, including the vulnerable area at her temples.

Hillary could guess what was coming next.

Sure enough, Monica tightened the screws in the headgear little by little while verbally abusing the girl, who seemed to be willing herself to die. Hillary watched, fascinated, as the screws eventually did their work, punching through the thin bone in the girl's temples, sending a clear pinkish fluid running from the girl's nostrils, which Monica reached over hurriedly to lick away. She stared back at Hillary, her eyes shining.

"Brain fluid," she said.

In the corner, Degas began to retch.

She helped release the girl from the stool and watched as Monica lifted the girl effortlessly over her shoulder and carried her to a leather chaise in the corner of the playroom. She laid her out on the chair and began to undress, motioning for Hillary to join her. When they were both naked they stretched out on either side of the dead girl, who lay staring sightlessly up to the vaulted ceiling. Hillary could feel her heart pounding with excitement, pounding until it nearly felt as if it would burst from her chest, her passion choking her.

Hillary watched as Monica stroked the dead girl, as she bent her head to one of the small bruised breasts. When she lifted her face her lips were red with blood.

"Taste," Monica said heavily.

Hillary leaned forward, the blood blooming on the girl's breast like a dark fruit, and licked it away, only to watch the blood bloom there again.

"The forbidden," Monica whispered. "Taste. It is the wine of life."

Nothing could have prevented her from doing so. The thirst had risen in her like a monstrous winged shadow. Hillary leaned forward again, and this time she did not sip tentatively, but drank deeply, as if to drain the girl dry, as if to drain the world dry, as if hoping to leave it a bitter grape hanging in the cosmos. She tasted the blood pouring into her mouth, but more than blood she tasted the girl herself—her memories, her dreams, her hopes, her fears—all of it washed over Hillary, leaving her dizzy with ecstasy.

Hillary fell back, surfeited at last, her eyes swimming with visions.

Monica shook her arm, waking her from her drugged dreams of the temple, of the statues lining the colonade, of the marble woman.

"This poor girl," Monica said, "has given you her life. Her pain and blood she has offered to you in prayer. You must give thanks for what you've taken. You must give her the ecstasy she seeks."

"She's dead," Hillary said wearily. "What can I do for her now?"

"Make love to her."

Hillary felt the passion grow in her again. Yes, that was it, wasn't it? The forbidden desire she had always dreamed of consummating. She looked up at Monica and saw the evil in the other woman's eyes and knew it was only the reflection of her own.

"How?"

Monica took Hillary's hand and laid it on the girl's charred breast. She moved it over the girl's soft belly, between her bruised thighs, onto her cooling sex.

"Our power extends beyond the gates of death," Monica said. "Ours is the dominion over life itself."

"Oh, yes," Hillary breathed. "Oh, yes."

She could feel the excitement building inside her, frightened only by the possibility that she would be struck dead, her body unable to withstand it all. She stretched herself upon the girl's corpse, placing her

266

mouth over the girl's cold lips, moving herself over the lifeless body beneath her, remembering the Vampire's performance at the Theater of Pain. She suddenly knew what to do without being told, as if the information had always been stored somewhere deep inside her, awaiting only this moment to manifest itself. She kissed the dead girl passionately, moving her mouth along the side of her neck, placing a string of poisonous kisses inside her shoulder to the soft rise of her left breast. There, she lifted her head, feeling the teeth slide out from under her gums, and lowered her head, closing her mouth over the girl's breast.

She moved against the girl's cold body, feeling it move beneath her, obedient to her desire. She felt the energy galvanize the flesh beneath her like an electric current, rising up her spine, pouring from her mouth into the girl's chest, jolting her heart to life. Her hand reached down between the girl's thighs, and Hillary felt the moisture there. At first she thought she had only imagined it, thought the movements merely the response of lifeless flesh, until she felt the arms around her head, legs wrapped around the small of her back, the breath in her hair.

Hillary felt confused and then frightened. But the instinct had already taken over, turning the fear into excitement as she felt the throbbing of the girl's heart inside her teeth. The girl began moaning, her body growing rigid with impending orgasm. Hillary held it off for a few heartbeats more and braced herself as the force of the girl's orgasm blindsided her, blinding her with a rapture unlike any she'd ever known. When it was over Hillary pushed herself away from the corpse as if she'd just escaped from death herself. She lay back on the chaise, her body lathered in sweat and blood, trying to figure out what had just happened to her.

"Look," Monica said.

Hillary looked up and saw the miracle that had transpired. The girl's body was no longer a roadmap of pain and death. Her bruised lips had healed, her mangled breasts were white and pink, her ravaged thighs restored to innocence. But what was more amazing than that was that the girl's opened eyes were no longer staring soullessly into eternity. Instead, there was the unmistakable light of consciousnessness there, even though it was dimmed to the blaze of a single hunger.

"We take men mortal," Monica said, "and we give them immortality."

In her confused state it had made a warped sense to Hillary, the way things made sense in dreams or when drunk, though the same things made no sense in the morning.

Though her sessions with Monica had been exciting at first, Hillary had begun to grow frightened that things were spinning out of control. Monica had told her not to worry, that there was no way they could trace the girl back to them, and besides, hadn't she seen the girl alive with her own eyes? Whatever it was that Monica was doing, she was messing with Hillary's mind. Hillary knew the girl was dead, that she couldn't have survived the torture they had inflicted on her, and yet, sure enough, she had seen the girl alive and whole again. She had made love to her, had felt her body responding, had seen her dress and leave the mansion.

So what had happened to her afterwards?

Hillary couldn't help but worry. If she were found out now, all of her plans would be destroyed. Lately, the things she and Monica did in the playroom had begun to scare her. She felt her hold on sanity slowly but steadily slipping away. Hillary thought of the dead Italian countess and the mysterious circumstances surrounding her demise and began to wonder if her death were really an accident after all.

Yet there was no easy way for her to end her relationship with Monica. Not now. Hillary was indebted to her. The woman knew enough to destroy her. She had set out to become a master and now found herself the slave of this strange and enigmatic woman.

Hillary turned back to the first page of the *Times*, where a picture of Edmund headed column one with an article listing him as ahead in the polls by twenty-one percentage points.

The magic, the pain, the blood. It was all working. But if anyone found out what she was doing, she would end up in prison.

She felt the Vampire's hand on her shoulders, pushing away the thin material of the nightgown and massaging the bare flesh. Her voice was like a song in Hillary's ear, her perfume sweet and intoxicating as raw meat. *Since when did raw meat seem intoxicating?* A slow, insinuating fog passed in front of Hillary's mind.

"You overtax yourself," the Vampire whispered in her ear. "Why don't you put the paper down now and come to bed?"

The Vampire's hand slid down the front of the negligee, playing with the rings in Hillary's pierced nipples.

"Come to bed now," Monica whispered again, and Hillary found herself rising from the chair, putting down her paper, her body already responding to the mere suggestion of the Vampire's embrace.

THIRTY-TWO

Kelly walked around the spacious loft while Connor fixed dinner in the kitchen area.

The walls were covered with Connor's work, framed photographic studies of nudes and nature scenes, still-lifes and everyday objects beside portrait studies of celebrities and politicians. Kelly recognized the faces of Ronald Reagan, Pope John Paul, and Madonna among shots of ordinary people going about their daily business. Kelly stopped at one such photograph in which a beautiful model type stood smoking a cigarette while her female poodle lowered her backside to pee. Ostensibly, it was a vulgar subject, but through Connor's lens it had taken on an elegance that raised it from its meager origins and imbued it with the indefinable and yet unmistakable air of sublimest poetry.

She remembered the photos he had shown her at the gallery. In the hands of a less talented photographer the dominatrices he had snapped would have seemed no different than the cum shots she had seen in the magazines at Captive Hearts. Somehow Connor had managed to capture the feline grace of the leather-clad women, the atavistic power of their sexuality, the sensual allure of their dangerous feminism. In his photographs the leather costume and bondage paraphernalia were not simply a sexual kink, but the vestments of a sacred sorority of high priestesses whose goal was the liberation of the human spirit.

Somehow Connor had captured what for Kelly was the essence of domination.

"Dinner's ready," Connor called out from the kitchen.

He was wearing an apron tied around his waist, protecting a pair of jeans and a white cotton shirt rolled up at the sleeves. His hair was still damp from the shower.

Kelly felt an almost irresistible urge to run her fingers through his mussed hair, to kiss him on his full, sensuous lips.

She had already decided that tonight would be the night if he made the first move. Actually, Kelly had already prepared to nudge him in the right direction. Her work at Captive Hearts gave her firsthand experience in the subtle power a woman had over a male's sexual response. Tonight she had chosen her outfit carefully: a short black evening dress, smoky seamed stockings, black high-heeled sandals, and a triple-strand choker collar of faux pearls. The ensemble was a little too dressy for a quiet dinner at his place, but that was exactly the point.

There was something maddening about Connor's cool and distant manner. She was sure that he was attracted to her; she had felt it since their first meeting at Captive Hearts. Yet he seemed to be holding himself back, as if afraid to express his feelings for her. She could sense the almost supernatural control he kept over himself, and it fascinated and frustrated her at the same time. Most men she had known, including Eric, couldn't wait to get into her panties. The possibility that Connor might be gay flashed through her mind. After all, he was artistic, good-looking, and cultured. It was a sad commentary on the male population in general that those three characteristics immediately called into question a man's masculinity, but it was unfortunately an observable fact, learned after several painful past experiences. She was sure, however, that Connor wasn't homosexual. There was something so irrevocably male about him that made the thought ludicrous. She remembered the look that had come over his face when she had hit him with the whip during the session at Captive Hearts. It was the look of a ravenous tiger—the look of a man who wanted to eat her up. Just the memory of it made her feel like Jell-O inside. So what was it that he was hiding?

Kelly sat down at the whitewashed oak-and-tile table in the dining area. Connor took out a slim gold lighter and lit the two tall candles in the center of the table. He filled their glasses with a pale red wine and sat down opposite her.

A vase of fresh flowers stood between the two burning tapers.

"I hope you like Vivaldi," he said, referring to the music on the stereo.

"Yes," Kelly said. *"Four Seasons,* isn't it?"

Connor smiled, looking pleased. "That's right. I heard it performed in Rome three years ago when they were making this recording."

The same words in another man's mouth might have sounded like braggadoccio. Somehow, Connor made it sound so matter of fact.

"I like music that aids the digestion when I'm eating. I'm not sure Vivaldi would take that as a compliment of *Four Seasons,* but—"

They both laughed.

"What are we having?" Kelly asked. "It smells delicious."

"Gnocchi," Connor said. "Have you ever had it?"

Kelly had seen it on the menu of an Italian place Eric

used to take her to, but neither of them had ever ordered it.

"It's a kind of dumpling," Connor explained. "Some consider it the original pasta of Italy."

He handed her a large flat plate on which a line of golden doughy crescents lay on a bed of grated parmesan. Over the top he had ladled fresh tomato sauce seasoned with parsley and oregano. He passed her a second small bowl, containing a fresh green bean salad with a rosé vinegarette dressing.

"How is it?" Connor asked as Kelly sampled a forkful of the gnocchi.

"It's delicious," Kelly said. "Really. Out of this world. Where did you ever learn to cook like this?"

"I studied at a cooking school in Paris for two years. My bohemian years, I call them, before I decided to do something practical and enrolled at Leipzig University to study German philosophy. My parents still can't figure out how I make a living taking pictures of nude ladies and park benches. They wonder when I'll get a real job."

"Do you see them often?"

Usually only around the holidays. They live in a condo in Florida now. Doing the retirement thing. My dad was a banker, so you can understand his concern over my unorthodox career. And your parents?"

"My parents died when I was six," Kelly said quietly. "I was raised pretty much by foster parents and the nuns of St. Peter's Catholic school in Dayton, Ohio."

"That must have been rough."

Kelly shrugged. "It was a long time ago. Kids are tougher than most people think."

She didn't want to go into the story again; not yet, anyway. It seemed she had just gone through the whole painful but mandatory process of opening up the old wounds of her past with Eric, and it was too soon to do it all over again. She just didn't have the stomach for it. She realized then that she wasn't really ready for a new relationship with anyone. She just wanted to take it easy for the time being and see where things went with Connor.

"In a way, I suppose it gives you a certain freedom," Connor said. "I mean, to do what you want and not have to explain yourself to anyone."

Kelly had often reflected on just that, but whenever she attempted to explain her situation in those terms to someone their reaction made her realize that they thought she sounded cold and heartless. People expected orphans to feel unloved and unhappy, and to carry the hurt and the bitterness around with them for the rest of their lives. Generally speaking, people liked to pity other people's misfortunes; it made them feel more fortunate themselves. Yet in spite of what Connor had said, Kelly discovered that even without family, there was always someone around to disapprove of what you were doing with your life. All she had to do was think of Gwen. Or Eric. Better yet, not think of Eric.

"Speaking of which, how is your story coming along?"

Kelly took a sip of her wine. "I still have a way to go on the writing," she said. "But the research is going quite well. I just had an interview with the woman who runs Captive Hearts. Her name is Ilana."

"Yes, I've heard of her."

"You *have?*"

"You don't have to look so surprised. You're forgetting, I'm not a complete square. After all, I am a photographer, part of the demimonde, too, you know." Connor grinned.

"Sorry," Kelly said. "Where did you hear about her, anyway? She keeps a pretty low profile from what I can judge."

"She's one of the city's true characters. She owns an underground theater so exclusive it is almost impossible to get a ticket. I've been trying for months. It's called Domination, I think. They present live S-M shows for the rich and famous. From what I understand, it's pretty heavy-duty stuff."

"I went," Kelly said. "Ilana herself invited me the night before last. Believe me, everything you've heard about Domination is true. And then some."

"Really," Connor said. He filled his glass with wine and reached across to refill Kelly's. "What did you think of her?"

Kelly toyed with the wineglass, letting her finger trail around the edge.

"She's a strange woman. It's hard to tell whether she's serious about half the things she says. If she is, I'd have to say she's a monster. Certainly a fascist. I keep trying to see the sense of humor, the spirit of play in what they do at Captive Hearts, and though sometimes I can spot it under all the games of pain and discipline, more often than not there seems to be something grimmer and darker at work that fits right into Ilana's might-makes-right philosophy. She's either one of the most clever women I've ever met or the most evil."

"Do you think she'd sit for a photograph?" Connor asked. "She'd be perfect for my S-M series. Could you get me an interview with her—or perhaps an invitation to Domination?"

"I doubt that she'd be open to such a thing. Besides, I'm still undercover. She has no idea I'm writing a story on her or Domination. I don't suppose she'll be happy when she finds out. I'm trying not to think about that. I understand she's got quite a reputation for making things nasty for her enemies. I've been reminded more than once that she's a relative of the Hungarian countess, Elisabet Bathory. As far as she knows, I'm just another one of her leather girls."

Connor nodded. "I understand. I wouldn't expect you to jeopardize your story." He finished his wine and ate another forkful of gnocchi. "I think you're undestimating yourself, though."

"What do you mean?"

"Why do you suppose she called you in of all the people to interview, or gave you an invitation to Domination if she thought you were just another leather girl?"

"I don't know," Kelly said. "I've wondered that myself. At first I thought that perhaps she might have found me out, but I don't think so. I don't think she would have let me see Domination if she knew I'd write about it. I mean, some of the people I saw there are very powerful, very influential. If it got out that they frequented such a place, knew what went on there, the philosophy behind it—" Kelly shook her head. "I get the strange feeling that I'm being recruited for something, but what it is I can't imagine. Valerie said it was because I'd shown a lot of promise at Captive Hearts."

"Maybe that's all it is," Connor suggested. "Perhaps she thought she'd found a kindred soul."

Kelly shook her head. "You wouldn't say that if you were there during our interview. I argued against her theories every step of the way. Valerie is better suited to her temperament. She is a far more knowledgeable proponent of the Domination ideal than I am."

Connor shrugged. "You know what they say: A doubter always makes the most fervent convert."

"Maybe," Kelly said. "But my instinct tells me that there's something underneath it all." She saw the amused look on Connor's face. "Okay, it's probably just paranoia, but I've got to find out."

"Yes," Connor said. "You must."

"Thank you," Kelly said.

Connor looked surpised. "For what?"

"For understanding why I have to do this," Kelly said. "A lot of men wouldn't."

"Well, I'm not a lot of men," Connor said quietly.

After dinner Kelly helped clean the table over Connor's protests and sat on the couch while he fixed dessert only after he protested that he couldn't cook with an audience. A short time later he joined her with two tall parfait glasses filled with a chocolatey-looking confection topped with whipped cream and shaved walnuts.

"What's that delicious concoction?"

"Tiramusa," Connor said, handing her a glass and a long spoon.

Kelly licked the velvety-textured cream off her spoon. "Hmm," she hummed with satisfaction. "Out of this world."

"Glad you like it."

Connor surreptitiously watched her as she ate the dessert. He hardly touched his own. Chocolate was a poison, albeit a minor one, but it still caused subtle changes in the body, and so he seldom indulged his taste for it, or his taste for alcohol, cigarettes, or any of the other common and toxic substances to which so many were addicted. Instead, he contented himself with observing Kelly. There were so many things one could learn by watching how someone smoked a cigarette or ate a rich dessert. As Kelly ate, he recognized the subtle signs of decadence that he fought so hard to purge from his own character. At the same time, he could tell that she did not indulge herself often. But that only made it more dangerous. When she did yield to temptation it put her at risk of losing control. He was afraid that the same thing would happen with her involvement in Domination.

Connor was relieved to find out she hadn't tried to

hide her visit to Ilana or her invitation to the club. Of course, it hadn't come as a surprise. He had followed her to both places. The night she had gone to Domination he had been sitting six rows behind her, having gained admission under the pretext of being a powerful Washington lobbyist on a visit to New York to speak to the governor on behalf of a large pharmaceutical company. But her openness suggested that she had no idea what she was getting herself into. It was her best claim to innocence in a situation that had no innocents and that was growing more ominous by the moment.

Across from him on the couch, Kelly had her legs crossed, letting her black dress ride up over her thighs so that he could see the tops of her black stockings, the feminine machinery of her garters, and a glimpse of her soft white flesh.

Was the move calculated or not, Connor wondered, as he put down his dessert, contemplating the unspeakable beauty of the pale flesh against the leather of the couch. He could feel himself responding even as he weighed the possibilities that the movement might be a trap. There was no doubt that either consciously or subconsciously—or more likely, in that strange hybrid state of consciousness that was the peculiar domain of women and the source of their legendary powers of intuition—she was drawing him close with the age-old cues more powerful than any defense derived by man or magic because it was linked to the very instinct for self-preservation and the only way to deny it would be to cultivate a will to die.

They made love twice that night.

He carried her into his sleeping area, laying her on the bed and lighting the candles he had placed around the room that afternoon in preparation. He undressed her slowly, ritualistically, until she lay naked against the

278

crimson satin sheets, the flickering candlelight painting her nudity with tantalizing brushstrokes.

He stood by the bed and undressed, staring down the length of her body, breathing slowly and attuning himself to her psychic aura. He could feel the heat and power coming from her body, sense her wild, undisciplined excitement, and knew that he'd have to be careful, for even an expert swimmer must respect turbulent waters.

She reached for him as he climbed onto the bed, but he eased her back, taking her firmly and gently by the shoulders and laying her against the satin pillows.

She didn't fight him.

He cupped her face in his hands and kissed the top of her head. He bent forward and gently kissed her throat. Then, taking her hands, he placed a kiss in each of her open palms.

He worked his way down her body, his mind focused on a mantra of protection as he sealed the trantric openings of her body. He kissed the soft curve of her belly and she moaned, reaching for his shoulders to push him down where she wanted him most, but instead he moved farther down, kissing her knees and, finally, the soft soles of her feet. No doubt she understood the gesture as foreplay, perhaps even as a sign of submission, but, in fact, it was an ancient tantric rite known as Nyasa, designed to strengthen the astral body against psychic attack. As he worked his way back up between her thighs, he visualized a golden egg of light surrounding them both, the light intensifying with her growing excitement. He felt the orgasm building inside her like a swell on the horizon, growing larger and more powerful as it moved ashore, finally washing over him and leaving him amazed at its strength, and, like a wave—which was not the water itself, but the energy that moved the water—the energy moved through her again, building once more on the horizon.

"Inside me," she murmured, trying to pull him up by the shoulders. "I want you inside me."

Connor had thought it might come to this. Although he had no intention of indulging in his own orgasm, he reached into the drawer of the nightstand for the condoms he'd also bought that afternoon. Kelly took the foil square from him and, smiling playfully, tore open the corner with her teeth, pulling out the small circle of lubricated rubber. She smoothed the condom along his shaft, feeling his penis jump eagerly in her hand. She drew him toward her, and Connor did not resist, entering her with one smooth stroke, as if they were two halves of a single being.

Connor moved slowly inside her, his eyes closed. In his mind's eye she was the Scarlet Woman of Revelation, clothed with the sun, her skin red as blood. He was the Lamb descending from the clouds, bearing the sword that kills and heals, his body the white of the spirit, both beautiful and terrible. He felt the pressure building in his loins and recited the incantations from his alchemical studies for the mixing of the Blood of the Red Lion with the Tears of the White Eagle. The elaborate impenetrable formulas, he'd learned, were merely glyphs for sexual union, the ancient grimoires a kind of magical sex manual designed to lead to the true philospher's stone: sexual ecstasy.

Beneath him, Kelly was moaning, offering her breasts like forbidden fruit to his lips, and he leaned forward to take them, sucking greedily on her nipples. She had reached behind him, locking her fingers behind his buttocks, as she drove him deep inside her. She gasped, feeling the whole length of him, and once again he had to fight against the urge to abandon himself to the need of his body.

He focused his attention just below his navel and saw a golden-red chaos, a field of energy and light like what must have existed at the formation of the universe. He watched, fascinated, as the red chaos divided into a blazing red sun and a bone-white moon, each ascending up his spine to the base of his skull. They held their place in the neural sky of his imagination, two immense spheres of energy: one fiery, active, masculine; the other cool, passive, feminine.

Kelly was arching her back now, bent like a bow poised to deliver an arrow, her body trembling with suppressed energy. He had slowed his thrusts until he'd stopped entirely, knowing that he couldn't last a moment longer. He lay motionless above her, afraid even to pull out of her, waiting for the need to subside before beginning again. Yet in the end it was his heart that betrayed him, throbbing once, the pulse in his penis triggering Kelly's orgasm, her body slamming forward against his, her desire delivering its final shaft, piercing the one chink in his armor of self-control.

He groaned, his body convulsing, and with the sun and moon standing side by side in the heavens of his mind, he felt the life leave him in a rushing torrent of ecstasy.

THIRTY-THREE

Gwen sat at the bar sipping a vodka gimlet and every once in a while raised her eyes to the dance floor. Two drag queens in sequined black cocktail dresses and glitter heels were spinning around to an old Donna Summer record. Cisco, the owner, let the male homosexuals come in to liven things up. As for the rest of the crowd, they looked pretty much like the usual Thursday-night fare.

A couple of biker dykes in leather, chains, and short pomaded hair sat a few stools down sipping Budweisers out of the bottle. They seemed to take great pride in looking even dirtier and talking even cruder than the male counterparts they professed to despise. In a booth near the back a couple of overweight women in business suits sat sipping martinis.

Was this what her social life had come to?

Why couldn't she find someone to love?

Either they came on too strong or they were wispy young things who just lay there like patients at a gyne-cological examination. Why couldn't she find the woman of her dreams: a woman who could join her in discovering the deep feminine mystery she was certain was the birthright of two women in love?

Sometimes Gwen wished she weren't gay.

Stupid wish.

As if she'd ever had any choice in the matter.

Ever since she was young enough to know the difference, Gwen had known she preferred girls to boys. In grammar school her first crush had been on a pretty dark-haired girl named Marsha who sat in front of her in first grade. Gwen was heartbroken when she exchanged valentines with a little boy Gwen played kickball with at lunchtime. Her mother had laughed good-naturedly that night when Gwen had told her what had happened. She tried to explain that little girls gave valentines to little boys and vice versa. To Gwen it hadn't made any sense whatsoever. She didn't love any of the boys in her class. She loved Marsha.

In high school it was even worse. She listened to her friends talk about boys at pajama parties and pretended interest when all the while she found herself sneaking glances at the other girls and fantasizing about the school's head cheerleader. How could she explain to her mother why she had no interest in the senior prom? Luckily, she secured a date with Leonard Fox, the only gay boy in her class. Her mother still didn't get it when three years ago she called to tell Gwen that Leonard had died of AIDS.

Berlin, Indiana, was not the best place in the world to discover that you were gay. There were places you could go, as there are in most small towns, even in Indiana, but for the most part they were hard places for hard-living women, alcoholics, prostitutes, even women who'd spent time in the nearby correctional facility for women.

Gwen had been introduced to the place by her gym teacher, who had divined her interest after noticing that Gwen spent more time in the shower after physical education class than was strictly necessary to achieve cleanliness. That night Gwen had received her initiation into the arts of Sappho in the cab of a semi from a three-hundred-pound female trucker from Atlanta with a buzz cut and skull tattoos. The experience had not been the wondrous female mystery Gwen had always fantasized it would be. Instead, it was something sordid and dirty and painful through which she had closed her eyes while praying for it to be over as quickly as possible.

Shortly after graduation she had packed her bags and shocked her family by announcing that she was heading for New York City. That had been over ten years ago.

Hard to believe.

In all that time she'd had her share of one-night stands, but somehow love had always eluded her. The closest she had come was her brief affair with Kelly; for a short time she thought she had found the mystery and power of feminine love. But Kelly had merely been curious, led into the affair by Gwen's insistence and her own sheer hunger for experience. Kelly had made no secret of the fact that to her it was just an expression of friendship and comfort. While Gwen said she understood, she nonetheless convinced herself she could somehow convert Kelly by the sheer force of her desire.

Since then Gwen had sworn off sex for the sake of sex. What she was looking for was magic. She'd had a taste of it with Kelly. She would rather wait than except anything less ever again.

She was staring at her face in the mirror behind the bar when she heard the voice at her shoulder.

"Can I buy you a drink?"

She turned, about to tell whoever it was to bug off, when she saw Ilana.

Gwen opened her mouth to speak, but it was as if her throat had been cut, and the blush spilled over her breasts like blood.

The woman was beautiful. She was wearing a leather

dress with laces across the bodice that barely contained her full breasts.

Too beautiful for me, Gwen thought ruefully.

"Are you looking for Kelly?" she said.

The woman smiled, raised her finger, and Cisco came over to take her order.

"Stoli on the rocks," she said. "And another of whatever she's having."

The bartender nodded, winked at Gwen, and turned away to fix the drinks.

Ilana turned to Gwen. "No, dear," she said. "I've been looking for you."

They moved to a booth at the back of the club.

It had grown more crowded, noisier, but Gwen hardly noticed any of the distractions. She was fixated on the woman. It was as if the rest of the bar were nothing more than a swirling gray fog and the only two people who existed in the world were she and Ilana.

"Tell me," Ilana said. "Do you believe in fate?"

"Huh," Gwen said, her mind cloudy. "I'm sorry. I think I've had a little too much to drink."

"It's not the alcohol, Gwen," the woman smiled knowingly. "Try to follow what I'm saying."

"I'm sorry," Gwen said. She fixed her attention on the woman's dark eyes. She could hardly have done anything else. She felt almost as if she were being hypnotized. "What did you say?"

"I asked if you believed in fate."

"I don't know," Gwen said, confused. "I-uh-suppose so."

"Well, I do," the woman said. "In fact, I know it exists. From the moment you stepped into my dressing room, I knew we were fated to meet."

"We were?" Gwen gulped another sip of her drink,

realized it was empty, and set the glass down clumsily on the table.

"Yes, we were. When you've lived as long as I have you learn to recognize these things."

As long as . . .

It was a peculiar thing for her to say. Gwen studied the woman closely: her face, her throat, her incredible dark eyes. The woman didn't seem to be any older than Gwen herself.

"I know you felt it, too, Gwen," Ilana said. "I saw it in your eyes. The way you looked at me. The way you tried *not* to look at me."

Gwen ducked her head. "I feel like I've known you a thousand years."

"Ah, but you have," Ilana said, reaching out to stroke the side of Gwen's face with her fingers. They were cool as snow. "You have."

"I don't understand," Gwen said, feeling deep down that she did.

"You and I," Ilana said, "have very old souls. We aren't like the others. We want something the others will never have. A relationship bound in mystery, joined in blood, blessed by the moon. A meeting not just of bodies but of souls, a love that extends beyond life and death itself."

Gwen felt her heart quickening as she listened to the woman's words, words that seemed to be engraved on her very soul. She felt an almost irresistible urge to throw her arms around the woman's neck as if she were her long-lost twin, and yet something held her back.

"You've been waiting for me for such a long time, haven't you?" Ilana said.

Gwen could only nod, her throat choked with emotion, her eyes spiked with tears.

"Poor dear," Ilana said. "It would be cruel to keep

286

you waiting any longer. Let's go somewhere where we can be alone, shall we?"

"Please," Gwen managed to say, her voice naked with hunger.

Gwen felt as if she were in a dream.

They left the bar and climbed into the limousine waiting at the curb. When she climbed inside Ilana touched the button on the console and spoke to the driver on the other side of the smoked glass.

"Home, Henrik," she said.

Gwen watched the streets unravel on either side of the limousine as they headed uptown. This wasn't just a dream, she decided, it was a real-life fairy tale.

Home was a penthouse apartment in one of the oldest and most distinguished buildings in Manhattan. They took the elevator to the top of the building and were greeted at the door by the beautiful woman who Gwen had seen with Ilana backstage at the club. She immediately felt a twinge of jealousy.

She remembered the kinky display Ilana had had her actors put on in the dressing room and began to wonder what kind of scene she had stepped into by coming here. Her heart sank at the prospect that her dream lover was just a bored and jaded aristocrat looking to spice up her sex life. Maybe at another time in her life, but tonight Gwen just wasn't in the mood for a three-some.

Her spirits picked up, however, when Ilana off-handedly told Paulette to fetch them some wine. Was it possible that the exquisite creature was just what she appeared to be: a maid and nothing more?

Ilana led Gwen to the sitting room and bid her sit down on an elegant armchair. Ilana took the chair across from her. A moment later Paulette came in with a tray on which stood a crystal bottle half filled with wine and two ornately cut goblets filled with the dark red liquid.

"I don't think I should have any more to drink," Gwen said, feeling a little light-headed. She took the goblet from the maid anyway and was surprised to feel the bowl holding the wine was warm.

"Nonsense," Ilana said. "The wine will help to clear your head. It's a very rare vintage." She sniffed the goblet. "1968. Summer of love."

She reached out her glass.

Gwen touched her goblet to Ilana's. She sipped the wine.

It had a strange flavor; fruity and tart and alive, it seemed to go straight to her head. Ilana was right. Her senses seemed turned up a notch, as if some filter had been lifted from between her and the world. The room seemed to sparkle and dance. She took another sip of the wine. And then another.

"I'm feeling—"

"Yes," Ilana said, her eyes calm and steady above the lip of her own goblet. "What are you feeling?"

Gwen placed the goblet on the end table with exaggerated care, as if she were on a ship plunging through rough seas. She rubbed her forehead. "I don't know. I'm so—hot."

"Why don't you take your clothes off, Gwen?"

"I don't—"

Gwen looked down and saw her hands already moving up the front of her blouse, her fingers on the collar button, fumbling it open. Ilana kept watching her, her eyes incredibly level, emotionless.

Meanwhile the hands moved down the front of Gwen's blouse, laying it open. Gwen watched them, horrified and fascinated at the same time, as if they didn't belong to her, as if they were the hands of a stranger. They tugged on her belt, released the snap on her jeans, and pulled them down her legs. She bent over and pulled off her shoes and socks. A moment later her underwear was gone and she was sitting naked in the armchair, her body warm and tingling, responding to Ilana's intimate gaze.

Ilana snapped her fingers and Paulette materialized out of the shadows. She stood behind her mistress's chair, and she, too, stared down at Gwen's naked body.

Gwen wanted to cover herself, but she couldn't move. Something in the wine had paralyzed her will, had released some deeper desire inside her that could no longer be denied, the desire to expose herself to these two strange but beautiful women.

"Call Henrik," Ilana said. "Have him take her to the club. I have something special planned for her."

THIRTY-FOUR

The priest lifted the ceramic teapot from the small hotplate behind his desk. He carried it over to a table buried under a pile of books and pages torn from yellow legal pads covered with an indecipherable scrawl.

"Please excuse the mess," he said. "I'm in the middle of researching a new book. It's about witchcraft within the Church. Turns out, while they were actively encouraging the persecution of witches, the Church Fathers were in the process of building the largest and rarest occult library in the world, as well as charging certain priests with the duty of becoming adepts in the magical arts."

He held up the teapot. "Will you join me?"

"Is it legal?"

The priest laughed. "It's only chamomile. I promise. Good for the nerves. Helps me sleep nights."

He carefully poured tea from the ceramic pitcher into a pair of small cups. He set the pot down on a short pile of books topped by a hardbound edition of Trevor Ravenscroft's *The Spear of Destiny* and slowly lowered his considerable bulk into the chair on the other side of the round table.

"So, what brings you here, my friend?"

Rossi had met Father Martin for the first time during

the weeks following his undercover assignment as Master Rod. He had heard about the priest from a veteran on the force, one of the old-timers who'd helped break the Son of Sam case back in the seventies. Rossi had been released from the hospital and given a clean bill of health by the police department psychiatrist. But Rossi knew that he was far from all right. He still had the dreams and the desires. He had seen part of himself that he had rather not known existed, like a relative you never knew you had until he shows up at your door one fine day and will not go away, knowing that blood gives you an unimpeachable obligation toward him.

Instinctively, Rossi had sensed that his problem was spiritual, not psychological. Though never a religious man, Rossi had gone to Father Martin for advice as a last resort. They spent more than a few late-night sessions over shots, and sometimes something stronger, talking about everything under the sun, but mostly about the nature of evil and how each human being had a dark twin skulking in the shadows of his or her life. Father Martin was not your typical priest. Even for a man of the cloth, he was a man of prodigious appetites, both intellectual and sensual. He stood only five-seven or -eight, but he must have weighed close to 250 pounds. Nature had given him a monk's tonsure, his exposed scalp as pink as a baby's bottom, but it was girdled with a fringe of snow-white hair. He was also a man of some dexterity and cruelty. Rossi had once seen him catch and strangle a mouse that had invaded his study with his bare hands.

In the end, Father Martin had not exorcised the dark twin who possessed Rossi, but he had taught him how to live in peaceful coexistence with him.

Rossi had called the priest up from the station after he'd gotten the coroner's preliminary report on Nancy Li. In spite of the fact that they hadn't spoken in nearly two years and that it was half past midnight, the priest hadn't seemed to be inconvenienced by the call, or even particularly surprised to hear from Rossi. Instead, he invited him over to the rectory of his small church on Staten Island, where Rossi and the old man were now sitting, enjoying a pot of sweetened chamomile tea.

"I'm sorry to disturb you at this hour," Rossi said.

The priest waved his hand, slurping from his cup.

"Don't mention it. As I said, I am awake most nights." He shrugged. "Old age."

It always surprised Rossi to remember that Father Martin was almost seventy years old. He had the smooth, rosy complexion peculiar to most men of God he'd met that always made them seem twenty years younger than their actual ages.

"Still, I appreciate it—"

"What's troubling you?"

Father Martin was never one to mince words. It was Rossi's turn to take a sip of tea.

"Have you ever heard of the Assassins of Christ?"

"The AC? Of course."

"What can you tell me about them?"

The priest's blue eyes twinkled. Church history was his passion, the more arcane and seemingly trivial, the better. Though he knew that Rossi must have an official motive for asking about the AC and that it would eventually be revealed, Father Martin was just as happy to have an excuse to discourse on his favorite topic.

"As far as anyone can determine, the AC originated with the formation of the Order of the Knights of the Temple in A.D. 1118. The Knights Templar, as they came to be called, were a fraternal monastic order founded by a Burgundian knight named Hugues de Payens, or Hugh the Pagan, and based on the Saracen fraternity of hashish takers, more commonly known as Assassins. Their beliefs are not entirely known, but they were most certainly heretical from a strictly papal point of view in that they believed, among other other things, in honoring the feminine principle of godhead and in the individual's ability to directly experience God without priestly interference. From the earliest times, the Knights had a paramilitary function, undertaking the holy duty of protecting wealthy Christian pilgrims on their journeys to the Holy Land, often inheriting the pilgrim's property, incidentally, if they did not return.

"As a result, in spite of the fact that each Knight took a strict vow of poverty, they became a very wealthy and influential order. Under some pressure, they offered their services to the Church and received a papal sanction from Pope Innocent II after Saint Bernard came to their defense, in exchange for the position of Templar Grand Master. Throughout the thirteenth century their power was unparalleled. They became one of the foremost money-leading institutions of the Middle Ages, serving kings, princes, and important merchants. Quite naturally, their power came under the scrutiny of an increasingly disapproving Church, and eventually the Knights became the object of envy and conspiracy. In the fourteenth century it all went bad. Pope Clement IV and King Philip of France, both in desperate need of money, conspired together to bring down the Templars.

"The Knights were accused of devil worship, sodomy, blasphemy, and the most horrendous forms of sexual perversion and human sacrifice. They were arrested en masse with their leader, Jacques de Molay and confessed, under torture, to the most heinous crimes against God and humanity. Later, they recanted their confessions, but those were feverish times, and their recantations made little difference to either the authorities or to the general public. The Templars were condemned to death and publicly burned at the stake as heretics and devil worshippers. In the following years, the Knights were effectively destroyed as an organization. Those who survived the persecution were scattered throughout Europe, hunted down by agents of the Church, which brought many of them to justice. To this day you'll find evidence of their survival in remote areas of Scotland and Wales, where many were buried under plain stones marked only with one of their favorite devices: a simple broadsword."

Rossi recalled what the FBI agent had said about the possibility of the murder weapon being just such a sword.

"Now here's where it gets tricky," the priest said. "It is rumored that a small remnant of the original Templars, seeing the handwriting on the wall early on, capitulated in the persecution of their brethren and aided both Pope and Crown. These Knights, practical and clear-sighted survivors as all traitors are, saw where the future lay. They were absorbed into the Church, which sought to gain the Order's hidden wealth and occult knowledge for its own. The Church, you see, did not become so powerful simply by crushing heresies. No, it incorporated them into its own system. Like the primitive warrior who draws strength from eating the heart of his dead enemy, the Church devoured its enemies and made its strengths its own.

"Pope Clement, in his devious way, saw that a paramilitary order such as the Templars could be of great use to him, as has every pope since that time. Over the years the Order of the Knights Templar has been one of the most secret and feared instruments of Church influence. Though no one has ever been able to prove they actually exist, their machinations have been detected in revolutions, financial crises, political and religious movements, and assassinations for the past five hundred years. Their proficiency at the latter has earned them the name under which they are said to operate today, the AC, or Assassins of Christ. But that is merely a front to make them look like a group of right-wing fanatics. It is a beard to disguise who they are really working for. Underneath, they are the same old Knights Templar. Whoever within the College of Cardinal controls the AC controls the Vatican. Remember the speculation surrounding the sudden, unexplained death of the first Pope John Paul? He was assassinated—poisoned by the AC. Rumor has it, he wanted to break the back of the organization once and for all."

"Incredible," Rossi whistled. "It's hard to believe that all this goes back so far."

"I've only scratched the surface, my friend," Father Martin said. "The roots of this evil feed the very roots of humanity. May I ask what NYPD's interest is in the AC?"

"The FBI tipped us to them."

Father Martin snorted. "Since when are they interested in stopping an agent of imperialism?"

"Since he's a suspect in a series of serial murders."

Father Martin raised his shaggy eyebrows. "Really?"

Rossi explained about the murders in Chicago and about the two recently found dead woman.

"Yes," the priest said thoughtfully. "I read about the murders. Tragic."

"Well, they think this guy may be an ex-priest who joined the AC, or vice versa, who went off his nut and started killing innocent people."

"Highly unlikely," Father Martin said. "If he's AC, he's got a purpose."

Rossi shrugged. "They think the Church may be protecting him out of loyalty, or out of fear that he'll reveal what he knows. Ordinarily, I'd think it was all a lot of mumbo-jumbo except I've got an informant who claims he's seen a character prowling the nightlife who dresses like a priest and drinks blood. It sounds crazy, I know, probably just some kind of fag fad, like sticking hamsters up their asses were a few years back, but it's the only lead I've got. What I need to know is if you've heard of any priests who've been in trouble lately. You know what I mean. Diddling around with the choir boys, screwing the deacon's wives, urinating in the baptismal fonts, that sort of thing."

Father Martin looked thoughtfully into his teacup.

"The Church guards its secrets fiercely," he said. "Some more fiercely than others. Secret organizations, assassinations, mystic cabals are one thing. What you are asking me . . ." He shrugged.

"It's very important," Rossi said. "Lives—innocent lives—are at stake."

"I can't promise you anything," he said finally. "I will make some inquiries. I have a connection in the Archdiocese Bureau of Records. He may be able to get me a list of the kind of priests you're talking about. I counseled him after he got into a similar jam some time ago and he owes me a favor."

"Thank you, Father," Rossi said.

He rose from the chair and reached across the table. The old priest's hand was plump and soft as a young girl's, but surprisingly strong. Rossi remembered the mouse.

"Be careful," Father Martin said, fixing Rossi with eyes like two blue pins. "It's an ugly business that you're embarking on. If you remember nothing else, remember this: There's nothing more dangerous than a righteous man."

THIRTY-FIVE

The sun was coming through the barred window and pooling around Kelly's bare legs, which were lying outside the bedclothes.

She woke up to its warm caress, stretching slowly, careful not to awaken Connor, who was still sleeping soundly beside her. He looked so handsome and peaceful lying there with his sandy hair falling over his clear, untroubled brow.

She gazed over the smooth muscles of his recumbent form, remembering the first time she'd seen him naked that afternoon at Captive Hearts, and how she had first responded to the sheer power and terrible beauty of his body with a dizzying mixture of fear and desire. She had compared him then to a large and dangerous cat, and sure enough, with the dark shadows from the barred window striping his body, the comparison only seemed more apt. However, right now, sated by sleep and sex, she would have to say that he looked to her more like a fallen angel than anything else.

After last night she was almost willing to believe he was an angel—an angel of love fallen to earth to teach her the art of eroticism.

The last several weeks had begun to wear on Kelly, leaving her with a strange feeling of unreality. Finding herself a character in the fantasies of others, feeding on the excitement she inspired in her clients, Kelly feared she was losing the ability to feel for herself. At first she welcomed the opportunity of escape that the work provided, as well as the outlet for her frustrations after the breakup with Eric. But lately she had begun to grow worried that she was hooked on the vicarious thrill of role-playing at the expense of truly living herself. She worried that perhaps she had become one of those vacuous voyeurs she had seen at Koski's happening, and again at Domination, incapable of feeling an authentic emotion of their own, a mere bystander at the play of life, observing with a cold and critical eye the all-too-human actors playing their flawed roles upon the stage.

Last night, however, Connor had given her back her soul.

She still felt him inside her, his mouth on hers, his hands healing her body. She suddenly wanted him again and reached out her hand to wake him, only to pull it back at the last possible moment.

She wouldn't be selfish.

But later. There would be time again later.

Kelly slipped out of bed and put on the white button-down shirt Connor had discarded the night before. Her own clothes were draped over an armchair by the bed. She could smell the familiar scent of his body trapped in the fabric, surrounding her, engulfing her, becoming a part of her, as he had surrounded her with his flesh the night before. The tails of the shirt were just long enough to fit her like a dress, covering her in front, and barely falling below her buttocks. She buttoned the shirt up and then, biting her lip in debate, unbuttoned it halfway down again, leaving just enough of her breasts exposed so that Connor would get the idea. She grinned, looked slyly back at his sleeping form, and padded barefoot across the loft to the kitchenette.

She found the coffee and filters in the well-stocked cabinet over the Braun coffeemaker. From a half-dozen varieties on hand, she selected a bag of freshly ground dutch chocolate beans, shoveled three heaping teaspoons of the rich dark blend into the filter, and filled the pot with cold water from the cooler by the refrigerator. She turned on the orange switch at the base of the coffeemaker and heard it immediately start to gurgle.

Opening the door to the refrigerator, Kelly located the eggs in the side door and took out four, as well as a carton of milk and some feta cheese she found in the cooler bin. Kelly gazed in wonder at the full but immaculately organized shelves. One shelf on the inside door held condiments alone: hoison sauce, Bengal chutney, and a bottle of something with an orange label written in Japanese. Kelly was impressed. She had never seen such a well-stocked bachelor's kitchen. She had finally gotten used to Eric's refrigerator, which usually contained little more than a half-killed six-pack, some green Oscar Mayer chicken franks, and a take-out box of whatever he hadn't finished the night before.

Kelly kicked shut the door and carried the omelet-makings back to the counter. She'd start cooking the minute Connor woke up.

In the meantime she walked back through the loft.

She gazed again at the photographs lining the walls like windows into another dimension in time. She thought that in each of the photographs she could see a little bit of Connor, some flash of his humor, his joy, his gentleness. Like a kaleidoscope, they offered little bits and pieces of how he viewed the world. Against the east wall she saw the Soloflex machine he used to keep himself in such wonderful shape, as well as a small black punching bag hanging from an iron chain suspended from a ring in the ceiling. She touched the soft leather, sensing the power of the man who had beaten it and feeling another surge of arousal.

She looked up and saw the door to the darkroom.

Aside from the door to the bathroom, it was the only door in the loft.

She walked toward the door, standing uncertainly before it, turning back to the bed where Connor still lay sleeping. She knew she shouldn't go inside, that it would be an invasion of his privacy, the equivalent of someone looking through her notes. She knew how jealously she guarded her own work-in-progress, unwilling to let anyone read it until she had polished it to meet her own exacting standards. She supposed Connor was just as possessive of his unfinished work, but she couldn't help but satisfy her curiosity. She wanted to know as much as she could about the man with whom she had spent the night. The man with whom she suspected she was falling hopelessly in love.

She grabbed the doorknob, turned it, and pushed open the door.

The overhead light came on automatically, casting a strange red glow over the wooden table, the trays of developing fluid, photographs clipped to what looked like a clothesline looped from one wall to the other.

Kelly waded through the red murk, feeling a strange sense of misgiving, her subconscious urging her to turn back. Connor could awaken at any moment and if he found her in here . . .

She moved forward, tentatively, trying to ignore the unshakable sensation that she was being watched. She dismissed it as simple paranoia. She would have a quick look around and then she'd leave—

Kelly froze, self-conscious of the eyes upon her.

Her own eyes.

She saw herself spread throughout the red room,

thumbtacked to the wall, staring up from the tray under the fluid, pinned to the clothesline.

She saw herself buying a newspaper, sitting in a booth at Gus's having lunch, standing outside Domination with Gwen.

Kelly suddenly felt sick to her stomach.

He'd been *watching* her.

And then, against the far wall, she saw a small black table set up like an altar with candles, stones, and feathers. A small votive candle flickered beneath a close-up of her face.

"You shouldn't have come in here."

Kelly whirled toward the voice and saw Connor standing in the doorway. He hadn't dressed, his naked body looking Satanic under the red light. She felt a jolt of fear.

"Get out of my way," she screamed so loud it made the fluid in the developer trays ripple.

She didn't wait for him to respond. She charged straight forward, afraid he might try to stop her, but to her relief he stepped to the side and let her pass out of the darkroom.

"Let me explain," he said.

She rushed through the sunny loft, feeling more secure, grabbed her clothes from the easy chair, and rushed into the bathroom.

She locked the door behind her, painfully aware of the flimsy doorknob lock. He could easily kick open the door if he chose. She stripped off his shirt in disgust. The smell of it, so intoxicating before, now gagged her. It disgusted her now, as if it were made of clinging, cloying flesh. She threw the shirt on the floor and bent over the sink. She ran the tap and splashed cold water on her face and stared at herself in the mirror. She was surprised to find that she was crying. He knocked softly on the door, his voice bringing her back to herself

"Please let me explain. It's not what you think."

She threw the dress over her head and worked it down over her hips, reaching behind her awkwardly to zip it up. She grabbed her high heels off the sink, preferring the mobility of bare feet until she got outside, as well as the option of using the spiked heels as a weapon should the need arise. She wouldn't hesitate to drive them into his groin if he tried to detain her.

"Get away from the door, Connor. I want to leave."

"Kelly—"

She refused to look at him as she hurried out of the bathroom, his nakedness no longer arousing, but obscene and threatening. She kept him fixed in the corner of her eye, where she could make sure he kept his distance. The elevator was at the other end of the loft, which seemed a thousand miles away. He followed along at her side, several paces away, and Kelly felt her heart hammering in her chest.

"You don't understand, Kelly. You're in danger. You've gotten yourself involved in something bigger than you think. I don't even know what it is yet, myself. I've been watching you for your own protection. You must believe me."

Kelly felt the words dragging at her like a net, tangling her in their warped logic. He was sick, obsessed. She should have known, having met him in a place like Captive Hearts. He was trying to rescue her from some kind of imagined evil that he believed existed at the club when it was his own crusading moralism that was the only evil. He was like Eric, only worse. Lord save her from men who wanted to save her soul.

She was less than ten feet from the elevator now, her mind already working out how to lift the screen. She was still afraid that he would try to prevent her from leaving at the last moment.

"I don't ever want to see you again, do you understand?" she said as she slid open the heavy screen. To her relief, he made no move to stop her. "If I find out you've been following me again, I'm going to call the cops and have you arrested. I know a detective on the NYPD. He'll make sure you don't fuck with me again. He doesn't always go by the book. Do you understand what I'm saying, Connor?"

Kelly stepped inside the elevator, dragged the screen back in place, and pressed the button down. They stood on opposite sides of the metal screen. Naked, he looked more than ever like a beautiful but dangerous animal. But who was really the prisoner? She remembered the first time she'd seen him—he'd been cramped inside the dog crate. Ironic that it should end like this.

"Kelly," he said in that maddeningly calm voice. No anger. No passion. Somehow his reasonableness made it worse. "You don't understand what you're doing."

The elevator started down.

Echoing in the shaft above her, she heard a slight trace of desperation creep into his voice for the first time.

"Please," he shouted after her. "You don't even know who you are!"

THIRTY-SIX

Connor stood in the gathering gloom of a cold New York City afternoon in Central Park and watched the seals. They were swimming purposely through the dirty water of their concrete habitat, smooth and sleek as large rubber bullets, traveling around and around, going nowhere.

He checked his watch.

It was already half-past three.

They were late. They were never late.

It wasn't a good sign.

He had made an emergency invocation yesterday after Kelly had fled from the loft to report that the Spell was broken. He knew that there would be repercussions, but he tried not to think about that now. His first responsibility was to the Operation, to make sure that it succeeded at any cost. Perhaps they could still find some way to salvage the situation.

Connor still had no idea what had gone wrong. This was the first time anything like this had ever happened to him. He had run through the events of the last several days a thousand times in his mind. Had he forgotten a crucial incantation, neglected the propitiation of some peevish demon or other, or had it just been a failure of Will? That darkroom door should have been

304

locked; the fact is, it was *always* locked whenever he wasn't using the room. Could someone have penetrated the protective pentagrams with which he'd sealed the loft, knowing that his concentration would be diverted during the ritual of love magic he would be performing with Kelly?

On the surface it was such a minor thing: an unlocked door.

But for the want of such a minor thing governments have toppled, whole races perished, and many a magician has lost his life.

It pointed up the importance of mantaining at all times a constant magickal vigilance over all that was in one's circle of influence, for you could never tell when or where the Adversary would enter. Ordinarily, Connor would have been awake long before dawn that morning, long before Kelly, and therefore able to prevent her from opening the darkroom door, even if someone else had purposely left it unlocked. However, the erotic exertions of the night before had exhausted him and sent him into a comalike sleep that had thrown off his natural defenses.

He thought now of the strange presence he'd felt following Kelly, hovering just at the corner of his eye, and wondered if that was where the interference came from. Of course, the Craft itself would have known his plans; it would have been easy for them to strike him at his most vulnerable. Had they sent a magician in to check up on him? Some fool who, on exiting the loft, had forgotten to undo one of the spells he'd cast. A small thing . . . like unlocking a door?

And then another thought crawled sideways into his mind, as cool and dry as a snake, its black eyes expressionless as stone, sparkling with sly wisdom.

Was it possible that they had planned it to go down like this all along? That they *wanted* him to fail? That his failure would actually be success in the overall Operation? The interference had all the earmarks of their particular brand of Machiavellian subtlety. It would be the way they would have done it.

Connor felt a hot flash of anger.

They had cost him an Illusion he had worked hard to create. Of course, he knew it was all part of the game, but this time he couldn't help but take it personally. Something had happened that night with Kelly, something that shouldn't have happened, but that had happened nonetheless. He hesitated to call it love. Love was too shallow a concept for what he had exchanged with Kelly in the midst of their love embrace. Rather, it was an exchange of energy, of essence, of life itself that bound him to her by magical compact. Whether he liked it or not—and he most assuredly did not like it one bit—he and Kelly were *possessed* of one another.

The blood pounded at Connor's temples, his blood pressure rising beyond its customary one-twenty over eighty. He did a quick yogic breathing exercise to dispel the adrenaline pumping through his system. Rage would do him no good. Like all powerful emotion, anger fogged the mind, made it easy to make a mistake, and that could be fatal. When dealing with the Craft experience showed that only cold, reptilian logic prevailed.

Connor glanced quickly at the people surrounding the concrete seal pool.

There was a young mother with a stroller; a businessman, looking haggard and preoccupied, and a mumbling street person clothed in a pile of oily rags, stamping his feet and blowing on his hands for warmth.

Could one of them be his contact?

A light snow had begun to fall like dirty confetti.

The mother pulled the stroller away from the pool

and started toward one of the inside exhibits, leaving only the businessman and the vagrant.

After a while the businessman also left, hands thrust deep in the pockets of his open trenchcoat, weaving toward the tropical bird aviary to sweat off the effects of his three-martini lunch.

Connor waited for the homeless man to approach, to make some kind of sign, but nothing happened. He merely stood where he was, blowing on his hands and stamping his feet, staring straight ahead into the endless corridors of his madness.

Maybe they weren't coming at all. But weren't they compelled to come if he made the proper invocation? Maybe this was their way of telling him that he was through with the Craft, that his invocations were no longer effective, that his magic had left him. Or maybe that was only what they wanted him to think. Maybe it was all part of the master game plan he was not supposed to know.

Dammit. He had to stop thinking like that.

It was the shortest road to insanity.

Still, how could he continue to operate if he didn't even know if his magic had effect or not, if he were a member of the Craft, or just some deluded, superstitious fool who believed in the power of spells and incantations?

He was about to turn away when he heard the voice.

"Good afternoon, Mr. Scott."

Instinctively, Connor turned in the direction of the voice.

There was no one there.

Of course there was no one there: He was looking into the seal pool.

Connor turned around, confused. He looked toward the homeless man as the only logical source of the voice when he heard it again, low and insistent, coming from behind him.

"Over here, Mr. Scott," it said.

Connor whipped his head back and found himself staring at a sleek black seal sitting on a concrete island above the foul water. The seal turned its pointed head to one side, its white whiskers making it look almost professorial. "Really, I wish you wouldn't act *so* surprised," it said. "After all, I am one of the higher social mammals. It isn't like you'd heard a cockroach reciting the Gettysburg Address."

The seal laughed in a series of barks, clapping its flippers in appreciation of its own joke.

Connor surreptitiously scanned the surrounding scenery, but even the homeless man had edged away, leaving him alone by the pool. There was no doubt some reasonable explanation for the illusion. As a magician himself, Connor knew that magic once discovered is the most real thing in all the universe. It wouldn't have been hard for a cleverly hidden mage to throw his voice so that it appeared the seal was speaking. Or perhaps they had implanted a transmitter somewhere in the concrete habitat, or on the animal itself. There was a darker possibility, however, that Connor didn't want to think about, but had no choice than to consider, and that was that they were somehow messing directly with his mind. Either through long-range hypnotic possession or by means of psychotropic drugs administered to his food, they might be controlling his thoughts and perceptions. Even so, there were strategies he could use to beat them at their own game. In dreams, for instance, one encountered illogical situations that defied the conventions of both physics and common sense all the time. But even there one could gain control of the situation if one stopped thinking in terms of absolutes and adapted to the rules peculiar to each particular dream. It was simply a matter of exchanging one set of illusions for another and living accordingly, like speaking a different language when one entered a foreign country.

"She's gone," he said to the seal, willingly entering the surreal. "She found the photographs. You bastards blew my cover."

"We know," the seal said, confirming Connor's suspicions that it had been planned all along.

"Why did you do it?"

"Why ask why? You know the rules, Mr. Scott."

"It's different this time. I need to know."

"It's never different, Mr. Scott. It's always the same. The Work is One."

Connor knew that the seal was right. He had heard the Code often enough in his years with the Craft; he'd even repeated it himself on countless occasions to frustrated 1=10 apprentices. The microcosm and the macrocosm were identical. As above, so below. The Law of Hermes Trismigestus.

"So that's it. I'm out of it?"

The seal nodded sagely. "The Operation is over, Mr. Scott. Mission accomplished."

"And the girl?"

"She has served her purpose."

"I see. So that's that, I guess. I just walk away."

"Yes," the seal said. "Oh, by the way. There is one last thing."

"What's that?" Connor asked, sensing the hook a half second before it jerked him awake.

"Seeing as you grew so close to Ms. Mitchell, we want you to be the one to close her file. It only seems fair, to both of you."

The seal slid off the concrete island, disappearing into the dirty water before Connor could answer, joining the other seals in their relentless pursuit of nothing.

The snow had stopped as well, and there was a terrible stillness in the cold brown air.

They might as well have asked him to commit suicide.

In a way they had.

They wanted him to kill Kelly.

THIRTY-SEVEN

For the next three days Kelly concentrated on finishing her article on domination. She spent most of the time holed up in her apartment, staring into the blue glare of her word processor, taking breaks only to go down to Gus's for coffee and the occasional burger.

Not that she was complaining.

The work was good for her.

Therapeutic.

She was still shaken by what she had seen in Connor's darkroom, and the few times she had left the apartment she couldn't escape the uneasy sensation that she was being watched, even though she knew it was probably all in her imagination. She found herself constantly looking behind her and out the window of her apartment, but to her relief she had seen no sign of Connor. She still got the creeps when she thought of how he had been stalking her without her even knowing, photographing her every move, even the night she had gone to the club. It made her feel vulnerable and angry at the same time. Connor was sick and she was lucky to have found out about him before it was too late.

Kelly needed someone to talk to, but she was reluctant to call Gwen. The last thing she needed to hear was "I told you so," which Gwen had every right to say. She called her eventually, steeling herself to take the bitter pill, but Gwen wasn't home. With the Thanksgiving weekend coming up, Gwen had probably already flown back to her parents' home in Indiana. Kelly felt a twinge of loneliness. The holidays were always the worst. Even if you didn't get along with your family—and most of the people she knew didn't—it was still nice to have somewhere to belong.

Kelly shook off the feeling of self-pity.

Strangely enough, the breakup with Connor had stirred up her feelings for Eric all over again. She had used the excitement of the new relationship with Connor to distract her from the pain she felt over losing Eric. It was the coward's way out, and now she was experiencing anew the heartbreak she had tried to avoid as she compared her comfortable old lover to Connor. Suddenly, she began to think she'd made a terrible mistake turning away as decent, strong, and solid a man as Eric. As a result, look at what she had wound up with—

A few times that afternoon she nearly picked up the phone to call him. Once she even went so far as to dial the station, but she hung up when the desk sergeant answered. The week before she had come home to find a large manila envelope in her mailbox without stamps or a postmark. When she tore it open the slim silver lighter slipped out and fell to the floor. Kelly looked at it through a screen of tears, so angry she tossed the lighter into the trash. Later she fished it out, shoving it into her pocket, feeling a connection she wasn't ready to sever. Now she told herself that she only wanted to explain things to Eric better than she had the night they'd broken up, that she wanted to apologize for hurting him, that she wanted to set things right. Yet deep down she knew that was only an excuse. What she really wanted was to hear his voice again.

It was all so juvenile.

At twenty-eight she would have thought she was well beyond such schoolgirl histrionics. In the end she decided she wasn't going to put herself through the humiliation, and through sheer force of will stuck with her decision.

Still, she couldn't help second-guessing her decision to stop seeing Eric.

Perhaps she had been too inflexible. Maybe she hadn't made enough of an effort to see things from his point of view. After all, he was older, more conservative, set in his ways. If only she'd been willing to compromise a little, to adapt to his needs. . . .

Bullshit.

She'd made the right decision. She loved her work and he had no right to ask her to give it up. She made no similar demands on him and would never dream of doing so. It was clear to her now that he could never accept her work or understand that it was every bit as important and rewarding to her as being a cop was to him. Better to have found out now, she told herself, than a couple of years down the road. She knew his character and knew there was no way to change him. Ironically, it was his solid, stubborn character that she liked best about him and what at the same time made it impossible for her to live with him.

She had worked too long and too hard to get where she was in the free-lance writing business to throw it all away. She thought of what Gwen had said. She wasn't ready to move to the suburbs and become the barefoot and pregnant wife of a homicide cop.

But it still hurt. Even though everything told her that breaking up had been the right thing to do, she couldn't help but think of all the good times they'd shared together, feeling aching emptiness at the realization that those good times were gone forever.

Kelly stared back at the computer screen.

Thank God for her work.

She scrolled through the document on the PC, unable to resist making a few last-minute corrections, even though she knew such changes were rarely for the better. It had been tough going at first, but she had finally gotten a handle on the piece, channeling some of her own frustration over the last week into her reflections on domination. Of all the pieces she had ever written, this one had undoubtedly been the most difficult. She had found the experience both disturbing and enlightening and, as with all her writing, she had discovered a lot about herself in the process. Nonetheless, it felt good to finally be done with the article, as if she had unburdened her conscience of some dark and long-hidden secret.

As she watched it roll down the computer screen, she was sure that it was some of her best work. Now if only Joan agreed—

Kelly reached the end of the document, saved it to file, and then keyed in the printer commands. She went to the refrigerator, pulled out a bottle of Evian, and watched the expensive laser printer she had splurged on after her first *NiteLife* feature type out the story. As the paper came out the top, she carefully gathered up the computer pages and arranged them in order inside a black plastic binder.

She checked the clock.

She still had a little over an hour before her appointment with Joan, so she decided to take a shower. She had lived for most of the last three days in her bathrobe.

After her shower she dressed in a pair of jeans and a Black Crowes sweatshirt she had bought at a concert last summer. She sat on the edge of the bed and laced on a pair of Reeboks. She looked up and saw her reflection in the mirror on the back of the door and smiled at the familiar person looking back. Without the high heels, tight skirts, and clinging blouses, she looked like her old casual self again. She had experienced the power and allure of her femininity and it had both awed and frightened her. She felt she was a better and stronger person for the experience, but she was done with domination. She was ready to get on with her life. She stuffed the binder inside her knapsack and took the elevator downstairs to the street. The only concession she made to the look she had cultivated over the past few weeks was the black motorcycle jacket she threw on over her clothes.

She took the Number Seven train into midtown, and in spite of the cool autumn weather, which was perfect for walking, decided to treat herself to a cab. The streets were crowded with pre-holiday tourists whose considerable ranks were swelled by office worker on the tail-end of their lunch hours, making their reluctant way back to their desks. Kelly never failed to see the latter, dressed in their suits and ties, their pumps and skirts, without pausing to be heartily thankful she was not one of them.

Sure, it was sometimes tough getting assignments, and there were the usual tax and insurance hassles, but she wouldn't give up the freedom she had as a free-lance writer for the security of nine-to-five slavery. She couldn't imagine being tied to a desk like most of the people she knew. They always seemed so tense and up-tight, in a hurry all the time, living by someone else's schedule, unable to even finish a night's sleep without being jarred from their dreams by the morning alarm.

Kelly arrived at the Madison Avenue office of *NiteLife* at half-past two. She waited in the tastefully appointed lobby until the receptionist informed her that Ms. Rosenberg was ready to see her and was escorted back to her office by a young male intern.

Joan sat behind her large glass-topped desk, surrounded by walls full of framed covers of *NiteLife* maga-

315

zines. Behind her the large window that made up the wall of her corner office gave a panoramic view of the East River. She was forty-something, attractive, and smart. From her blond, shoulder-length hair to her blue contact lenses to her nose job, she had carefully calculated a look appropriate to the publisher of the hippest magazine in the city. With a clientele that favored the young and the beautiful, it was essential. To that end, she had enlisted the best plastic surgeons in the city and had undergone the latest procedures to maintain an illusion of beauty. If you looked a little too closely, you could see the strings that held the whole thing together. There were times that Joan's carefully planned face looked like a plastic mask.

There was a desperation to Joan's swim against the inevitable tide of time that Kelly found profoundly sad. But at twenty-eight, Kelly was just old enough to see the first insidious signs of age on her own face. Nothing dramatic; just a line or two in certain lights, from certain angles. A little puffiness around her eyes if she didn't get enough sleep the night before. A hint of what she would begin to look like in ten years or so. Kelly wondered if she would grow gracefully into middle age, or if she would fight it every wrinkle of the way, as Joan had.

"So," Joan said, smiling. "You have something for me?"

Kelly slid the black binder across the glass-topped desk. This was the worst part, no matter how many times she'd been through it, despite the fact that she knew she'd done good work. Joan picked the binder up off the desk, opened it, and started skimming the first page. Kelly squirmed in her chrome and mauve seat, letting her eyes rove over the walls, stopping at the framed cover of the issue in which her first feature appeared, hoping to give herself confidence.

It didn't work.

No matter how many stories she wrote, how much success she had, it would always be like the first time every time she handed in a new story. That was the beauty of the creative process.

And the terror.

You could never write the same story twice. Each time you had to prove yourself anew.

Kelly turned her attention back to the window. Just over the custom-tailored shoulder of Joan's red blazer she watched a tiny tugboat pushing mightily through the sluggish brown water. She tried to fix her concentration on the boat's efforts, tried to ignore the pages falling between the perfectly manicured fingers of Joan's hands, tried not to read the expression on her inscrutable plastic face.

It took her less than ten minutes to skim through the story, but it couldn't have seemed longer to Kelly if she were hanging by her neck from the ceiling. Finally, the last page fell from Joan's hand, sliding gracefully along the surface of the glass-topped desk, and she looked up and fixed Kelly with eyes whose only fault was that they were too damned perfect.

"Genius," she said, her red, collagen-enhanced lips stretching over her capped teeth in what could almost have been a cover girl smile. "It needs a little cutting, but it's fantastic. I knew you could do it."

So that was it, Kelly thought, as she left the *NiteLife* offices.

She was done with domination once and for all.

THIRTY-EIGHT

Kelly decided to celebrate finishing the article by putting all her other projects on hold long enough to enjoy a few days off. She'd earned enough money on the domination piece to put some aside in the bank, and Joan had been so pleased with the story that she'd immediately offered Kelly another feature.

One of the downsides of free-lancing was that there were no scheduled holidays, no formal weekends. Every day was as much a potential workday as a day off; and every day you didn't work was a luxury that could cost you somewhere down the line. The free-lance world operated solely on the basis of feast or famine: Either there was too much work or not enough to go around. As a result, free-lancers were by necessity an opportunistic lot, never saying no to an assignment, even if it meant working day and night for days on end, taking on more work than they could reasonably handle in order to counterbalance the long dry periods in between. Kelly couldn't remember the last time she'd taken off more than two days in a row.

After some consideration she decided to spend at least part of the day at the Metropolitan Museum of Art. She hadn't been there in months, and she always enjoyed wandering through the labyrinthine halls filled with paintings, artifacts, and exhibits. No matter how many times she'd been there, it always seemed as if she discovered something new every time she went.

Kelly took the N train into Manhattan and then got on the Number Six to Eighty-sixth Street and Fifth Avenue. The Museum was across the street in Central Park.

She entered the huge marble hall, already filled with tourists and teachers herding students on class trips, paid her admission, clipped the tiny purple pin to the collar of her blouse, and headed straight to the Egyptian room. She was awed by the ornately decorated sarcophagi and the delicately rendered hieroglyphics preserved behind the climate-controlled display cases. To contemplate the antiquity of the pieces and to imagine the unknown craftsman who struck the marks upon the stone that were all that remained on earth of his soul and spirit left Kelly with a dizzying sense of time. Upstairs, she visited the Arms and Armor exhibit, where her awe at seeing the armor that men fought and died in was somewhat tempered by the surprise she always felt upon seeing how short in physical stature were the warriors of the Middle Ages. Afterwards she took a casual stroll through the modern art wing to take a look at the Jackson Pollock canvases on display. She was standing there taking in one such canvas, a great expanse of swirling, free-form patterns, when a woman appeared at her shoulder. She was dressed in black, a large black hat and dark glasses framing a pale beautiful face. She had that natural charisma that all famous people seemed to have, but Kelly couldn't place where she had seen her before.

"Quite amazing, isn't it?" the woman said. "To think a mere mortal could conceive such a work."

"Yes," Kelly said.

"It's almost enough to make you believe in man's divinity."

"They say his paintings anticipated the photographs that scientists are now taking of subatomic particles."

The woman laughed.

"Is that what they're saying? What fools the scientists are. So blind to reality they can only see through microscopes and telescopes."

"What do you think he was painting?"

"He was painting me," the woman said. "At the moment of his death."

Kelly turned, startled, and the woman smiled before she walked away across the floor, her high heels echoing through the hush of the high-ceilinged room like a pair of hammers.

She must be some kind of nut, Kelly thought.

After countering the chaos of Pollock's paintings and the conversation with the strange woman with a dose of the sensible Old Masters, Kelly took the elevator downstairs to the museum cafeteria and had lunch, a fairly credible chicken curry and an all-natural raspberry soda, costing more than it should have, but somehow worth it all the same.

Lunch over, she decided to take advantage of the weather to take a walk along Fifth Avenue to the Strand Bookstalls, set up near the entrance to the park. As she walked along the tree-lined street she became aware of the unmistakable sensation of being watched. She had felt it first at the museum, but it had passed, and she had not given it a second thought, attributing it to an understandable paranoia after her experience with Connor.

Now it was back again.

She turned around abruptly to see if anyone was following her.

Just a businessman staring past her. A woman pushing a baby carriage. Another woman walking three Pekingnese. An old man on a park bench.

No sign of Connor.

Or the woman at the museum.

The old man looked up from his paper, as if to say what the hell are you looking at?

Kelly shrugged and kept walking.

She browsed through the stalls of used books, buying a couple of tattered paperback mysteries, but her uneasiness took all the fun out of it.

By the time she got back on the subway she felt threatened and depressed. Her day off had been ruined.

All because of Connor.

Damn him.

On Friday night Kelly threw caution to the winds and went out with Marc Barclay. She had spent a quiet Thanksgiving at home, watching the Macy's parade on television, reading one of the mysteries she'd picked up at the Strand, walking down to Gus's in the afternoon for a hot turkey sandwich. On the whole, she didn't mind spending a quiet day alone, had even chosen to in a sense, turning down an invitation to spend Thanksgiving with one of her neighbors from the building. Nevertheless, by Friday she was starting to feel the first symptoms of cabin fever, and knowing Gwen probably wouldn't be back in the city until Monday, she had accepted Marc's well-timed invitation for a night on the town.

Marc was one of the staff writers at *NiteLife*, whom she'd met on several occasions when she came in to talk to Joan, as well as at the magazine's annual Christmas party. He'd called her a couple of times, asking for a date even though he knew she was seeing Eric and had turned him down in no uncertain terms each and every time.

He was good-looking enough, but Kelly found his obnoxious and egotistical personality abrasive; nonetheless, she decided to give him the benefit of the doubt and accepted his gracious offer of dinner and a show. She didn't bother asking Marc where he'd heard the news that she was available, assuming that it was Joan who'd told him. In addition to being a thoroughly modern businesswoman, Joan was also a natural *yenta,* unable to resist the temptation of playing matchmaker between her unattached friends. She claimed it was in her blood. She'd been trying to fix her up with Marc ever since she told her about her break up with Eric, claiming that they'd be perfect together.

It really didn't make any difference where he'd heard the news, or if he'd heard it at all and just happened to call at the right time. Kelly could use the company, and she found herself reasoning that perhaps she had misjudged Marc. After all, he really did seem interested, in spite of the fact that she had turned him down so many times. Who knew? Maybe he knew something she didn't.

Kelly met him at a small Thai restaurant in a fashionable part of the Village, close to where he lived. He was dressed in a pair of cowboy boots and a black duster, his shoulder-length reddish hair tied back in a ponytail, a calculated growth of two day beard sprinkled over his chiseled features. He kissed her on the cheek as she came to the table and informed her that he had already taken the liberty of ordering for her.

Throughout the dinner he kept up a constant infield chatter that revolved entirely around what was obviously his most favorite topic: himself. He talked about his current writing projects, his ex-girlfriends, his plans to go back to school, his extensive connections in the

New York avant-garde scene. When he asked her about herself he listened with an exaggerated attentiveness that convinced her of two things: He'd seen at least one Alan Alda movie and he wasn't listening to a single word she said.

She was glad when dinner was finally over and it was time to head for the theater.

He had already told her that it was an off-off-Broadway play; he hadn't said just how far off. It turned out the "theater" was a converted loft owned by one of Marc's friends. A collection of mismatched lawn chairs were arranged on one side of the room and a sheet of paper painted to look like Dealey Plaza covered the wall on the other side. In front of the scene was parked a large Cadillac convertible, in which sat a nude woman in a pillbox hat and a man wearing nothing but a rubber JFK mask. There were others in the car, including Fidel Castro and Marilyn Monroe. The play was apparently a reconstruction of the sexual fantasies of all the participants on that dark November day in Dallas in the last moments before the assassin's bullet, fired by a rouged Lyndon Johnson in drag, warped the American psyche forever.

Kelly found her mind drifting throughout the tedious and tasteless performance, wondering how in the world they managed to get the huge car into the third-floor loft in the first place. After it was over, signaled by a climaxing Jackie "O" tossing confetti into the audience to represent her dead husband's brain tissue, Marc introduced Kelly to the author/producer/director of the play, who had also starred as JFK, and who proceeded to launch into a fevered half-hour monologue on the sexual symbolism of assassination and the validity of current conspiracy theories.

Later, Marc took her to a coffee shop for espresso and invited her up to his apartment. Kelly refused at first and then relented when he pressed her, not sure why she had agreed to go even as she found herself walking the half block to his building and taking the elevator up to his loft.

He fixed them both a drink, which she didn't want but took out of courtesy and pretended to sip as she sat on the couch. She turned on the television, feigning interest in some guest Arsenio Hall was supposed to have on that night, and before she knew it, Marc was sitting beside her, his hands all over the front of her body, pulling up her shirt and trying to undo the snap on her jeans.

She pushed his hands away gently but firmly and told him in a quiet voice that she wasn't interested.

He wasn't discouraged.

He grabbed her wrists and pinned them above her head in one of his hands, his body suddenly taking on an alarming new strength, his breath heavy with purpose.

"You love it, don't you, baby," he whispered hoarsely.

Behind them, Arsenio was leading his audience in a round of wolfish grunts.

"Let go of me," Kelly said, trying to squirm out from under him.

Marc pressed closer; his lips finding her mouth, his tongue pushing against her pursed lips.

"So you want to play hard to get," he said, puffing with excitement.

"Stop it," Kelly grunted, twisting her face away, gasping for breath.

"Yeah, baby," Marc muttered, losing himself in a private state of passion. "You like it like this, don't you?"

He had somehow pulled his penis from his fly, and was rubbing its hardened length against the inside of her thigh. With one hand still holding her wrists, he tried once again to undo the front of her jeans, his clumsy fingers unable to manipulate the button, yanking on it in frustration.

"Damn," he muttered, realizing he'd need both hands to undress her.

She felt him reach around to his back pocket with his free hand and, straddling her body, come up with a pair of silver handcuffs. Kelly felt one of the cold steel bracelets snap shut around her left wrist.

Kelly was so shocked, she just stared at it for a moment. Meanwhile, he groped for her other wrist.

He's going to rape me, goddammit.

It had all seemed so unreal up to that moment; the idea that anything truly bad could happen, that he could actually rape her, had seemed absurd. After all, she knew this man, had just been to dinner with him, would see him again this year at the *NiteLife* Christmas party.

He's actually going to rape me.

Like hell he is!

Kelly swung the arm with the dangling handcuff out of his grasp, catching him over the eye with the steel. He jumped back, touching his brow, which bore a widening crescent of blood.

"What the fuck—" he said, staring in disbelief at the red on his fingers. "Why the hell'd you do that?"

"Get these off me," Kelly growled, holding up her arm. "Now!"

"Okay, okay," he said, sounding genuinely scared. "Just let me get the key."

"Hurry up," Kelly warned, hardly placated.

Marc rummaged around in his pocket for the key to the handcuffs. He seemed completely changed, as if some kind of temporary madness had passed and left him without any memory of his actions of a moment before. He found the key and nervously jabbed it into the lock on the handcuffs, wiping away the blood that was now dripping from his right eye.

"I didn't mean anything by it," he said, popping the lock. "I thought you were into it."

"Into what, you bastard?" Kelly said, rubbing her wrist. "Being raped?"

"You know—" he struggled. "Rough sex."

"What the hell gave you that idea?"

"The article. Domination," he said, the handcuff dangling from his hand, incriminating. "I just thought—"

"Well, you thought wrong," Kelly snapped. She pushed him off her and got up from the couch, straightening her clothes. She grabbed her coat and headed for the door. She turned back and saw him sobbing on the couch.

"I'm sorry," he said, wiping away tears diluted with blood. "I really didn't mean to hurt you."

In spite of herself, Kelly felt a pang of sympathy.

"Forget about it," she said brusquely.

She opened the door and turned back once more.

"Hey, you better put something on that eye."

"Yeah," Marc said, trying to smile. "Thanks."

On the subway home she thought about what had happened, feeling a mixture of anger and guilt. Had she been asking for it? Did the fact that she'd written an article on S-M give him the right to presume she'd respond to his forceful advance?

Of course it didn't

The problem was, she could also see how it might seem that way to him.

She leaned back on the seat and let herself be lulled by the sound of the train rumbling over the tracks. There were only a few other riders on the car beside her. A young Hispanic couple were kissing near the doors and an old homeless man was sleeping off a drunk at the back of the car.

Through slitted eyes, Kelly watched the two kids making out. They were seemingly oblivious to her and the world outside their embrace, their love innocent and sweet, with nothing to be ashamed of.

Jesus, Kelly thought, how long since it had been that way for her?

Had it ever been that way for her?

THIRTY-NINE

After Kelly got home she was still wired.

Her doctor had given her a prescription for Xanax a few months before, when she'd had a bad case of insomnia. She found the remainder of the prescription in a small brown bottle in the upper right-hand corner of her medicine cabinet, behind Eric's Lectric Shave. She had swallowed two of the mild sedatives, but still she hadn't been able to calm down.

She had already undressed to get ready for bed when she pulled the cord that turned on the closet light and saw the leather jacket hanging at the end of the pole.

It was a good three inches from the rest of her clothes, as if purposely segregated, guarding her secret alter ego.

Behind it lay the leather skirts and pants, the latex bodysuits and corsets, the harnesses and masks that had become a part of her new personality.

Kelly thought of the special outfits that priests, judges, and soldiers donned to symbolize the fact that they had shed their ordinary, everyday identities and taken on special powers. Costuming was essential to the assumption of authority, as any superhero worth his or her salt could readily illustrate. Without their mitres, their solemn robes, their medals and golden epaulets, what was to separate the man of power and distinction from his humbler fellows? One of the first lessons she had learned as a dominatrice was the importance of ritual clothing and that a slave should always be kept naked, or attired in some humiliating fashion that accented his or her nakedness.

Naked.

That was exactly the way she had felt the last few days. First Connor, tracking her with his camera, and tonight Marc, with his smug assumptions about her sexual life and his crude attempt to dominate her. She had hoped that after Eric she would be able to straighten things out for herself, but what she had found instead was that she was still being controlled and abused by the men around her. What was the answer? To give up men altogether? For one wild moment she thought about calling up Gwen. But deep down she knew that really wasn't what she wanted, nor would it have been fair to Gwen. She thought she had found a piece of what she was seeking in domination. Had the new sense of power she had felt at Captive Hearts only been an illusion?

She reached out and touched the leather, cool and impersonal, letting her fingers trace the zippers slashed across its surface. She needed to feel empowered again, in control.

Kelly stood in front of the mirror on the back of the bedroom door to watch her transformation.

First she pulled on a pair of black silk micropanties that snapped along the crotch to allow a lucky slave to pleasure her with his mouth, if she so chose, but most likely just to tease him with the possibility that he'd be offered such an honor. Next there were the dark seamed stockings, which she unrolled slowly up her legs, fastening them to the garters at the tops of her thighs. She stretched her legs, admiring them, pointing her painted toes, imagining her naked slave kissing each toe with ceremonial reverence and sincere gratitude. She felt a shiver of anticipation. She stepped into the leather skirt, zipping it up the side, so tight it felt like a second skin. She pulled on a brief leather middy corset that closed on the side with tiny hooks and that had a studded collar that snapped securely around her throat. The forbidding leather garment pushed up her breasts and left her midriff bare, instantly transforming her natural charms into weapons of erotic power. To finish off her outfit she slipped her feet into a pair of four-inch PVC pumps. She slipped into her biker jacket, studded, belted, and slashed with zippers, the leather having long ago conformed to the shape of her body so that the jacket fit her like a shell.

She looked at herself in the mirror and felt a familiar surge of power.

Once again she was no longer Kelly Mitchell.

She was Lady Domina, Mistress of Pain.

She left the apartment by the backstairs, avoiding the elevator and the chance that she might be recognized, and walked hurriedly down the street to the subway entrance on the corner. She took the M train into Manhattan and then the F into the Village. On the way she found herself in a car with a couple of punk types, their sexes nearly indecipherable beneath the leather, spiked hair, and pierced and tattooed flesh. Their aggressive, defiant posturing visibly melted when then saw Kelly and they gazed after her with forlorn puppy dog eyes. She remembered encountering a similar couple on the train several weeks ago and how she had felt threatened and vaguely violated under their sneering scrutiny. She realized how far she had come since then.

She exited the train in SoHo. In the first bar she went to she received a proposition from a sweet-faced topless woman in leather hotpants and a pierced navel and a flabby, shaved, middle-aged business type, stripped down to a pair of frilly pink panties.

Neither of them were what she was looking for tonight.

In the second bar her luck was much the same.

She was approached by a handsome young preppie who wanted to be treated like a naughty dog and a husband who offered his pretty wife as a love slave for the evening. She sent them on their way. She had seen their type all too often at Captive Hearts, men and women whose drive toward submission brought them to the brink of letting go but who lacked the courage to go all the way.

Tonight she needed the real thing.

It was in the third bar that she finally hit paydirt. Located near the meat-packing district in one of the most dangerous sections of the city, the Dungeon was notorious for its hard-core action and was definitely not the place for novices or the weak of stomach.

He was standing by the bar sipping something red, half turned to watch a live-action domination display.

Tied to a whipping post under a hot spotlight, a large bare-breasted, bottle-blond amazon was beating a muscle-bound male submissive with a steel-tipped cat-o-nine tails.

The slave must have been a serious pain freak because the woman was obviously holding nothing back, giving it to him for all she was worth. His rippling, studio-tanned back was already covered with bloody stripes where the whip had reopened the scars of old wounds.

Unlike what happened at places like Captive Hearts, where most of the pain was simulated and the mistresses made sure not to leave permanent marks that might be detected by girlfriends or wives, the action at the leather club was brutally real. Ordinarily, Kelly found it hard to watch such displays, but lately she had begun to discover her tolerance had increased. She thought of what she'd read about the ancient Romans and how they needed ever more violent displays to amuse them. Was it true what the proponents of television censorship so often asserted—that violence was an addiction that required ever-increasing doses for the addict to receive his accustomed kick?

Kelly watched both the man at the bar and the domination tableau, switching her eyes from one to the other. He was a large, well-built man, his dark clothes complementing his black hair, which fell raggedly over his pale forehead. His face was handsome but rugged, his mouth stretched in a thin line below a distinctive hawklike nose. His strong jawline was darkened by a shadow of beard. He brought the drink to his mouth and Kelly saw his powerful hand around the tumbler, his index finger decorated with a large blood-red stone.

He drained the remainder of what was in the glass in one swallow, his head back, the muscles in his throat working.

His eyes, however, never left the whipping post.

Kelly felt an immediate attraction to the man. There was something about him that called to something corresponding deep inside Kelly, that made her blood thrill with excitement, that made her *hunger*. She motioned to the bartender and had him bring the man another drink. She saw the bartender explain the situation, nodding in her direction, and the man turned and looked Kelly directly in the eyes.

His eyes were as black as his hair, as black as night, as black as leather.

There was a sadness in his face that caught her by surprise. It was the sadness of a man who had seen much in the world, who had lost much. At the same time she recognized the arrogance of a man who was used to wielding power. It was the unmistakable combination she had seen countless times in those she had met at Captive Hearts, as well as in the leather clubs, both slaves and masters. It was the look of superiority that came from transcending the conventions of morality and sexuality, not to mention the threshold of pain it was necessary to pass that separated the general population from those chosen few initiated into the cult of domination.

To such men and women, it was a matter of pride how much pain they could endure—and how much they could dispense.

In his glance, Kelly felt the electricity pass between them, a subtle transferral of energy that registered at the seat of her sexual being. She felt its effect in the sudden arousal of her erogenous zones. A fantasy scene flashed before her mind's eye, and she was sure that somehow he was sharing the exact same fantasy.

Her heart beat double-time.

He looked away, back at the whipping, and then to her again.

Kelly smiled coolly, though she felt like a woman being burned at the stake. She slid off the bar stool and made her way through the crowd of half-dressed people to the door. She waited outside for less than a minute before he emerged from the bar. He glanced her way only briefly, then started up the street as Kelly followed.

He crossed Ninth Avenue into what Kelly realized was a neighborhood of abandoned tenements and crumbling warehouses. Ordinarily, she wouldn't be caught dead here in broad daylight, not to mention after midnight. There were routinely any number of assaults, rapes, shootings, and stabbings in this part of town, and the police themselves were reluctant to patrol the area. She knew from Eric that they considered that anyone caught down here after dark, except for the most obtuse tourist, must have pretty much deserved whatever it was they got.

By all rights she should have been scared. But the sense of invulnerability she had felt in the subway carried itself over even to these mean streets. It was as if Kelly had crossed some inner line within herself that separated the predators from the prey, and she suddenly saw the world through new eyes. She moved with the easy confidence of an animal that had no natural enemies and knew instinctively that it was safe wherever it might go, because it had the respect of the other predators, who recognized her as one of their own.

Up ahead, the man had stopped at an abandoned brownstone next to a drab gray church. He paused for a moment, as if waiting to make sure she was still following, and then slowly climbed the crumbling stairs of the porch to the peeling door at the landing. He reached into the pocket of his dark coat and took out a key, unlocked the door, and disappeared inside.

Kelly stood at the bottom of the stairs and stared up at the black doorway. He had left the door open for her to follow.

She knew that what she was doing was dangerous—if not downright suicidal—but she couldn't help herself. The need she felt was so powerful it swept everything else before it on a raging hormonal tide of desire. Suddenly, she understood that all that separated the predator from the prey was the strength of appetite. Tonight it was her appetite that made her a predator.

Kelly climbed the broken concrete, careful to keep her balance in the high heels. She reached the landing and without hesitation plunged into the dark pool of the open doorway.

She found herself in a small vestibule.

Underfoot, the linoleum floor was gouged and pitted, while the plaster walls were rotted away with great cancerous holes. There was a smell of dampness in the stale air, as well as the telltale odors of mold and old urine. As her eyes became acclimated to the dark, she shut the door behind her and saw the mail slots on the wall to her left, the tiny cubbyholes thick with dust and cobwebs. In one of the slots a few letters still leaned, delivered by a postman long ago, to a recipient who never received them. There was a short hall to the right lined with trash cans, and straight ahead a stairway leading up to the second floor. She could see the landing where the stairs doubled back above her to the second floor. On the wall above the landing was a window through which the moonlight shone, casting a thin, nervous light on everything. As she listened in the silence she heard the sound of his steps on the stairs above her as he reached the second floor and proceeded down the creaking floorboards of the hall overhead.

Kelly climbed the first flight of stairs, pausing at the landing, and stared up to the second floor. The light from the window at her back was brighter here. As she mounted the second flight she could make out more of the hallway. Her high heels were loud in the silence of the building until she reached the top of the stairs, where they were suddenly muffled by the worn carpet covering the floor. She walked slowly down the hall, staring at the doors on either side of her, each of them shut except for the door at the very end of the hall, which stood slightly ajar.

She pushed the door open and found him inside.

He was stripped to the waist, his arms raised over his head, shackled to the ceiling by a pair of stainless-steel cuffs. In a circle around where he stood he had lit several small black candles.

On the wall, Kelly saw the rack of torture tools.

She took down a long leather bullwhip well worn by

use. She turned and walked back to the man in the shackles.

Standing a few feet away, she saw his splendid musculature in the flickering candlelight. Slowly she unfurled the whip and with a fluid motion she brought it forward, the heavy leather cracking across his shoulder blades. He gave a sharp intake of breath and she saw the muscles of his back shudder in response. Kelly felt the sweat break out across her forehead, her heart hammering beneath her sternum, the moistness between her legs. The connection between them had been made, the spark ignited.

She drew the whip back again as he steeled himself for the next blow.

It followed shortly thereafter, marking him diagonally to the first, forming a red *x* across his trembling flesh. In the silence of the room she heard his hoarse voice.

"Harder," he said.

The next blow caught him across the lower back. She saw the sweat fly from his body in tiny crystal beads. His head was thrown back, his eyes closed, as if he were savoring the pain of the stroke.

Again the gruff command. "Harder."

She remembered his fixation on the bodybuilder and the amazon in the bar. He was obviously a heavy pain freak, and while Kelly was not as big or as strong as the bottle-blonde, she would give the man a beating he would remember. She was in just the right mood. She drew back the whip and brought it forward with all her might, hearing it crack over his shoulders like a gunshot. Each time she whipped him he made the same reply. He wanted it harder, harder than she could deliver it. She lost count of how many times she hit him until she heard him counting off the blows. She had stopped to catch her breath when he shouted at her not to quit. His back was striped with sweat and blood, his face white and haggard, and yet he begged for more. Kelly had begun to grow scared that she might seriously hurt him. She had heard of slaves who in the passion of the moment got carried away to the point of harm. Sometimes in the throes of ecstasy they might even be blind to their own survival.

"Thirty-five," he muttered. "Five more!"

He counted off the final strokes. At the count of forty Kelly felt the whip take on a life of its own and fly out of her hands, coiling in the corner like a dangerous snake. She stared dumbly after it, turning only in time to see the man burst from the handcuffs as if they were mere toys. As quickly as that the assurance she felt earlier was gone. She no longer felt the immunity of a predator among predators. Now she felt the trembling, helpless paralysis of small prey. The man had turned to her, his body heaving with the exertion of the whipping, his eyes burning like two black holes, sucking everything inside them.

"Don't come closer," Kelly threatened.

She reached inside her jacket pocket for the small keyring canister of Mace she had learned to carry while at Captive Hearts. She held it up as a warning. He hadn't moved a step toward her. Instead, it was his eyes that posed the danger. Somehow his eyes were drawing her toward him.

Don't make this harder than it has to be.

The thought came into her head without a word being uttered. It had merely blossomed there, like a flower, out of the fertile soil of her brain. Kelly was so stunned that for a moment her fear vanished.

"Who—"

I am here to help you. But first you must submit yourself to me. Trust me.

"Stop it," Kelly said. "Stop."

Come.

"No!" Kelly shouted, trying to shake herself from this bizarre enchantment. She squeezed the button on the canister and a thin stream arced between them, splashing against the man's face and chest. By all rights he should have been incapacitated, the fluid causing intense burning in the tender tissues of his eyes, nose, and throat, not to mention the open stripes across the front of his chest. Instead, he stared at her, completely unaffected. She squeezed the button again, and once again the stream of Mace looped across his face without effect.

Kelly felt her hand involuntarily loosen around the canister. Her keys fell to the floor. She tried to object, but the words came out in a low moan. She felt the darkness cocooning her, wrapping her in shadows, numbing her even as her brain remained wide awake, shouting its protests. She stood there, unable to move, unable to speak, as he walked calmly past her and toward the door into the hall.

Follow me.

She felt herself turn and follow him obediently out the door, as if he were leading her on an invisible leash. *Wait,* she thought, remembering the keys attached to the Mace canister lying on the floor a few feet away. *My keys.*

The next words that flashed through her mind chilled her to the bone.

You won't need them anymore.

PART FOUR

BAD BLOOD

"A woman came in with white eyes of ivory,
holding out arms to me and smiling: she had
in place of teeth bits of red flesh."
—Rene Daumal

"Nature is cruel. If man is to survive on this planet
he must be even crueler."—Johannes Streicher

FORTY

Kelly surfaced in the darkness.

She had no idea where she was or how long she had been under. The darkness that surrounded her covered her like a hood, so that she could no longer distinguish between the black inside her head and the black without. Her world had been brutally reduced to the senses of sound and smell alone.

The smell of damp and stone.

The sound of dripping water.

She remembered little of what had happened after leaving the abandoned brownstone, following the man down the stairs and into the night, drawn after him by some irresistible force, his will leading her helplessly along. She had fought to break the hold he had over her and, when that failed, to hold on to her consciousness, but it had faded, slipping away by halves, until all that remained was a tiny throbbing ember in the growing darkness of her submission.

Now she lay on a thin cot somewhere in the vast sleeping heart of the city.

Abducted by a madman.

Damn, it was cold.

She tried to move but found that she couldn't, her arms and legs strangely unresponsive, leaden. She didn't seem to be tied. She felt the way one does sometimes in the split second before waking, when the mind returns to consciousness before the body, and in that strange disquieting moment you experience what it is like to be dead.

She panicked, struggling futilely to overcome the paralysis that gripped her body like a swimmer fighting against a powerful current.

Don't panic.

She heard the thought in her head and knew it wasn't hers.

She tried to speak, to answer back, but her vocal chords were locked. Nonetheless, the thought resonated inside her skull.

Let me go.

I can't do that.

Why not?

I want to help you.

He was in here with her, somewhere, moving around in the darkness. She heard the sound of a key scrabbling around in a lock, the outraged screech of a door opening on rusty hinges.

Footsteps ringing on the stone floor.

Then the scrape of a match and the sharp tang of sulfur teased her nostrils.

She saw his hollowed features as he touched the match to the wick of an oil lantern. He carefully trimmed the flame and an orange-yellow light slowly crept up the walls to fill the room.

Her captor stood behind the lantern, his dark, obsessive eyes regarding her with sadness and pain. But the thing that disturbed Kelly most of all was the fact that beneath his dark suit the man was wearing the collar of a priest.

Again she heard the voice inside her head.

I'm going to let you speak.

Kelly felt a portion of the darkness relax its grip on her brain, like the talons of a huge black bird, and flap off into the distance, her nausea gripped in its talons. The feel suddenly rushed into her arms and legs, and she stretched them, testing them, lifting her hands to her face, examining them as if she were seeing them for the first time. Slowly, carefully, she swung her tingling legs off the cot, put her feet on the floor, and sat up.

She appeared to be in a small cell of some kind, unfurnished except for a small wooden table, a straight-backed chair, and the iron cot on which she was sitting. There was an old-fashioned ceramic commode by the cot and a large plain wooden cross hanging from a nail on the wall above the table. The black iron grillwork of the cell door was also decorated with crosses.

"Where am I?" Kelly asked.

"In the basement of St. Jude's church. These cells were built nearly two hundred years ago to aid in prayer and meditation. It seems our ancestors had a markedly more austere attitude toward their vows then we do nowadays. Later, in the years preceding the Civil War, they were used as part of the Underground Railroad to help slaves on their way up north to Canada."

"You are really a priest?"

The man nodded.

He poured some water in a clay mug and carried it to her.

"Are you thirsty?"

Kelly looked suspiciously at the water until he took the mug from her and drank some of it himself. She took the mug from his hands and gulped the cool water greedily, nearly choking.

"Easy," the priest said. "Not so fast."

Kelly coughed, cleared her throat, and drank again, only this time more slowly. When she was done she handed the mug back to him.

"How long have I been here?"

"Two days," he said matter-of-factly.

"Two days!" Kelly said, shocked. She would have guessed several hours at most.

"Please don't be alarmed," the priest said. "It was necessary to keep you here to ensure your safety. There are people, powerful people, who mean you harm."

Kelly felt a sharp *v* of pain in the place between her brows.

"God," she muttered, rubbing the hurt away. "What did you do, drug me?"

"No. A simple matter of mind control. All beings of our kind possess such powers."

"Beings of our kind," Kelly said, trying to keep the fear out of her voice. If he were insane, it was best to understand the nature of his delusion as soon as possible. "I don't understand."

"Come," he said, indicating a heavy earthenware bowl on the table. He removed the cover and the redolent smell of broth filled the tiny cell. Kelly instantly felt her mouth water. "You must be hungry. Eat."

Kelly rose carefully from the cot, taking a few tottering steps before he caught her arm and led her to the table. She sat down, took up the spoon, and fell to eating the thick, delicious soup. She'd hardly realized just how hungry she was until she started eating. She was halfway done before she lowered her spoon to ask him to explain what he'd meant earlier abut someone being after her.

"Who," she said quietly, "who is after me?"

"In time," he said, "it will all be made clear to you."

He looked up toward the ceiling of the small cell, but as if he were looking straight through the stone to the moon that must be shining in the heavens beyond, or listening to a whisper beyond the range of human ears to hear, the kind of whisper that only madmen hear.

Once again Kelly felt the fear scamper up her spine like a red centipede.

He glanced back to Kelly, and his eyes bore the stamp of insanity.

"But now I have business to attend to."

"Please," Kelly said. "Tell me what you want from me."

"It's not what I want," the priest said cryptically. "But what She wants."

He cocked his head, as if he could hear the woman he was speaking of even now.

Some lover who had jilted him?

His mother?

He took the lamp from the table and turned abruptly to the door of the cell.

"Please," Kelly said again. "Leave the light?"

The priest seemed to debate her request for a moment and at last relented. He returned the lantern to the table, took up the empty soup bowl, and pushed open the heavy iron door to the cell. He scraped the door back across the stone floor, and it shut with a loud, hollow clang. He fished a large antique-looking skeleton key from the pocket of his black suit and turned it inside the rusted lock.

He stood there a moment, staring at her through the bars of the cell, and then turned and made his way up the stone stairs.

Kelly heard another door opening and closing on the floor above.

And then the sound of dripping water.

Suddenly she was alone again with nothing between her and the dark and cold but a lantern filled with less than a half inch of oil.

FORTY-ONE

Father Sylvestri moved through the mean streets of the city, following a sixth sense he was hardly even aware of, he'd had it so long.

He prowled the streets of the Village with its all-night clubs and after-hours counterculture, moving like a native among its predominantely gay inhabitants, brushing past bewhiskered, musclebound men in oiled blue-black leather who might have been bikers except for some indecipherable look of longing in their eyes. He passed through the Lower East Side and Alphabet City, where, if you didn't walk fast enough, someone was liable to kill you for your shoes, and down into Little Italy, where the mobsters and wiseguys viciously protected their shrinking neighborhoods from the Chinese on one side and the blacks on the other.

He zigzagged across the city at random, from Gramercy Park to midtown, from Upper Manhattan to Tribeca, sometimes by subway, most often on foot, following nothing but his own instincts.

In Washington Square Park dark figures leaned out of the shadows, whispering conspiratorially, offering him crack and seeds.

In the Port Authority bus terminal underaged male

hustlers loitered around the reeking men's room stalls, selling sex.

In Central Park a man huddled in the bushes, waiting for some unsuspecting female passerby to become his next victim.

He ignored them all.

They were not the one he sought.

From one end of the island to the other he felt the desperation burning off them like a fever, their hungry eyes sticking to him like leeches.

Humans.

They disgusted him.

He had renounced the human race over two hundred years ago. In a small, windowless cell of the insane asylum at Charenton, he had whispered his lurid confessions to a short, sandy-haired French nobleman imprisoned by his mother-in-law for falling in love with his wife's sister. The poor man had thought the confession a figment of his own imagination, scribbling away furiously in the rat-infested darkness, aghast at the horrors he discovered in his own subconscious, unwilling to acknowledge the reality of his supernatural visitor.

He published the confessions under his own name, novels penned in blood, chronicling every act of violence and perversity imaginable. His books were condemned as the blasphemous ravings of a lunatic, banned, and finally burned. Meanwhile, he lived up to the charges of his critics by slowly going insane. He was set free after the Revolution, but somehow he always found his way back to prison. The record showed he'd been arrested for sodomy, flagellations, and once for attempting to poison several prostitutes at an orgy with tainted sweets.

He was innocent of most of the charges.

Sentenced to die on at least two occasions, he somehow managed to survive, writing plays inside the asylum, which he produced with the help of the other inmates. He died behind bars an old man: penniless, discredited, and grotesquely obese. Yet the terrible confessions that the Marquis de Sade penned for his strange, "imaginary" visitor would earn him a place in history as one of literature's most diabolical and influential writers, linking his name forever to the practice of forbidden passion.

Sylvestri was standing on the deserted platform of the Lexington Avenue line waiting for the train when he saw from the corner of his eye the three shadows peeling away from the darkness behind a stone piling.

They were young, so incredibly young, they seemed creatures of a totally alien, inconsequential species.

Like mayflies.

Born in a pond to live but a day and die.

They came toward him, their sweet young blood thundering in their veins, spiced by adrenaline and testosterone. Their movements were exaggerated, almost stylized, like the movements of a dance, but it was a dance of violence and aggression, practiced a hundred times, each pass designed to produce a flinch of fear and submission in the face of their intended partner.

The priest watched with detached interest as they approached, their ebony faces glaring as angrily as those he'd seen carved on totems in Africa over a thousand years ago.

"Hey, man," said their leader, a tall, thin kid wearing a bulky jacket that stretched nearly to his ankles and was designed to make him look twice as big as he really was. He was missing two teeth in the front of his mouth and his nose looked like it had been broken recently. "What you lookin' at?"

"Yeah, what you lookin' at?" asked one of the other two. He stood within a foot of the priest, so close Sylvestri could smell the cheap vinyl of the coat, and glared from beneath the rim of fake fur. The kid thrust one hand significantly into the parka; the other he pushed into the priest's face, thumb and pinkie extended, his wrist twisting for emphasis, his fist bristling with chunky rings. His other arm was shielded in a ragged plaster cast.

"He axed you a question, you white mutherfucker," the third one asked, as if they all had a part to play in this age-old drama. "You hard of hearing or somethin'?"

They all laughed, a high-pitched, nervous laugh, full of cruelty.

"Please leave me alone," the priest said. "You don't know what you're getting into."

The calm voice seemed to unnerve them, even as it served to infuriate their leader. "What's in the bag, mutherfucker?"

"You think because you're a fucking priest you safe down here?" one of the others sneered.

They had taken up positions on either side of the priest, edging out of the range of his peripheral vision. Sylvestri didn't need to see them; he could smell their blood in the air around him, hear it howling in their veins, feel the warmth of it against his skin. With the subtlest of unconscious signals, almost a form of telepathy, they grabbed him on either side. The boy in the long coat pulled his hand from his pocket and the priest saw the knife gleaming in the dirty station light. The boy lunged forward and drove the knife into the priest's stomach as he grabbed for the bag.

Sylvestri, however, had already dropped the bag on the platform, caught the two boys by the throat, and lifted them off the ground, his arms effortlessly extended to either side, as if he were doing the iron cross. In his powerful hands he strangled both of them in seconds, crushing their windpipes as if they were no more than cardboard tubes.

The boy in the long coat realized something was wrong the minute the knife had gone into the priest.

It didn't feel right. Like sticking the blade into a fucking cheap cut of meat.

He looked up at the priest, his hand still on the handle of the knife, *dry as a bone, not slick with blood as it should be* and tried to pull it out to stab the priest again. Instead, the priest brought his knee up, smashing the boy's teeth back into his throat and sending him hurling backward off the edge of the platform onto the tracks below.

The priest dropped the dead boy he still held in his hands and walked to the edge of the platform. The boy in the long coat was lying on his back on the third rail, having what looked like a hundred-thousand-watt epileptic fit, his eyes boiled white and bulging from their sockets, his lips flapping and frothing, his head haloed with bright blue sparks.

Sylvestri exited the station and walked several blocks before a homeless man near Times Square who'd approached him for some spare change stopped dead in his tracks, his head clearing for the first time since the Carter Administration.

"Hey, man," he said, from out of a cloud of delirium and stench. "Are you—all right?"

The priest followed the man's startled gaze and saw the handle of the knife sticking out of his abdomen. He calmly pulled it from the dry flesh and slapped it into the fingerless glove covering the bum's filthy hand.

"Keep it," the priest said. "It'll bring you luck."

Near dawn, Father Sylvestri found what he was looking for on South Street, not far from the Seaport.

She was dressed like the other streetwalkers working the block: short shorts, fishnet stockings, tattooed breasts spilling out of a tight leather jacket. Her hair was bleached, teased up in short spikes, long bangle earrings brushing her shoulders. Her thin face looked hollowed out, as if burning away from the inside, her dark, kohl-lined eyes windows to her blacked-out interior.

They recognized each other instantly.

He didn't think she could have been dead for long. She still had that dazed, unfocused look they always had on first being brought back.

She was doubtlessly one of Hers.

Some poor soul she had turned into one of her eternal slaves and sent out into the world to slake her insatiable hunger for domination. They usually didn't last long before they were hit by a bus or raped or beaten to death.

Although they never died.

Not really.

They were eternal victims.

They just kept on going unless someone chanced upon the one way to put them out of their misery and lay their souls to rest.

The ultimate domination.

She held his gaze for a moment, then dropped her eyes. She turned slowly, coquettishly, and sauntered off down the block in what only he recognized as a parody of the way the others walked, rolling her dead buttocks seductively as she balanced herself atop the thin high heels.

The priest followed her down the street, through an alley thick with shadows and across an abandoned lot of dirt and shattered glass. She stopped every fifty yards or so to make certain that he hadn't lost her, turned toward him and smiled, her lips painted thick and red, exaggerated against her white face, glowing like a lantern in the moonlight.

He stopped when she stopped, and they regarded each other across the distance like two beings without language locked in a complex and ancient ritual of mating.

In a way, that was exactly what they were.

He followed her down to the river and found her waiting for him under the bridge. She had already removed her coat, spreading it on the damp ground and kneeling on it as she pulled down the front of her blouse.

Her breasts were small and hard as baseballs without the red stitching.

The tattoo was two small puncture wounds weeping blood.

She shimmied out of her shorts and torn stockings and knelt there, naked and stupid in the moonlight, the dark water lapping the concrete pilings behind her like all the blood in the world. She was holding her breasts up in her hands, offering them to him, rubbing the gray, unresponsive flesh that moved beneath her thumbs, and mouthing an imaginary penis, but it was the dead-fish stink of the water, its unmistakable aroma of bloat and decay that he found intoxicating.

Overhead, he heard the occasional hum of a car on the bridge into the city, the sound vibrating in the air like the string of a bass.

The city was awakening.

Out in the gray fog he could hear the sound of the first ferries making their way from the Highlands, carrying commuters from New Jersey.

The sun would be up in less than half an hour.

It was time to get to work.

He put down the leather bag, unzipped it, and reached inside for the orange rubber ball gag. She opened her mouth and took it gently between her lips, reminding him of the way his parishoners took Holy Communion from him on Sunday morning. She bowed her head almost reverently as he cuffed her hands behind her back in what always struck him as a mockery of prayer.

"Mashter," he heard her mumble through the gag.

He turned back to the leather bag lying on the damp earth. When he returned he stood over the kneeling vampire, bowing his head to the east, the blotchy light of the fog-shrouded sun burning the back of his neck, and prayed as he lifted the silver cross in the air, one hand on each of its cross bars like the hilt of the sword Excalibur.

I am not your Master. He forced the words into the dead girl's brain. *Your Master is in Heaven. I send your soul to Him.*

Only then did she look up, puzzled, her eyes widening, her sharp teeth biting into the orange rubber ball between her distended lips as the vampire-priest drove the sharpened point at the base of the crucifix through the vulnerable place between her shoulder blades, all the way through the dead meat of her empty heart.

Later, he lashed her ankles together and hoisted her up in his arms, hanging her from the bridge's infrastructure. With a small but lethal silver scythe that the Druids once used for castrating the yearly Oak King, he cut off her head, propping it up at the base of one of the pilings, the staring eyes looking soullessly in the direction of the rising sun.

From out of the severed neck, the round flesh pink as bologna, not a single drop of blood spilled.

FORTY-TWO

"When are you going to let me out of here?"

The priest had returned, unlocking the door to her cell, clutching in his hand a white paper bag. He closed the door behind him and walked to the table where the lantern had long since burned out. He took from his pocket two small votive candles, set them on the table, and lit them with a match. In the flickering yellow light Kelly recognized the trademark golden arches.

"I brought you some food," he said.

Kelly eased off the cot and approached the bag warily. She opened the top and smelled the warm food inside. She pulled out a sausage McMuffin, wrapped in greasy yellow paper, a hash brown nestled in its cardboard sleeve, and a large cup of black coffee.

Not counting the broth she'd had the night before, this was the first real food she'd had in three days.

She tore the paper off the sausage sandwich and folded half of it into her mouth.

Unlike the first two days, she was no longer under the priest's mind control, and she had spent the previous night wide awake. She had paced back and forth across the tiny store cell more times than she cared to count, and after testing the gate and walls to satisfy herself that there was no way to escape, she had finally lay down on the cot. She hadn't intended to fall asleep, just in case the priest came back, but out of sheer boredom she'd done just that.

As she finished the sandwich, licking the grease from her fingers, and began on the hash brown, Kelly gazed at the priest, who had meanwhile backed up to the gate, his arms spread out to either side, fingers laced around the bars.

He looked exhausted, his dark good looks etched with lines, his fierce eyes dulled, his complexion even in the yellow candlelight gray and waxy.

Even his clothes looked rumpled and worn.

He looked to be about twenty years older than he had last night. Kelly wondered if perhaps the priest had been up on another all-night bender, kidnapping more young women. He certainly looked it—

She tore open the three packets of sugar she found at the bottom of the bag, dumped the contents into the coffee, and mixed it all together with a plastic stick.

She washed down the last of the hash brown with a swallow of the hot coffee and looked up again at the priest, who seemed to be studying her with great interest.

"Thank you," she said, warming her hands against the cup. It suddenly seemed to be a lot colder in the cell.

The priest nodded. "You're welcome."

He stepped toward the table to take up the remnants of the breakfast, and Kelly shied backward in her chair.

The priest froze, a look of embarrassment on his face.

"There's no need to be afraid," he said. "I'm not going to hurt you."

He seemed genuinely offended.

He proceeded again, only this time more slowly, to gather up the paper on the table. He turned back toward the gate.

"You haven't answered my question," Kelly said. "When are you going to let me out of here?"

The priest looked down at the refuse in his hands and then up at the ceiling of the cell. He slowly turned around to face Kelly. In his eyes there was an incredible sadness that terrified her even more than the earlier glint of madness, for it betrayed bad news that he himself felt powerless to change.

"That's not a question easily answered," he said.

"Why not?" she asked, unwilling to let him off easily.

The priest put the garbage back down on the table and walked to the far wall, his face averted from hers, his eyes staring through the stone as if to a time and place he could still see.

"It's a long story," he muttered. "Old and sad."

"I've got the time," Kelly said sarcastically.

She was shivering all over now, but it had nothing to do with the cold. The priest looked as if he were debating whether to tell her the truth.

He sighed, and Kelly knew he had.

"It was in the year of our Lord nineteen-sixty-five," the priest began, "that I met her for the first time. I was serving a parish in a small suburban town in New Jersey, where I taught at a Catholic school for girls. I had never heard of the town before, but I had been sent there by the Church after several years in Germany. It was not the kind of place one would have expected to find such a woman, but then, in the most remote corners of the world grow the rarest flowers. She was sixteen at the time I first laid eyes on her, a young woman beautiful as a madonna, in the way a woman is beautiful only once in her life, when no man can resist her.

"I know what you're thinking," the priest said, glancing sharply at Kelly. "That a sixteen-year-old is only a child, but I've lived in times and places where a girl of sixteen was already an old maid or a mother four times over. She was an innocent, this girl, but she was no child, and the blood in her womb tempted me like the sweetest of wines, for it was clear to anyone who had sense to discern such matters that her finest year had come and it would have been a sin against God and Nature to let her sour in the bottle."

"But you are a priest," Kelly said, unable to help herself.

"Do you think that priests have no desires? Have you never thought that perhaps we become priests precisely because our desires are stronger than most?"

"But your vows—"

"It is true that I had forsaken humanity years ago, the fever-sweat of passion seemed so tawdry and bestial to me with the passing of the centuries, but this girl burned with a cool and holy flame that tempted me like a moth to its own immolation. I followed closely her academic career, laying hold of her papers and essays as if they were the testaments of the great philosophers, taking the greatest delight in watching her thoughts struggle for expression like green shoots in the hard reality of the world. I stood at the window of my office and watched her in the schoolyard during lunch hour as she chatted with her friends or played kickball, but mostly sat by herself beneath an old willow tree, reading a book about the martyrdom of the saints or the passion of our Savior, for in spite of her popularity, she was a singularly solitary girl who took such things close to her heart.

"Every Wednesday afternoon there was confession, and naturally I contrived that I should be her confessor. It was there, in the darkness of the confessional, that I fell in love with her soul. She spoke to me of her dreams and desires, of the worries, fears, and hopes of adolescence, and yet underneath it all there was the seriousness of someone three times her age. She had that rarest of human sensibilities, which enabled her to be both revolted and fascinated by the passionate images boiling in her overripe imagination. I had recognized in her a soul in torment, and though it sounds trite, I saw in her a great deal of myself as a younger man. She spoke to me in greatest confidence of wanting to become a nun, and the seriousness in her voice chilled me to the bone. I tried to dissuade her from that calling: A woman of such beauty and sensibility had no business retreating from the world, and I told her so.

"I brought her to my room after school and read to her from my library of books and papers, chronicling the true history of the Church, which no catechism would ever teach. I taught her about the heretics, the mystics, and the saints more holy than those who persecuted them in the name of God. I taught her the horrors of the Inquisition and the Witch Trials and the moral condemnation that perpetuated more horror and misery upon humanity throughout the centuries than all the so-called enemies of the Church combined. I taught her the greatest heresy of all, which was that the Church had declared a spiritual war on an enemy that didn't exist except by its own creation, for it had labeled man an outlaw to be hunted down and crucified for no other crime than being human. Was my intention to save her from a path of tears and thorns or was it merely to corrupt her? Perhaps the two paths have always been but one.

"It was obvious she was falling in love with me, and yet I did nothing to discourage her. The black flame of my soul leapt at the prospect of consuming such a creature. I knew her dreams and fantasies, and when she came to me I did not turn her back, but let her believe she had found a kindred soul in me. It was at the end of March, just before the school staged its annual Easter Passion Play. She was to enact the part of Mary Magdalene, though only modesty kept her from the more im-

358

ortant role of the Virgin. One evening, while I was working late in the auditorium preparing for the show, he slipped into the building on the pretext of having forgotten something at the rehearsal that afternoon. She had been drinking a little—I could smell it on her breath—and beneath the yellow rain slicker she wore I could sense the electricity of her naked flesh. She kissed me quickly and awkwardly, a girl's first sweet kiss, and when she saw I did not mock her she kissed me again, only this time with a tenderness and wonder that once would have melted my heart.

"She smiled shyly and crowned me with a wreath of flowers she had woven with her own hands and proceeded to undress me with such awe and reverence you would have thought she were pulling aside the veil concealing the holy of holies. She kissed my hands and feet, soft fluttery kisses, as if she were entrusting rare butterflies to my care, and laid me down upon the crude wooden cross we used for the crucifixion scene. She tied me to the cross with silken scarves and, trembling as if she had the ague, shed her raincoat and stepped above me in the semidarkness, her body cool and lovely as an angel's. I knew what was in her mind as she made love to me among the props and symbols of history's greatest moment, thinking, through the misdirected passion she felt for me, to express her holy love for the man who loved humanity so much he died in pain and suffering.

"I made love to her only once, but as fate would have it, once was enough to doom her. She kept our forbidden liaison secret until not even the bulky sweaters she wore into the summer could conceal her secret. Her parents were beside themselves with grief and anger, for they had never expected such a thing to happen to her, so sweet and mild a child she had always been, their favorite. Unable to turn their wrath against her, they sought the name of the man who had defiled her, but in spite of their threats and cajoling she wouldn't give up my name. Even though illegal at the time, her parents had the means to procure her a safe abortion, but she wouldn't agree to the procedure, horrifying her parents by her resolve to bear the baby. They put her instead on a plane to California, telling the neighbors she was visiting a relative for the summer, and sent her to a special home for unmarried mothers where the child would be born and put up for adoption. She would return as if nothing had happened, their little girl again.

"I knew nothing of what happened, not that I would have changed events if I had. Shortly after the incident in the auditorium I was transferred from the school to Argentina. Not until years later did I learn the fate of my all-too-human lover. To mix the blood of our races is considered a sin, and insofar as I had taken a vow of chastity I was damned twice, but it was she who paid the price. After a long and difficult labor she died in childbirth, without ever having laid eyes on the fruit of her misplaced love. The child, a girl, was quickly placed with a couple out of state.

"For years I sought to follow the trail of paper to its source, but the bureaucratic maze surrounding these matters is such that not even an immortal has the time to penetrate to its source. At last, however, a few lucky breaks lead me to those who had the answers I sought, and once they understood who it was who sought them they readily gave up their secrets in exchange for their dying breath. I found you in a Catholic orphanage outside Chicago. Your adoptive parents had just been killed in an auto accident. They told you I was a nightmare, but you knew better, lying terrified in your bed as I stood over you, gazing in fond wonder at the miracle I'd wrought, for you were the very reflection of myself in your mother's loving face. Don't think it wasn't hard to refrain from taking you right then, nor would it have been forbidden, for nothing is taboo for a vampire. Yet something held me back—to this day I don't know what—and I swore I'd leave you to live and die outside my shadow, finding what mortal happiness you could.

"I was a fool to think that such a grace was possible, for inside your veins the blood of an immortal flows, and sooner or later you must wake to who you are. I must do now what I should have done before."

"I don't believe you," Kelly said, awed and terrified by the man's words, the more so because they bore the ring of truth. Not the talk of immortals and vampires, of course, but the intimate details of her life. How, for instance, had he known about the orphanage, her adoptive parents' death, the nightmare man. "I don't believe you're who you say you are."

"You don't have to believe me," the priest said. "It is probably better that you don't."

"Why me?" Kelly asked. "Why are you doing this to me?"

"You are a vessel into which I have unwisely poured my blood and soul, and there is One who would take advantage of that weakness to mock and gain mastery over me in the witness of Christ. She will warp you toward the evil and awaken the bloodlust within you so that you, too, become a creature of the damned."

"Ilana?" Kelly asked.

"You are surrounded by vampires. She is but a disciple of the Goddess of whom I speak."

"You are the one who's been killing all those girls, aren't you?" Kelly said with terrible certainty.

"I've killed no one," the priest protested, "who wasn't already dead. I merely laid their souls to rest."

"And that is what you intend to do to me, isn't it? That's what you're going to call it. Putting my soul to rest so that I don't become a vampire. What you really mean is that you're going to murder me in cold blood."

The priest shook his head sadly.

"You are making far too big a deal of this. Death is not hard. What is hard is to live without hope. Without peace. Without the promise of death."

He turned to the gate, opening it and locking it behind him.

He stood by the bars for a long time, looking in at his prisoner, his face once again filled with sadness.

"If you only knew what I was saving you from," he said. "You'd fall to your knees and thank me."

FORTY-THREE

Ilana lay facedown on the massage table as Paulette ran her oiled hands over the dead muscles of her shoulder blades, working out the stiffness.

Ilana closed her eyes and sighed.

The girl may have been mute, but her fingers spoke all the forgotten languages of pleasure.

Her hands helped move the sluggish blood Ilana had recently ingested from a mother and daughter, coaxing her inner organs into functioning. Paulette alternated her long, smooth strokes with a short chopping assault that loosened the acidic wastes and pollutants, awakening the burnt-out nerve endings. Ilana could feel the dirty, distressed blood becoming oxygenated.

It began moving through her body as if it were her own, giving her a momentary semblance of life.

Exhilarating.

The hands continued to move, rubbing, thumping, cupping as the girl poured more oil into her palms, her fingers melting as if they were made of warm butter.

They feathered lightly over the small of her back, the firm white globes of her ass, and gently stroked the soft flesh at the back of her thighs.

As she lay there she replayed that evening's performance before her mind's eye.

The mother and daughter had been quite extraordinary, better than she could have expected, especially the mother. The way she had changed from selfless parent concerned only with her daughter's safety to savage she-devil determined to ensure her own survival had added an extra frisson to the proceedings, especially at the end when the mother cut the teenager's throat in a desperate and ultimately futile attempt to ingratiate herself with her captors and save her own life. If she could have criticized anything, however, she wondered if she had made them feel enough pain. Certainly the duration of their suffering had been sufficient, but had they suffered intensely enough?

Perhaps she was just being too critical.

The audience had seemed to enjoy the performance, judging from the applause. But Ilana was a perfectionist; that's what made her so good at what she did. Well, practice made perfect. She would get another opportunity soon enough.

Ilana allowed herself to concentrate fully on the exquisite sensations emanating from the very cradle of her being as Paulette had teased the withered nerves in her vagina into jangling life. She could feel the atrophied parts there grow swollen and warm with borrowed blood as the girl between her legs breathed heavily with the labor of her exertion.

Ilana felt her own breath grow heavy as Paulette replaced the hands between her legs with the warmth of her face, her lips seeking the tiny piece of dead flesh that was the trigger of all pleasure. She felt the girl coax, plead, and finally forcibly try to pull the trigger—to no avail. For a moment Ilana poised on the edge of orgasmic rapture, but just as suddenly the sensation faded, leaving her with nothing but memory, intangible as the echo of a beloved voice.

The girl labored on, but the feeling was lost. In spite

of her earnest efforts, she was doing little more than licking at dead flesh.

"That's enough, Paulette," Ilana said, annoyed.

The girl stepped away mutely, her face shiny with her own saliva but showing no sign of the distaste she must have felt for the act of necrophilia she'd just been required to perform.

Ilana rose from the table.

"Leave me alone." She waved off Paulette, who bowed to her mistress and turned to leave the room, her head lowered.

Ilana watched the long, sinuous curve of the naked girl's back, the suggestive roll of her rosy-pink buttocks, the delicate placement of her feet as she walked, and felt the slightest twinge of jealousy.

Ilana turned and walked across the room to the tiled floor surrounding the inlaid hot tub. She descended the three steps into the warm bubbling mineral water. She crouched down into the water, letting it lap against her chin, splashing up on her cold porcelain cheeks like someone else's tears.

With her eyes wide open, Ilana slipped off into a kind of death.

She was roused an indeterminate time later by the sound of scuffling and muffled shouts, her consciousness surfacing slowly behind her staring eyes, like a diver rising from a bone-crushing depth.

In the water Ilana was aware of something dripping red, the drops burgeoning in the water like roses in time-lapse photography, blooming and disappearing in a matter of seconds.

Ilana knew they weren't roses, though to her they were as fragrant.

She looked up and saw the Vampire standing at the

edge of the Jacuzzi. So entranced was Ilana by the woman's commanding beauty that she momentarily failed to notice the object she was carrying.

In the Vampire's right hand, dangling from its long brown hair, swung Paulette's severed head.

The Vampire let the head fall to the tiles with a soft crunch, and it rolled over onto its cheek, the pretty eyes staring into nowhere. She kicked the head into the tub with the steel-toed tip of her leather boot. The head rolled and tossed in the violent water like a cabbage.

"You've killed her," Ilana said stupidly. If she could have sorted out her feelings at that moment she would have realized that her shock wasn't so much due to the fact that the girl had been killed but that no one had the right to kill her but Ilana.

"You know how the game works," the Vampire said.

The head bobbed to the surface, eyes staring at the ceiling as if in ecstasy, and then disappeared once again.

"But—why?"

"You have no need for servants anymore," the Vampire said ominously.

Already Ilana felt the Vampire's mind inside hers, a dark gloved hand stroking the ghost of nerves long dead, eliciting a response that existed only in memory, one that not even Paulette, with all of her training in the sensual arts, could attain.

Suddenly, the presence was withdrawn.

Ilana shivered with anticipation, her body arching like a bow with tension, pulled by an invisible hand.

"No," she whimpered. "Not yet."

"No, you don't want to die," the Vampire asked, amused, "or no, you don't want me to stop?"

"Please," Ilana said, unsure herself what she meant. "I've done everything you've asked."

"Yes, you have," the Vampire said. "But then again, what choice did you have? I need your energy, Ilana. I have an appointment with an old, old friend, a man of God, as it were. He's more important to me than you. It's as simple as that. Now, come."

And Ilana felt herself coming.

She moved through the water, pulled along like a fish on a powerful, inexorable line. She crawled up the steps of the Jacuzzi, over the tiles, lying naked at the steel-toed boots, under the imperious gaze of her godlike mistress.

"On your belly, *slave*," the Vampire mocked.

Ilana felt the word on her back like the lash of a whip, but it did nothing to stop the burning in her loins; if anything, the humiliation only added fuel to the fire that was consuming her. She lay there naked on the tiles at the feet of the Vampire and felt a strange sensation, a sensation she hadn't felt in the nearly four hundred years since she'd been changed. It was strange and exciting and terrifying all at once.

It was the touch of cold, of something colder than herself, of death itself.

She had little time to register the sensation before another more powerful one jolted her system, leaving her squirming indelicately on the tiles, as if she were being electrocuted by pleasure. She looked up, breathless, in gratitude and terror, and saw the Vampire towering over her. She shimmied forward and kissed the tips of the woman's boots, leaving two lipstick prints on the polished steel.

She felt the jolt again, only this time there was no release; it was as if her nerves had been overloaded, her body's dead circuitry shorting out, catching fire. She tried to beg for mercy, but her teeth were shattering, her bones rattling, and a feeling like a great black wave was rising inside her so immense that she immediately realized the hopelessness of any further resistance.

In that instant Ilana knew the ecstasy of the slave, the

sacrifice, of all those who gave their lives to something greater than themselves.

In that instant of orgasmic release, she felt a joy unmatched by any she had ever known.

As her head was lifted into the air by the hair and her bulging eyes saw the indignity of her abandoned body still writhing on the tiles below, Ilana had just enough time to register the forbidden pleasure she was tasting for the first and last time, the thought shuddering through her with the force of personal apocalypse that here was something greater than domination.

submission . . .

The Vampire laughed, kissing the lips on which the dying word was formed, tasting each delicious syllable, the nectar of immortality itself.

She laid the head on the edge of the pool and slowly undressed, removing her leather gear with the self-conscious artistry of a stripper, knowing that the dead vampire could still see through dimmed eyes, that the severed head would live on a while yet.

When she was naked the Vampire stepped into the roiling water of the Jacuzzi and let herself drift to the far end as she closed her eyes and dreamed of another dead lover in a similar situation four hundred years ago, Ilana's former mistress, Elisabet Bathory.

FORTY-FOUR

The candles had long since burned down and drowned in their own pools of wax. Meanwhile, Kelly lost track of time, of space, of whether she was awake or asleep.

She brushed away imaginary insects from her face and tried not to picture the mice that might well inhabit such a cellar, in spite of the telltale squeaking she occasionally heard.

She kept her feet up on the cot, her arms folded across her body, hugging herself for warmth.

In the darkness she'd had plenty of opportunity to contemplate what the mad priest had said about her past. It was insane, certainly, and yet as the uncounted hours passed and she tried to make sense of what was happening to her, her mind could conceive of no more rational explanation and so had seized compulsively upon what the priest had said.

Some of what he'd said was undeniably true. She could not deny that the story of her life seemed to have been mysteriously shaped by an unlikely series of accidents. Still, she couldn't allow herself to believe that the tragedies she'd experienced had all been some kind of grand conspiracy, though in the darkest moments of her life it was true she had often entertained her share of paranoid fantasies. Nor could she believe that her wild-eyed kidnapper was, in fact, her father. Yet how else could she explain his intimate knowledge of her life? Certainly the possibility that the man was her father was the most believable aspect of this unbelievable turn of events.

She had never seen her real father, and this man might be him just as well as the next. But if he were her father, why had he kidnapped her? What had she ever done to him?

His talk of vampires had convinced her of his insanity, but at the same time it struck a resonant chord deep inside her. The fact was, her interest in domination pointed to a strange and aberrant taste. She remembered how Ilana had called sadists vampires at the Theater of Pain. She wondered if that was why he had tracked her down. Kelly shuddered as she thought of the way she'd wielded the whip against her own father. And yet even with the knowledge of who she was, he had encouraged her to follow him back to the abandoned building. Perhaps he was some kind of religious fanatic who, upon discovering that his daughter had inherited his tainted blood, was now intent on destroying her.

She remembered, too, the day she had fled Connor's loft. What was it that he had yelled down the elevator shaft as she headed for the street? Something about not knowing who she really was . . .

At the time she had taken it merely as the accusation of a desperate man who thought he knew what was best for her better than she did herself.

Now she wondered if he really did know something she didn't.

Had he been following her for a good reason?

Suddenly, she heard the scratch of a match. The

sound scared her, for she hadn't even heard anyone enter the cell.

She put up her hand to shield her eyes against the light. He had changed into the long purple robes that he probably wore to administer Sunday mass. On the table, surrounded by a circle of fresh votive candles, he had set a tray on which stood a silver chalice and a small plate containing a single white wafer. The sight struck a special kind of terror in Kelly's heart.

The priest bowed before the chalice and looked at Kelly, curled up on the cot.

"Come, child," he said.

"What are you going to do to me?" Kelly asked, trying not to sound as frightened as she felt.

"I am going to give you communion. Come."

Kelly didn't move from the cot.

"Don't make me force you," the priest said quietly. Kelly knew he could do it. She remembered how he'd invaded her mind earlier, the helplessness and nausea she'd experienced as he manipulated her body as if she were a puppet, pulling the strings through the force of his will alone.

She rose from the cot and reluctantly approached the priest.

"Kneel," he said.

Slowly, Kelly lowered herself to her knees, her hands folded together as if in prayer, but really to keep herself from trembling.

Above her, the priest lifted the wafer to the ceiling, his eyes staring up reverently, reciting in Latin the incantations that Kelly vaguely remembered from Catholic school. Around his neck, hanging from a long cord, Kelly saw a large silver crucifix catching the light of the candles, its lower end tapering into a nasty point.

She was contemplating the cruel-looking crucifix when the priest continued the ritual of transubstantiation in English. At first she thought she was hearing him wrong, his words twisted into a nightmare gospel of evil.

For he hung upon the cross at that hour, close to death he was when the Vampire approached. She offered him eternal life and dominion over all the kingdoms of heaven and earth and showed him the fate that awaited him. She showed him the fate that awaited him if he chose life and the fate that awaited him on the other side of the grave. The thirst was great upon him, raging through his dying body, and yet he did not weaken.

Even at that last hour he did not weaken. The Vampire sought to tempt him with the cup of life, holding the blood before his parched and cracked lips, tempting him with her body, even the body fashioned by the Goddess Herself, Astarte, and Isis and the goddesses of the secret groves of love.

He did not weaken, no, not even at that hour of greatest need, but mastered himself and the angels around him, so that all the world might see how this man conquered himself and how his death opened the way to the peace hereafter. Selah.

When he was done the priest held the wafer to her lips.

"Body of Christ," he intoned.

Stunned, Kelly opened her mouth obediently and took the Host.

She bowed her head. "Amen," she whispered.

Even though the priest was mad, she drew some comfort in the hope that something of the ritual retained its power, that her last conscious act on earth was to take holy communion.

She'd taken the sacrament only once since her days in the orphanage, and that had been her first Christmas in New York, when she'd gone to a mass at Saint Patrick's Cathedral. Yet all at once the postage-stamp taste of the wafer brought back a storm of memories from those early days, memories of her overwhelming feelings of piety, solemnity, and humility at the realization of what it meant to take communion. Kelly waited for the Host to dissolve on her tongue until it was soft enough to swallow, as the nuns had stressed, not to touch or tear it with her teeth, remembering that through the magic of Catholic ritual, the wafer of bread had quite literally become the flesh of the Savior, Jesus Christ.

In the meantime, the priest had consecrated the wine, kissing the chalice and closing his eyes in almost sensual rapture.

Kelly wanted to run, to bolt from the dungeon room, but fear transfixed her to the spot.

Fear—and something else.

The priest lowered the chalice and Kelly took it, the silver cold between her hands. She stared up at the priest, who looked down at her with a strange benevolence. His face no longer bore the expression of pain and suffering it had before. In the flickering candlelight, Kelly might have mistaken him for a man her own age.

"Drink," he said.

Kelly lifted the chalice to her lips and was surprised at the *warmth* of the wine inside. She stared up questioningly at the priest, who nodded, smiling, at the chalice.

"Drink," he said again.

Kelly took another sip of the wine, this time prepared for the warmth of the beverage, and she closed her eyes in appreciation of its intoxicating flavor. She lifted the chalice, greedily gulping its contents, afraid that the priest might try to take the cup away from her before she'd had her fill. Instead, he let her drink, watching approvingly as she suckled from the silver pap of the holy vessel. For her part, Kelly felt the warmth spread through her limbs like liquid fire. It was not just the warmth of the alcohol, but something more intimate, more sensual—something *alive*.

Kelly felt as if her senses had been turned up a level. Suddenly, the sight of the flickering candlelight, the aftertaste of the wine, the smell of the burning wax, the sound of the priest's voice, the damp, cool air on her face opened stunning new avenues of sensation throughout her body. She was seized with a series of erotic tremors as wave after wave of sense impressions swept over her, leaving her trembling with ecstasy. In a part of her brain she realized that the wine must have been drugged, and yet soon even this last island of logic was swept away in the warm, erotic sea that rose over her, filling her lungs with its suffocating perfume, her ears with its siren's song of oblivion.

When Kelly opened her eyes she found herself staring up at the towering figure of Jesus Christ, twisting in agony upon his cross.

She felt the coolness of the marble beneath her and realized that she was lying on the church altar. All around her candles burned, lapping at her exposed flesh like warm orange tongues.

She must have passed out before he carried her up from the dungeon to perform the sacrifice. She came to this conclusion with a strange detachment, as if it were happening to someone else. She was still under the spell of whatever had been in the wine, a prisoner in her own body, enchanted by the sensuality of her own enhanced senses.

She turned her head lazily to the side and saw the priest. He was feverishly mumbling some prayers, his eyes staring up at the dying god on the cross, as if speaking directly to him.

"Forgive me . . . Father . . ." Kelly whispered, her lips forming around the words like a kiss.

The priest ignored her.

He continued his prayer to the marble Christ, and for the first time Kelly noticed the huge, shining crucifix he held before his face, the big brother of the one he wore around his neck, the light traveling down its channeled length, pulsing in a point above her bared breastbone.

"Take care of my daughter, Lord," the priest intoned. "Admit her back into your Kingdom. She is innocent of the evil in her blood. I gave her life in darkness and I take it away in the name of the Light ..."

Kelly understood that the time had come for her to die, and yet somehow she didn't care. In a way, she welcomed the cruel and swift penetration of the blade, her breath quickening as her father raised the cruciform sword above his head and began to bring it down with a terrible cry of pain.

Kelly had closed her eyes, waiting for the rapturous blow, but it never came.

When she opened her eyes again she saw the priest staring into the palms of his hands, as if they were burned. The cross-sword had flown off, traveling end-over-end and clattering to the floor at the base of the Holy Sepulchre.

The priest turned sharply and saw the Vampire standing in the center aisle between the pews. Over her shoulder, she saw a large man in a black suit standing guard at the door.

"How dare you blaspheme this Holy Communion?" he thundered.

"I see you've found her for me," the Vampire said, staring past him to the girl on the altar. "I knew you would. After all, blood *is* thicker than water."

The priest started forward, swinging a censer of incense.

"I cast you out, unclean spirit," he shouted. "In the name of the Father, the Son, the Holy Ghost. I cast you out!"

The Vampire ignored him.

Instead, she came closer to the altar, her boots echoing loudly on the marble floor. In the alcoves the votive candles flickered, the saints looking terrified.

"She is quite pretty," the Vampire said. She looked

375

from the girl to the priest and back again. "I can see the family resemblance. She's certainly well worth waiting for. You should be proud of her, Sylvestri. I promise I shall enjoy corrupting her immensely."

"You can't take her. You don't have the power. Not here."

"Oh, but I do," the Vampire replied casually. "You see, I just paid a visit to another old friend."

"I'll kill you," the priest roared. He threw away the censer and started forward, his fists doubled up like maces at his sides.

He hadn't gotten within ten feet of the Vampire before he was stopped in his tracks, his hands on either side of his head, clutching his skull as if he were afraid it would explode. He fell to one knee, his eyes squeezed shut in pain, tears of blood running down his weathered cheeks. He felt her hand inside his brain, squeezing his mind like a sponge, releasing the foulest images from his memory.

"I—renounce—you," he muttered, forcing the words through a jaw clenched against the mounting wave of pain.

He raised himself to his feet, struggling against her control like a weightlifter against a bar full of iron, his body trembling with the supernatural effort. He staggered forward, his arms extended, as if walking through a firestorm. He felt the flesh peeling from his face, his bones splintering, his cells dying. His fingers touched the white skin of her throat, the very ridges of his flesh describing dizzying heights of pleasure. He closed his hands around her windpipe, breathless with passion, and felt her yield within his grasp. It seemed almost impossible how easy it was, after all this time, to destroy her. He felt a pang of sympathy, even of love, and he opened his eyes to gaze upon her face one last time and was shocked to see the mockery there.

"Goddamn you," he cried, and crushed her windpipe in his powerful hands.

He had killed before—so many times before, he had lost count—but it was never quite like this. He felt her life between his palms, twisting like some elemental thing, a powerful snake, all muscle and bone, her indomitable will to survive more terrifying than death. He redoubled his efforts, calling on his deepest reserves of faith and strength, but the evil thing in his hands turned on him, and suddenly it was as if he'd been struck by lightning, the bolt paralyzing him where he stood and then throwing him violently backward, hurling him clear across the room and into a pew, which shattered into a million shiny splinters.

The priest knew then that he couldn't kill her, not if he were given a hundred lifetimes. He looked wildly back to the altar on which Kelly still lay and jumped to his feet, hell-bent on reaching her in time.

As he approached the altar his hand clutched for the sharpened crucifix around his neck, ready to drive it into his daughter's heart, but froze halfway there, opening and closing spasmodically in the empty air. The cord snapped and the beads scattered across the marble floor. The cross followed with a hollow clang.

Kelly saw the look of terror in his eyes.

The priest felt the robes shredding from his body as if he were set upon by a host of invisible claws. He screamed as if he were on fire as the demons stripped him naked, sweeping him off his feet and hurling him back against the cross. He was held there, crucified by tension, for what seemed like an eternity, before he felt the invisible nails methodically being driven into his feet, his wrists. He bellowed in pain, his crucified body superimposed on that of his Lord, twisting in pain as he was lashed by a sudden storm of invisible whips.

"My God," he shouted, his eyes rolling upward. "Why hast thou forsaken me?"

On the altar, Kelly reached down sleepily and picked up the crucifix that fell from her father's neck. She slipped it inside her coat, over her heart, thinking it might protect her, and then she lost consciousness.

The Vampire stood under the cross and stared up at the crucified priest. She called back to the man in the black suit guarding the door, unwilling to take her eyes from the pain on her victim's face for even a moment.

"Take the girl to the car, Daniel," she said. "I want a few minutes alone with the good father. We have nearly two thousand years of catching up to do."

FORTY-FIVE

Officer Patrick Brannigan heard the call while he was sitting at the counter of his favorite twenty-four-hour coffee shop on East Twelfth Street. The night manager had a television above the refrigerated case that he usually had tuned in to whatever sport was in season, and he let Brannigan eat for free in exchange for the security of having his own police protection.

For his part, Brannigan had turned the stool on which he sat into his own informal headquarters. Everyone in the precinct knew where they could find Brannigan if they needed him; he'd be sitting right there at the counter, sipping coffee and having a nosh, monitoring his radio for calls he couldn't avoid answering.

He was doing just that when the call came in about the trouble at the church.

He didn't remember ever seeing a church in that area, but he recognized the address immediately because it was in one of the most notorious high-crime districts in the city. The cops avoided it whenever they could, and when they couldn't they made sure that the action had cooled down before they went in to assess the damage and count the casualties, and even then they usually waited for suitable reinforcements.

So Officer Brannigan hardly leapt off his stool to

head for the scene of the crime. On the contrary, he calmly finished the last of his ham sandwich and ordered another cup of coffee and a piece of Vic's famous cocoanut custard pie before reluctantly hoisting his twenty-year-veteran ass off his stool and heading for the patrol car to answer the call of duty.

Meanwhile, a few blocks away, Devon Hilliard was sitting in his patrol car, talking to a couple of prostitutes who were playfully leaning in at his open window. He was having a nice time flirting with one, a cute little mocha-colored number in tight gold hot pants and a sequined tube top when he heard Brannigan on the radio, responding to the call at the church and requesting backup. Hilliard, too, had heard the earlier call and had decided to sit on it awhile until someone else picked it up. He knew that being a native of these parts was no immunity to the hatred the neighborhood people felt for the police. If anything, his pigmentation made him even more of a target insofar as a lot of folks felt a lot more comfortable shooting one of their own. They didn't really see him as a cop, just another nigger masquerading in a blue uniform.

"Sorry, girls," he said, rolling up his window as the girls groaned their disappointment. "Duty calls."

The little mocha princess leaned forward and planted a big wet kiss on the window, leaving a pink lipstick stain on the glass.

Cute, Hilliard thought.

They both pulled up in front of the church at approximately the same time. Brannigan climbed out of his car when he saw Hilliard come up behind him.

"What's up?" Hilliard asked, noting that Brannigan had already unbuttoned the snap on his holster.

He knew Brannigan from his first days on the force, when the lard-bellied, donut-eating cop was charged with the duty of teaching Hilliard the ropes and skills necessary to staying alive on the streets. Those skills amounted to developing an instinctive sense of locating where trouble was most likely to occur and then contriving to place yourself as far away from it as possible without breaking any departmental regulations. Brannigan had undoubtedly developed the skill to perfection, and Hilliard felt extremely fortunate to have studied at the feet of the master.

"I don't know," Brannigan said. "Someone called in trouble at the church. Front door's ajar, but I don't think anyone's inside. If they're still in there after all this time, their too fucking stupid to be dangerous."

"Are they sending backup?"

"Should be here in a few minutes."

They had both arrived at the scene with their lights and sirens off so as not to attract a crowd. In this neighborhood, any time a crowd gathered there was always the possibility of stray gunfire.

"Should we go inside?" Hilliard asked, already pulling his gun.

"Let's check it out."

They advanced slowly up the stairs of the church, which was dwarfed between the surrounding tenements, looking like a wedding cake made of soot and grime. They reached the top of the stairs and stood at either side of the large double doors, guns drawn, and looked at each other. Brannigan nodded, and the two officers shoved open the door and slipped inside the church, crouching low to the floor.

"Police!" they shouted in unison.

There was blood everywhere.

Blood filled the holy water fonts, pooled on the marble floors, dripped from the pews. The stained-glass windows were smeared with blood and the holy statues in the alcoves on either side of the church were wet and scarlet, as if they had been painted with it. The votive cups in front of the statues were overflowing with blood, and at the end of the aisle the altar itself was slick with blood, as if all humanity had been slaughtered there in one monstrous satanic sacrifice.

Brannigan and Hilliard stood at the head of the aisle, too stunned to move, their mouths gaping, their guns lowered to the floor. The magnitude of what they saw defied all description. Had someone been waiting in the shadows behind the door, they would have been able to cut both their throats without the least resistance.

"Holy shit," Brannigan whispered.

Together, he and Hilliard stared at the priest crucified above the altar as if they were gazing at a holy vision.

And then Hilliard doubled over and puked.

FORTY-SIX

In her dreams, Kelly was burning, the flames wrapping her legs in orange light, licking at her belly and breasts. The sensation was so vivid, she was sure she had experienced the real thing in a previous life. Only when she heard the voice of her Inquisitor was she able to awaken, staring into the bank of hot Kliegl lights that scrubbed her in their omnipotent glare.

"Hello, Kelly," the voice said. "It's so nice to meet you at last."

"Where are you?" Kelly shouted into the lights. She knew that she had been brought to the Theater of Pain. She stared up at her manacled hands, the chain pulling her up so that her weight rested uncomfortably on her toes, making it difficult to keep her balance in the high heels, her ankles locked in a thirty-six-inch spreader bar. A few feet to her left she saw a stark iron rack from which hung whips, paddles, and other instruments of torture that someone had wheeled out and left there, no doubt to give her food for thought. It was Valerie who had taught her the importance of building a sense of anticipation in her victims. Kelly remembered the couple at the show several weeks ago and wondered if behind the lights there was an audience watching her. She wondered if Ilana had somehow found out that she had written a story about her experiences and this was her punishment.

"Ilana?" she said, squinting into the light. "Is that you?"

"Ilana is dead."

The light seemed to part, as if it were a curtain of fire, and a shadow slipped through. She was dressed in the black leather bondage outfit that Ilana had worn the night of the show, but Kelly could tell that the woman behind the mask was not Ilana. In her hand was a leather crop that she lifted to Kelly's face. Kelly gazed at the woman in the mask with a mixture of defiance and awe. She was flawlessly, incredibly, indescribably beautiful. Her gray eyes seemed to hold the enigmatic mystery of God Himself, while her lips seemed to promise the most ecstastic secrets of the flesh. Kelly already felt the powerful urge to submit to this strange and commanding woman undermining her will power, but she fought against it with all her strength.

"Who are you?"

"I am the woman you've been searching for your entire life, the woman poets speak of, and of whom lovers dream. The Bible called me Lillith. Keats called me la belle dame sans merci, the beautiful lady without mercy. Stoker called me a vampire."

Kelly didn't know whether the woman was serious or whether this was all part of the show—or, even more terrifying, both. She looked toward the light. "Are there people watching?"

"Whenever there is pain there are always beings present. Suffering is consciousness, as the Buddha said, but what he didn't say is that it feeds consciousness. From the bystanders at the scene of an accident to the visitors at the bedside of a dying cancer patient, suffering creates a well in time from which creatures both seen and unseen draw their life."

384

"Is that what you intend to do to me?" Kelly asked defiantly, determined not to let the woman see her fear. "Make me suffer?"

"In a manner of speaking," the Vampire said. She moved out of Kelly's line of sight, standing behind her, and Kelly braced herself for the bite of the riding crop. In the past several weeks she had administered a lot of pain, all of it, of course, inflicted upon more than willing victims. She saw how acceptance enabled her slaves not only to endure the pain but to derive intense pleasure from it. Yet now that it was her turn to be on the receiving end, Kelly knew she would not submit, no matter how much she suffered. She waited for the first blow to fall, but it never did. Instead, the Vampire had walked all the way around her and now stood before her again, the crop held under her chin as she considered Kelly.

"Why don't you do what you have to do and get it over with?" Kelly growled.

"It's not going to be that easy, I'm afraid," the Vampire said. "You see, Kelly, I understand your nature better than you do yourself. I might break your body, but I could never break your spirit, for in your veins flows your father's blood, the same sacred blood that flows in mine. What I seek is not your submission but your enlightenment. I want to awaken you fully to who you really are—a Vampire who lives on the pain and suffering of others."

"Never," Kelly cried. "You'll never turn me into such a monster. Kill me now and get it over with."

"Not so fast, Kelly," the Vampire said. "The show has only begun." She looked up into the rafters. "Lights!" she shouted.

The bank of lights in front of her suddenly shut down and another bank came on with the sound of a thousand wings, illuminating her from behind. She blinked back the temporary blindness and made out the full-

385

length mirror standing a few feet in front of her. Kelly saw herself trussed up and wearing the domination outfit she'd put on several nights before. Her stockings were torn and her hair needed washing. She averted her eyes.

"Look into the mirror, Kelly," the Vampire said. "What do you see? I'll tell you what I see: A pretty young woman at the height of her physical and mental appeal, a strong healthy body that many men lust after and many women envy, a quick and lively intelligence that seeks to understand the meaning beneath experience, that challenges what most fools only take for granted. But all of these qualities are fleeting, like the shadow of a bird across a lake at evening, from darkness it comes to darkness it goes. Just so, what I see in the mirror is passing even as I speak. For nothing in that mirror remains the same. Look, Kelly, look into the mirror at the face of what's to come."

Reluctantly, Kelly lifted her head, and this time when she looked into the mirror she could see her naked body beneath the clothes she wore, but even as she recognized the nude woman in the mirror as herself, the image began to change and shift. She saw her breasts and belly visibly begin to sag and fat pad her hips and thighs. She saw bags collecting under her dimming eyes and lines spread across the once smooth skin of her face. Almost imperceptibly at first, and then more rapidly, her hair grew in white and brittle. At the same time, her joints began to swell, red and painful, and flesh hung down from her jaws in a fleshy dewlap. She tried to turn her head away before she could see more, but it was as if she were riveted to this time-lapse projection of her life. Suddenly, her vision shifted again, and it was as if her flesh had become transparent, and she could see through to the inner workings of the anatomy underneath.

"Do you see that dark mass in the lower left quadrant

of your abdomen?" the Vampire said. "That is the beginning of the cancer that will kill you. It will start in your uterus and grow secretly for nearly two years before the first painful symptoms send you to your doctor. By then it will have spread throughout your body like wildfire, mestastisizing in your liver, your lungs, your brain."

Even as the Vampire spoke, Kelly saw the dark mass growing, sending off its silent emissaries of death through the limbic system of her body, until it was posted at every vital site. Then, as if by quiet and malignant consent, they rose up in revolt, demanding their own life and survival with single-minded fanaticism, overthrowing the very life off which they lived. She watched in terrible fascination as the destruction raged, unable to tear her eyes away from her dying body, the flesh rapidly melting away like snow in the sun, as the cancer inside her burned out of control and left her nothing but a soulless sack of bone and ash. And still it didn't end, for death stripped her of what the cancer couldn't steal, and she saw the grinning skeleton advance from the ruins like the one assassin you never expected because he was hiding inside of you all along. And then it was as if years had passed and she saw the casket in which she lay rotted by dampness and plundered by mice and insects, the bones inside, tossed unceremoniously by successive cycles of freeze and thaw, scattered pell-mell beneath the orderly green lawn of the cemetery.

The image in the mirror faded, and Kelly once again saw herself as she was, yet shadowed by what she knew she was becoming.

"It doesn't have to be that way," the Vampire whispered. "You can stop time, avoid the mortal inevitability."

"How?" Kelly said numbly.

387

"Daniel," the Vampire shouted, and suddenly the lights illuminating the mirror shut down and another bank came on to replace them. Kelly turned her head to the right, the manacles clanking overhead, and drew a sharp intake of breath when she saw Gwen bathed in the unforgiving light.

She was on her knees, bound to a short T-shaped cross, her arms spread out on either side along the cross bar, her ankles crossed and lashed behind the upright. Her naked body bore the marks of severe mistreatment, her skin sheathed in sweat, sweat plastering her hair to her skull. She lifted her head, and Kelly was shocked to see the expression stamped there, her nostrils flaring, her lips parted, her eyes glazed over, it was the look of a woman in the most extreme throes of passion. She looked at Kelly as if it were only natural that she'd be present, for in the logic of her fantasies, Kelly had been there all along.

"Take me," Gwen sighed, her breasts heaving with pent-up desire, the small silver bells attached to her nipple clamps jingling merrily.

"Stop it," Kelly shouted trying to wake Gwen out of this nightmare. "Don't do this!"

Gwen worked her sweat-slicked body up the post as best her bonds would allow, wriggling in a lewd come-hither dance.

"Stop it," Kelly said again, feeling something dark building inside her, threatening to break through. She tore her eyes away from Gwen.

"Only you can stop it," the Vampire said, her tone sly and cool, dripping with insinuation. "Only you can save her life. Look."

And in spite of herself, Kelly turned her head back to her friend, knowing full well that once she did she would be pushed past the point of no return.

Gwen knelt there as before, only now Kelly could see

inside the abandoned body of her friend, could see the exchanges made between her cells, the blood orbiting through her body, the synapses firing in her brain, and all of it timed by the beating of her heart. At the same time, Kelly could see how the cells grew weaker with each exchange, more vulnerable to injury and mutation, the age and disease coded inside the genes. She saw how the blood deposited its fatty substances inside the arteries around her heart like silt laid at the mouth of a river, how the synapses fired less efficiently each time, deadening thought and feeling by such incremental measures one hardly noticed the slow slide toward senility. And behind it all, through it all, Kelly saw her friend's heart beating with the terrible precision of a metronome, each beat taking a moment from her life, leading her to the grave, a countdown to Doomsday. Suddenly, Kelly saw the phantom of time behind all phenomena, the dark angel mocking her with each passing second, the sands of life spilling away through her fingers, her friend dying before her eyes.

"Take me," Gwen said.

And Kelly was moving across the stage, free of the manacles, crouched over the moist, trembling body, her specialized incisors sliding out from under her gums where they'd always been, hidden behind her human teeth, waiting for this moment of recognition and revelation when she kissed Gwen and discovered who she truly was.

FORTY-SEVEN

Rossi got the call from Graham at half-past midnight.

Graham got the story from an off-duty uniformed cop who was sitting at the same neighborhood bar that Graham frequented, soaking up a beer. A priest had just been found in a church in the meat-packing district, close to the warehouse where the first body was found. There wasn't a lot of information available, except that the two cops who'd found him hadn't stopped puking yet and nobody was giving the priest much chance of surviving.

Rossi told Graham to sit tight and he'd pick him up in fifteen minutes.

It was raining as the old Grand Prix zipped along the wet streets. Rossi remembered the priest from St. Jude's Church. They had interviewed him about a week earlier. The name on the list that Father Martin had given Rossi was Father Paul Bettinger, but the priest at St. Jude's informed them that Father Paul Bettinger had been suddenly transferred out of the parish. When they asked why he'd been transferred, the priest said enigmatically that Bettinger was on sabbatical. The suspicious nature of the transfer left Rossi sure that Father Paul was the man they were looking for, and he'd expended most of his efforts in the past week in trying to locate him, with no success.

Rossi slowed at a red light and went straight through.

Now that Rossi thought about it, he hadn't liked the looks of the priest at St. Jude's from the start. There was something about him that wasn't quite kosher, if you could forgive the expression. Unlike Father Martin, the priest didn't have that plump, pink, cherubic look that even the rotten ones seemed to have. Instead he was a big, rawboned, haunted-looking man. He wondered what the priest—he couldn't remember his name—had known about the murders, for Rossi was pretty certain that it wasn't a coincidence that he'd been attacked. He remembered what the FBI man had said about the AC and what Father Martin had said about how the church like to protect its dark secrets.

Rossi turned down Prospect Avenue and spotted Graham standing on the corner, his hands thrust deep in the pockets of his overcoat, the rain plastering his already thin hair to his large, bony skull. Rossi reached over and unlocked the door as Graham climbed inside, shaking himself all over like a dog.

"Jeezus, it's a crapass night," he said. He stretched his hands over the vent to warm them. "What, have you got the air conditioner on?"

"No," Rossi said. "Thermostat's bad. Takes a long time to warm up."

"How long?"

"August."

"Shit."

Graham reached into his overcoat and produced the stub of an old cigar. He stuck it in the corner of his mouth and pulled out the lighter in the Grand Prix's dash. He touched it to the cigar, puffed, touched it again, and stared in disgust at the cold coil inside the lighter.

"Why the hell didn't you tell me it was broken?"

Rossi shrugged. "Didn't know until just now."

Graham grunted in disgust and tossed the lighter into the ashtray.

Rossi coasted through another red light as he headed for the bridge.

"Brakes work on this thing?" Graham asked drily, putting the cigar back in his pocket.

"Last time I checked."

"Use 'em lately?"

Rossi slammed on the brakes, throwing Graham forward. Graham slapped his meaty hands on the dashboard just in time to keep from hitting his forehead.

Rossi grinned.

"Wiseguy." Graham grinned back coldly. "Do that again and I'll kick your ass."

They turned onto the bridge, the tires humming over the grated pavement, the stanchions rising all around them as if they were driving through the skeletal remains of an apatosaurus, the sulfur lights and the rain giving it all an even more surreal look than usual.

"What else do you know about the priest?"

"Not much more than I told you on the phone, and all of that secondhand from Kendrick. You know Kendrick, Jack's son, good kid. He said they brought the priest in around midnight, thought he was already dead and sent him directly to the morgue, when one of the ghouls down there heard kicking and moaning and all kinds of carrying on from inside one of the drawers. They ain't rocket scientists down there, but you got to hand it to them, they could tell right away something was wrong."

"Ha ha."

"Yeah, anyway, when they opened up the drawer the priest was still alive. They rushed him back up to the

ER, where they tried to sew him back together again. It's a long shot, but I figured I'd call you."

"I'm glad you did," Rossi said. "There's something about that priest that never did sit too well with me. I just hope he hangs on long enough for us to talk with him."

They arrived at Manhattan Central Hospital about twenty minutes later.

The ER was in chaos, but that was the normal state of affairs for a big-city emergency room on a Saturday night. The place was as crowded as a snowed-in airport full of stranded travelers. There were people sitting and lying all over the sprawling ward, clutching bloody limbs and broken bones, some waiting patiently for their turn, others moaning so loudly the inexperienced would think they were dying right then and there. They passed one such man curled up on a gurney, grabbing his chest, his face clenched in pain like a fist, screaming at the top of his lungs. Rossi couldn't tell if the man was suffering a heart attack or just a bad case of heroin withdrawal. Either way, his predicament was apparently not the most important the overworked medical staff had to handle.

Rossi stopped a harried-looking nurse carrying a bag of some fluid the color of raw liver. She impatiently directed him to a warren of screened-in cubicles and rushed off before he could ask any more questions. It was Graham who spotted the young uniform standing guard outside a cubicle at the end of one of the rows. As they approached, the fresh-faced cop blocked their path.

"This area's restricted. Authorized personnel only."

Rossi flashed his detective's shield.

"I'm sorry, sir," the cop said again, this time apologetically. "I can't let anyone through but Inspector Coughlin. He should be here within the half hour. He wants to take the statement."

Yeah, Rossi thought, as soon as he squirms his way

out from under that fat whore he's got stored away up in the Bronx.

Rossi reached into his pocket, pulled out a sheet of paper, and passed it in front of the young cop's face for a couple of seconds. He stuffed it back into his pocket.

"That's my authorization," Rossi said. "Now step aside, junior." He didn't wait for the cop to move but pushed right on past.

Graham nodded significantly at the young cop, who still looked uncertain, and followed Rossi into the cubicle. He recognized the piece of paper Rossi had waved in front of the kid's face: it was the out-of-court settlement agreement from his divorce, impressively stamped and notarized, but absolutely meaningless in the present context. Nevertheless, it had gotten them past more than one intimidated guardian of the gate. Graham had seen Rossi pull similar tricks on countless occasions and knew the best thing to do was to keep his mouth shut and play along.

They were met inside the cubicle by a bearded doctor who looked like a college kid who'd been up for the last thirty-six hours preparing for final exams. The front of his green scrubs was covered with the distinctive graffiti scrawl of a spurting artery.

"You here to take a statement?"

"Yup," Rossi said.

"It's about damn time," the doctor snapped. "We've been waiting for you guys for the past two hours."

Rossi ignored the attitude. "How's he look?"

"Well, he's not going to die of old age, that's for damn sure." The doctor shook his head. "I'm sorry, it's been a tough night." He lowered his voice to a whisper. "The chaplain was just in here to give him his last rites. To be quite honest with you, from everything I know about medicine, the man should be dead. We did our best," he shrugged, "but he's all torn up inside. I've

394

never seen anything like it; it looked like a badger had gotten loose inside him. Frankly, I don't know how he's still alive. He's only held together by sweat and a few stitches. I think he's been holding out for you guys. He must have something real important to say."

"Where can I find you if I need a medical report for the record?" Rossi asked.

"I'm on duty until six this morning," the doctor said. "Then I collapse in the doctor's lounge for three hours before my next shift. Ask for Dr. Harakian."

Rossi nodded and the doctor left him and Graham alone with the patient.

The priest was lying on his back, his body swathed in bandages like a mummy, stained in places where the blood had already soaked through in large red splotches. He had enough wires and hoses running from his body to supply a small aircraft. He looked as if he were already dead, his eyes staring blankly up at the ceiling, except for the horrible tic that worked his right cheek, curling his bloodied lip up on one side in a rictus sneer. Rossi was no doctor, but he didn't see how the irregular line running across the screen of the monitor above the bed could be broadcasting anything but bad news. The priest looked to be holding on to whatever life he had left with all his might.

Rossi crouched down beside the bed, grabbing the cool metal rails in both hands, his face close to the face of the dying priest.

"Father," he whispered. "Can you hear me?"

The priest blinked, as if clearing away some private vision, his eyes filling with fresh pain. He tried to turn his head, but Rossi stopped him.

"No," he whispered urgently. "Don't move. I just want you to answer a few questions. Can you do that for me? Can you speak?"

The priest's mouth opened, his lips working over the

words, fighting the tic for control of his jaw muscles. "Yes," he said at last.

"Who did this to you?"

"She did," the priest said. "Her."

"Who's she?" Rossi asked, trying to sound patient, but knowing that the man didn't have much time left. In his line of work, Rossi had been around enough dying people to recognize the symptoms. "What is her name?"

"Legion," the priest said. He grimaced as pain knifed through his body. He gasped for breath. "Too many names. Goddess. Vampire."

The priest was edging toward delirium. Rossi felt his heart sink. They obviously weren't going to get much from him.

"Daughter. Save her." The priest coughed, pausing again to catch his breath, the pain rattling his teeth. "Stop. Save. Kelly—"

Rossi heard the last two words and felt his blood turn to slush. Of course, it could have been any of a thousand, ten thousand Kellys who lived in the city, but something inside, some instinct he'd long since learned to trust, told Rossi that the woman the priest was talking about was *his* Kelly.

"Kelly who?" he asked.

"Daughter. My daughter."

"Where is she?" Rossi pressed, urgent now, the monitor over the bed flatlining, the shrill tone already bringing the sound of rubber-soled feet squeaking down the hall. "Where is Kelly?"

The priest's words were drowned out by the sound of the monitor, but Rossi could read the priest's lips as if he had drawn the word in blood in big block letters across his pale white forehead.

Domination.

FORTY-EIGHT

For perhaps the first time in his life, Rossi was thankful for the experience that had once brought him to Domination. He knew the club was not located in any guide of the city, nor did it advertise in the trade papers, not even those catering to the S-M crowd. It was strictly the kind of place you discovered by word of mouth.

During his undercover operation, Rossi had found his way into the club, having heard about it from a wealthy society woman who liked to hire him to discipline her gigolo tennis instructor. Rossi hadn't returned to the club since his days as Master Rod, but he'd been back to the club twice since the murders began, and had found no one who was willing to talk with him. The people in the S-M scene were as clannish as any cult, and as unforgiving when they felt they'd been betrayed.

He realized he'd been right all along. Kelly had somehow gotten in over her head. Of course, he had tried to warn her. If he had only told her about his own experiences, perhaps he might have prevented this from happening.

Bullshit.

Kelly would have gone ahead anyway.

Something in her blood had called her to explore that world and nothing could have stopped her. He knew from experience. He had long since given up the illusion that it was police work alone that led to his immersion in domination.

Outside the windshield the wipers slapped away at the rain, which had begun to fall harder. He raced down Eleventh Avenue, past Thirty-fourth Street, and into the lower Twenties. Beside him, Graham was uncharacteristically silent, staring impassively out the window, the shadows of the raindrops rolling down his heavy face like dark sweat. What they were doing was not exactly according to regulations, but it was hardly the first time they had thrown away the book. Going by the book kept your ass safe, but it seldom broke a case or saved a life.

They rolled up in front of the old theater and Rossi shut off the engine of the Grand Prix.

Graham already had his gun in his lap.

"You don't have to do this," Rossi said.

"Wouldn't miss it for the world." Graham shrugged. "One for all and all straight to hell."

They climbed out of the car and approached the dilapidated building, skirting the boarded-up marquee and heading directly down the side stairs to the basement entrance. Strangely enough, there didn't seem to be any party in progress tonight. The red light at the bottom of the stairwell was out and there was no sign of the leather-clad bouncers that usually guarded the door.

Rossi glanced back at Graham, nodded, and started down the stairs.

When they got to the bottom Graham prepared to kick the door before Rossi held up his hand. He pushed gently on the door and it swung back on its hinges.

Rossi pointed at his chest, waited for Graham to indicate that he was ready, and ducked into the building. He took up a position just inside the doorway, his heart pounding in his ears. Graham followed right behind him, crouching on the opposite side of the door.

"Holy shit," Rossi whispered.

The only light in the huge room was coming from the horror movies that were still running against the walls. But the scene before them was worse than any horror film. In the gray twilight, they could see the bodies scattered throughout the room. There must have been at least fifty of them. They were hanging by their heels from leather manacles, bound upside down to x-frames, locked in medieval-looking stocks or inside man-sized coffin cages. Each bore the unique markings of the extreme and unusual tortures they'd been subjected to before they were allowed to die. The one and only thing they had in common was that they were all stone-cold dead.

The sight reminded Rossi of photographs he'd seen of Jonestown and the concentration camps of Nazi Germany on a smaller scale. There was something of the cult about it, of organization, of ritual. Such wholesale butchery could not have been the work of one person. There must be several killers.

"I'm going in the back," Graham muttered, his face hard, grim. "You check things out here."

Rossi nodded, thankful for Graham's tact and understanding. His partner was giving him the chance to study the bodies by himself, to see if he found Kelly. He waited for Graham to disappear into the shadows before beginning his search.

Rossi passed before the grim tableaux, staring from one victim to the next, until it almost seemed as if he were looking at an exhibit in a wax museum, rather than the ruined bodies of the real men and women who'd lost their lives here. The magnitude of the slaughter had overloaded his moral circuitry, made it almost impossible for his brain to process the reality of what he was seeing. He gazed critically into the faces of the women, skipping over the men, looking carefully at their wildly distorted expressions, knowing full well that death changes a person.

Slowly, methodically, he checked the face of each dead woman, ready at any moment to lose his mind.

Graham moved swiftly along the wall to the back of the club, walking through the movie *Invasion of the Blood Farmers*.

He felt a strange coldness in his body as he thought of the slaughter. He'd only seen its like two or three other times, and that was in Vietnam. The VC had murdered an entire village in the belief that one of its inhabitants was giving shelter and aid to the Americans. When Graham had come with the local ration of supplies he regularly delivered as payment for information about guerrilla troop movements he'd found the heads of every man, woman, and child neatly stacked in a small pile outside the village. The sight of those faces had haunted his nightmares for years. He hoped for Rossi's sake that he didn't find what he was looking for, and that if Kelly were dead, Graham found her first.

He saw the door to the main theater and stared up the hallway of stairs leading to the second floor. There was a single red bulb at the top of the landing, casting the hall in a dim red light. Graham knew that if someone were covering the landing, they could pick him off as easily as plugging a pig in a barrel.

He had two choices: either take each stair with the slow deliberation of a major assault or launch a blitzkrieg on the landing.

He decided on the latter.

He took a deep breath, let it out, and jumped the

stairs two at a time, his trigger finger ready to spray the landing above at the first sign of movement.

He waited for the bullet to smash his forehead, but instead he reached the top without trouble, heart pounding, huge crescents of dampness spreading like wings under his armpits. He stood with his back to the door, fighting to catch his breath, his fists wrapped around the revolver in front of his face.

He took one last deep breath, ducked low, and rounded the corner, and found himself squinting into a hard white light.

"What the fuck—"

He was standing in the back of what at first glance seemed a typical theater except that on the stage, centered in the spotlight, was a short wooden cross upon which hung the body of a naked woman. Unlike the people in the outer room, however, this woman was clearly still alive. Graham could see her labored breathing, her mouth moving, her body trembling against the harsh bondage.

Graham took a step into the theater, his eyes glancing quickly around to the darkened balconies on either side of the stage. He was painfully aware that he could be walking into a trap, that an assassin could be lurking somewhere in the darkness above. If that were the case, he was dead meat already.

Graham took a second step, glancing nervously down the aisles on either side of him.

He looked back to the stage. The woman on the cross lifted her sweat-soaked head and fixed Graham with tortured eyes.

"Help me," she pleaded.

Graham felt something inside him give way when he heard the woman's cry, something that had been weakened when he first saw her bound there and that needed only the sound of a human voice to shatter completely.

It was Graham's infallible instinct for self-preservation and it was his ability to break through this wall when the occasion demanded that made him a hero instead of a mere survivor.

Graham ran to the front of the theater, the gun nearly forgotten at his side, and jumped onto the stage.

Sure enough, the girl was not only still alive but, aside from some superficial wounds, she didn't appear to be seriously hurt.

Graham knelt before her, putting his gun on the floor, gently lifting her face in his hands.

"You're going to be all right now," he said, staring into her face, enunciating each word carefully, as if she might not understand English.

He reached around behind her to loosen her lashed ankles, his head close to her cold shoulder, the side of his throat almost completely exposed for the time it takes to blink an eye when the bound woman's head snapped forward in a blur of movement. Graham felt nothing but stared in shocked incomprehension at the meat and vein hanging from the woman's mouth, recognizing it instinctively as his own.

He scrambled around on the floor, trying to grab his gun, which slipped hopelessly out of his hands, slick with blood.

Just before he lost consciousness, Graham managed to scream one last time, even though it was medically impossible.

He no longer had a throat.

Rossi heard Graham scream.

He had finished checking out the corpses, satisfying himself that Kelly was not among them, and was standing by the door leading to the theater.

Now he charged up the stairs, entered the auditorium, and saw Graham slumped on the stage. Above him, Rossi saw a bound woman struggling to reach him, her teeth bared, her face and breasts covered with fresh blood. Only when he got closer did he recognize the woman's rabid, twisted features as those of Gwen. Dammit, it figured she was in on this somehow. Rossi had always known there was something he hated about the woman. Why couldn't Kelly have listened to him?

Rossi didn't waste a moment. He brought his revolver up and fired at the bound woman, striking her six times in the center of the chest as he ran down the aisle.

He climbed onto the stage, slipping on the blood, coming to a stop on his knees in front of Graham's body.

"Don't die on me now you stupid Irish bastard," Rossi sobbed, struggling to turn Graham over onto his back. His partner's face was white as bleached bone, his eyes staring, his lips peeled back in the cold grin characteristic of someone meeting death for the first and last time. From his torn throat the blood leapt in long, intermittent jets.

Rossi put his hands over the wound, but the blood sizzled through his fingers, and with it the life of his friend.

Tied to the cross, the naked woman thrashed furiously from side to side, trying to free herself. Around her neck, set starkly against the cold alabaster skin, was a necklace of six dry black bullet holes.

FORTY-NINE

Connor raced up the Long Island Expressway, which twisted before him like a wet black eel. He fought the wheel of the silver Mazda Miata, wrestling to keep the small car on the road as it was buffeted on all sides by the gusting wind. He had stolen the car from an underground parking garage near Rockefeller Center about an hour earlier.

He let the limousine slip out of sight several miles back, following only what could best be described as the astral trace it left along the wet road, like a phospherous trail he could read with his instincts alone. Another gust of wind struck the car on the left, forcing him onto the shoulder of the road, before he muscled it back onto the highway. The rain washed over the windshield as if it were an incoming wave.

Tonight was the night the whole Operation was coming to a crisis; he could feel it in his bones. He had been watching over Kelly ever since they had broken up, trying to discover some clues as to the truth of the danger surrounding her, and what made her so important that the Craft had wanted her destroyed. More importantly, he was making certain that they hadn't dispatched anyone else to carry out the order he'd been unwilling to carry out himself. He no longer believed that she was just a loose end, but the whole Gordian knot itself.

He had followed her every step, watching her apartment, her trips to the grocery store and the museum, even her date with that obnoxious asshole from *NiteLife* Magazine. He was her invisible bodyguard—her guardian angel, as it were—determined to protect her from any and all harm.

Of course, he had been there when she left her apartment to go to the leather bar. He had followed her and the priest to the abandoned building, watched the scourging and the subsequent kidnapping, and finally Kelly's imprisonment in the basement of St. Jude's Church. He could have rescued her at several points along the way. The priest had an aura of formidable magic surrounding him, but he had left himself vulnerable on more than one occasion. The fact, however, was that rescuing Kelly outright would interfere with the karmic order of events before they'd had a chance to run their proper course. It might be necessary to interrupt the flow at some point and suffer the consequences later in order to save Kelly's life, but the longer he waited, the least disruption it would cause, and the more he would be able to discover the Craft's true purpose. As it was, the fact that they hadn't yet sent out any assassins to destroy Kelly or punish him for his insubordination was clearly evidence confirming his gut feeling that he was still doing the Craft's business, whether he liked it or not. They had probably calculated on his rebelliousness, and as a result he was behaving in exactly the manner they required in spite—or rather because of—his disobedience. It was frustrating. They knew him as well or better than he knew himself. In any event, his self-discipline had been rewarded upon the appearance of the woman in black leather who had destroyed the priest and stolen Kelly herself.

405

He turned off the expressway, following a narrow, even more treacherous stretch of road that snaked its way around the rocky coastline toward the northeast end of the island. If he hadn't intuited where they were going before, he was sure of the destination by now. He remembered the talk with the strange bald man in the limousine in the middle of the Jersey swamp, the photograph of the mysterious European heiress. *We think she may be in the country to commit an act of political terror. Maybe even the assassination of a major American political figure.* On the northeast tip of the island, on a rocky outcropping facing the cold green Atlantic, sat the fortified mansion of Senator Edmund Erion Stanton.

Connor still had no idea where Kelly fit into this whole scheme. Was she part of the plot to assassinate Stanton, or was she merely a device to draw Connor into a collision course with Monica Caron? He couldn't believe the former and he couldn't explain the latter. What was the connection between Monica and Kelly? He remembered what the bald man had said about Monica's predilection for S-M, but she generally confined her affairs to the rich and famous. Was it possible she had fallen in love with Kelly?

Connor turned off the highway and onto a narrow drive, cutting through the woods and marked with signs informing trespassers to turn back or to risk prosecution. Connor switched off the headlights and followed the road about half a mile in before driving the car into the surrounding woods, concealing it behind the heavy wet boughs of a stand of fragrant pine trees.

He climbed out of the car and quietly shut the door, standing in the rain, listening for trouble. He knew he couldn't risk taking the road in case it was under camera surveillance from the house. He would have to make his way through the woods. He slowly lowered his heart and breathing rates, picturing a graph from Abramelin, and imagined himself slowly dissolving into the wind. When he was finished he turned toward the thickest part of the woods, belted his long black raincoat tightly at his waist, and headed in the direction of the mansion.

He moved through the woods like fog, picking his way surefootedly over the wet logs and leaves, instinctively avoiding the chuckholes and exposed roots that might trip him up. In spite of the rain there was a full moon above, and it cast its light through the thick cloud cover, throwing the rocks, trees, and groundcover in a velvety blue twilight. He moved so swiftly and quietly, he had come within inches of a deer before it even sensed his presence, its eyes rolling wildly before it bolted off madly into the underbrush.

Connor came to the edge of the woods and crouched down behind the slick trunk of a huge oak tree. About fifteen feet away he saw the compound. It was surrounded by a cyclone fence and behind that another fence of black iron spikes at least eight feet tall and no doubt electrified. The area between the woods and the fence had been meticulously cleared and the trees trimmed back to prevent anyone from using an errant branch to clear the fence.

Leaving the cover of the woods, Connor took the cyclone fence at a run, scrambling up its side, vaulting over the top, and landing in a crouch on the other side. He sprinted alongside to the interior fence, looking for imperfections in the ground where the earth might have worn away from the bottom of the fence, leaving enough room to shimmy under. He finally stopped and attempted to scoop the mud and rock from near the base of the fence, careful not to get too close, hoping to scrape his own shallow pit beneath the electrified spikes. But just as he feared, the iron spikes had been solidly set into a thick slab of concrete. There was no way under without dynamite.

Connor returned to the cyclone fence, aware that the narrow corridor was probably under video surveillance. He climbed the fence again, dropped to the other side, and jogged along the edge of the woods, slopping through the mud and wet grass. He emerged on the east side of the compound, the land rising dramatically in a jumble of broken boulders, black and slick in the rain.

Connor wiped the sleeve of his poncho across his eyes and stared up at the rocks.

Whoever had planned the security layout of the compound had known their business, but there was nothing they could do about the boulders. With the rain falling in his face, Connor gazed up to the top of the pile to a small outcropping of stone. If he could make it safely to the summit, he just might be close enough to jump and clear both the cyclone fence and the row of electrified black spikes.

Connor picked his way carefully up the treacherous rock face, each foothold threatening to send him tumbling backward toward unconsciousness. With every gust of wind he clung desperately to the rock, his body pressed against the cold body of the stone. After the wind died down he continued on up the jumble, making his way hand by hand. By the time he made it to the top, the skin on his knuckles was torn and raw, his muscles sore with exertion and the strain of holding himself in various unnatural positions against gravity.

He pulled himself over the side of the top rock and rolled over on his back, letting the cold rain refresh him a moment before climbing to his feet. The wind, unblocked, was even stronger up here, buffeting him like a boxer, driving him perilously close to the edge. Behind him, somewhere in the dark, he could hear the waves crashing against the shore in white violence.

Connor moved toward the end of the flat rock, staring down at the outcropping about fifteen feet below. It was less than a hand's breadth wide, water running off the end and down over the jagged edge of the rock slide. If he missed by so much as an inch, or if he slipped, he would plunge down the side of the rocks and wind up breaking bones, if not killing himself outright. He closed his eyes, visualizing the grid for transforming oneself into an eagle, when he heard the scuff of a boot behind him and whirled around to see a black-clad man on the other side of the rock.

He was the man Connor had seen with Monica at St. Jude's. The tails of his black coat were flapping in the wind blowing off the ocean. In the occasional lightning Connor could see the man's face, stone and cold and white, the rain running over his features as if they were carved in marble. The man came forward, and Connor was surprised at the awkwardness of the man's movements. He was obviously not trained in the killing arts. He would be easy to dispatch.

Connor dropped to the ground, sweeping his legs in front of him, taking out the legs of the man in black. Connor jumped to his feet to deliver the chop to the back of the head that would render his attacker unconscious when the man came up, driving his fist into Connor's sternum, the blow so heavy it momentarily stunned him, and threw Connor gasping onto his back. Once again the man came forward, grabbing Connor by his coat, attempting to lift him from the ground, when Connor struck the man across the bridge of his nose with his forehead. The man staggered back, his nose smashed against his face like bloody putty, but he recovered quickly and started forward once again with the mindless determination of an automaton. When he came within striking distance, Connor sent a sidekick into the man's solar plexus, spun, and landed a solid roundhouse to the man's temple that sent splinters of bone into the soft tissues of the man's brain.

The blow was perfectly timed and forcefully delivered and should have dropped the man where he stood, and yet still he staggered forward. Expecting the man to fall, Connor inadvertently let his guard drop; he let it drop for only a heartbeat, but a heartbeat was enough to get you killed. The blow came from the left side, and he caught it out of the corner of his eye just in time to avoid its full force. He rolled away, the side of his face throbbing, and came up on his knees, his heels hanging off the edge of the rock. He reached inside his coat and pulled out the ninja *shiruken* he kept in a small leather holster strap beneath his left arm. With one fluid motion, he hurled the three razor-sharp metal stars at the vulnerable areas in the man's throat, groin, and wrist. The *shiruken* struck home, penetrating the flesh with a sodden *thunk,* as if they had struck dead wet wood, severing the veins as they were supposed to, but the life did not leap from the man's body, spooling away in red puddles on the rock. And that's when the truth became clear to Connor.

This man is already dead.

Connor had heard that some magicians had mastered the arts of necromancy. He had even seen how some tribal shamans in Africa had worked their voodoo to turn otherwise healthy men and women into soulless slaves, which popular culture called zombies, and who were capable of enduring almost superhuman levels of pain and hardship. But what appeared to be the raising of the dead was a mere psychological trick synonomous with hypnotism in which the magician supplanted the will of his subject with that of his own. Yet the man who stood before him now was not merely a zombie, for a zombie was not really a reanimated corpse but an ordinary human body and, therefore, in spite of its greater tolerance for pain, bound by all the normal physical

410

laws binding any other physical body. In other words, if you cut the throat of a zombie it *should* bleed to death.

The man before him now seemed to be animated by an evil that transcended the body in which it was contained. Connor had never quite believed it possible before, but he considered that what he was encountering was a true case of demonic possession.

He didn't have much time to plan his next form of attack when the man had closed on him again, throwing a wild right at his face that Connor blocked with his left arm, feeling the bone in his arm snap like a dry white stick, the pain driving up his shoulder and lodging in the side of his neck like an iron spike. Connor tried to scramble away, the man's boot catching him in the side, knocking the breath out of his lungs. He saw the man coming again, hop-stepping, preparing to finish him off with another kick. Connor waited for the man to come, knowing he had only one chance to guess right or it was all over. He waited as the man's leg went back, swung forward, and caught the heel of his heavy boot in his right hand, going with the blow as far as he could, letting the man's momentum carry him to the edge of the stone, and as his body passed above him, Connor gave him the extra push that sent him sailing overhead, arms spread in the air like an oversized bat, actually seeming to glide through the air for a moment, and then giving in to gravity, stronger than death itself, which sent him hurtling down onto the black iron spikes of the fence below.

Connor crawled to the edge of the rock and stared down.

The dead man was pierced through the throat, chest, stomach, and crotch, his transfixed body flopping around on the electrified spikes, outlined in a thin blue light packing a jolt of thirty thousand volts. The electrocution seemed to last forever. Connor could read the pain in the man's face as the electricity surged through his body, and the expression on his face was unmistakable: it was that of someone who wanted to die—and couldn't. Suddenly the body seemed to explode in a shower of blue tears as the fence shorted out and the compound was plunged into momentary darkness before the emergency generators kicked in and restored power to the house. The dead body, no more than charred bone and tattered clothes, hung on the fence that was no longer electrified.

Connor stared down at the remains of the ghoul and then up at the compound. He sure as hell hoped there weren't more like him inside the house.

Protecting his injured arm, Connor carefully picked his way back down the rock face, which was even more dangerous than climbing up. A few minutes later, he had broached the cyclone fence and the black iron gate and entered the grounds of the compound. At the very moment he did, in the power plant that ran the compound, the short circuit caused by the electrocuted vampire had started an electrical fire.

FIFTY

Inside the main house, Degas saw the security breach on the monitor. At first he thought it was simply a malfunction resulting from the loss of power caused by the storm, but after the emergency generators kicked in and he saw the path of broken sensors, Degas knew that he wasn't looking at the tracks left by simple coincidence.

He pressed the alert button on the house intercom and waited for Hillary to answer in the bedroom. He hated to disturb her when she was with Monica. That bitch was real bad news. Hillary had always been more than a little crazy, but Monica had pushed her clear over the edge. Degas had tried to warn Hillary, but the woman was completely captivated by the countess or heiress, or whatever the hell she was supposed to be. Degas had backed off, shocked and a little jealous to find that he no longer had his mistress's closest confidence. He'd been replaced. But that wasn't the chief among his worries. Lately, he'd begun to wonder if eventually Hillary would turn against him altogether.

What if Monica suddenly decided that he knew too much to live? He knew Monica only had to give the word and he'd be history. Even worse, he didn't want to wind up charged with what she and her lesbian girlfriend were doing in their basement torture chamber.

413

His fear of the latter was what kept him from running
out on the situation altogether. If he weren't there to de
fend himself, Hillary and Monica could blame him for
everything.

He pressed the intercom again, and heard Monica's
voice on the other end.

"What is it, Degas?"

He felt his blood chill.

"Can I speak to Ms. Stanton?"

"She's indisposed just now," she said, a faint trace of
irony in her voice. "You can speak to me."

"I think we may have a problem outside. It may be
just the power outtage, but I don't think so."

"Where's Daniel?"

Degas remembered the strange, silent, glassy-eyed
man who served as a kind of personal bodyguard to
Monica. In spite of the fact that the man was a real
hunk, Degas could feel nothing but repugnance for him
the way one would feel for dead or corrupted flesh.

"I don't know. Outside somewhere—"

"Get up here immediately," Monica snapped, her
voice suddenly cold and urgent. "We have a possible assassin on our hands."

Hillary looked up from the chair by the window, her
face streaked with tears.

She heard Monica's exchange with Degas over the intercom, but not even the talk of assassins moved her
Right now she didn't care if she lived or died.

Lying on the four-poster bed was a woman Monica
had brought back from the club. She was still unconscious, looking pale and beat, her clothes dirty and torn
She was pretty, younger by fifteen years or so, but no
raving beauty. Certainly Monica could not love this
common woman more than her. Yet the evidence was

414

here. The long periods of time Monica spent away, her old and detached demeanor, her disinterest in making love.

"Why?" Hillary asked for the hundredth time. She hated the whining, desperate tone in her voice, but she couldn't help herself. She felt like she was breaking apart inside. "What has she got that I haven't?"

"I've told you," Monica said coldly. "She knows how to love."

"I can love," Hillary protested.

"You love no one but yourself."

"That's not true," Hillary cried. "I love you."

"You don't love me," Monica sneered. "You love what I can give you. Power. Fame. Immortality. The minute you didn't need me anymore you'd drive a stake through my heart."

"That's not true. It's not true."

"Of course it's true, Hillary dear. You love like a fourteen-year-old girl loves. All tears and drama, but always with one eye in the mirror. You've never loved anyone in your life. Not your father, not your mother, not your husband, and no matter what you've told yourself, not even me. You've never known what love is and never will, that will be your punishment through the endless hell of your life."

Monica's words pierced Hillary like arrows, each one finding a vulnerable place in her defense, leaving her on the floor in a softly sobbing heap at her cold lover's feet.

"Please," she murmured, barely audible. "Don't leave me."

Monica patted Hillary on the head like a dog. "Not to worry, love," she said. "I still need you every bit as much as you need me. I won't leave you. Not yet, anyway."

There was a knock on the door, and Degas's voice loud and urgent on the other side.

"Come in," Monica said.

Degas looked from Monica to Hillary, lying on the floor in her nightgown, and back to Monica again. He could hardly keep the disgust and disapproval from his face, though it was suitably covered by a mask of raw fear. No matter what his resolve, his first unstudied glimpse of Monica always terrified him, which was just as well, because he was sure the woman could read his thoughts as clearly as if he spoke them.

Monica continued patting Hillary absently on the head, fixing her gaze on Degas.

"Look after my little pet," she said. "I've got business to attend to downstairs."

Are you okay?" Degas whispered softly.

Huddled on the floor, Hillary nodded.

He reached down and helped her to her feet. She felt so light, so frail. Degas was shocked. Had the cancer come back, burning her away from the inside? Or was it just a case of lovesickness?

"She's no good for you," Degas ventured, sensing Hillary's vulnerability, gambling that she might be more receptive to his argument in her current state. He waited for her to protest, and when she didn't he continued. "You have to let her go. She'll destroy us both. She'll destroy everything we've worked so hard to get."

Degas looked with distaste at the woman lying on the bed. No doubt she was tonight's victim. Over the last several weeks he'd dumped enough of them back in the city, circling the deserted streets in the early morning hours, making sure no one saw him. When was it going to end? How long before his luck ran out and someone traced the damaged girls back to the compound? How many years would they give him? Twenty? Thirty? Fifty? No doubt he'd spent the rest of his life in prison

"I can get rid of her for you," Degas said, laying it out gently. "Make some calls."

"No," Hillary said sharply, cutting him off. "Not Monica. Her."

Degas stared back at the woman on the bed.

"Who is she?"

Hillary shrugged, pouting. In a woman her age, it was not a flattering expression. "How the hell should I know? Some whore she picked up and claims to love. I want her dead."

Degas looked doubtful "It won't end with her. You know that."

"I don't care. She won't cheat me out of what she promised. She's not going to give this bitch the power that is rightfully mine. Kill her."

Degas walked to the bed and looked down at the unconscious woman. He knew that killing her wouldn't solve anything. There would only be another, and another after that. Hillary was out of control. She had become a kind of cancer herself, voracious, consuming, destroying everything in her path and corrupting everyone around her. There was only one way to stop her, but it was too late for that now. Degas had discovered the malignancy inside himself.

"Kill her," Hillary growled. "Do it *now.*"

He was afraid to disobey her, afraid she'd turn on him. His only hope was to have her on his side against Monica, to make himself Hillary's indispensable ally. Degas reached down, staring at the hands emerging from the sleeves of his Armani suit, a murderer's hands, *his* hands. He placed them around the unconscious girl's throat, his thumbs over her fragile windpipe, and, slowly expelling the air from his lungs, squeezed.

FIFTY-ONE

Conner entered the house through an entrance in the garden, kicking the door off its hinges. Either the short circuit knocked out the surveillance system or they already knew he had penetrated their defensive perimeter. Either way, the time for subtlety was over.

Connor raced through a short hallway, past the gardener's quarters and up a narrow flight of stairs to the main floor of the house. He could feel the electronic eyes following his progress, cold and impersonal, like the distant eyes of God.

So the system was still working.

Fine, let them see him coming. Perhaps it would draw them out of their holes.

Connor felt the adrenalin surging through his bloodstream as he opened his third chakra in preparation for the battle ahead. The change in body chemistry sharpened his instincts, making it possible for him to sense the subtle traces left in the aethyr marking the path where Kelly had recently passed. He vaulted across the giant great room with the sunken conversation pit and the wraparound window with the magnificent view of the Atlantic surf, slid across the polished marble floor of the circular entrance hall, and grabbed the ornate imported Italian railing of the east wing stairwell, sprinting up the tightly winding stairs to the second floor. As he did so he focussed his attention on his Yesodic center, opening up his extrasensory channel, trying to tune into the mental link he'd forged with Kelly during the night of ritual love-making. If she hadn't rejected him entirely in the weeks that followed, there would still be enough of a residual sympathetic bond between them, the kind of bond that under normal circumstances would have caused a delight-fully embarrassing series of apparently "coincidental" encounters in crowded department stores, restaurants, subways, or parties thrown by previously undiscovered mutual friends and business associates.

Sure enough, Connor had tuned into her thoughts, which seemed murky and unfocused, like someone asleep or unconscious, but which were strong enough to give him an instinctive sense of the hands around her throat, the Victorian wallpaper, the carved acorn orna-ments at the top of each wooden bedpost.

Connor bolted down the second-floor hallway to the staircase at the end and raced directly up to the third floor, making a dash for the bedroom he knew to be lo-cated at the back of the house. He lowered his shoulder and drove the door back on its hinges, the wood shrieking, startling the large, ponytailed man leaning over the bed, his hands already closed around Kelly's throat. Kneeling beside the bed, staring raptly at Kelly's purpled face, was a middle-aged blond woman in a sheer negligee. She looked up at Connor as if he were nothing more than a minor nuisance.

The man, however, realized the danger instantly and turned from the bed, his trained body easily falling into an attitude of attack that Connor recognized as the po-sition of the Deadly Mantis, a fighting pose from an ar-cane and exceptionally lethal form of Tibetan martial arts rarely taught to westerners. Connor had studied the form himself during two years in the Himalayas and knew well the murderous prerequisites for admittance into the discipline. The man moved toward him expertly, his forearms raised, cutting hypnotic patterns in the air, dangerous as sharpened sword edges.

If this man were dead, Connor knew he'd be in trouble. With his combination of skills and endurance, the man would be indomitable.

To all appearances, the man seemed to be alive, but Connor still didn't know for certain until he launched a snap-kick to the inside of his groin and saw the pain twist his features. The man recovered quickly, however, spinning inside Connor's flat-handed thrust to the chin and delivering a forearm that caught Connor on the shoulder, sending a nauseating current of pain down his damaged arm. Ordinarily, the blow would have been minor, but the nerve and tissue damage occasioned by the broken bone nearly paralyzed him. In spite of his attempt to mask his pain, Connor could read the eagerness in his opponent's expression as the man saw Connor's face blanch and, smelling blood, moved in for the kill.

Connor used the man's killer instinct against him, stopping him with an elbow to the ribs, snapping his arm up at the elbow and clubbing him in the temple with his fist. Having thrown his opponent off balance, Connor had time to set his position, driving the man backwards with three successive sidekicks to his midsection, the heavy band of muscles across the man's abdomen the only thing protecting him from internal hemorrhage.

The man hit the wall behind him and slid down, gasping for breath, while Connor paused for a moment to let the pain from his injured arm subside. Meanwhile, the man, realizing that he'd met a superior adversary, rose from the floor, holding in his left hand a long, bone-handled switchblade he'd pulled from inside his cowboy boot. The moment he saw the blade, Connor knew the fight was over.

The man did not lunge forward, retaining enough presence of mind to remember the basics of effective knife fighting, dealing Connor several painful cuts on the hand and one deep one across the left cheek, but there was enough desperation in his parries to provide an opening that Connor took full advantage of, catching the man's knife hand between his own forearm and hip, breaking the delicate bones inside the man's wrist and sending his teeth scattering across the floor like dice with a knee to the jaw. The man staggered back, his eyes wild with fear, his hand fluttering at his side like a white flag, blood drenching the front of his John Weitz suit and Enzo Fabriccio silk necktie.

Connor felt no pity.

He might have killed the man with a single sword thrust to his throat, crushing his windpipe like a paper cup.

Remembering the sight of him crouched over Kelly's helpless body, he instead delivered a brutal sidekick to the center of the man's chest, the force of the blow disturbing the rhythm of his heart, launching the traumatized organ into a violent tachychardia that left him dying on the floor of heart failure.

Connor turned back to the bed.

The woman in the negligee had disappeared.

Kelly had meanwhile regained consciousness, fighting to draw air through her damaged windpipe, the white flesh of her throat bearing the scarlet print of ten determined fingers.

Finally, she caught her breath, her eyes cleared, and she took in her surroundings, as if awakening from a bad dream.

"Connor?" she said.

FIFTY-TWO

By the time Connor led Kelly out of the bedroom, he could hear the shrill tone of the smoke detectors and smell the acrid stench of smoke. They ran down the stairs to the second floor and the smoke grew thicker, stinging their eyes and filling their lungs like steel wool.

Kelly started choking on the smoke, raising her hand to wipe her tearing eyes.

"Don't," Connor cautioned, grabbing her wrist. "You'll only make it worse."

"I can't breathe," Kelly gagged.

"Take short breaths," he said. "Like this."

He demonstrated the rapid shallow breathing pattern known to martial artists as Sparrow Breath. He didn't expect her to master it then and there, but even an imperfect application of the technique would be enough to get her through the blinding, suffocating smoke.

"Grab my hand," he said. "And stay close to the ground."

They moved slowly along the second-floor hall only to find the situation worse than they'd expected. Thick black smoke rolled toward them like angry storm clouds from the direction of the spiral staircase, blocking off their route to the first floor. Connor peered through the roiling darkness to his left and saw a molten room, its ceiling sagging under the weight of fire.

"What do we do now?" Kelly rasped, her face blackened by smoke, her eyes white and afraid. She was holding her hand over her nose and mouth, trying to keep out the toxic fumes.

"Wait here," Connor said.

He waded through the thick, suffocating waves of black smoke, sipping from the narrow current of fresh air along the floor. He came to within ten feet of the end of the hall before the heat blocked him, singeing the hair on his eyebrows. The center tower around the stairwell was functioning like a chimney, creating a draw through which the fire clawed its way greedily through the house. From where he stood, Connor could see the stairwell fill with a howling, twisting fire, as if the stairs led to hell itself. From below he could hear the sound of men shouting furiously at each other, the shadows moving behind the wall of fire like those of demons. Connor wondered if they were additional private security forces or if the local fire department had already found its way to the compound.

Friend or foe, he had to get Kelly out of the building and spirit her safely away, and he'd already decided to kill anyone who got in his way.

Connor made his way back up the hall, finding Kelly crouched under an antique table by the wall.

"Is there another way down?" he shouted over the flames, which howled all around them like a hurricane wind.

"I don't know," Kelly shouted back.

"Think," Connor said, trying not to sound desperate, even as he felt the heat of the flames licking at the back of his neck. "How did you come up here?"

"I don't remember," Kelly said, crying. "Stone. I remember stone."

Connor looked down the hall toward the stairs, leading back to the third floor. He thought of the woman in the negligee he'd seen by the bed. Where had she gone? There *must* be another way down. He suddenly had a flash of intuition.

"Let's get back upstairs."

They ran down the hall to the staircase and made their way back to the third floor.

Connor dragged Kelly by the hand back to the bedroom and saw the door to the huge walk-in closet, standing open just as he'd pictured it. He shoved the clothes aside, pounding his fist against the back wall of the closet until his hand struck hollow wallboard and he found the concealed door. He pulled it open and stared down into the concrete fire tower. He saw a narrow staircase lit by battery-powered emergency lights that were bolted to the sweating concrete walls. From where he stood he could see two landings down before the stairs turned beyond his view.

"Come on," Connor said.

Kelly had thrown herself down on the bed, looking completely exhausted.

"I can't," she moaned.

"There isn't much time," Connor said. "We've got to keep going."

He helped Kelly off the bed, leading her toward the closet. He stepped through the doorway, leading Kelly in after him, and carefully shut the door behind them. It was cool and damp in the tower, the flame and smoke unable to penetrate the thick stone walls built to absorb the impact of a nuclear explosion. The fresh air seemed to revivify Kelly, who reached down to remove her high heels, clutching them in her hand, before proceeding down the stairs. Connor followed closely behind her, taking an occasional quick glance behind them to make sure that they weren't being followed. In the closeness he could smell a trace of the senator's wife's perfume lingering in the air.

At the bottom of the tower they came to a forbidding-looking steel door, made to resemble the old-fashioned doors of medieval dungeons but forged out of the high-tech alloys from which modern bank vaults were made.

Connor felt his heart sink.

If the fleeing woman had the presence of mind to lock the door behind her, they were trapped, imprisoned inside the tower of the burning building.

Connor stepped in front of Kelly and put his hand on the cool steel door. He shoved it, gently, and it moved backward on its hinges with the smooth precision of high-tech German engineering.

Connor breathed a sigh of relief, only to have the breath catch in his throat when he saw the scene inside the room.

What he saw was a torture chamber—there was no other name for it—worthy of the Grand Inquisitor himself. At a glance Connor took in the grim machinery of human suffering, designed and perfected throughout the centuries, as only human genius could, to produce the optimum of pain in its victims. There was a suspension tackle, slant tables, stocks, and cages, every possible device for rendering up the delicate parts of the human body to cruelty. On the walls and tables he saw displayed thumbscrews, mallets, whips, pincers, chains, and bone saws, as well as more modern instruments of pain, including a nail gun, a dentist drill, and a chain saw.

"Good evening, Mr. Scott."

Connor spun round in the direction of the voice.

From out of a curtain of iron chains and hooks hanging from the ceiling stepped the Vampire. She was wearing a dark hooded cloak that covered everything but her face, which gazed at Connor with a strange mixture of peace and *hunger*. In the flickering light of the candles on the walls her porcelain features gave her the appearance of a Madonna. Connor let his eyes linger along the aristocratic line of her long white neck. Above her cheekbones, her eyes were the most unusual shade of grey he had ever seen. She had the eyes of a goddess, the kind of eyes that might be watching a storm over the Mediterranean or a fatal automobile accident on the autobahn. She slipped the hood off her head, and he saw her hair like sunlight shining all around her. She was saying something to him, but he hardly heard a word she was saying. Instead, he watched the way her mouth moved as she spoke, imagining her red lips moving over his body, consuming him.

"What are you?" he said.

"I think you know the answer to that better than most men, Mr. Scott."

Connor felt the sweat breaking out all over his body, felt the hair standing up on the back of his neck. He knew this was the woman the bald-headed man was talking about, the woman the Craft had wanted him to find. They had said that she was a terrorist, a possible assassin, but standing in her presence Connor knew that she was far more than that. She was within arm's length of him now, moving toward him without taking a step, or so it seemed, until he realized that it was he who was walking toward her, his body obeying her silent command, or, perhaps, having for the first time developed a will independent of his mind.

"Stop it!" Kelly screamed, stepping in front of him, coming between Connor and fate. "Leave him be. It's me you want."

"No!" Connor said, still half-dazed from his reverie. "Get back."

"It's no use," Kelly said. "She's already ruined me. I'm one of them. But you still have a chance. Let me go, Connor. Let me go to her."

The Vampire clapped her hands slowly and deliberately. "Bravo," she said mockingly. "How touching. The lovers seek to sacrifice themselves for each other. Have you forgotten the lesson I taught you earlier, Kelly? Have you forgotten what it is to die?"

"I don't care," Kelly said. "I don't care if I die. I was wrong to choose life. All things live and die. It's the natural order of things. I was a fool to think I could change it."

"You are a fool to deny who you are," the Vampire said simply. "The aristocracy of the spirit runs in your veins, not blood. Self-sacrifice is not in your nature. You can love, but your love is cruel and heartless. It is a vampire's love. Mortals such as these were meant to serve us. Their prayers are their love poems to our kind, their breath our incense, their flesh and blood our meat and drink. They have built whole religions around this principle. Their greatest achievement in art and architecture, literature and philosophy, are expressions of their single highest spiritual principle: submission. As you shall see—"

She turned back to Connor, letting the cloak fall open. He caught a slice of the body underneath, the flesh as white and exciting as lightning. He thought of the Song of Solomon, the forbidden hymns of Cybele, of the dog priests of Astarte, who cut off their own genitals in ecstatic worship of the Goddess. He thought, too, of the salmon that swims to its death upstream, of the spider who stings her mate in her web of love, of the sacred king who lives seven years in the Queen's favor and then is hung from the limbless tree.

In her presence, Connor knew that all effort of Will was meaningless, all Magic impotent, all resistance futile. She was the source of all power, the one who he sought behind the veils of a thousand women, who took his life from him the way another woman took his essence. She was positive and negative, black and white, good and evil, and he yearned to return to her as if to a severed twin. For a brief moment Connor thought of the woman who had tried to save his life and felt a pang of sorrow. He had felt genuine love for Kelly, of that he was sure, but what he'd felt for her could not compare with what he'd felt for the woman who stood before him now. It was the difference between lighting a match and falling into the sun. The woman who stood before him now was his destiny.

Connor wondered if this had been the Craft's plan all along; that he should immolate himself to this woman, to sacrifice himself once and for all to some greater, unseen cause. To be sure, it had always been implicit in his oath that he might one day be called upon to do just that. In fact, the art in whose pursuit he had so singlemindedly devoted his entire life had at its center the seed of his self-destruction. For the paradox of magic was that though one sought to change the course of events in accordance with Will, the greatest magical act any magician could perform was to learn how to make his own ego disappear. In the western tradition it was called achieving the Knowledge and Conversion of the Holy Guardian Angel, and its accomplishment meant death. It was what Connor was attempting to do now.

He fell to his knees like a knight before his Lady, and the woman cupped his head in her distant hands and averted his face from the horror of the Abyss and the unseemly hunger of the grave. He felt the teeth in his throat, but to him it was the song of the future, the fruit of the garden, the ecstasy of freedom after long bondage. He was conscious of his blood and rose up to meet her lips, pouring out a libation to the Goddess, who appeared before him in a vision of apocalyptic beauty.

Kelly watched in horror as Connor lost his soul to the Vampire, seeing his will to live slip slowly away, his blood pumping in silent praises of the goddess.

Her hand went to her own throat, and that was when she felt the silver cross under her leather coat. She pulled it out, the metal cool as ice in her hands, reflecting the dim candlelight as if it were made of fire.

She remembered how the cross had had no power in her father's hands, how the Vampire had easily disarmed him of it when he tried to drive it through the monster's heart, and knew that she, too, would have no more success in destroying her with it. And that is when the truth dawned on her with all the terrible finality of a condemned man's last day on earth. In her ears she heard again her father's crazy sermon about the god who let himself be crucified in order to show mankind the way to death, and for the first time she truly understood the meaning and the necessity of His death.

She stared at the cross in her hands and knew that it had been given to mankind not as a weapon, not as a means of protection, not even as a symbol of faith.

It was the key to the prison.

Connor wept.

He had been only inches from the revelation, from the truth he had sought all his life, when the vision died and he felt himself thrust out into the darkness, reliving in his cells the trauma of being pushed from the safety of the womb, of being cast out from the garden, of being forced to earn his bread from this day forth by the sweat of his brow.

He was hurled forcibly across the room, landing in a leap against the wall, staring up, stunned and horrified. The Vampire was transfixed to the spot, her mouth moving soundlessly, red with promises of rapture he now knew to be all lies.

Red with his blood.

"What have you done!" the Vampire roared, turning around, her teeth bared in a feral grimace. She was looking at where Kelly stood in the shadows, the shaft of the silver crucifix emerging from between her breasts, the blood dripping along its length, over her fists, which clutched it to her bosom.

"You forget that I am human, too," Kelly said through gritted teeth. "And as a human I know what it is to die for love. For though an immortal god himself, the vampire died on the cross so men might live."

The Vampire growled and leapt toward Kelly, pushing her hands out of the way to yank the cross from her chest. Kelly spread her arms and wrapped them around the Vampire as if to embrace her, pulling her close and driving the other end of the cross into the Vampire's dead heart.

Connor rose to his feet, staggering to the wall where the chainsaw hung.

He turned back and watched as the two women shuffled across the floor of the basement, locked in a macabre dance of death. He wiped the sweat from his eyes and pulled the cord of the chainsaw. The tool sputtered, belched black smoke, and finally came to life, its low gutteral roar sounding strangely comforting.

The Vampire had staggered back off the blade, pushing Kelly away from her, the steel sliding from the wound with a dry rasp. The injury had deeply affected her, as had Kelly's unexpected act of self-sacrifice, and as she attempted to recover, her body seemed to change, shuffling through a thousand appearances, like playing cards, each one different and yet all recognizably part of the same deck.

As she straightened up to come for Connor, he saw no more seduction in her smokey eyes, only murder, plague, genocide, and extinction. He brought the chainsaw around and severed the rabid head cleanly from her delicate white shoulders.

Connor watched in disgust as the body continued to move out of force of habit, but blindly, stupidly. He stepped out of the way and it continued on past him, crashing into the wall, turning, and falling to the floor. It began to melt away, growing gelatinous, sloughing off like an old sack, and the air reeked of smoke and old Vaseline. Connor instinctively averted his eyes an instant before the thunderclap and the bone-white lightning struck that surely would have left him blind. Yet from the corner of his shielded gaze he saw the figure rise from the light: its body soft and larval, covered with weak, vestigial limbs, its long dolorous face all mouth, its eyes blind and shrunken like healed wounds. Yet surrounding the creature were a magnificent set of wings, feathered with flame, that bore it toward the ceiling, where it vanished altogether in a drizzle of acid tears.

Connor gazed in awe at where the angel had stood only moments before and saw Kelly. In one hand was a silver lighter; in the other hand, a silver crucifix dripping blood one drop at a time, like a clock striking midnight.

FIFTY-THREE

Connor wasted no time making good their escape.

He leapt across the room to where Kelly stood, still clutching the bleeding cross and staring at the pink puddle of bubbling gelatin that had once been Monica Caron. As if wakened from a trance, Kelly dropped the cross on the floor, held her face in her bloodstained hands, and screamed. Connor grabbed her roughly by the arm and propelled her down a short tunnel at the back of the dungeon, stopping at another vaultlike steel door.

He released the locking mechanisms and pulled open the door. The cold rain fell on his face and he breathed in deeply the crisp, fresh air. As he suspected, the tunnel led to a secret entrance that opened outside the grounds of the compound. The entrance would have made it easy to bring victims in and out of the dungeon without being seen. Down below, Connor spotted a narrow muddy path that looked innocuous enough but that was, no doubt, used for just that purpose. Connor had accidentally discovered the road in his earlier reconnaissance of the area and, though he hadn't suspected its purpose, he'd nevertheless thought it a good place to conceal the Mazda. It was parked about a hundred yards away.

"Come on," he said.

He climbed carefully onto the slippery gray rocks and turned to help Kelly. As he did, he took a quick look around back to the main house.

The air above the mansion was illuminated in a hard white glare as helicopters stitched in and out of the roiling, smoky sky. The chop of their blades was all but drowned out in the relentless whine of sirens. Below, the house was completely engulfed in flames, firefighters from six different stations reduced to the role of mere bystanders as the structure slowly collapsed under the sheer weight of the light.

Even from here, Connor could feel the terrible heat of the flames.

At his side, Kelly sagged heavily against him. Connor caught her as she fell, carrying her the rest of the way down the rocky outcropping as the rain washed the blood and ashes from their faces.

FIFTY-FOUR

Rossi stood on the beach and stared at the black sea, tossing like a giant sleeping fitfully in the moonlight.

The rain had turned to snow, the white flakes streaking momentarily in front of his eyes before disappearing into the water. The flakes struck his flesh and melted instantly, stinging him like countless small hypodermic needles, numbing his expressionless face. Behind him, the fire department had finally gotten the blaze under control, which meant that it had burned itself down, the mansion little more than an acre of red-hot embers. Even now inspectors were sifting through the wreckage, trying to come up with some clue as to exactly what had happened.

Rossi had heard about the attack on the mansion while he was at the hospital. Graham was dead. He'd bled to death within minutes on the stage at Domination, in spite of Rossi's frantic attempts to save his life. By the time the paramedics arrived, Graham's body was already cold. Rossi drove with them to the ER anyway, going a little crazy, offering his own blood for a transfusion, demanding they do something to bring his partner back. Of course, it wasn't until later that Rossi realized just how hopeless it had been: Most of Graham's throat was *gone*. They had Gwen in custody for the murder: It had taken four men to subdue her enough to administer the tranquilizer, and even then they'd had to force a rubber bit between her jaws to keep her from biting. They had her under observation in the psycho ward at Bellevue. Lacking a pulse, a blood pressure, and decorated with six ostensibly fatal bullet wounds, no one had yet figured out how she was still alive.

To make matters even worse, the priest had vanished into thin air. Rossi had driven back to Manhattan Central on the long shot that the man might still be hanging on and that he might be able to suggest where Kelly might have been taken. Instead, he had found out that the priest had apparently walked out of the hospital under his own power, leaving his police guard disemboweled in his place. The last time Rossi had seen him the priest had been dead, and now he was a fugitive. The whole thing was weird and getting weirder.

When Rossi heard about the trouble at the senator's mansion he raced to the scene. There was nothing he could do for Graham but catch his killer: He might still be able to save Kelly's life, even if it turned out that she was somehow implicated as a suspect in all this. At this point, anything was a possibility. By the time he arrived the place was swarming with law-enforcement officials from the FBI, the NYPD, the Rockland County Sheriff's Department, the Coast Guard, and the Secret Service, among others.

The prevailing opinion so far was that they were looking at an assassination attempt. So far they had found two dead bodies on the premises, both charred beyond recognition, though it was clear that neither of them was the senator, who was safe and sound in the Capitol and, until twenty minutes ago, was enjoying some late-night aerobics with one of his favorite DC mistresses. The senator's wife had somehow miraculously escaped the blaze and was sitting in the back of an armored limousine, speeding on its way to a Connecticut safe house. They wouldn't know the identity of the two charcoal bodies until tomorrow, after they examined the dental records.

"Detective?"

Rossi looked up and saw an overweight detective in a black raincoat backlit by the orange glow coming from the compound.

"What is it?" Rossi said.

The officer pulled his hand out of his pocket and held out his arm.

"They found this in the ashes," he said. "One of the detectives said you probably dropped it."

Rossi looked down at the silver lighter in the man's hand. Even in the dim light he could see the delicately scripted monogram engraved in the metal.

Rossi felt the tears sting his eyes.

"Thanks," he managed to say.

He took the lighter, and the cop turned away and made his way back up the beach.

Rossi stared at the lighter in his hand as if it were a souvenir left by an alien. It raised almost as many questions. To be sure, it proved that Kelly had been present at the mansion. Had she perished in the fire? If not, was she part of the assassination conspiracy? Was she responsible, in part, for Graham's death? Or was she being held against her will? Was it possible that she had left the lighter there on purpose as a message to Rossi? He cocked his arm, ready to throw the lighter into the sea, but something held him back. Slowly, he brought his hand down, opened it, and stared again at the lighter, so small, so light, so elegant.

He fished around in his coat pocket for his pack of Camels, shook loose a cigarette, and held it in the corner of his mouth. He thumbed the lighter to life, cupped it in his hand, and touched the flame to the cigarette.

He snapped the lighter shut and slipped it back into his pocket.

He'd find her, dammit, one way or another. He'd find her if it was the last thing he ever did.

He finished his cigarette, staring into the cold black heart of the sea, and flicked the butt away like a tiny orange star arcing into oblivion.

Tomorrow morning he'd drive to the station and turn in his badge.

EPILOGUE

BORN
AGAIN

"I sought a soul akin to mine,
but I could not find one.
I searched every corner of the earth;
my perserverance brought no reward.
Yet I could not remain alone.
Someone had to approve of my character;
someone had to have the same ideas as I."
—Lautremont

"There is no law beyond Do what thou wilt.
Love is the law, love under will."
—Aleister Crowley

The bus that was to take them out of the nightmare was parked outside gate seven in the concrete heart of the Port Authority.

Connor stared out the dirty window as two last-minute passengers handed their tickets to the driver. One was an elderly black man in a long green corduroy coat; the other was a middle-aged fat woman with a blue suitcase covered with oil stains. Connor watched them carefully as they came down the aisle. The fat woman squeezed into a seat near the front of the bus next to a teenage girl in a bulky goosedown coat, while the black man continued down the aisle to lay full length across the empty seats in the back. Connor could find no crack in their masks to suggest that they were anyone other than the anonymous travelers they appeared to be.

Beside him, Kelly was sleeping fitfully. Her breath came in ragged gasps. The wound in her chest, though grievous, had not proved fatal, but Connor was still worried about her.

They had raced back to the city after leaving the burning mansion, making it across the island before the authorities could erect roadblocks leading in and out of the compound. Connor drove like a madman, returning the Miata to the garage from which he had originally taken it, leaving it parked in the exact same place from which he'd first seen it, careful to completely erase his trail.

They took a cab the rest of the way. The early-morning streets were nearly empty, except for the omnipresent tribe of homeless people and a few sidewalk Santas of questionable ethics, standing beside their cardboard chimneys, hoping to get an early start. Around them all the snow fell merrily. Connor caught the cabbie glancing in the rearview mirror, his eyes on Kelly's breasts, or rather, at the red material she clutched in her fists. Her face was pale and she was trembling slightly, but whenever Connor asked her how she was she only smiled weakly and told him she was fine. The cabbie shrugged when he saw Connor's eyes on him in the mirror.

"Ain't none of my business, pal," he said.

It was good, for once, to be in New York City, able to depend on the apathy of strangers.

He had the cabbie stop in front of an all-night clothing store on Eighth Avenue, paid him, and sent him on his way. Inside the store, Connor bought Kelly a pair of jeans, sneakers, and a bulky gray sweatshirt. She changed into the warm, dry clothes in the store's bathroom while Connor settled the bill at the register. They discarded the heels and the torn, bloody dress in a trash can outside the Port Authority, where both would be taken by a rummaging homeless person inside of fifteen minutes.

In the bus terminal Connor headed directly for the Greyhound ticket window and bought two tickets to a small town in South Dakota he'd chosen completely at random, hoping thereby to make it impossible for anyone following them to deduce where they might have gone through a computerized analysis of his Craft file. It was bad enough that sooner or later they would be able to determine their destination psychically. He'd have to do his best to jam the astral circuits.

Connor looked at his watch.

His arm throbbed, but that was the least of his problems. The moment they were safely on the road, he'd do a quick Hatha yoga meditation to ease the pain. The bone would set all right. He'd bought two *People* magazines at the newsstand and a package of shoelaces. In the men's room he rolled the magazines around his arm and tied them in place with the shoelaces to form a makeshift splint.

The bus was scheduled to leave in less than a minute and the driver had not yet boarded. Connor looked outside and felt his blood go cold. The tall, skinny driver was talking to a policeman in a wet black poncho who was twirling his black nightstick between his fingers with the dexterity of a high-school baton twirler. Connor immediately scanned the bus, once again checking out the emergency exists, visualizing the quickest route of escape. He looked back to the two men standing at the gate and carefully read their lips. He was somewhat relieved to find they were talking about the Jets' chances in the upcoming game on Sunday against the Buffalo Bills.

Right on cue, the driver glanced at his watch, bid the policeman good morning, and climbed the stairs into the bus. He settled himself behind the wheel, checking the mirrors. Connor saw the driver's eyes in the rearview mirror as he scanned the passengers in the double-row behind him. His eyes rested on Kelly a moment too long, flicked to Connor, and then returned to the sideview mirror as he released the air brakes and slowly backed the bus out of the parking spot.

Connor made his own survey of his fellow passengers. Two seats up there was a lean, raw-boned man in a pair of Levi's and a denim jacket poring over a dog-eared leather Bible. Across the way was a man in a rumpled suit, his tie stuffed into his jacket pocket, his hand over his eyes. Behind them, to the left, was a washed-out woman in a kerchief and her eight-year-old son, hunched over a Gameboy. Any one of them could be the one sent to assassinate them, including the driver.

Connor knew what he had done had certainly marked him for death. Even if he could have argued that his earlier insubordination might be part of the Craft's plan, there was no doubt in his mind that his failure to give himself up to the angel was tantamount to his betrayal of his most sacred vow. It mattered little that it was Kelly who had prevented his sacrifice; the fact that Kelly was still alive was his fault. Connor was equally certain that the creature he had seen escaping from Monica Caron's ruined body *had* been an angel.

He could no longer deny it. He had been stunned to see the real form of the being. In all of his scrying into the astral world, he had never encountered anything like it. Of course, he should have been prepared for such an alien manifestation. After all, he knew well the awesome visions of prophets such as Isaiah and Moses, to whom the celestial agents had appeared in flame and terror. Connor understood that the point of the vision was to shatter the ego's preconceptions, expectations, and desires, for godhead was quite beyond any mortal effort to conceive of it. That is what it meant to surrender to God. Terror, Connor could have lived with: It was what he was trained to do. What he had seen, however, had filled him with a sick revulsion.

It was Alien and it was Evil.

He had pulled back the veil and seen the awesome secret. Humanity was herd to a race of superior beings who milked them for their suffering.

Now the Craft would come after him with everything

444

it had. They would follow his tracks from one place to another, tirelessly and relentlessly. No witness-protection program, no plastic-surgery technique, no safe house or maximum-security prison ever devised would be able to hide him from them. They would hunt him down through the years of his life, and when his life was over, straight across the border into the realm of death itself. By turning his back on the angel, he had condemned himself to eternal damnation. The Craft would have their revenge.

Connor gazed at the woman who had saved his life.

How much time did they have? Where would the fatal blow be struck?

Kelly moaned, twitching in her sleep, her pale face frowning.

She would no doubt be haunted for as long as she lived by what she had been through, for no mortal was meant to see what she had seen and live. Connor wondered if the evil that had been released upon Monica's demise had found a home in Kelly. It was quite true, as Einstein said, that energy could not be destroyed, but only transformed.

Had Kelly been transformed by the evil she'd released?

They were halfway through the Lincoln Tunnel when Kelly woke with a start. The yellow sulfer lights shining through the windows were shuffling across her face, reminding him of the way the Vampire's face had changed, reviewing each of her incarnations before she died. She stared listlessly at the yellowed tile walls of the tunnel, filthy from the accumulated exhaust of years of mortal traffic, and saw the painted line that separated New York from New Jersey. She turned to Connor, and for a moment it was as if she didn't know him.

"I just had the worst dream," she finally said. "I was in ancient Rome. There was a bald-headed man, an

445

emperor I think he was, dressed in women's clothes, and hanging from a pair of leather manacles was a girl who could have been his sister. He had a whip in his hand, slick with blood, and he didn't want to hurt her anymore, but it was me who was telling him to do it, promising him he would become a god. The worst part was that when I looked closer at the girl she had Gwen's face. . . ."

"It's over now," Connor said, trying to comfort her. There would be time enough later for the truth.

Kelly shook her head. "I don't think I can live like this. To feed off other people, their weakness, their love, their pain. It makes me sick."

"Cherish that sickness," Connor said. "It is your humanity that makes you sick."

"No, you don't understand. It's not the thought of the blood that makes me sick. It's my hunger for it."

"We all have hungers, Kelly. We all feed off other people to survive. It's the way of the world. It's the way we're made. The best thing we can do is to survive as humbly as we can and be mindful of those who sacrifice their own lives that we might continue on."

Up ahead he could see the end of the tunnel fast approaching. The sun had come up in the meantime, and the light at the end was white and thick with snow.

"I'm scared," Kelly said, facing the light.

"Take my hand."

Kelly grabbed Connor's hand in her cold one with the desperation of someone drowning, who'll reach out to anyone, friend or foe. Together, they sat quietly side by side as the bus raced from the tunnel and plunged headlong into the fire.

ABOUT THE AUTHOR

Michael Cecilione lives on the Jersey Shore with his wife, Christine. He is the author of two previous novels, *Soulsnatchers* and *Deathscape*. He is currently working on his fourth, *Easy Prey*, which will be released by Zebra Books.